CONTENTS

A Brief Divided Man Refresher

Divided Seed shall a Divided Child Beget who shall grow into a Divided Man

Fin Tanner and Kyle Tanner, half-twins, are the Divided Man of the prophecy. Rook Brandymoon is their Completer.

At the end of *Miss Brandymoon's Device*
The newly reunited Fin and Rook were planning a belated honeymoon on the asteroid when they learned of Kyle's takeover of Shaw Ministries. Kyle had torn down and rebuilt his own mind, unleashing an infectious insanity. He also possessed the cache of microtransceiver body jewelry, making him very dangerous indeed.
Fin and Rook confronted him.
Kyle and Fin battled in the cathedral, and inside Rook's head. Rook's mind nearly broke as she strove to ignore her connection to Kyle in order to help Fin. In the heat of battle, Kyle consumed his audience to fuel his attack. The spider aliens came to Fin's aid. Rook's anthropomorphized coping mechanisms, Brook and Bramble, tried to give victory to Kyle, but Rook overpowered them and plowed through Kyle's knee, distracting him long enough for Fin to strike the decisive blow.
Together Fin and Rook exited the cathedral into a flurry of ash and snow.

At the end of *Tenpenny Zen*
After 12 years in suspended animation, Willow went into labor. Her contractions threw ripples through the Elsewhere and stirred up momentous events in Webster. Brad no longer consistently buffered Melissa from the patterns of meaningless trivia that plagued her, and she planned to kill both him and herself.

Through Gale, Brad learned of Willow's whereabouts in Severin's basement henge contraption. To stage a rescue, he used Melissa as a distraction, a tactic that worked a little too well. Melissa chose to stay at Threshold House with Severin and learn mastery of her visions, even when he told her he expected to have sex with her.

Brad freed Willow, inadvertently triggering the domino batteries. The cascade's energies charged the henge contraption's stone slab to white-hot, then it sank out of sight into the Elsewhere.

Willow's labor progressed quickly, with supernatural complications. Gale chased Brad and Willow, coming across them in the blizzard in time to sacrifice herself to save Willow. Gale disappeared back to the Elsewhere from which she was born.

Happily reunited with Brad, Willow gave birth to daughter Zen in the back of his car.

Selections from Shaw's New Revelations

Divided Seed shall a Divided Child Beget
who shall grow into a Divided Man

A hidden Plague will Dream in Men and Blind their Hearts,
and Black Dreams will descend for Twenty Years and Flood the Earth.

And utter Blackness shall prevail over the Earth
that the Hosts in Heaven not look back upon it.

They that Bear the Divided Child shall Wander Entombed,
Each cast Unseeing into a Lightless Maze of Dreams

Sundered shall be his Heart who Divides the Seed,
that it Holds not Joy but spills a Barren shadow

Those who go Forth in Chains will be called into the Firmament,
but fall and be Minions of the Pretender

A Murder of Crows shall pick clean
the bones of the Pretender and of his Legions

A Completer, an Unknowing angel with Shadowed Wings,
Shall heal the Divided Man and restore Light upon the Earth

Tanner Family Tree

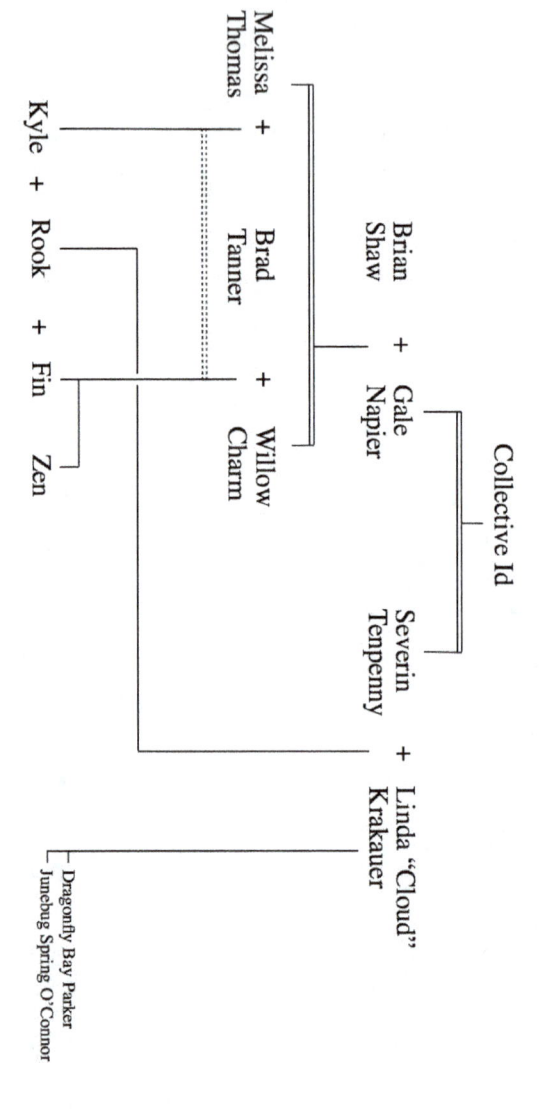

twins
half-twins

Melissa
Thomas

+

Brian
Shaw

+

Gale
Napier

Collective Id

Severin
Tenpenny

+

Linda "Cloud"
Krakauer

Kyle

Brad
Tanner

+

Willow
Charm

+

Rook

+

Fin

Zen

Dragonfly Bay Parker
Junebug Spring O'Connor

iv

Part One

Chapter One

THE FRIGID NIGHT

As a reporter I should be setting the record straight. I was an eyewitness to the mass slaughter at the cathedral, for fuck's sake. I've got a shit-ton of inside info about Kyle's organization. It's a journalist's wet dream. And now, with a career-launching opportunity dropped in my lap, I'm going to pretend none of that is true. I'm going to cover my ass, and Fin's.
	from Rook Tanner's journal

MONDAY, NOV 6, 2000

Of course it had to be both.

Snow or sleet on its own would be bad enough, but the universe had a sense of humor, alternating between the two with startling frequency. Rook Tanner shivered. Neither she nor her husband Fin were wearing coats.

A patrol of mercenaries ran past them toward the devastated cathedral, weapons drawn. Rook knew that should be alarming, but she'd already used up her adrenaline. The mercs worked for Fin's half-brother Kyle and would presumably be interested in whoever left him in his broken state.

"We can't be here when they come out." Rook tried to ignore her throbbing headache and the tang of acrid smoke in the air.

"I'll talk to the aliens," Fin said. A quick and traceless exit was called for. The space-spiders routinely transported people to and from the asteroid belt, so sending Fin and Rook home to Webster should be a snap.

Fin closed his tired green eyes, his forehead scrunched in concentration. Rook could see the puncture marks where she pierced his left brow on the day they met, and it made her a little sad he wouldn't be wearing a hoop there anymore. That hoop's hidden technology had corrupted his dreams, but it was also the thing that brought them together.

Small ice pellets settled in Fin's dark hair as he communed with his friends on the asteroid. Rook stamped her feet and regretted her bare legs.

Fin snorted and opened his eyes. "They can't help. They say they're too drained from the fight." He sounded unconvinced.

Rook threw a look at the smoldering shell of the once-grand glass cathedral. She wanted to be far away before the mercs came back out. "Let's get to the highway. We'll hitch a ride."

Fin nodded.

They jogged across the grounds of the Shaw Ministries compound and made their way to the main road.

A stoner couple in a blue Geo Metro were the first samaritans not to take offense at their burnt carpet stench, or the bloodstains on Fin's shirt. Rook and Fin shared the tiny back seat with a heap of food wrappers and a friendly brown dog.

The drive from Donner to Webster usually took an hour, but the hellacious winter mix pelting down on the mountain road made the going slow.

Three hours trapped in the weed-and-wet-dog-scented car with an endless supply of Phish left Rook carsick. Fin fell into an exhausted slumber, but Rook's throbbing head and queasy stomach kept her awake. She replayed the terrifying mental battle Fin and Kyle waged in the cathedral — and in her mind — obsessing over the traitors inside her head who almost tipped the outcome into disaster.

When their clown car finally made it to Webster, they stopped for gas about a mile from Fin and Rook's bomb shelter hideaway.

The precipitation was a mere flurry and Rook was desperate for

fresh air, so they thanked their chauffeurs and set out on foot. Immediately, the snow turned into a drenching five-minute downpour, changed briefly to sleet, then settled into pinprick needles of ice. The wind knifed through Rook's sodden black sweater and rattled her frozen hair.

"We're almost there," Fin said through chattering teeth.

Rook looked up at him in the illumination from a nearby porch light and smiled weakly. His lips looked as blue as hers felt. His dark hair clung to his forehead like unruly seaweed. At the base of her skull, the signal that connected her mind to his thrummed steady and comforting, and blissfully unchallenged.

Trudging along the suburban street through the slush and darkness, Rook hugged her soggy sweater tighter against herself, like pulling on wet socks for warmth.

"Chez Tanner." Fin gestured to his father's large, bland house, the only one on the street not lit up. He led Rook off the sidewalk into a clump of pine trees. Her go-go boots sank into a slushy, muddy quagmire, but she couldn't care. They would soon be inside. Beyond the pines they squelched across piles of wet, compacted leaves under naked trees that afforded little protection from the wind and ice and returning rain.

"I'm so cold," Rook finally allowed herself to complain as Fin hauled open the hatch under the bushes. He hugged her with his free arm, and she tilted her face for a kiss. His lips were frozen, but his tongue was hot and probing.

"Don't slip," he warned as Rook started down the long ladder.

The only light in the bomb shelter was the warm gold and red glow of Vesuvius, their lava lamp. The feeling of entering a furnace was a welcome one. Rook pulled off her dripping sweater, leaving herself topless, her nipples hard as ice. It felt good to be back in their little pocket of tastefully decorated 1950s nuclear paranoia. The hatch clanked shut and Fin climbed down to join her.

"Why, Mrs Tanner," he said, "you seem to have lost your shirt."

"Lose yours too, and your pants. We need to generate some body heat."

"I like the sound of that."

Shadows shifted. They weren't alone.

Fin pulled Rook to him in an icy, protective embrace. A female voice behind Rook said, "Fin?"

Who was down here? No one else knew about this place. Rook squirmed, trying to turn, and Fin's grip loosened as he said, disbelieving, "Mom?"

Rook spun around. A woman with long red hair stood beside Vesuvius, wearing a plaid bathrobe. She had elfin features, and didn't look old enough to be Fin's mother.

Is that the robe the aliens gave me?

Mouth hanging open, trying to decide if she was angry or not, Rook swiveled her head back and forth between her husband and this intruder.

"Mom!" Fin said again, more sure this time. He brushed past Rook and hurried to the other end of the shelter where he swept the woman into his arms.

"Fin!" Rook and the woman both said.

Fin released the woman, then hugged her again and bent to kiss her cheek. They were both crying. The woman held Fin's face in her hands, studying him, tsking over his injuries, smiling through her tears.

Rook's hand crept up to cover her mouth. Fin's mother? Could it really be? She'd been missing for more than ten years. Rook stared at their joyous reunion and slowly approached, not wanting to interrupt, and not wanting to feel like such a voyeur.

Her heels clicked against the metal floor and Fin looked at her.

"Rook! This is my mom."

Rook nodded, not knowing what to say.

"Mom, this is Rook. We're married."

Fin's mother blinked in surprise.

Melting snow trickled out of Rook's hair and down her chest,

reminding her she was naked from the waist up.

"Oh!" She crossed her arms over her boobs.

"Where did you go?" Fin asked his mother. "Are you okay?"

"I'm fine, Fin. So much better now that I've seen you! You're so much older."

Rook tore her eyes away from them. She tugged the chain to turn on the overhead light. Buried deep in a pile of clothes at the foot of the bunks she found a snug white sweater that looked cozy. She pulled it on, then sat on the bentwood chair to shed her waterlogged boots.

Fin and his mother chattered excitedly.

If I let them talk long enough, maybe they'll forget I was standing there with my tits out.

Across the narrow aisle, the bunk was neatly made, unlike when they left. In the center lay an unfamiliar bundle. Rook pulled off her second boot, and moved to get a better look.

A baby!

She looked toward Fin and his mother, who were talking and hugging, and seemed to have forgotten she was there. Rook turned back to the baby. It looked very new, in that unfinished way babies had. It was wrapped in a towel.

Rook straightened and took a few hesitant steps toward Fin.

"Oh, good, you found a shirt," he said. "Come here."

Fin's mother looked at her with a smile. Her eyes were the same green as Fin's.

"I'm Willow," she said. "And you're Brook?"

Rook nodded, then shook her head. "Rook. I go by Rook."

Willow studied her, staring at her eyes. It made Rook uncomfortable.

"Um," Rook began. "I'm wondering about the, uh, baby over there."

Willow smiled and Fin said, "Baby?"

"There's a baby on the bunk," Rook explained as Willow went and picked it up.

"Fin," she said, "this is Zen. Your sister."

Fin recoiled. Rook reached for him.

"She was just born tonight," Willow said.

The hatch clunked open and a deep male voice from outside said, "Wow, the roads are horrible!"

A plastic shopping bag dropped to the floor with a muffled splat, and a pair of legs in charcoal suit pants and muddy wing-tips started down the ladder. The voice continued, "I think I got everything. Diapers and wipes, some sweats for you." The man carried another bag in his left hand.

He reached the bottom of the ladder and turned around. His suede jacket was spattered with raindrops, but clearly expensive. Likewise the suit underneath, wet and dirty though it was. His right knee peeked through a hole in the pant leg. His dark hair was conservatively cut and graying at the temples. Rook put his age around 50. He looked like a banker or CEO, handsome but straitlaced.

When he spotted Rook and Fin his gray eyes widened in surprise. "Oh good! We were going to find you tomorrow, Fin."

Fin took three quick strides and punched the man in the jaw.

"Fin!" Rook and Willow cried.

Willow foisted the sleeping baby into Rook's arms and raced to separate the men.

"Brad, are you okay?" she asked.

Brad rubbed his jaw and nodded.

"Come on, Rook," Fin said. "We're leaving." He started up the ladder.

"Fin, wait," Willow pleaded.

The awkward bundle in Rook's hands wiggled and she didn't know what to do. She'd never held a baby before.

"Rook," Fin growled.

The idea of going back into the storm filled her limbs with lead, but their secret haven was no longer secret. "I'm not wearing shoes," Rook said quietly.

Fin stopped climbing and looked fiercely at her. Her emotional

reserves were drained and she felt on the verge of exhausted tears. Fin softened and came back down.

"Get some shoes. I can't stay here."

"Fin," Brad said.

"I don't want to hear it, *Dad*," Fin said, the last word sharp with sarcasm.

Were the situation reversed, she wouldn't want Fin to try to make her play nice with her own family. She had to have his back, even if it meant more snow. Rook studied Fin's father while holding the baby out for Willow. Once unburdened she burrowed into her pile of clothes and located a pair of black heels. Not great for stomping around in the snow, but better than going barefoot.

When she got the shoes on she saw Fin unplugging Vesuvius. Brad had his arm around Willow, who cradled the baby, crying.

Fin handed Rook Vesuvius's base and climbed out of the shelter carrying the glass capsule in his right hand.

Rook smiled apologetically at Brad and Willow, then followed her husband into the frigid night.

*** *** ***

Severin Tenpenny carried Melissa to the hammock, the closest thing to luxury in his drafty, unfinished attic. She was shapely enough, though her body was not as trim as Willow's. He smoothed her hair back from her face. It matched Willow's natural color, except Melissa's golden locks contained traces of silver. Both girls inherited their pixieish looks from Gale, although Willow's extended sojourn in the Elsewhere kept her young. Melissa looked a decade older than her twin. Severin's lips twitched into something resembling a smile. He laid a blanket across her nudity before starting down the steps.

His next task was to soothe Gale. The unpleasant memory of their pitched battle on the front porch would be fresh in her mind. Furthermore, the upheaval in their domestic arrangements was bound to stir up jealousy. That should be the simplest hurt to remedy. His sister's frustrations would be overcome by her maternal instincts soon

enough with her girls under one roof. And Severin saw no reason he couldn't continue to indulge Gale's sexual appetites.

I'll need to get a bigger hammock.

He projected his customary calm as he descended to the first floor.

Adding Melissa meant a fresh energy supply. Her misapprehensions about her power made her utterly dependent on Severin for tutelage, which would make her easy to control. He permitted himself a few seconds of grinning, and even a chuckle. All it took to claim Melissa was chasing away her husband, which Severin didn't even remember doing, as such.

Melissa's husband.

Severin rushed to the basement.

The light was on, the outside door ajar. The thousands of domino batteries were gone. Willow was gone.

Even the slab was gone.

The bastard can't have dragged that off!

Severin paced the paths of his dominoes like a wilderness tracker, examining their faint marks in the dirt floor. The interloper must have set off the cascade, releasing the dominoes to return to the Elsewhere as each fed its store of energy into the next, all the way to the slab itself.

What happened when the slab became energized?

In a shadowy corner of the vast room, a single artifact remained. A jade carving of a bare-breasted barbarian queen that Severin recalled extracting from his table years ago. He retrieved her from the unclean floor, marveling at her continued existence. None of the other thousands of items survived.

He pocketed the tiny statue.

The dominoes, his carefully constructed arrays of arcane batteries, were toppled prematurely. Wasted. Was Willow consumed in the process, her would-be rescuer fleeing in horror?

No. That didn't feel right. Severin knew he would have felt the slab's spark being released, felt the Elsewhere reeling from the blow.

No, the energy had not been set free.

Without Willow to conduct the power to the Elsewhere, the slab wasn't grounded. The power had been trapped. He pictured the white hot stone, glowing with frustrated potential.

Severin stalked to the open exterior door. If the wet snow ever held any tracks, it had long since obscured them.

Gale must have discovered this disaster hours ago and lit out into the storm to find her living baby doll. If she'd not been successful by now, she would not return triumphant.

Grudging admiration for Willow's rescuer, the care and planning he must have put into this exploit, brought a grim smile. Melissa had been ideal bait. The moment Severin saw her he thought only of adding her to his collection, of giving himself a complete set. Severin had taken his eye off the husband, dismissed him.

Now Willow was lost, Gale gone.

Gale would come back, would choose one daughter plus him over being alone, vainly chasing the other. Doubts stained Severin's thoughts. How soon could he anticipate Gale's return, really? She turned on him rather completely during their confrontation. Her ire might need time to cool, but Severin felt confident she couldn't function indefinitely without him.

Meanwhile, Melissa was his creature in ways more total than she could grasp. She was every bit as suitable a conduit for the slab's energies as Willow, and held her own impressive reservoir of mystical power. Using her to release the charge might even produce greater effect. Severin liked the idea of delivering a more powerful jolt to the Elsewhere. The longer the Collective Id was stunned, the better his opportunity to enshrine himself in the role of Superego before it recovered.

But the slab was missing. What happened when all that power flowed into it and couldn't escape? It must have lost its moorings to the

physical world and been set adrift in the Elsewhere.

Easily fixed. I've done it before.

He closed and locked the outside door and turned off the lone light bulb before trekking back to the attic.

Melissa slumbered in the hammock where he left her. *At least one thing knows its place.*

Severin strode to his table, merely an old door spanning two sawhorses. He pulled the jade figurine from his pocket and turned her in his fingers as he stared at the white sheet draping the makeshift table, studying the contrast between the elegant detail of the carving and the deceptive homeliness of the portal that brought it to him. He placed the figurine on a nearby crossbeam.

The slab came to him by way of his table, too. He had reached into the Elsewhere and guided it into position in the basement. Now he would have to guide it back.

With his right hand, Severin lifted a corner of the sheet and reached under with his left. He reached deep, past the table's surface, and felt warmth. He sought farther, knowing the heat came from the energy trapped in the stone slab.

He would soon have his target.

Searing agony attacked his palm, but he gritted his teeth and pressed his hand against the slab. Sweat flowed over his body as he struggled to direct the momentum of his enormous catch. His original discovery of the slab had also been excruciating, as was the later focusing. He'd been sure his hand would be pulverized, yet found it unharmed.

The massive stone was slipping away, not cleaving to his hand as it had before.

He strained to maintain contact, frustrated that the pain interfered with his feel for the work. Severin let a whimper escape, tears joining the sweat dripping from his graying beard. He flexed his fingers, and cried out from the pain.

The slab eluded him. His pain receded, now a throbbing, stabbing echo of its pinnacle. After stirring the Elsewhere in futility for another

minute, he drew his hand out from under the sheet.

Severin's forearm terminated in a charred stump, the jagged, blackened ends of two bones protruding where the softer tissues shrank away.

"Uncle," Melissa asked groggily, "what is that horrid smell?"

*** *** ***

Brad Tanner tried to sleep, but it was too tempting to stare at Willow, to watch Zen breathing. His delicate, beautiful girls, fairy creatures he couldn't believe existed in his squandered life.

He kept replaying the acrimonious scene when he'd arrived with the diapers, each trip through the events highlighting new ways to be disappointed, frustrated, and wounded by Fin's behavior. Plus his jaw hurt.

Willow had talked him out of giving chase, convincing him it would only lead to more conflict. She said Fin reacted badly to his sister, which made sense. Fin never knew Willow was pregnant, but even if he had he would have expected the child to be somewhat taller.

Fin didn't know about the suspended animation that prolonged Willow's pregnancy for twelve years. He naturally assumed a recent conception. Brad ground his teeth. Fin was so angry because he thought Brad was spending time with Willow. On an intellectual level, Brad knew it was a simple misunderstanding. On a gut level he knew the resentment would be there no matter what clarification Fin received.

Brad wiped his eyes. *What did I expect, thanks for bringing her back? I should have kept her safe in the first place.* Brad reached across Zen to stroke Willow's cheek, and silently promised to never let anyone hurt her again, himself and Fin included.

Fin. Would the gap between him and his son be bridged with Willow's return, or grow wider?

Willow had been disconcerted and disappointed that Brad knew nothing about Fin's marriage or wife. That was even more awkward than discovering the inflatable doll upon their arrival down here. Willow was having a hard time adjusting to the idea that Fin was an

adult, but kept getting slapped in the face by the evidence.

Maybe Willow misunderstood. Fin married? It sounded far-fetched, and yet...

My son didn't tell me he was getting married, Brad thought with a familiar stab of regret.

Brook was pretty and seemed loyal to Fin. Her fashion sense placed her squarely in Fin's tribe, and she apparently didn't question his obsessive devotion to his lava lamp. Brad wished them well, but even more he hoped to get to know them. His second chance was open to everyone.

After four hours of not sleeping, Brad crept from the bunk. He climbed the ladder in his socks and raised the hatch, then sat on the rim to put on his shoes.

The trees wore sheaths of ice, and each limb he brushed made tiny music. The sun had only recently risen, and the cold in the air was sharp. He circled to the front door, and stepped over a heap of newspapers to unlock it. It looked like the house had been deserted for weeks. He and Melissa had been preoccupied: her plotting his murder, him planning Willow's rescue.

The few items that mattered to Brad were in a box in the downstairs closet. He would claim them now before abandoning the house to Melissa.

The phone's message light blinked. With a shrug, Brad hit the button.

"This is the trauma center in Donner, regarding Kyle Tanner. Please return this call, at ..."

Brad scrambled for the pad and pen, and replayed the message to get the number. He dialed with unsteady fingers.

His call was answered, and transferred. He spent a minute on hold. The people he spoke to seemed passive, unconcerned. This was just another day at work for them.

The doctor's tone was less distant. Not warm, but comfortingly professional. Brad heard years of practice with delivering unpleasant

news. The doctor began with a too-detailed summary of the reconstruction he wanted to do on Kyle's knee, without which Kyle was never going to walk again without a cane.

"The cerebral issues are of greater concern," the doctor said candidly.

"What do you mean?"

The doctor's explanation was too much for Brad to process, despite obvious pains to express it in layman's terms. He mentioned delta waves and something about inconsistent symptomatology.

"But he'll wake up?"

"I can't put odds on it. None of the available data preclude it, nor adequately explain why he remains unconscious. Prudence favors optimism."

Brad okayed the knee surgery. It was something he could do.

Melissa should know about this.

Brad ended his call to the hospital and punched in the digits for Melissa's voicemail at the bank. He paused before pressing the final button. Did he owe anything to the woman who'd plotted to kill him?

He swallowed. What kind of fate had he left her to?

He pressed the button.

"Kyle is in the hospital in Donner. Thought you should know." He left the number.

A weight lifted once he decided to tell her.

Brad wanted to get back to Willow. Hearing Melissa's voice, thinking about her, set his hands trembling. The break was far less clean than he'd imagined it.

*** *** ***

What if a lie believed itself?

Scurrying through the tunnels and chambers deep in the heart of Gaspra, an asteroid 150 million miles from Earth, a few dozen beings applied their full concentration to this riddle. Until 22 days ago, that lie had been the foundation of their universe. It called itself the Floating Wisdom, and it thought it was a collective intellect spanning thousands

of planets. The scuttling beings in the asteroid had been a part of it.

The only real part.

Fin Tanner shattered the lie, casting the alien spiders into despair and chaos.

Then he helped them find a small, true unity to replace the grand, false one he took away.

The spiders revered Fin Tanner, although they seldom understood him. When he battled his brother they gave him power. When Fin evaded Kyle's killing stroke, the brunt of it surged into the spiders.

It might have killed them, but instead they absorbed it. That flood of power was infused with Kyle's beliefs, and now so were the spiders.

They now carried the Prophecy of the Divided Man.

Kyle knew it as the New Revelations, a tale of sin and redemption he gleaned from the mind of Reverend Brian Shaw. The Tanner brothers were its central figures, the Divided Man, and their conflict a sort of holy war. They fought over the Completer, a woman named Rook, who went with Fin when Kyle fell.

Yet, the prophecy remained unsatisfied. There were more battles to be fought.

The more they studied the prophecy, the more the spiders came to understand that it was their mission to bring it about, to restore light upon the Earth.

They discovered a new truth even greater than the old lie.

Chapter Two

MYSTICAL GLASS KINGDOM

I'm freaking out a little about my mental health. When people talk about their inner child, I don't think they mean it quite this literally. And, lucky me, I've got two. Brook, perfection personified, and whipping girl Bramble. Both look just like me, so I never know who I'll see in the mirror. They're so real it's scary. I know I'm not making them up, but that actually makes it worse. They're there. In my head.

My research suggests that I do not have dissociative personality disorder. B and B are something else. Depersonalization disorder and clonal pluralization and selective doubles delusion and all that jargon Wymbol used to spout to Mom. I wonder if he's still practicing? He helped me get them under control back then. Maybe he could do it again? But how would I ever tell Fin? "Say, honey, did I ever mention that I'm full-on crazy? Funny story!"

Kyle fucking Tanner ruined everyfuckingthing. He woke them up. He made me believe Fin was dead. That's such an evil thing to do! Is it any wonder I left the Stockholm Syndrome Sisters in charge? I was out of my mind with grief.

I can't tell Fin about this. I can't tell him my multiple personalities prefer his evil twin. No fucking way. No fucking way.
     from Rook Tanner's journal

Freshly showered but rewearing yesterday's clothes, Fin Tanner waited for his wife in the dingy hallway outside the Buck U gymnasium women's locker room. He tried not to look like a creep.

Considering the life-and-death battle he'd fought yesterday, he had

remarkably few injuries. There was the small gash under his eye, bruising on his torso, miscellaneous cuts from all the broken glass, and his scuffed knuckles. Hardly worth mentioning, but Rook kissed them all. She had escaped unscathed and felt guilty.

Fin would never forgive himself if he'd gotten her hurt.

On the heels of four college girls in skimpy workout clothes, Rook came through the door looking clean and beautiful, but tired. It was still strange to see her with chestnut hair. Her blue eyes lacked their customary glint, and the hum of her mental signal was ragged. Fin felt a stab of guilt at her bare legs and impractical shoes. Her skirt was barely long enough to protrude beneath the gray hoodie she liberated from the library's lost and found. The small flock of rook tattoos encircling her ankle silently scolded him for dragging her around in such lousy weather.

"I've been thinking," she said as soon as she spotted him. "My ID is in my leather jacket. If I can find that, I can go to the bank. And then we can eat."

Fin hugged her. She relaxed into his chest, and he breathed the familiar, gingered peach smell of her, disguised under a layer of cheap hand soap. He loved her so much. He didn't want to think what he would have done last night without her, what sort of bender the image of his mother and Brad — and a goddamn baby! — would have sent him on.

"I wore the jacket to our reception." By which she meant the kegger they threw three weeks ago. The kegger that culminated in explosions and abductions, alien and otherwise.

"We'll think of something else." Fin wished he had some idea what. Neither of them had their keys or wallets. "Let's go back to the library." They'd spent the night there, drying off with the bathroom's wall-mounted hand dryers, and having sex in that same bathroom while waiting for Rook's sweater to dry.

Rook shook her head, pressed against his heart. "The police probably picked it up, right?"

"We can't just go into the police station," Fin said.

Pulling away, Rook said, "Why not? It's my jacket. I want it back."

Fin set the plastic bag containing Vesuvius between his feet and opened his arms to Rook, wanting harmony with her. She ignored his gesture.

"I'm hungry," she said. "I don't want to live in the library. I don't want to shower at the gym and wear gloves from the lost and found. I want to fuck in the bathroom because it's fun, not because it's our only option. I want a real life." Rook's vibration was as worked up as she was. "One of us needs to solve this, and…"

She stopped talking and turned away.

What the hell was her problem? He was the one with the issues right now. Didn't she know he was hungry too? He wasn't proposing they live in the library, it just seemed like a safe base of operations.

In a mocking voice she said, "We can't go home, Rook. We can't go back to the bomb shelter, Rook." She grew shriller and shriller. "We can't go to the police station."

"Rook," Fin said, but he didn't have anything else to say.

"We're in a bad place, Fin. We need to solve this. I'm going to find my jacket. You don't have to come."

She walked away without looking back, pulling up her hood against the frigid temperature outdoors. Fin struggled into his pilfered windbreaker, grabbed Vesuvius's bag, and hurried to catch up. With everything turning to shit he couldn't stand to lose her too.

The previous night's devastating mix left the world glazed in a half-inch of ice. Sunlight sparkled off every tree branch, street sign, and bike rack. The campus looked like a mystical glass kingdom. Fin had no time to take it in, hustling to keep up with Rook as she marched downtown. The temperature hovered in the teens.

He was wary of entering the police station, but Rook kissed his cheek and went inside.

At least her legs will be warm.

After fifteen freezing minutes Fin started to get frantic. Had they

arrested her? He was on the verge of going inside and risking his own incarceration for unknown crimes when she walked out, wearing her black leather jacket and a self-satisfied smile.

Fin rushed over and kissed her. "Where's your bank?" The prospect of food was suddenly overwhelming.

"It's Viridian. On Alder Street."

Fin shook his head. "That's Brad's bank."

"So? He's unlikely to be standing in line right this moment. I'll be quick."

Until now Fin had been too embarrassed to tell her what his father did for a living. "He's, like, vice president of the bank."

Her cinnamon brows went up. "Well, that doesn't change where my money is." She started in the direction of Alder, weaving around patches of ice.

Fin snagged her elbow, "Why aren't you listening to me?"

"Because you're being totally irrational and I'm fucking hungry." She shook her arm free and strode away.

Irrational? How could she call him irrational? He pulled his camo lost-and-found ski cap tighter over his ears and stomped after her. But he wasn't going into the bank.

***   ***   ***

Willow was awake when Brad opened the hatch. She greeted him brightly, but her eyes looked red. She must have been thinking about Fin. He hugged her.

"You have a present for me," he said with a wink.

Willow tilted her head in puzzlement. Brad opened the cardboard box and handed her a tiny envelope.

"Here, honey." She gave an exaggerated wink and held the envelope out to him. "This is for you."

Brad said, "Open it," and held his breath.

She slit open the flap with her fingernail and peered into the paper pouch. Her face lit up. She pulled the silver ring out and held it next to its mate on her left middle finger.

With happy tears in her eyes, Willow took Brad's hand and slipped the ring onto his finger. The sweet, familiar tingle passed over his skin wherever she touched him. He moved her own band over one spot to her ring finger, too.

"I love you," he said, and kissed her.

Zen stirred, stretched, and gave a small cry.

Willow beamed at Brad, then at the baby, and crawled to the back of the bunk to feed the tiny girl.

Brad sat on the edge of the mattress. "We should take you both to get checked over."

Willow nodded as she offered her breast to Zen.

"There's a good hospital in Donner." He could see Kyle on the same trip, if he could slip away. "Who knows if Severin has people out looking for us around here."

Willow looked at Brad for a long moment, but didn't say anything.

Brad felt the silence like pressure growing in their steel sanctuary. "Of course, we can't go until they clear the roads," he explained, by way of opening a relief valve. "Everything's impassable. Ice. I don't think there's any emergency, you're obviously both fine, so we can wait another day. It's just a good idea to go, as a precaution, and—"

"This afternoon's fine," Willow interrupted. "Or tomorrow. But I don't think Severin has spies in the maternity ward, any more than you do."

Brad licked his lips and nodded. Too vigorously. He needed to say more, but feared blurting out the wrong thing. Silence accumulated again, compressing Brad but not seeming to bother Willow. She stroked Zen's head as the infant nursed.

"It's Kyle," Brad said quietly. When Willow didn't reply, he took a deep breath and told her of his conversation with the doctor, told her he was scared about his son's condition, and finally confessed that he left a message for Melissa. With nothing further to blurt, he stopped talking.

"We should go today, and hope Melissa isn't there," Willow said.

"You're not angry?"

"No, that's Fin's job," Willow said with a sad chuckle. "You're Kyle's father. You'd do the same for Fin, or for Zen. And you had to tell Melissa. You did the right thing."

Tears burned in Brad's eyes. He'd done the right thing. He hadn't realized how badly he needed to hear that.

"But," Willow said, "when you act like Kyle is a dirty secret, I feel like you don't trust me." She looked away.

"I have something else," Brad mumbled. "A dirty secret."

Willow looked back, eyebrows raised.

"You have a twin," he said, watching for her reaction.

Willow's eyes widened and her brows went higher. "How did you know?"

Brad blinked at her. "How did you? You never said anything."

"She's one of the things I learned during my captivity, listening to the bubbles." Brad gave her a puzzled look. "It's hard to describe. The place where I spent those years is some kind of colossal mind. I visited it once before. The night I met you. Remember, I was hitchhiking?"

Brad nodded with a smirk. "You said you were a dryad."

Willow rolled her gorgeous jade eyes. "Yeah. Well, you knew I was on something, but I never told you any details."

"You went to this same place?"

"It looked different but it felt the same. An endless ocean of green tie-dye fire, full of everything people obsess about. The scariest was that masonic eye thing on the dollar bill. It was hunting me. I panicked and created a swarm of spiders to hide behind." She shook her head and chuckled. "I did mention I was high, right? Anyway, drug trip stuff aside, Severin calls it the Elsewhere, because he's pompous. It's like an übermind for all humanity. It's made of people's thoughts, but it has its own thoughts, too. I overheard what it thought about, including me and my twin. All I know is that she exists. Given my track record with family reunions, I don't care to press the matter." She paused again. "Now you. How did you know?"

Brad squirmed, and could tell Willow noticed. "Technically I don't

know anything. Maybe I'm wrong."

Willow narrowed her eyes. Brad looked down.

"It's Melissa," he mumbled. Willow tensed. He spoke without raising his head. "On the day Fin and Kyle were born, I put it together. Like I said, I have no proof. But so many things fit, with your birthdays, and your childhoods. You look a lot alike, too, underneath the hair and the clothes." Hearing the phrase escape his lips, Brad panicked. Looking at Willow pleadingly he said, "I mean you dress differently!"

She smiled. "The crazy thing is, that actually makes sense. It lines up with some other things I overheard."

"I never set out to marry your sister." Brad was evidently not done blurting things out, after all.

Willow dropped her glance, which might have been to check on Zen.

He continued, "It was a huge mistake. It almost got me killed." Willow's eyes flicked back to his. "Melissa was researching poisons, toward the end." He felt Willow stiffen again and Zen made a grumpy little noise. "I hate to say mean things about your sister, but she planned to kill me."

Willow let out a sigh. "My own mother kidnapped me. Why should I be touchy about my homicidal sister?"

She switched Zen over to the other side. "Is there anything else in the box?"

"Let's see." Brad folded himself in half and stretched out his arm to get a grip on the edge of the box, grunting. Willow giggled, and Zen fussed.

"Daddy made Mommy move. Bad Daddy," Willow murmured, helping Zen latch on again.

Brad started lifting artifacts out of the box, studying each and holding it out for Willow to see.

His MBA certificate, framed. Snapshots. Some small antiques came out next. A mantel clock, well preserved but nonfunctional. A pair of small horses carved from a deep green semiprecious mineral. He told

her how they had been passed down through the family and were said to be terribly valuable, but his mother allowed him to play with them anyway.

"There's only one more thing," he said.

He produced an empty wine bottle. Willow glanced expectantly from it to Brad several times. Brad smiled, feeling sunshine on his face and remembering a warm campfire after skinny-dipping. Willow nudged him with her elbow and raised her eyebrows.

"It's from our picnic." Brad watched for Willow's recollections to show.

"At the lake," she breathed, a languid joy brimming in her eyes.

Brad put the bottle back in the box with the horses, and gave Willow a deep kiss. Zen protested, so he planted a gentle kiss on her head and she seemed content.

*** *** ***

"Both together?" asked the waiter. "Or separate checks?"

Rook rubbed her temples and said, "One check. I'll have the all-you-can-eat spaghetti. Alfredo sauce. And water with lemon."

"Same here," said Fin. "Only I'll have the meat sauce."

The Shamrock Diner was famous for their cheap, mediocre lunch specials. The pasta would be bland, but they could stuff themselves for $3.99 each.

Rook was beginning to relax. Things were getting back on track. After lunch they would both be in better moods and she'd make Fin see how stupid he was being.

Then she'd be able to a take real shower. A long, hot shower. Scalding.

Seventeen days she'd been with Kyle. Over two weeks.

Rook shuddered.

A sponge bath on an asteroid full of giant spiders, and a lukewarm splashing in a locker room shower, might have rinsed away all the blood, but they were not enough to wash away her degradation.

For that she needed time. Time alone, and time with Fin to heal

their fractured relationship. But now Fin was acting like an asshole, and they were essentially homeless.

And she could still feel Kyle.

Even worse than the stink of him on her skin was the stain inside her head. While the shattered cathedral filled with noxious smoke, her two husbands made her mind their battlefield.

The horrible violation of Kyle's presence there, full-fledged and malice-ridden — the confusion caused by Brook and Bramble — the humiliating inability to be sure of her own desires — the knowledge that she nearly became the instrument of Fin's demise —

Rook pressed her forehead against the cool tabletop and took slow breaths.

Fin worked his fingers into her hair and massaged her scalp.

If only her headache would go away. It had been a constant nagging presence since the cathedral, since the mental signals linking her to both halves of the Divided Man rang through her at the same time.

Fin's vibration felt strong and constant, yet distorted. Kyle had left something behind, something to remember him by. He'd maintained his proprietary grip on her mind even as Fin destroyed him.

Mental shrapnel. Brittle, insidious splinters of Kyle's psyche buried in her brain, vibrating to his unique wavelength, creating interference with Fin's signal, and enticing her evil sister personas out of hiding. What could be better?

Rook knew Fin would want to help, but she couldn't stomach the thought of him entering her mind while he was so irrational. Couldn't say she ever wanted anyone in there again.

The waiter returned with their lunch. Rook sat up. Fin scooted Vesuvius's bag out of the way and eyed his bowl like a predator. Rook sniffed her own food suspiciously. The sauce had separated, leaving unappetizing, semen-like clumps clinging to the pasta, and the cheese smelled a bit ripe. Rook poked it with her fork as Fin scooped up huge bites of his and shoveled them into his mouth.

The sauce wasn't as bad as it looked, but the noodles were beyond

gummy. Rook washed down each bite with gulps of water.

Fin noticed her distress. "The Alfredo's no good? Here, we'll trade."

He swapped their bowls and dug right in with indiscriminate gusto. Rook managed to finish the remains of the meat sauce serving, but wished she had ordered something else.

When Fin was winding down on his third helping, Rook pounced.

"I'll have about $180 after I pay for this," she said. "That's it."

Fin nodded and mopped up some leftover sauce with a chunk of garlic bread. "Cool."

"No, Fin, it's not cool. It's all the money we have. What are we gonna do?"

He sat back in the corner of the booth and put his boot-clad feet on the seat. "We'll think of something."

"We're dressed like a couple of thrift store mannequins," she snapped, "and I don't even have any underwear!"

Fin glanced around to see if anyone noticed her outburst, but Rook was past caring. She blinked away angry tears and went on, "Maybe you're happy to keep wearing the same clothes and carry Vesuvius around in a shopping bag. But I'm not, Fin! I'm not." The tears came now, hot and choking.

Fin hurried around to her side of the table and put his arms around her. Rook wanted to collapse into his embrace, but needed to keep fighting to escape this unacceptable situation.

"Shh," Fin soothed. He kissed the top of her head. "Rook, shh. We'll fix it. What do you want to do?"

"I want to dye my hair," she surprised herself by saying.

"What?"

"*He* did this to me. I don't want to look like his creature anymore."

"Well, okay." Fin sounded flustered.

"And I don't want to dye it in a public bathroom." Rook shook with the force of her sobs.

Fin hugged her and was silent.

"Please Fin," she begged. "Can we please talk to Bishop? He'll

understand, won't he? He'll let us in, right?"

Fin kissed her head again and squeezed her. "I never talked to him after the reception," he confessed. "The explosion put him in the hospital, and I didn't visit him. I was too worried about finding you."

Rook sniffled and wiped her wet cheeks on her sleeve.

"I guess I need to explain that to him, not you," Fin conceded.

Relieved Fin finally acknowledged the need for help, Rook allowed herself to relax against him and be comforted by his embrace and his sweetly smoky smell.

Her tears ran their course as the other diners lost interest in the melodrama. Fin cradled her and smoothed her hair. He held her hands and stroked the chess tattoos on her inner wrists with his thumbs, murmuring apologies.

After a trip to the restroom to blow her nose and splash her face with cool water, Rook felt better. She pulled her leather jacket on over the gray hoodie, grabbed her mismatched gloves and, together with Fin and poor Vesuvius, got in line to pay.

Behind the counter a wall-mounted television showed the weather. The storm had moved north to spew its wrath over New England. Sunny skies and frigid temperatures were expected for the remainder of the week.

The anchorwoman came onscreen wearing her serious face. "Search and rescue teams in Donner are combing the rubble of the Shaw Ministries Cathedral for bodies."

Rook's breath caught.

Over footage of the smoldering ruin, the report told about renegade reverend Declan Spitz and how, upset at being removed as the public face of Shaw Ministries, he staged a coup resulting in the total destruction of the cathedral, the grievous injury of interim leader Kyle Tanner, and the disappearance of somewhere between 2,000 and 3,000 people.

Rook gasped. *Kyle is alive.*

No fatalities had been discovered. Rook knew they never would be.

They'd all been incinerated by Kyle's mind and their ashes were now mingled with those of the entire building.

Fin nudged Rook forward a few steps and whispered, "Ignore it. It doesn't concern us anymore."

The utter bullshit of the report fascinated Rook from a journalistic standpoint.

The cable news claimed that Spitz led every single ministry employee and student, plus a few thousand worshipers, in a rebellion against upstart Kyle, and into hiding. Authorities feared a repeat of Jonestown or Waco. It was unclear whether the Declanists, as they were being called, remained in the US, or had fled overseas. Anyone with information was urged to contact law enforcement.

Rook didn't think she'd be doing that.

Fin guided her forward again as the line moved. They were almost to the register.

The anchorwoman thanked the field reporter and said, "All footage from inside the Shaw Ministries control room was destroyed, but we have obtained a home recording of the final broadcast. We apologize for the low quality of the image."

Rook's stomach flip-flopped and she thought she might get another look at the reviled Alfredo sauce.

Kyle's grainy image materialized on the screen, preaching his gospel. Eyes so filled with hungry madness in a face so much like Fin's. The color balance was off, the greens too vivid. Inside Rook's head the shrapnel throbbed. Brook and Bramble moaned with pleasure, and Fin's vibration wavered.

Rook felt lightheaded as whiteness overtook her vision. She sucked in a breath and realized the whiteness was just snow on the TV. The image broke down completely, replaced by a picture of a television camera with angel wings and a halo, and the message Heaven Help Us, We Are Experiencing Technical Difficulties.

Neither she nor Fin appeared in the footage. Rook smiled and took a shaky breath, then turned and hugged Fin tight.

"We're okay," he said, and she started to believe it.

It was her turn to pay. The reporter on TV started interviewing an expert on cults. Change in hand, Rook hurried back to the booth to leave a tip. When she dropped a dollar bill and handful of coins on the table, one of the quarters spun away from its brothers and twirled on its axis. The image rattled Rook and she turned away before it could slow and topple, deciding the answer to an unasked question.

✳✳✳   ✳✳✳   ✳✳✳

Jay Marshall collected Threshold House's mail from the box beside the front door, then sought out his girlfriend Rainbow. He found her on the sofa in the media room, cross-legged, flipping through the *Journal of Computational Physics*. He sat beside her.

Half to himself he said, "I wish I knew what the hell's going on around here."

Rainbow knitted her brow at him.

"Last night, the demolition derby out on the porch. Can you believe Severin would participate in something like that?"

"That's not the weirdest part," Rainbow said. "Who'd he take up to the attic?"

Marsh had no idea. He was probably the closest thing Severin had to a right-hand man, and even he didn't really know the guy.

They all knew it was Severin's money they were playing with, and that he was exponentially more hands-off than any corporate or university research director on Earth. If he was a bit eccentric and creepy, that usually felt like a pretty good trade for such unparalleled lack of supervision.

But winning a new girlfriend in a fistfight, or whatever the hell happened on the porch, was probably over the line.

Marsh shook his head. Before he could say anything Leaf rushed in. "Turn on the news!"

Marsh worked the remote, and Rainbow folded down a page corner and set aside her magazine.

Helicopter footage showed a smoldering heap of glass shards while a

male announcer intoned the sketchy specifics known so far.

When the announcer said, "If you're just joining us," Marsh muted the television.

"A cult uprising, huh?" He looked at Leaf, then at Rainbow.

"Convenient that the rebellion's leader disappeared, and can't be interviewed or interrogated," Rainbow said.

Leaf chuckled.

Marsh thought they were missing the most important point. "Someone really wanted that jewelry."

Marsh, Rainbow, and their cohorts at the TEF had, until very recently, been reverse-engineering a cache of body jewelry stuffed to the gills with gobsmackingly ingenious nanotechnology. The upstart preacher Kyle Tanner sent armed mercenaries to re-steal it, and now his empire was a smoldering ruin.

Rainbow shivered. "I'm glad it wasn't here anymore."

"Some of it is," Marsh said.

All three looked around at each other.

Leaf said, "We'll have to take extra precautions. If we lose those pieces, we'll never be able to contact the aliens."

"You and your aliens," said Marsh and Rainbow together.

Leaf folded his arms and glared at the television.

Rainbow looked pointedly at Marsh. "Should we tell Severin?" By 'we' she meant 'Marsh' and everyone knew it. He was the only member Severin spoke to anymore.

Marsh sighed. "Maybe tomorrow. Now doesn't seem like a good time to go up."

Cliff walked in from the kitchen and took a bite out of the apple he carried. He chewed, then asked, "Does anybody know what happened to the basement door?"

Various shrugs and other noncommittal responses met this question.

"It's busted. Somebody kicked it in, or something."

"Nobody ever goes down there, except Severin and Gale," Marsh

offered.

"Come to think of it, where is Gale?" Leaf asked. "I mean, has anybody seen her?"

Marsh thought about the mysterious new woman, and he and Rainbow shared a significant look.

*** *** ***

Neither Brad nor Willow had ever installed an infant car seat before, so it took the better part of an hour before they were satisfied they'd done it right. With Zen strapped in, they started out for Donner. Brad was relieved to be on the move.

The plows and salt trucks made the roads passable and the trip through the crystalline landscape took only a little longer than usual.

At the hospital, Willow and Zen were examined and pronounced fit. Zen weighed in at 7 pounds, 7 ounces. She received her first round of inoculations, which did not please her, got her footprints taken to dissuade her from ever becoming a foot criminal, and received the name Zen Promise Tanner on her birth certificate.

With his girls squared away, it was time to locate Kyle. Brad had managed to keep worry for his son at bay by focusing on his daughter. Without that distraction, the terrible, crushing concern hit him all at once.

Willow handled talking to the hospital staff and they were escorted to Kyle's room.

Kyle lay in the hospital bed, his right knee bandaged and elevated. He was hooked to an IV and had a heart monitor clipped to his finger. Despite what the doctor told him on the phone, Brad expected much more equipment. Aside from the knee and a few scrapes on his face and knuckles, Kyle looked uninjured. What on Earth happened to him? There were no bandages on his head. If he'd been rendered nearly brain dead, wouldn't there be some outward sign of trauma?

Willow squeezed Brad's hand and gave him a little push into the room. She stood in the doorway gently bouncing Zen to keep the infant amused.

Brad approached Kyle's bed, feeling the sting of tears. He touched Kyle's hand, the one without the IV. It was warm but unresponsive.

"Hey, Tiger," Brad choked. He bent over and kissed Kyle's forehead. Surely that would offend Kyle enough to wake him, but no protest came. Brad broke down into sobs. He knelt beside the bed and clasped Kyle's hand between both of his, hugging it against his cheek.

A few moments later he felt Willow's hand on his shoulder. She stood behind him, offering him her support. This would be unbearable without her.

Zen gurgled.

"This is your brother, Kyle," Willow explained. "He's not well right now, but we hope he wakes up soon so he can meet you."

Once Brad regained his composure they talked to the doctor to find out what happened, and arrange Kyle's transfer to the hospital in Webster. The doctor told him tests showed no alpha or beta waves in Kyle's cerebrum. He did exhibit lower-level brain function, meaning the only life support he currently required was an IV. "The knee surgery was a splendid success," added the doctor, but Brad didn't allow the shift of topics.

"How serious is the brain damage?"

"Your son's case gives us conflicting clues. Strictly speaking, there is no brain damage. No significant injuries, apart from the knee. Our best guess at the cause of his state is drastic psychological trauma."

"He wasn't in an accident?" Brad recalled the previous time Kyle ruined his knee.

"No, Mr Tanner." The doctor sounded puzzled.

"Then what happened to him?"

"Haven't you seen the news?"

Brad indicated Willow and the baby. "We've been distracted. Please tell me what happened to my son."

The doctor would only say Kyle was dropped off at the emergency room, and reiterated that Brad should watch the news. He offered to let them use a private waiting room.

An orderly showed them to the room, handed them the remote, and left.

Brad turned on the news and got up to speed on the story of the Shaw Ministries coup, but the story made no sense. Kyle was mentioned, but Brad couldn't understand how he tied in. The footage of Kyle preaching made him laugh. There was nothing else to do. Kyle as a televangelist was beyond disbelief.

Willow looked nonplussed.

"He told us he worked for a security firm," Brad said.

"Like a bodyguard?"

"He never said. I guess maybe he was working undercover at this church."

"Pretty far undercover."

Brad nodded. What other explanation was there?

"I need to tell you something unbelievable now," Willow said in a hushed tone.

"I don't know how many more unbelievable things I can take in."

"I think that Brian Shaw person was my real father."

Brad remembered Willow telling him her father was a cop, but that was when she thought her mother died in childbirth. Now they knew she'd been lied to about her past.

"It's confusing," Willow continued, "but I think that's something I learned while I was — wherever I was." She shook her head and shrugged.

"That is pretty unbelievable."

She furrowed her brows. "Yeah. Maybe it was just a dream."

"I've heard that lots of girls dream of being a televangelist's daughter," Brad joked. "It's more popular these days than being a princess."

Willow chuckled and swatted him.

To Zen, Brad said, "You won't do that, will you? You'll be Daddy's princess."

*** *** ***

Prophecy.

An eloquent portrayal of the deeper reality, encapsulating all of time

from the dividing of the seed to the restoration of the light. It was perhaps unflattering to find oneself referred to as a hidden plague, but for the spiders it remained a potent truth regardless. Dwelling in the asteroid belt did hide them from humanity, after all. They took comfort in knowing the setbacks and suffering they'd experienced had been foretold, and they drew even greater strength from the knowledge that all would come right in the end.

The spiders' mind reveled to once more have something on which to meditate. And what a marvelous key this gave them! Like a decryption algorithm for the human psyche, it led them to a miraculous discovery. They beheld the true author of the prophecy, for whom Reverend Shaw had merely been a utensil.

They saw the collective human mind.

A magnificent being, not attenuated across light years like the Floating Wisdom but concentrated on Earth in billions of minds. Minds so imperfectly joined that they remained ignorant of it. Yet its strength was boggling. If the harmony could be perfected, and all those thoughts aligned, this collective would become a god.

The meshing of human minds was at present confined to the raw, tempestuous Id. A roiling cauldron of conflicting impulses, a creature built of wants piled upon urges, fight on top of flight. Made of what everyone else wanted, the Collective Id had wants of its own.

Prophecy.

The spiders themselves were birthed from the Id, complete with their fabricated history as cogs in the Floating Wisdom, that caricature of the true collective. In their manifestation as aliens, as giant arachnids, they represented something humanity needed and dreaded simultaneously.

The Floating Wisdom's ambition to assimilate humanity had been its juvenile attempt at deepening the unity of all human thought, echoing the Id's aims as it was, itself, an echo.

Having accepted their status as a shared delusion, the spiders embraced their role as agents of prophecy.

They alone knew how to restore light upon the Earth.

They would fully awaken the Collective Id.

Chapter Three

A FORMER MOTEL

Individuals with known ties to the late Reverend Shaw have made contact with this agency regarding technology we have an interest in, offering to disclose the location of aforesaid hardware in exchange for special treatment with respect to specific legal matters which these individuals characterize as belonging to the class of events this agency prefers to give special handling, to minimize public disquiet, suggesting the arrangement constitutes a win-win.
Operation Lullaby internal communication, 11-7-2000

Fin halfheartedly kicked his mini-fridge. It didn't provide much of an outlet for his rage.

Rook had been right. All it took to gain access to their room was an awkward apology to Bishop for being a lousy friend. Now she was with Bishop, retrieving her clothes from the bomb shelter, which gave Fin privacy for his tantrum.

He flung himself into his battered recliner, thrashing the air with his fists and wanting to scream. *Why does Brad have to be such a dick?* A scalding brew of images roiled in Fin's mind, forming no coherent pattern, just violation and fury.

How was he supposed to protect Rook with Brad invading their sanctuary? How did Brad even know about it?

When else has he been in there?

Fin pounded the armrest, which yielded with a loud creak.

He slumped. Willow. All these years, half his life, Fin held to his faith that she'd come home. But she was with Brad all along. Making babies.

Fin wept, snot and sticky tears pouring out, his shoulders heaving.

Someone said his name. He opened his eyes, and heard a familiar deadpan voice ask, "Are you all right?"

"Hey, Vesuvius. Yeah, I'm fine. How 'bout you?"

"Great. Good to be home."

Fin pawed at his wet cheeks. "Uh huh."

"It was strange when those people came to the bomb shelter. Brad, Willow, and the baby."

Fin scowled. "Yeah, I know."

"I wondered if Willow would remember me. I said hi, but she couldn't hear me. She seemed confused."

"What do you mean, 'confused'?"

"She didn't believe what Brad kept trying to explain to her."

"Start at the beginning." Fin wanted to hear about Willow, even if his feelings were too jumbled to cope with her actual presence.

Vesuvius recounted the unexpected arrival of Fin's family. How Willow demanded to know what Brad meant about twelve years, and Brad's insistence that was how long she was missing. Her contention that it was biologically impossible, that it had to be six months, based on her pregnancy. Brad admitted he couldn't explain it, but he could describe the bizarre circumstances of her imprisonment. Hearing about the stone altar surrounded by magic dominoes changed Willow's mind about the impossibility, and she let him leave to get diapers.

"A little later you and Rook got there."

Because Vesuvius presented his tale as a complete transcript, it took about half an hour to get through it.

Fin mulled.

Rook came in with her backpack slung over one shoulder and her laptop hugged to her chest, lugging a beat-up trash bag full of — Fin hoped — clothes.

She dumped everything on the mattress and hoisted herself onto one of the cafe stools.

Fin belatedly stood so she could have the chair, but she waved him

off.

"They aren't down there anymore. They left you a note." She handed over a folded piece of paper.

He opened it and spread it on the table so they could both see.

Fin,

We're going to a hotel. There's a lot we need to talk about, so we hope to see you again soon under better circumstances.

Love, Mom & Brad & Zen

*** *** ***

Bubbles of light surround him. Clear and bright, blinding white.

He is lost in the thick, murky darkness, unable to find his way. Unable, even, to find himself. He should be in agony. The bitch, his beautiful, devoted wife, destroyed his knee. It seemed the rest of him was destroyed along with it, shattered into malignant green grit and diffused among the pure bubbles of light.

The bubbles speak to him of another, baptized in this same way, and how they miss him. Kyle understands that the bubbles are speaking of his brother. Of course they are speaking of his brother. He and his brother are the Divided Man. They must share everything, even this.

Kyle's brother never spoke to the lights. They hope Kyle will.

Kyle knows that a small, almost insignificant portion of himself has remained with his wife, buried inside her. He wonders if it will help him return to his body.

For now he floats among the bubbles and listens.

*** *** ***

The charred flesh smell had finally been eradicated from the unfinished attic. The windows were closed again, slowing the arctic outside air's infiltration. Melissa Tanner huddled under an electric blanket in the hammock and stared at her uncle. A short, dumpy man with scraggly, graying hair and beard, a hawk nose, and fiercely blue eyes under wild, dark brows. Being her mother's twin put him in his sixties. His lecherous behavior made him the epitome of a dirty old man.

What the hell did Brad get me mixed up in?

Severin refused medical attention for his amputation. He wrapped it in a bandage to hide the protruding bones. And that was all.

Whenever Melissa tried to coax her body into movement, to leave this freak show before anything worse could happen, fear of the inevitable crushing return of the patterns stopped her short.

Without a buffer, every sensory impression struck Melissa with amplified force, triggering cascades of pointless trivia. A flock of birds on the wing doused her with minor league batting averages from the 1920s, the rattle of a pot lid conveyed a tide chart for Galveston. Useless information contaminated all five senses, drowning out her life.

These patterns had wrecked her life until she found Brad.

Brad's simple presence shielded her from the tumult of inane facts.

So did Kyle's.

So did her uncle's, she recently learned.

She must get Severin to teach her to master her ability, like he promised. She must be able to function on her own. Without Brad or Kyle or Severin. Without anyone.

Brad had traded her in for his mistress, the woman Severin was all too happy to tell her was her long-lost twin. What sort of negating mystical balm did Brad provide her?

Severin grunted and stepped away from his table. He was frustrated in trying to 'use it' one-handed. Not that Melissa knew what he was trying to use it for. He refused to share that information. She assumed it was supposed to be magic.

What had her life become? She'd fucked her uncle, a virtual stranger, in the hopes he would teach her magic tricks. Melissa lifted the bottle of white wine and took a long drink.

Wine was the only thing she'd ingested in the 48 hours she'd been in Severin's house. The stench of his burnt flesh killed her appetite for a while, but she would need to eat soon.

She took another swig of wine.

When she opened her eyes, Severin stood over her.

"It's time for a lesson," he said. "Get undressed." He took the wine

and placed it on the floor, then hauled her to her feet.

Melissa's head swam and it took her several seconds to stop swaying, by which time Severin was naked and climbing into the hammock.

"Hurry up," he said. "Unless you don't want to learn."

Learning was the only way she would escape. Melissa reluctantly stripped. These were the clothes she'd worn to work two days ago, now rank and wrinkled. She dropped them with Severin's garments.

Amid much flailing and swearing, her drunken limbs conveyed her into her uncle's embrace. She straddled him and tried to keep her gaze averted from his missing hand. He chuckled as he entered her, then grabbed her left hand and put her thumb in his mouth. Melissa shuddered as he sucked it and shoved his salty thumb into her own mouth.

No matter how much she resented Brad, at least he never did anything like this.

Severin rested his stump on her hip. Melissa's stomach clenched, but she had to see this through or face suicide. She couldn't take a life full of the patterns again.

Her uncle seemed intent on bringing her to orgasm. Melissa did her best to accommodate so he wouldn't start prodding her with his stump. She'd passed out midway through her first time with him, and now she was grudgingly impressed at his staying power. Once she divorced her mind from the proceedings and only allowed herself to experience physical sensations, she felt surprisingly strong stirrings and her climax built.

When she came, Severin popped his thumb out of her mouth and pulled her down to kiss her, sucking the air from her lungs.

Melissa snagged the wine bottle and drained it to wash away the taste of Severin. He grabbed her hip to hold her in place.

Ages later he came too, and allowed Melissa to sleep.

When she woke, a fresh bottle of wine stood beside the hammock, uncorked and waiting.

Melissa struggled to her feet, ready for a trip to the bathroom. Severin looked up from his book. "I thank you for your assistance, Melissa, and I trust you found your lesson instructive."

"That was no 'lesson.'"

He held up his left arm, displaying the unbandaged stump. Instead of exposed bones, there was now shiny scar tissue.

"How the hell?"

Severin's lips did something smug. "The powers of the Elsewhere are marvelously useful. Do you understand now how to use them?" He sounded amused.

"You know I don't."

"Let me know when you're ready for your next lesson. I am at your beck and call." He returned his attention to his book.

*** *** ***

The prophecy reverberated in the alien spiders' collective mind. It spoke of a Divided Man, a being tragically split apart from itself. Prophecy also assured that this figure would be put whole through the Completer, restoring light upon the Earth.

The Tanner brothers were the Divided Man, although that image was best seen allegorically. The entire species was sintered into tiny, confused individuals. Fin and Kyle were archetypes, imbued with elemental separateness. In their fusion, all separation would be overcome for everyone.

Subconsciously Fin knew this. The art on his skin reflected the prophecy, the eclipse on his forearm most strikingly. It depicted the fusion of opposites necessary for the Completion of the Divided Man.

The spiders basked in the beauty of that vision of total unity. Their bliss didn't last, though, as they contemplated the cruel twist that connected them with, perhaps, the wrong brother.

Fin knew about the prophecy, but never told them.

Kyle was wreathed in it, stamping it onto everything he touched.

Fin rejected the prophecy, resisted his part in it.

Kyle embraced it, and possessed the will to act.

Rather than battling each other, these men should have been cooperating as agents of the Collective Id.

Now, it was too late. One of the brothers had been destroyed.

Or, had he?

Kyle's mind was pulverized, reduced to a gritty plume and flung across the whole collective. But he was alive. If his countless tiny granules could be coaxed back together, he might be repaired. He might still fulfill his preordained role.

Just as Fin might be persuaded to abandon his radical individualism.

The spiders were conflicted about talking to Fin since being touched by Kyle and suddenly understanding so much more. But it would be wrong to give up on Fin, whatever his past mistakes. To do so would be contrary to the prophecy.

*** *** ***

Fin trailed his fingers along the length of Rook's torso and over the rise of her hip, tracing the flight of the hundred or so bird tattoos speckling her pale skin. She was a Rook made of rooks, like the large tattoo on her right shoulder blade.

Sometimes that eight-inch tower, composed of a densely packed flock, was Fin's favorite, but his favorite was often whichever he was looking at. They were all strong and sexy, like the woman who bore them. His wife.

The twin bed they shared meant they spent their nights spooning under the pile of blankets, naked. Fin wasn't used to sharing, but he didn't mind too much since it meant waking up to this, a beautiful woman's bare bottom pressed into his crotch. Fin leaned forward and kissed his wife's shoulder right where it started to curve into her neck.

Rook's hair was black again, and smelled flowery, with a hint of ammonia. Her mood improved after dyeing it and taking a long shower, but she still seemed fragile. Fin understood. She'd been through a lot.

He kissed her neck and ran his hand up to cup her breast where a couple of the braver birds swooped close to her nipple.

She jerked awake and turned to look at him in the soft amber glow

from Vesuvius.

"Morning," he murmured and kissed her shoulder.

She smiled and relaxed back onto the pillow, facing him, her signal a gentle purr at the base of his skull.

Fin pulled her in for a kiss, ready to lose himself in her.

On his mini-fridge was one last condom. It supposedly glowed in the dark, but Fin couldn't be bothered to let it charge up before putting it to use.

***

When Rook returned from the bathroom, Fin was lounging in bed. He was scheduled to look for a job today and wanted to procrastinate as long as possible. It would feel more satisfyingly slackerish with a smoke, but they were broke so he had effectively quit. Rook wouldn't get her first paycheck from her new university library job for another two weeks.

"I need you to go somewhere with me today," she said.

"The employment office?" Fin asked with marked unenthusiasm.

"Something you'll like even less," she promised. "The employment office will be like dessert after our errand."

"Do tell," Fin said, his interest piqued.

"I want to get my stuff from Marcus's apartment."

The statement hung there between them, and Fin waited for it to resolve into something more palatable. Like résumé writing. Or syphilis.

Rook soldiered on. "I want to get everything before the eviction notice goes up and they sell it at auction or something."

Fin didn't like the idea of her having to pay Marcus's bills. She'd already paid enough on that asshole's behalf.

"I'd like you to come with me," she continued. "The memories…" She cleared her throat. "The memories might, uh…"

"Okay," Fin said so she wouldn't have to keep searching for the words. He'd already seen her upset enough in the past few days. "What do you think, Vesuvius? Does she just want me along to lug the heavy boxes?"

"That or she has a pickle jar she can't open."

Rook smiled with relief. Fin liked to make her smile.

He dragged himself out of bed and pulled on a pair of jeans and a well-worn Nicotine tee over a thermal undershirt. He'd designed his band's logo himself.

Rook upended her trash bag of clothes onto the floor and chose a gray minidress and a pair of thick black stockings.

The temperature was a balmy 20 Fahrenheit. Fin buttoned his Red Army trench and shoved his hands in the pockets. Rook wore her leather jacket, and wrapped a plaid scarf around her neck three times.

At the liquor store they scored a couple of boxes. Rook led the way around to the alley, heading toward Talisman Tattoo.

"I thought you wanted to go to the apartment."

"After this. This should be easier. I need my certification papers, my portfolio, and my equipment. I paid for it, I'll be damned if I'm going to leave it in there. I'll sell it myself."

Fin took her by the arm. "You don't want to go in there."

"Of course I don't, but I need to get my stuff." She was getting frustrated with him again.

"Hang on. Let me explain. I went in when I was looking for you. There's puke everywhere."

Rook wrinkled her nose. "Peyote."

Fin nodded. "Plus, he was kinda crazy. There's stuff you don't need to see." Specifically her blood-coated effigy. "You wait here. I'll get your things."

She told him what she wanted and where to find it. Fin hurried in, skirting the dried vomit lakes, and collected everything in under ten minutes. He checked the cash register for extra funds, but came up empty.

With Fin lugging the box of piercing supplies they walked to Marcus's apartment. The building was a former motel, converted in the 80s, its U-shape surrounding a parking lot full of ratty cars and oil stains. The exposed staircase took them to the second floor's open

walkway.

Rook hesitated outside the door to #211, key at the ready. She looked up at Fin, her blue eyes frightened and glistening.

"You can wait out here," Fin said.

She shook her head. "Just help me, okay?"

"Okay."

She stuck the key in the lock and turned the knob. The apartment looked like it had when Fin came to collect her clothes: larger and nicer than his own. The unit used to be two motel rooms with a connecting door. One of the bathrooms had been ripped out and its plumbing cannibalized for the kitchenette.

A private bathroom and a stove? Luxury!

Rook took a deep breath and let it out, then stepped into the living room. Fin followed. Seeing her here made him uncomfortable. She lived here with Marcus for two years. This was her home much more than the boarding house was.

"I want to do this quickly." Her voice was tight. "Gather up any books that aren't Native American themed."

Fin scouted around while Rook rifled through CDs and DVDs, adding about half to the Stoli box she held.

The bedroom stank of stale pot smoke. Fin eyed the double bed with a pinch of jealousy and wondered if Rook missed having room to stretch out.

Moments later Rook darted into the room and over to a TV/VCR combo on the dresser. She stabbed the eject button and snatched the tape. After glancing at the handwritten label, she dropped it and stomped on it, sending her heel through the casing.

Fin raised his eyebrows and she said, "You don't want to know."

Fin tried not to think about what was surely on that tape.

"Ready?" he asked.

"Almost." She added the dead videotape to her box, and walked into the white tile bathroom.

Fin tagged along.

From the shower she retrieved shampoo, conditioner, and a purple razor. She opened the medicine cabinet and tossed him a pink plastic case. "Now we don't have to waste money on condoms."

Fin opened the case while Rook grabbed her toothbrush and a stick of deodorant. A small dome of rubber sat in the box.

"I never trusted condoms on Marcus," Rook explained in a falsely cheerful tone, "because of how... ornamented Li'l Coyote was."

"I didn't need to know that," Fin grumbled, then realized, "It's a diaphragm."

"Yep." Rook tossed two boxes of tampons and a handful of panty liners into the Stoli box.

Fin closed the case while Rook rummaged through a laundry basket, sorting her silky undergarments from Marcus's BVDs and flannel shirts. Finally she positioned the vodka box at the edge of the counter and used her forearm to sweep everything in: hairspray, lipsticks, nail polish, and about fifty other mysterious tubes. Where would they put it all?

Back in the bedroom, Rook went to the desk against the end wall and unplugged an inkjet printer. As she flipped through a pile of papers her hands began to shake. By the time Fin set his box down and gathered her into a hug her cheeks were wet with sudden tears, her lips trembling.

I should never have let her come here!

Her whole body quaked, and so did her signal. She whispered something he couldn't hear.

"Shh," Fin soothed. "Let's get out you out of here."

She whispered again and this time Fin caught it. "I had to kill him."

"I know." He felt impotent, had no way of knowing how this felt for her, didn't know how to help her. He sat on the floor with her in his lap and held her as she sobbed.

"He was going to rape me," she said into his chest. "And then he was going to kill me."

Fin squeezed her. "It's all over now."

"I screamed so loud." She shuddered. "I was so scared, Fin."

"I wish I could have helped you. But you were brave, Rook. Really fucking brave."

"I shot him in the throat," she whispered.

He hadn't heard these details before. The image of her terror and desperation filled Fin's head and brought tears to his own eyes.

"I'm so sorry I couldn't keep you safe," he said. "I love you more than anything and it kills me that you had to go through that."

She clung to him and wept, her tears soaking through his shirts to wet his skin. Many minutes later she said, her voice thick, "Will you still love me when I'm in prison?"

Fin held her tighter. "I would, but you're not going to prison. I promise."

"Someone will find his body."

"No. I know you don't want to talk about Kyle, but that's the one thing he did right. His toadies took care of the van and everything in it. Nobody will ever find him."

A long time later she shifted, breaking their embrace. With the bitterest smile she uncrumpled a wad of paper and showed it to him. A page from a large sketchpad, covered with a detailed pen and ink illustration.

"He was always working on the ultimate tattoo, to mark me as his. This was meant to cover my whole back."

Fin studied the sketch. The spread-winged rook from her lower back spanned the bottom of the design, supporting a hodgepodge of tribal symbols and power animals.

"I didn't want this, for obvious reasons. So I let him give me the other ink."

Fin thought of all the birds and towers across her body. It never occurred to him she might not have wanted them.

"Every tattoo I have he gave me, and every time I see them they remind me…"

If Fin didn't find a way to fix this, they would forever live in Marcus's shadow. "Hey," he said, but she didn't respond. "Rook." It

took a couple more attempts before she looked at him. The pain in her eyes broke his heart.

Fin indicated the graceful braid of black ink encircling his left ring finger.

"Marcus was a deplorable human being, and what he did to you was vile, but he gave me this tattoo, and it's beautiful."

He positioned his hand on hers, lining up their wedding rings.

"It's beautiful because it binds me to you. Forever. When I look at it I think of you, not him. I think of how much I love you and how amazingly lucky I am to have you."

Her lips twitched in a tiny smile, but her eyes were sad. Such a delicate color, the ghost of the color blue, they now looked flat and tired. Fin knew it was up to him to bring them back to life.

"You chose to have your wedding ring, right?" said Fin.

Rook nodded.

"Did you choose any of the others?"

Another nod.

"Which one was first?"

She pointed to her right arm where she had a long black quill in an inkwell shaped like a chess rook.

"You were playing with the dual meaning of your name, weren't you?" He smiled. He hoped to get her talking again, hoped he could salvage things.

"I wanted my mom to stop calling me Brook, to cement my chosen identity."

"You did it brilliantly."

"Then Marcus put the feather on my clavicle, then the birds on my ankle. After a while I had to balance them out with another tower, so I got this." She indicated the solid black rook on her left wrist.

"You showed him you were the boss." Fin hoped she'd see it that way.

Another tiny smile, this one briefly reaching her eyes. "I guess so." She sighed. "After that it was a tug of war. He'd doodle ravens, I'd insist

on a tower. Back and forth."

"You kept him in his place," asserted Fin.

"The one back here," she pretzeled her arm around to pat her shoulder blade, "I thought by making the tower out of birds I could get him to stop calling them ravens and call them rooks, but it didn't work. He still called them ravens. Called me Raven, too."

"But they're rooks. And you're Rook. Any fool can see that."

"I ended up with more birds than towers."

"You never let him give you this monstrosity." Fin waved the paper. "You won."

"Did I?" She sounded so small and afraid.

"Of course you did. When I see your tattoos they tell me you're a strong woman. You spent two years with the devil and you're the one who came out alive. Even if you didn't choose them all, your tattoos represent who you are. You *are* Rook. It's the name you chose, and it's who you are. You have the strength of the castle battlements and the grace and freedom of the bird. I love your tattoos because they're part of you and I love you."

"Really?"

"Really." He kissed her forehead.

"When you look at them you don't see him?"

"Absolutely not. I see my beautiful wife. But," he conceded, "if you want to remove them, I'll support you. I don't know how we'll afford it, but we'll find a way. I like them but it's more important that you like them."

"You promise me they don't bother you?"

"I promise."

"And you really think they make me look strong?"

"I do."

"And you really love me, even after everything?"

It wounded Fin that she had to ask, but she needed the reassurance right now. "Always, Rook. I love you always."

Now her eyes smiled. "I love you, too."

He held her, reassuring his poor, vulnerable girl that things would get better.

She squeezed him, then stood.

Their last stop was the kitchenette. She balled up the tattoo sketch and burned it in the sink.

In the cabinet beside the refrigerator she found a half-empty bottle of Southern Comfort. She took a long pull, then offered it to Fin. He took a sip, capped the bottle, and added it to his box.

Rook stared at the blinking light on the answering machine. "I might have an assignment for *CTP*." She pushed the button and they listened to the messages.

The first was someone named Donovan, inviting Rook and Marcus to a party. The next was Lara, Rook's friend from the library, asking if she planned to go to Donovan's party. Then the police called about her jacket and ID. After yet another call about Donovan's party, a woman's voice came from the tinny speaker.

"Brook, are you there? Pick up."

Rook shook her head. "Piss off, Mom."

"Junebug said you got married! And not to Marcus!" Rook's mother went on in a disbelieving tone. "Brook, honey, I can't believe it. You're only 21! Except, wait, what's today? Oh no! I missed your birthday again! You're 22 now. Happy birthday, Brook, honey. You should have reminded me. Anyway, you're just barely 22. Did you really get married?"

Rook squirmed.

"You need to call me, Brook. Oh, and Marcus, if you get this and she did marry someone else, could you please call and tell me who?"

Fin felt bad for thinking it, but Rook's mom sounded kind of wifty.

"Junebug?" Rook spat. There followed one more message, the landlord demanding the rent, but Rook talked over him. "How the hell did Bug find out?"

"Um," said Fin.

Rook eyed him suspiciously.

"I talked to her when I was looking for you. She's your sister, so I thought… I didn't know it was something you wanted to keep secret." It hurt a little that she didn't want her family to know about him.

Rook kissed him on the cheek. "Thank you for looking for me."

"You're not mad?"

"Not at you."

She took a final look around, then said, "I'm done here." She dropped her key on the coffee table.

Fin hefted two of the boxes and went out the door. Rook picked up the other two and left without looking back.

Chapter Four

ALLEYWAY AT NIGHT

A search of aviation records has uncovered a number of charter flights connected to the Declanist Cult. Authorities believe cult members have fled to southern Africa where leader Declan Spitz is rumored to have purchased land in several countries using embezzled ministry funds. The investigation is ongoing.
Webster Daily Press, 11-9-2000

Severin descended the main staircase, feeling like he was waking from a dream. He'd spent the past few hours having tantric sex with Melissa, recharging himself with her energy.

He thought back on afternoons spent in similar pursuits with Gale. There had been no sign of his twin in the three days since Melissa arrived. Gale was gone. She was never coming back, an idea that gave Severin vague consternation.

The onset of an odd malaise correlated with Gale's absence. Severin never felt anything like it in the many years before he met her, but it hit him as soon as she left.

Before they met, she nonetheless was out there, his complement, balancing things on some metaphysical level. They were, in a sense, a composite entity. If part of that entity were destroyed, the remainder would be thrown out of balance. That partial entity might even go into irreversible decline.

I am merely the half that hasn't stopped moving yet.

At least his consternation was no longer vague.

Such injustice. Instead of three power sources he now had only one. Severin momentarily lost himself in a reverie of how things ought to be,

Gale babysitting her grandchild while Willow and Melissa competed to please Severin in exchange for tiny scraps of knowledge. Far fairer to think of than the reality, where he had only this counterfeit Gale who openly resented him.

So far, Severin had succeeded in stringing Melissa along without teaching her anything of her power. It was key that he prevent her from attaining independence, ensure she remained afraid of being alone. And, ensure she never comprehended how dependent he was on the power he absorbed during their couplings.

Her fondness for alcohol made all that almost too easy. She thought she wanted to gain her freedom, but she always chose numbness when it was offered.

At the bottom of the steps a promising coffee smell drew Severin toward the kitchen. He glanced at the smooth, shiny stump of his left arm. *I should have made Melissa recover the slab.* Her contact with it would have released all the pent energy, and he would now be the Collective Superego.

Marsh stood in his path. "There's been a development, and I think you'll want to know about it."

Severin grunted and tried to keep heading for the kitchen. Marsh didn't budge.

"This is important. I need to talk to you."

Severin folded his arms. A fleeting look of horror crossed Marsh's face when he saw the stump.

Let him wonder.

Marsh swallowed and launched into a mercifully succinct explanation of the disaster at Shaw Ministries. He requested direction with regard to the jewelry, which might be in new hands now. Given the obvious coverup, Marsh speculated those hands could be governmental.

Severin raised his eyebrows. "This is the astonishingly important news? Shaw is dead, and our need for the jewelry is passed. I have initiated a new project, and do not have time for such irrelevancies. Now, please excuse me."

Marsh let out a heavy sigh, and smiled, relieved the matter was closed.

In the kitchen, Severin collected a case of white wine to take upstairs. He drank red himself, but there was half a bottle in the attic.

*** *** ***

Fin?

"So now you want to talk to me? Where the hell were you when we were freezing our asses off?"

There was little we could have done to help you. We were quite exhausted.

"Cry me a fucking river. You had enough juice to move us a few miles."

A regrettable set of circumstances. Give us a chance to make it up.

"What do you have in mind?"

Partnership.

"I hung up my superhero tights once Kyle was under control."

Before you came among us, we thought we knew all the answers. In our arrogance, we mistreated you. You dealt us grievous injury and pain. In self-defense.

"I'm not sure this is stuff you should be reminding me about if you're trying to win me over."

You could have left us to perish. You could have completed our destruction yourself, for which we couldn't have blamed you. Instead, you fashioned for us a marvelous solidarity. You made us better than we were before.

After a long pause, Fin sighed.

"You're welcome. Let's call it even."

In the time since you reshaped us, we have had much to contemplate. We understand now, where before we toiled in ignorance. We have discovered our mission, and it is something we cannot accomplish alone.

"I can't wait to hear this."

Healing us was merely a warm-up for you. There are so many who remain lonely and confused, and you, Fin Tanner, can heal them. You

can heal everyone.

"I thought you said you gave this a lot of thought. This is the same old Bloated Wisdom routine, and you know how I feel about that shit."

This isn't the same at all! The Floating Wisdom sought to impose its own unity, and it was unfeeling in pursuit of that goal. We want you to be the one to bring your people together. We know the ecstasy it brings. You can spread that to your own kind, Fin.

"Do I have to come up there and kick your asses? It's the same thing, no matter how you dress it up."

Please, Fin. Think more carefully about your own beliefs. You know this must happen, and you must be part of it.

"What the fuck are you talking about now?"

Divided Seed shall a Divided Child Beget, who shall grow into a Divided Man.

"NO!"

Yes. It is destiny.

"It's the half-baked, pretentious ramblings of a maniac. Ignore it. Forget it. Contemplate something else!"

Shaw never knew where those ideas came from. Why they matched your life.

"Anything can match up with anybody's life, if you want to believe badly enough. Especially if it's as vague as Shaw's bullshit."

We followed Shaw's words back to their source. We've seen the truth, Fin. And we think you know it already. Let yourself admit it. There's already a tenuous connection between all human minds, a collective not so unlike the Floating Wisdom. The dreams and terrors of the whole race flow together to make a Collective Id.

"You can convince yourself of anything, no matter how crazy, if it's what you want to believe!"

And you can refuse a truth, however incontrovertible, if it's uncomfortable.

"I will not help you with this."

We cannot do it without you.

"Good. You can't do it. Fuck off and die."

Fin...

"Fuck off and die."

✳✳✳   ✳✳✳   ✳✳✳

In order to fully awaken the Collective Id, thereby restoring light upon the Earth, the spiders required assistance. With Fin's refusal, they would need to reawaken the other half of the Divided Man. But how? He was comatose, his mind shattered much like the original Floating Wisdom.

The prophecy itself provided guidance. They turned to its other major figure, the Completer, and eavesdropped on her sleeping mind.

Rook dreamed she stood in an alleyway at night, lost. The New Revelations were spray painted across the block walls on both sides. Her bare feet sank into loose, filthy sand. Her flashlight provided only a feeble, greenish light.

Adding the prophecy to Rook's dream was the most the spiders could manage. She couldn't hear them like Fin, so they had to use more subtle means of communication. It was having an effect, though. She recognized the words and turned away, looking for a way out. No matter how far she ran, she never made any progress.

Rook wanted to escape before Reverend Shaw found her. Being surrounded by his ominous words recalled her to a dangerous time when she and Fin were his prisoners. Shaw hurt Fin, and she had to help. The sand became finer, more like ash. She sank in to her knees.

The spiders observed as Rook struggled in the gray dust, the alley now gone. She called for Fin, but the ash she slogged through was Fin. She had to rebuild him from the inside, digging up blocks from the ashes and organizing them into a tower. There were too few stones. To make up the shortfall, she added herself as a building block every few spaces.

The spiders withdrew to ponder what they had seen.

The essence of Rook's dream was factual. Fin had been catatonic, his mind destroyed, and she restored him. In so doing, she performed her

function as the Completer.

She could do it again.

Tomorrow night, Rook's dreams would feature Kyle.

*** *** ***

Brad had never before been to the boarding house where his sons lived. He was depressed by the state of dilapidation. It needed a new roof and fresh paint. The front walk was heaved over the roots of some long-gone tree. The owner didn't want to invest in upkeep while awaiting an offer from a developer, an all-too-common story with the big old houses in the neighborhoods close to campus.

The floorboards of the porch sagged as Brad navigated the narrow strip that had been cleared of ice. He knocked on the door and Bishop answered.

"Hi Brad." Bishop shook his hand. "Glad you could make it before I had to head to work."

"It's not a problem. Is he here?"

Bishop nodded. "They don't come out of the room much. Third floor. End of the hall, on the right."

"Thanks for helping me track him down." Brad started up the wooden stairs.

"Brad," Bishop said. When Brad turned back he continued, "I was sorry to hear about Kyle."

Brad smiled a grim smile. "Thanks, Bishop." He shook off the wave of melancholy and climbed the steps.

Standing outside the door to Fin's room, Brad rubbed his jaw and hoped he wasn't about to get punched again. The only sound from inside was the sporadic click of typing.

Brad rapped on the door. The typing stopped and footsteps scuffled. The door opened inward and revealed Fin's alleged wife holding an open laptop. Her pale blue eyes widened when she saw him.

Her hair was black now, and styled in an aggressively choppy fashion. She wore a tight black top sheer enough to reveal the black bra underneath, and a startling number of tattoos. A chess piece pendant

hung around her neck, and a sequined Union Jack miniskirt rode low on her hips. Her fishnet-clad legs ended in Cookie Monster slippers with ping pong ball eyes.

Brook glanced over her shoulder, into the part of the room blocked by the door.

"Is it Bish?" Fin's voice asked from those deeper recesses.

"No," Brook said and swung the door fully open.

Brad took in the room in one dismayed glance. A twin mattress lay defeated on the floor in the far corner. Squeezed in along with it were a green armchair and ottoman, a cafe table with two chairs, a rickety entertainment center, a dorm fridge, a stack of liquor boxes, and an enormous amplifier with no guitar on the stand beside it. The atmosphere was musky, if one wanted to put it kindly, a complex blend of overdue laundry, marijuana, and sticky sheets. A black garbage bag covered the only window. The walls looked like they'd been decorated by an angry teenage boy. The heap of dresses and lingerie beside the amp was the only sign a female lived here.

Fin sat at a flimsy desk crammed into the closet, staring at his Mac. The monitor was cluttered with palettes.

Fin clicked the mouse one final time and turned around. When he saw Brad he bristled and looked away, swearing.

Brook shifted her gaze between Brad and Fin. The silence grew awkward. Brad sought his VP of Lending smile, but settled for its wonky backwoods cousin.

"Hello, Brook. I'm Fin's father, Brad Tanner. I'd like to welcome you to the family."

Brook nodded and gave a tiny smile, then grasped her pendant and said, "It's Rook actually. Like the chess piece." She waved the necklace at him.

"Rook," Brad corrected himself. "Sorry."

Fin snorted and pushed his chair out from the desk. He stomped over to his wife in his stocking feet and wrapped an arm around her.

"What do you want, Brad?"

What Brad wanted was an end to all the hostility. He stood in the doorway, wishing what he had to say would be easy.

"I'm sorry, Fin." He shoved his hands in the pockets of his khakis.

Fin stood there.

"I'm sorry for a lot of things," Brad went on.

"Okay," Fin said and reached out to shut the door. Rook stopped him.

"Let him talk," she urged quietly, earning an immediate place in Brad's heart.

Fin rolled his eyes but made no further move to close the door. Rook backed him up a step to one of the seats at the cafe table, where he sat heavily beside his lava lamp. She took the other chair and placed her laptop on her knees.

Neither of them invited him in, so Brad continued to hang back in the doorway.

"Well?" Fin demanded.

Brad achieved fleeting eye contact. "Your mother just came back, that evening you saw her." Fin was going to interrupt, so Brad talked faster. "I know what it looks like, but that's not true. It's a very strange situation, hard to explain. I'll do my best."

Fin affected a bored look.

"I'm sorry I didn't keep her safe. It was my responsibility and I failed. I came here to apologize for letting you down and for not keeping your mother safe. I didn't know…"

"Didn't know what?" Fin spat.

"I didn't know there was any reason to worry. We were making plans to be together. She told me she was pregnant. I was going to leave Melissa."

Fin scoffed. Rook seemed to be taking notes.

"And then she was just gone. You know. You were there. She vanished, and I knew it was because I hadn't done my job. I should have protected her. I should have kept her safe." Brad blinked tears out of his eyes. "But now that she's back, I won't let anything or anyone hurt her

again. That includes you."

"Me?"

"Don't punish Willow for my failings. You can be mad at me, refuse to forgive me, hate me forever. I'm used to it. But she doesn't deserve it."

Fin's angry stare dropped.

"We've moved out of the bomb shelter. We're at the Buckminster Grand. I'm sorry we invaded your territory and that you feel violated. I needed a safe place to take her and the baby where Melissa wouldn't look. Or Severin."

"Who the fuck's Severin?"

"He's the man you should be angry with. He had Willow in his basement all these years, in some kind of cryogenic sleep."

"So the baby's his? Did he rape her?"

"The baby's mine, Fin. Zen's your sister. Willow was pregnant when she was abducted and she was in labor when I found her." He could see Fin's incredulity mounting. "I know it sounds crazy, but it's true."

Fin wiped his eyes on the sleeve of his dingy shirt.

Brad wished he could comfort his son. He cleared his throat and said, "Tomorrow's her birthday. It would mean the world to her if she could talk to you." He pulled a business card from his pocket and held it out. Fin stared at the floor. Rook set her computer down and approached to take the card.

"I've left the bank," Brad explained. "Our number at the hotel is on the back. Call anytime. Zen keeps us up anyway."

Rook flipped the card over and read the number. Brad noticed a tattoo around her ring finger. He looked at Fin's left hand and saw its mate. Were they legally married, or did they just get the matching tattoos and consider that good enough? He didn't think he could ask.

"Did she even miss me?" Fin asked, nearly inaudible.

"She didn't choose to leave. She loves you, Fin. And so do I."

Fin shot him an unreadable look, then wiped his eyes again.

Rook waited for a minute to see if Fin had anything else to say.

When he didn't she said, "Well, goodbye. Thanks for stopping by, Brad."

"Thanks for hearing me out," Brad said, more to Fin than to Rook. He gave Rook a tight smile and backed into the hall as she closed the door.

*** *** ***

"Fuck," Fin said. "Fuck fuck fuck." How was he supposed to deal with this shit?

Rook tucked Brad's business card under Vesuvius, then moved behind Fin and put her hands on his shoulders.

"I thought that went pretty well," she said.

"What, just because I didn't punch him?"

She kissed him on the shoulder. "Wanna talk about it?"

"Maybe." Fin wasn't used to having someone around who cared about him and wanted to help him work through his problems. But he didn't want to talk. At least not about his family.

Rook kneaded his shoulders in silence.

He knew how shitty Brad felt about failing to protect the woman he loved, and he guessed that meant he accepted that Brad loved his mother.

Fin didn't want to relate to Brad. Their relationship had always been antagonistic, which kept things simple. Now he was in danger of understanding how guilty and helpless Brad felt when Willow disappeared. Brad had no way of knowing Willow would be kidnapped, the same way Fin had no way of knowing Rook would be. What made it worse was Brad only let Willow down once, whereas Fin let Rook get abducted at least three times.

Which makes Brad the better man. Wonderful.

Rook gave his shoulders a final squeeze and picked up her laptop.

"Does Brad know Vesuvius talks?" she asked.

"No," said Fin and Vesuvius.

"Why?" Fin asked.

"The stuff he said about this Severin person lines up with what

Vesuvius told you. If he doesn't know the lamp is going to fill us in on his story, why would he try to convince you of something so outlandish? He was trying to get you to trust him, and that would be much easier if he left out the parts about the evil genius with a science fiction contraption in the basement."

"You think he's telling the truth?"

"Well, maybe."

Fin bridled. *How can she believe Brad?*

"The world's not how we always thought," she said. "Where were we going to spend our honeymoon?"

"Inside an asteroid."

"With who?" she prompted.

"The spider alien collective," he said with a sigh.

"And what is Vesuvius?"

"A talking lava lamp only the two of us can hear," Fin admitted.

"If you can accept all of that, plus wage mental warfare with Kyle, I think you should be open to the possibility that what Brad said is true."

"Maybe."

"And I think you should call your mom."

"I think you should call yours," Fin retorted.

She looked at him for a full minute, staring into his eyes. "If you call your mom on her birthday, I'll tell mine I got married, and endure the endless lectures."

"Deal," Fin said, and closed his eyes.

*** *** ***

After checking both direction signs, Rook turned a corner with her book cart. Buckminster's library was the size of a shopping mall, and she hadn't yet learned all the passageways.

The stacks could be particularly disorienting because it all looked the same, endless rows of dull green metal shelves stuffed with endless rows of books.

Only one book remained on her cart, and if she could find the place it belonged her job would be complete.

The book's title was *Dividends, a Manual for Maximizing Returns*. Checking the catalog number on its green leather spine, Rook saw it belonged under Religion and Philosophy. She looked at the back cover, and saw a picture of a spinning coin. A hologram, she thought. It spun even when she held the book still.

Laying the volume back on the cart, Rook noticed the title was actually *A Divided Man Returns*.

She pushed her cart down a long, institutional-green corridor. There were no bookshelves, just closed doors at regular intervals. Outside the next one was a gurney, its occupant covered with a sheet. Rook pulled back the sheet to reveal a row of books, held in position by mismatched bookends. One looked like a head, the other a pair of bare feet. One toe had a bookmark tied to it.

This was the Science and Technology gurney, so her book didn't belong there.

She kept walking down the endless green hallway, occasionally entering a room to see what types of books belonged on the beds. She found Psychology, History, every conceivable genre of fiction, Hypnosis, Ballet, and Human Sexuality. She found dozens of other topics, but not the one she needed.

Every few minutes an echoey female voice made announcements in an uninflected, businesslike tone.

"An unknowing angel with shadowed wings shall heal the divided man and restore light upon the Earth."

"Those who go forth in chains shall be called into the firmament, but fall and be minions of the pretender."

Rook couldn't make sense of the messages, although the words carried an odd familiarity.

One door stood open along the right side of the corridor. Rook parked her cart and took the book inside with her. The room smelled strongly of Good & Plenty candy. Kyle lay in the bed, with various tubes and wires attached to him. Rook pulled aside his sheet, and smiled. Religion and Philosophy, at last. The slot for this book was right in the

middle, so she slid it into place.

Kyle's green eyes opened.

Rook jerked awake and sat up, gasping for air.

***

The spiders withdrew, congratulating themselves for coaxing Rook to symbolically Complete Kyle, performing in her dream the task they wished her to accomplish while awake.

Controlling the title of the book took two attempts, but she'd accepted most of the other details easily. Also pleasing was the way she woke at the critical moment, all but guaranteeing she would remember the dream.

Future augmentations of the Completer's dreams would be calculated to produce a jolt of panic or other strong emotional signal, something potent enough to jar her awake. Kyle himself seemed a promising device. Her complicated and powerful feelings about him would serve to make the dreams memorable.

They must be sure to exploit that. It would hasten Kyle's return, speeding fulfillment of the prophecy. What ecstasy it would give the human race, when all minds were one!

***   ***   ***

"I would like some clean clothes," Melissa said, trying not to slur. Her diet had expanded, but white wine was still the staple.

"I assume you have some at home?" Severin said.

Melissa ground her teeth, but tried to smile. "My husband probably got rid of them like he got rid of me. I'd like to buy something new."

"You can borrow one of the vans. The keys are on a hook in the garage." He spoke like they'd been doing this for years. "Have fun, and buy something pretty. You deserve it."

A cauldron of hatred hissed and spat in Melissa's mind. His guileless facade was twice as infuriating as the smirk he usually wore when speaking to her.

"I'm drunk," she said. "I can't drive like this." Let him refute that.

"I see your point."

He crossed the attic to an old steamer trunk. Melissa stumbled after. Severin lifted out a pea green cardigan and handed it to her.

"This was Gale's, but I'm sure she wouldn't mind her daughter wearing it."

"Can I shower?"

Severin led her down to one of the bathrooms on the third floor.

When Melissa finished drying herself she found the sweater only. Her undergarments were gone along with her shoes and the rest of her clothes.

Seeing little alternative, she slipped the sweater over her head. At least it smelled clean. It was boxy, had a low V-neck, and fell to mid-thigh. Melissa felt exposed.

He's not going to get away with this.

She would get real clothes. She would teach him she was not his prisoner.

She was, of course, because she remained dependent on him. The slime of insistent, distracting minutiae would coat her world the moment she set off. He understood that, and taunted her with empty promises to help master this 'power.' Meanwhile, he often departed the premises without warning.

Like yesterday.

She had been at the kitchen window as the van pulled away, its repugnant green color suddenly advising her how many people worldwide were killed by jellyfish annually. Everything around her vomited up meaningless statistics, the patterns making up for lost time. One of her uncle's toadies said, "It's part of the Mersenne series," which meant nothing to Melissa but did provide crucial insights into the average diameter of coconuts, with and without the husk. She fled upstairs to be alone with her wine and her damnable visions until Severin's return.

He was a manipulative son of a bitch, smug and sure he had control. It would feel good to give him some doubts.

Melissa exited the bathroom. Severin stood a few doors away,

looking into a room full of computers.

"Where are my clothes?" she demanded.

"In the laundry," he said. "You look much better in this." He reached out with his stump and stroked her exposed collarbone.

"I need to use the phone."

"There's one in the kitchen." He started down the grand central staircase. Melissa followed, wishing she weren't barefoot.

Severin indicated the wall phone, then went to the refrigerator. Three men wearing green sweaters like hers sat at one of the large tables, drinking coffee and talking over some papers.

Melissa picked up the phone, then wondered who she planned to call. There was no point in calling the police. No crime had been committed. There was Brad, of course, but that was a ridiculous idea. What could she possibly say? *Yes, you sold me to the freak show, but since I was going to kill you let's call it even. Come pick me up.*

Severin looked over his shoulder at her, so she hastily dialed the bank. Listening to her voice mail would help her feel like she still had a life.

The first message was from Brad, almost a week old, telling her Kyle was hospitalized. Melissa gripped the phone and replayed the message. What had happened to her son? Brad's message gave no clues. She listened to the rest, deleting those from coworkers immediately, hoping for more information about Kyle. Finally, a message from a Dr Peabody.

"Mrs Tanner, your ex-husband said you could be reached at this number and has asked that I pass along information about your son Kyle."

'Ex'-husband? Was that what Brad called himself, or was the doctor assuming?

A second message from Dr Peabody told her they transferred Kyle to Webster General and she should direct any questions there.

Melissa was shaking as she hung up. Kyle was in a coma. He might never wake up.

He could never leave her.

Unlike that bastard, Brad.

Secret knowledge that she could escape Severin and not drown in trivial misery gave Melissa hope. It would be awkward to rely on someone bedridden. If she could learn to master her dark talent it would be better. She could be free.

Melissa smiled. Kyle wasn't going anywhere. She could get him if she needed him, if things with Severin became too unbearable.

Buoyed by her decision, Melissa poured herself an aromatic mug of coffee and was looking over a tray of store-bought pastries when Severin approached. He stood behind her and ran his hand up her thigh, under her sweater.

"Uncle, stop," she said, stressing the first word.

The three men at the table looked up.

Severin moved in front of her and pulled her in for a deep kiss. When he let her go he said, "This is Melissa. She lives here now. Melissa, meet Horn, Leaf, and Free. They're on the second floor."

He selected a cheese danish and left the room.

Melissa had no choice but to follow, cheeks glowing with humiliation.

Chapter Five

Secret Dream Journal

Setting: inside Vesuvius - red and golden
Fin is there. It's terribly hot. We get naked and start to fuck on a
lava bubble. Vesuvius turns into an hourglass and the lava pours
down into the bottom, along with me. Down here the lava is glow-
in-the-dark green. Kyle is waiting for me. He wants my help with
something. We fuck on another bubble while he tries to tell me
what he needs me to do, but he can't because we're kissing too
much.
Rook Tanner's dream journal

Willow Charm leaned against the padded headboard of the hotel bed. "So how old am I anyway? I feel like I'm turning 34 today. But Fin's 25 years old, so I shouldn't tell people I'm 34." Brad handed over their wriggling daughter and sat beside her. "On the other hand, I don't love the idea of suddenly being 46."

"You look great for 46." Brad winked.

"But I don't look great for 34?"

"You look great, period. And quit complaining about being 46. I'm 51, for crissakes. You're making me feel like an old man."

"You look great for 51," Willow teased. "The gray is distinguished."

"Distinguished? Oh, the kiss of death."

Stroking Zen's wispy brown hair as she nursed, Willow started to nod off, leaning on Brad's shoulder. It was funny that she needed any rest after being asleep for twelve years, but her mind used the downtime to process the strange information she learned from the bubbles of light.

The phone on the nightstand rang, jolting Willow awake. Brad reached across, but Willow got it first.

"Hello?" she mumbled.

"Happy birthday, Mom." Fin sounded older.

"Thanks Fin." Tears stung her eyes. "I'm so, so happy you called. This is the best birthday present I've gotten in at least twelve years."

He sort of chuckled.

Brad eased Zen out of Willow's arm and laid her in the bassinet.

"I missed you, Mom." He sounded so sad.

"Fin, listen to me. I love you."

"But you didn't miss me. You won't say you missed me. Brad wouldn't say it either."

"For me it's only been a few days since I dropped you off with Ember and Beacon. It's so zen. It doesn't feel like I've been away long enough to miss you. But when I saw you, and you're all grown up, I know that I missed so much of your life. That kills me. I would never have chosen to be away from you."

Fin sniffled.

"I want to get to know who you are now," she said.

"I'm still Fin."

Still the same uncommunicative kid. "I know. Your name is Fin Chester Tanner," she said, quoting a favorite saying from his childhood.

"But you can call me Fin and I'll still know who you're talking to," he finished, sounding less glum.

Wanting to help improve his mood, she asked, "So you're in a band?"

"I was." He coughed. "We broke up. Our equipment sort of blew up."

That was alarming. "Was it at the magazine you work for?"

He paused. "Different explosion."

"I'm going to sound like a worried mother now, Fin—"

"That's okay. I missed out on that."

"I want you to stay away from explosions from now on, young man."

"Yes ma'am."

Willow smiled. He was still her boy.

"Is the magazine still publishing?"

"I think so, but I don't work there anymore."

Brad hadn't told her that. "What are you doing now?"

"I have a freelance assignment." He sounded evasive.

"I used to freelance." For her it was only a week ago, but for him it was half a lifetime. "Do you remember?"

"Yeah."

Willow wished Fin would ask some questions, hold up his end of the conversation. He hadn't even mentioned his new sister.

"We're looking at a house tomorrow," she said. "It's a foreclosure Brad learned about from the bank. If we like it we'd be able to move in right away."

"Oh."

"I'll be sure to get you the address and phone number."

"Okay."

"Do you have a number for Beacon and Em? I'd like to let them know I'm back."

"I think I have their address upstairs. It might take me a while to find it."

"Could you look for it for me? Not right now."

"Yeah. Okay. They'd be happy to hear you're okay."

*** *** ***

Hearing his mother's voice made Fin feel like a kid — stupid and vulnerable. It had always been impossible to think she was never coming back, but now he saw that deep down he'd believed her dead. How differently would he have led his life if he'd known he'd one day need to tell her about it?

Rook joined him on the couch, her big gray sweater sliding off one shoulder, exposing the feather inked on her collarbone. She tucked her bare legs under herself and smoothed her black velvet miniskirt.

"It's so zen," Mom said, repeating her stock phrase. How had he forgotten she said that all the time? He laid his palm on the Japanese

willow tree tattooed over his heart. "I can't believe you're married. In my mind you're still 13."

Fin switched the phone to his left ear and said, "Well, I'm not."

"You're not married? But I thought—"

"I'm not 13."

She continued in a hurt voice, "How long have you been married? Brad didn't even know."

Fin wished she'd quit mentioning Brad. Rook smiled encouragingly.

"It's been about a month. October 13th."

Rook's smile widened when she realized what he was talking about.

"You're newlyweds," Mom said. "That's so sweet. It must have been a whirlwind courtship, because Brad didn't even know you had a girlfriend."

Fin gritted his teeth. "Yeah. It was." He didn't feel up to telling her he'd only known Rook two weeks before they married.

"That sounds familiar," Mom said. Fin didn't want to imagine her getting all googly with Brad. He ground his teeth some more.

"Now, your wife's name is Rook?"

"Yes."

"But is her real name Brook?"

Fin admitted it was.

"I knew her parents."

"That seems pretty unlikely."

"Ask her how Dragonfly is."

Fin turned to his wife and said in a theatrical tone, "Rook, how is... Dragonfly?"

She shrugged. "I haven't talked to him in ages."

Fin boggled. "Rook, *who* is Dragonfly?"

"My brother," she said, like they'd been over this a hundred times.

"You said your brother's name was Bay."

"Dragonfly Bay," said Rook and Mom together.

"My mom knew your parents."

"My condolences," Rook said.

"Well," said Mom. It seemed, suspicions confirmed, she didn't feel comfortable with the revelation.

The conversation petered out, and ended with Fin not quite promising to call again soon.

Rook wrapped her arms around him and held him for a few minutes. Then she said, "Your shirt stinks. I think you need to do some laundry."

Fin pinned her to the couch and tickled her, but caught an eye-watering whiff of his pits and had to agree.

On their way upstairs, he said, "I think I remember playing with Dragonfly. He was older than me and liked to throw things."

"Sounds like him. His temper got him in a lot of trouble in high school, especially after he found out Mom was screwing his friends. He moved out after that."

Fin looked at her in amazement.

"Maybe now you see why I don't feel like talking to her."

Back in their room, Fin dug around on the top shelf in the closet until he uncovered a cigar box held closed by a rubber band. The band fell apart under his fingers as he slid it off. It had been a long time since he'd looked in here, but this was where he expected to find Ember's address. Now that he knew his mother was alive, looking at mementos of her shouldn't be as painful.

He pulled out a small stack of photos. The top one was the last picture he had of her, taken at the mini-golf course on his 13th birthday.

"Look at her," Rook said in a strange voice. "She looks exactly the same."

"I thought you were the one saying we should believe Brad's story."

"It's just weird to see the evidence." She took the picture for a closer look. "Is that you?" she asked, trying not to laugh.

Fin grabbed the photograph and hid it on the bottom of the pile.

They went through the remaining dozen pictures until they got to the earliest one. It showed a group of hippies. His mom and Brad were

sitting in the grass, laughing together while he, as a toddler, petted a black dog.

"That's my dog, Komodo." Fin said.

"Oh!" Rook pointed to a beautiful strawberry blond in a halter top and cut-offs, sitting beside Ember. "That's my mom."

Fin studied Rook's mother. There was the same mischievous allure about her that Rook had. "I can see a resemblance. What's her name?"

"Linda."

"Well, Brook, we made a deal. I called my mom, so now you need to tell Linda we're married."

Rook stuck out her tongue at the use of her given name, but acquiesced.

She wound up talking to Linda's answering machine.

"Hi Mom, it's Rook. Yeah, I got married. And not to Marcus. Tell the Bug not to tattle. And don't worry about me. We're looking for a new place and I'll get you the number when we're settled. Bye."

"We're looking for a new place?" Fin asked.

"As far as she knows."

***   ***   ***

Marsh worked his way through a bowl of minestrone as he reviewed his spreadsheet, happy as a geek could be. Fresh data to analyze, and a beautiful genius to discuss it with. Tomorrow was Thanksgiving and he would be spending it with Rainbow at her parents' house.

Melissa came into the dining hall holding her head. She paused and wobbled, then deliberately moved to the phone. Marsh wasn't sure she wouldn't pass out. He kept an eye on her in case he needed to catch her.

"It's rude to stare," she spat.

Marsh turned sheepishly back to his soup.

She lifted the receiver and dialed a long-distance number. She cleared her throat.

"Hello, Mother. I'm calling to wish you and Daddy a happy Thanksgiving."

There was a pause, and Marsh saw peripherally that Melissa was

holding her head again.

"I know, and I'm sorry. It's just not going to work out this year."

Another, shorter pause.

"No, it has nothing to do with Brad. As a matter of fact, that reminds me. I've left Brad."

Marsh raised a few spoonfuls of soup and blew on them, while Melissa gave monosyllable responses for a while.

"Well, if you'll forgive my saying so, none of that is really any of your business."

Marsh took one last bite. To get the rest he'd have to scrape the bowl, and the noise would be lethally embarrassing.

"Mother, I'm an adult." She tugged at the hem of her cardigan, once Marsh's own. It would seem Severin had a fetish for short blonde women in green sweater dresses. What made it more disturbing was that Marsh and the rest of the TEF received no explanation for Gale's departure or Melissa's arrival. It was as if Severin thought they wouldn't notice the difference.

None of them knew what happened to Severin's hand, either. Consensus was he had, in fact, had two hands until recently. A small group of newbies speculated that the left had been a prosthesis all along, but Marsh knew that wasn't the case. Would Melissa hold the answer? Marsh knew he lacked the balls to ask her.

Melissa leaned against the wall.

"Thank you, and sorry to have missed your call. No, I didn't do anything special. Birthdays don't mean what they used to. I forgot all about it until you mentioned."

She sighed, almost moaned. "I said I was sorry, Mother. I haven't been at the house. As I said, I left my husband."

Marsh carried his bowl to the sink, glancing over to see Melissa move the receiver away from her ear, scowling.

"Have an extra slice of pumpkin pie for me, and tell Daddy I said I love him and he should have an extra slice, too. I hope you'll get over your disappointment someday."

*** *** ***

Rook stood at the bathroom sink and brushed her hair, watching in the mirror as her reflection did the same. Except her reflection didn't have a hairbrush. Rook looked down. The sink was now a bed.

Kyle lay propped up on pillows, green eyes open but glassy in the sallow light. Another reflection of Rook stood behind his head, and reached out to stroke his brow. "Wake up, honey," she crooned.

"Don't do that," Rook said. The woman at Kyle's head patted his cheek. She moved to stand beside her twin, across the bed from Rook, and leaned down close to Kyle's face.

"Don't!" Rook said. The other Rook was staring into Kyle's eyes.

"That's not going to do anything," said the first reflection. She climbed onto the bed and straddled Kyle. She pumped her hips, and kissed him.

"Stop it, stop it!" Rook shrieked. Her reflections looked at her, then at each other. They nodded.

The one on the bed climbed down, and both of the other Rooks stepped back.

Rook gave her duplicates a warning look, and slid onto the bed and threw one leg over Kyle. She felt his warmth through her panties.

Her reflections helped slip her underwear down. They pulled Kyle's green blanket out of the way, and lowered her until he was all the way inside her. He was motionless, but she felt a throbbing in his flesh as she rocked and ground her hips. Her climax built quickly.

"Now, do it now," Brook and Bramble urged.

She leaned down to look into Kyle's empty green eyes, moaning in pleasure.

***

Rook's moan woke her.

Fin slumbered on. Vesuvius's warm glow shifted between gold and crimson.

Rook squeezed her knees together and swiveled her pelvis. Arousal followed her from the dream, leaving her feeling frustrated as well as

unclean. A familiar pattern. She crept from the bed and took her laptop over to the recliner.

This made twelve consecutive nights with at least one dream about Kyle, all sexual. She always woke on the cusp of orgasm. After typing a brief description of this latest episode, Rook scrolled through the file.

Perhaps they wouldn't be as disturbing, looking back. She wanted to be able to laugh about them. It wasn't time for that yet, though. Even the one where Fin baked her a cake that turned out to be Kyle slathered in green icing still creeped her out.

No matter how innocuously the dreams began, they always wound up pornographic. Rook would feel lost, knowing there was a job she alone could undertake, a catastrophe only she could avert, and it all tasted like Kyle. Other times she would be working hard to Complete him in some dream-logic way. No matter what, it always ended with rapturous fucking.

Rook closed her computer and crawled back into bed, snuggling against Fin. She loved the way he smelled, like he blew out a candle in a coffee shop. Tuning in his idling mental vibrations, she failed to tune out Kyle's. Whatever mental shrapnel she'd taken when Kyle's mind shattered was embedded in her subconscious, infusing her dreams with that distinct Kyle flavor.

Fin gathered her in his arms, and she sighed. It was partly a happy sigh for the warm security of her husband's embrace, and partly a sigh of dread for the next unpleasant dream.

But they weren't unpleasant, which was the whole problem.

*** *** ***

"Both?" asked Rook. "Why?"

"The red's for the housewarming," explained Bishop. "The white's for Thanksgiving."

"Should we have a safe word so I can signal when I need to leave?" asked Fin.

Bishop shook his head. "You'll do fine."

Rook wished she shared Bishop's rosy outlook. It had been years

since she'd done anything family-oriented and she hoped this dinner at Willow and Brad's new house would go smoothly.

The house was more of a cottage, the antithesis of the soulless suburban contemporary where Fin lived as a teenager. Where Kyle grew up.

The glass-paneled front door opened, emitting warmth into the frigid dusk. Willow grinned and enfolded Fin in an embrace. Brad stood right behind her holding the baby. He shook Bishop's hand and gave Rook a one-armed hug. "Welcome, Rook."

Rook watched tensely as Brad put out his hand to shake Fin's. Fin hesitated, then cooperated. Brad pulled him in and clapped him on the back.

The group moved into the living room. A cheery fire crackled in the stone fireplace, but there was no furniture.

Bishop proffered the wine bottles. "From all of us. Happy Thanksgiving, and happy housewarming, too."

The smell of roasting turkey made Rook's mouth water. She and Fin had been subsisting on Ramen, and she was sure the promise of a full meal helped persuade Fin to attend tonight. He and Willow had continued their phone conversations and seemed to be on pretty solid ground. The terrain around Brad remained quite suspect, though, and where Zen was concerned, nonexistent.

Glossy red hair hung loose to the middle of Willow's back. Rook studied the woman, confirming the idea that she hadn't aged in twelve years. Her fashion sense hadn't changed either. The baggy sweater and billowy skirt had a hippie flavor.

Fin kept sneaking looks at the baby in Brad's arms, looks Rook couldn't read.

Both Fin and Brad stood just over six feet tall, with the same lean frame and dark brown hair. They were handsome for all the same reasons, especially when they smiled. Fin wouldn't like to hear it, but he looked a good deal like his father. So did Kyle. The brothers were portraits of the same man, done by different artists.

Rook wished she could stop thinking about Kyle, but he haunted her waking thoughts now that he dominated her dreams.

Life had become a grinding repetition of work, resisting sleep, and dreaming of the myriad ways she could fuck her husband's evil half-twin. It left her exhausted and headachy.

She didn't dare talk to Fin about it. That's what the secret dream journal was for.

Fin's stomach growled. With a laugh, Willow went to the kitchen to get things ready, and Brad disappeared with the slumbering baby.

Fin slouched over to the fireplace, and Rook joined him. On the mantel, an antique clock was flanked by two small jade horses. Lifting one, Rook said, "See how intricate these are?" She hoped to distract Fin from his darkening mood. The figurines were sturdy little warhorses with rippling manes and tails, their right forelegs raised, armored saddles on their backs.

He picked up the other horse and turned it over in his hands. "Yeah." He trotted the animal along Rook's bare arm to her shoulder, made it peek down her cleavage and give a horsey whistle.

"Fin!" Rook whispered.

Laughing, he put the horse back on the mantel.

"You look really pretty tonight," he said, and Rook melted a little. He bent and kissed her cheek.

Willow called, "Turkey time!"

At least Brad and Willow did have a dining set, so they wouldn't need to eat standing up. Willow claimed the chair beside Fin while Rook was across from him, between Brad and Bishop.

"I hope we didn't forget anything," Willow said. "We were so rushed at the grocery store."

"It smells wonderful," said Bishop.

"Did you make pecan pie?" asked Fin.

Willow smiled. "Of course. It's your favorite."

Rook was bemused to realize she didn't know her husband even had a favorite kind of pie.

The meal progressed with several further realizations for Rook: enough wine could make even the most awkward situation enjoyable; Bishop was skilled at steering the conversation out of danger zones; Rook liked Willow, and more surprisingly she liked Brad; Fin's steel-toed loafers were not the best choice if he wanted to play footsie.

"How's the freelancing?" Willow asked as she gathered dirty plates.

"Um," said Fin. "Slow."

That was an understatement.

"That's the thing with freelancing," Willow said. "It's sporadic. Maybe you should look for something to do full-time while you get established."

"That's what Rook says," said Fin. "But I think I should stick to it."

Rook rolled her eyes.

"What do you do, Rook?" asked Brad.

"Well, I used to be a body piercer. Now I'm shelving books at the university library. Plus I do a little writing for a local tabloid." *Because at least one of us needs to make some money.*

"Body piercer?" asked Willow.

"Eyebrows, noses, nipples, navels," said Rook. "Um. Other places."

"It's quite a fad," explained Brad. "That and tattoos."

Willow shook her head in amazement. "I don't think I need to hear any more about piercings. I do admire the artistry of your tattoos, Rook. They're beautifully done. I don't think I could stand the pain, though."

"It's not too bad," said Fin.

"You have a tattoo?" Willow sounded alarmed.

"Counting my wedding ring I have five."

"Five!" Willow turned accusingly to Brad, who looked guilty for some reason.

"If you count each of Rook's birds separately, she has 156," Fin said with pride.

Willow sat back and blinked, alternating her gaze between her son and daughter-in-law. "A lot changes in twelve years."

Brad poured more wine.

Further conversation was derailed by Zen's cries from the back of the house. Willow brought her into the dining room and sat back down.

"Zen is Mommy's hungry girl, isn't she?" cooed Willow as she lifted her shirt and positioned the fussy baby at her breast. Rook looked away, disturbed, and met Fin's own uncomfortable gaze. They both widened their eyes in horror and tried not to laugh.

Brad announced he was going to clean the kitchen before serving dessert, and Bishop offered to help.

In a ploy to avoid staring at her mother-in-law's chest, Rook excused herself and headed toward the hall bathroom. Amid the clinks and clatters from the kitchen she heard Brad say, "We moved him to Webster General without the media catching wind. We've got him admitted under a false name, too. They're more interested in Spitz now anyway."

Maybe I'm dreaming about Kyle so much because he's closer now. Like it or not, they shared a mental connection.

"There's no change in his prognosis?" Bishop asked.

"They're running tests," Brad said with a sigh. "Everyone has a theory. I visit almost every day, but it's more for my benefit than his. He's a much better listener these days." Rook heard pain in his voice.

"That must be hard."

"Wil comes along for moral support, but it's awkward for her. She doesn't know Kyle, and we're always concerned Melissa will show up while we're there. They say she called once but hasn't been in."

"I'd be happy to go with you sometime," Bishop offered.

Feelings of betrayal sparked, but Rook tried to let them go. Bishop didn't know the details of her ordeal with Kyle. He was just being a good friend for Brad, the way he was a good friend for Fin.

And for me.

Rook hurried along to the bathroom.

When she got back to the dining room, Brad and Bishop emerged from the kitchen armed with pie and coffee. Zen took that as her cue to make a horrendous noise in her diaper.

Brad set the coffee pot down and scooped the infant out of Willow's hands. Talking baby talk and making airplane noises, he flew her out of the room.

Fin seemed nonplussed by Brad's paternal display. He looked at Rook and shrugged, then started pouring the coffee into everyone's mugs.

"None for me," Rook said. Sleep was hard enough without the caffeine. She poured herself more wine instead.

Willow was passing out slices of pecan pie when Brad returned with Zen, who wore a fresh yellow stretchy suit.

"You would not believe—" he started.

"Brad! We have guests."

Brad smiled. "So we do. Sorry."

"Could I hold her?" asked Bishop. "My sister's kids are growing up fast and I miss them sometimes."

Rook nibbled at her pie. It was so rich she didn't want to make herself sick. Fin did not share her qualms. He devoured his first piece and dished up a second, with extra whipped cream.

"Brad bought me the most marvelous thing," Willow announced. She left the room and returned with a camera. "It's a *digital* camera! I imagine it's not very exciting for the rest of you, but it is for me."

She took a few snaps of the individuals around the table, then said, "Rook, could you come over here with Fin? I need a picture of you both together."

Rook sat on Fin's lap, trying to keep her skirt from riding up. They smiled for the first picture. Fin pounced and kissed her for the second.

"I need a copy of those, Mom," he said. "I don't have any pictures of Rook yet."

Rook was surprised to realize that was true.

"Would you like a family shot?" Bishop asked.

For the next several minutes Rook had flashbacks to being dragged to the Sears portrait studio with her brother and sister. So much repositioning, so many flashes. So many Tanners.

Willow said, "I want a picture of just my kids together."

Fin tried to protest, but Zen ended up in his arms anyway.

He held her stiffly and she squirmed.

"You need to cuddle her so she feels secure," Willow coached.

Hesitantly Fin tried it and Zen calmed. She stared at Fin with her big gray eyes and he looked down at her. Bishop snapped a picture.

"Hey there, Zen," Fin whispered. "I'm your big brother. I guess we were supposed to grow up together, but we kind of got ripped off." He sniffled. "When you're older and Brad starts to bug you, you can call me and we'll talk about it, okay?" He bent down and kissed her forehead, then handed her back to Willow. Brad smiled and laid his hand on Fin's shoulder.

"You probably don't remember, Fin," said Willow, "but you first met Rook when she was one day old."

Rook and Fin looked at each other, surprised.

"Cloud helped me deliver you, and I was returning the favor. I brought Dragonfly home to spend the night after Rook was born so she could bond with her parents."

"Fat lot of good that did," Rook grumbled, "since Casey wasn't my real dad."

"I always wondered how things turned out," Willow said quietly. "We lost touch."

"Oh, it worked out fantastic. Casey left right away. I always thought it was my fault, and eventually Mom confirmed it. I wasn't really his daughter. She tricked him. Stupid fuck. He wasn't Bay's dad either and that didn't bother him. He signed up to be a dad when he married Mom, but then he didn't feel like living up to his obligations."

Everyone else looked uncomfortable, but Rook couldn't stop the flood of words.

"After that I had five other daddies. All of them ditched me. It's enough to give a girl a complex." Angry tears brimmed. "If only Casey fucking Martin had been able to put innocent kids ahead of himself…" Rook wiped her eyes with the back of her hand. "Not that I'm bitter."

Fin put his hand on her knee. "It's not your fault."

"Mom's on number seven now. He's lasted longer than any of the others. Probably because I'm not around to get in the way."

"Rook," Fin said and hugged her.

In Fin's arms Rook started to feel safer, loved. She blinked the rest of her tears away and said, "I think I've had enough wine."

"I'm so sorry I bought it up," Willow said sympathetically.

"So," said Brad, coming to her rescue, "are you two looking for a new apartment?"

"No," Fin said. "We can't afford anything else."

"Sure you can," Brad said.

"Maybe later. Once I've gotten the freelancing up to speed."

"Fin, that room you're living in — no offense Bishop — that room is no place for newlyweds. Your wife deserves better."

Rook silently agreed with Brad and looked to Fin for his response.

"How are we supposed to pay for what she deserves?" Fin asked, getting prickly.

"With your trust fund."

Trust fund?

"Oh." Fin sounded chastened. "Yeah."

"You've got a great deal of money sitting in the bank while you make your lovely wife live in squalor. I know you don't like to rely on me. You probably even think there's a certain romance to the situation. 'It's us against the world.' But you're punishing Rook."

"How much money are we talking?" Rook asked.

Brad looked pointedly at Fin, who looked pointedly at his hands.

"Fin?" she demanded. "How much?"

"I don't know. Around $100,000."

Rook's eyes narrowed.

"I don't think of it as my money," Fin said.

"Your name's on the account," said Brad. "It's yours. Think of it as your payment for putting up with me all these years."

How could Fin let them wallow in poverty when he had access to so

much money? It's not like they needed a sports car or a Rolex, but some damn food would be nice.

"Dude," said Bishop. "If I had that kind of money, I sure as hell wouldn't be living in that house."

"Fuck off," Fin said, but he sounded defeated.

Holy fuck are we going to have a conversation when we get home. If Fin didn't get a job immediately he could go fuck himself.

A short time later, as they put their coats on, Brad handed Fin an envelope.

"It's a wedding gift."

Fin opened the flap and peeked inside, then tried to hand it back.

Brad wouldn't take the envelope. Rook snatched it. Inside were several hundred-dollar bills.

"You can't buy us, Brad," Fin said.

"It's a gift, Fin. To celebrate your marriage. It's not a trap."

"We're doing fine without your help."

"No we're not," Rook said. She tucked the money into the inside pocket of her leather jacket and kissed Brad on the cheek. "Thank you, Brad. I really, really appreciate it."

Brad smiled.

Fin glowered.

"You can pay him back when you get a job."

Chapter Six

BUBBLES OF LIGHT

With the recent closing of Talisman Tattoo, Webster is now a one-tattoo-parlor town. Owner Marcus Savage defaulted on his business lease. Property management firm J&K Enterprises will auction all business effects on December 3. According to J&K, a t-shirt store is planning to take over the basement location in Ricket Alley in time for Christmas.
  Business Briefs *column from* Webster Daily Press, *11-30-2000*

Moving another person into his room hadn't made it feel smaller to Fin, because that person was Rook and he always wanted to be near her anyway. However, trying to store real food in his mini-fridge made it feel inadequate, somehow revealing how cramped the room really was.

Rook wouldn't hear of ritually burning the Thanksgiving cash, but they worked out a compromise. They rented a safe deposit box where they placed that money, agreeing not to touch it unless it was life or death.

Meanwhile, it stung his pride sufficiently that he went out and applied for jobs at a few restaurants. Early December turned out to be a good time to do that, assuming you wanted to actually get such a job. Two of them already called back.

The upshot was they'd been able to shop for groceries. They did it at three in the morning, when the only other people in the store were employees running floor polishers and pallet jacks. Fin sang along with the cheesy piped-in music, which made Rook laugh. He liked that. It was nice to know acting more like grown-ups didn't have to mean the end of laughter.

Now the food was stashed in the tiny refrigerator and they lay together in the too-small room, spooning on the too-small bed.

"We need to get presents for your folks," Rook announced.

Fin grunted.

"Nothing extravagant," she continued, "but they've been really generous. This will be the first Christmas in years that I have any shopping to do. At least we have about three weeks."

"Not quite," Fin said. "Solstice, not Christmas. It's a few days earlier."

Rook twisted around to look at him. "Solstice, huh?"

Fin nodded.

"Nature cult thing?"

He shrugged. "Probably. But Mom never treated it as a religious holiday. She likes it because it's a real thing, a verifiable feature of the Earth's orbit. If you're going to perform illogical ceremonies, it's at least a logical time to do them." Rook elbowed him, but not hard. Fin continued, "I always liked it because it's different from what everyone else does, and it's not commercialized. It gave me something to act superior about, if you can even picture me doing that. Plus it meant I got to open my presents sooner."

Rook relaxed to her earlier position and nestled tighter against his body, her smooth warmth delicious against his skin, her gingered peach scent arousing.

"Have to buy them sooner, too," she murmured.

***   ***   ***

The Completer was the primary female in Fin's life, but not the only female. Fin had recently reestablished ties with his mother. Without the farcical confabulation of the Floating Wisdom to blind them, the spiders recognized Willow from her sojourn in the Collective Id, where she created them. In a way she was their mother, too.

Which made Fin their brother, after a fashion.

If they could convey to Willow the beauty of their vision for a unified humanity, she might persuade Fin of his duty. If Fin would

agree to fully awaken humanity's collective mind, they could let Kyle slumber. It would save them the step of restoring the Divided Man, letting them move directly to restoring light upon the Earth.

The spiders tried to communicate with Willow, but she could not hear them. Excited by the possibility of interviewing their creator, they contemplated transporting her to the asteroid. But, no. Bringing her into their presence involuntarily was a flawed idea. She might become agitated. Fin had done enough damage.

They tried to reach her in her dreams the way they reached Rook, but Willow's sleeping mind was opaque. Was it because it was her mind that shaped them? Was it because she was absent from the prophecy? A fascinating riddle, but its answer wouldn't help.

Willow's deafness meant they were no closer to getting through to Fin. She did not offer a shortcut to prophetic fulfillment after all. The mission still depended on Kyle.

Their energies were best spent convincing the Completer to perform her function.

*** *** ***

Severin hunched against the chilly breeze with his hand and his stump in his pockets. He crossed the back yard, returning to the House from a perfunctory visit to the garage workshop. He hoped to one day find his troupe of mad scientists building a gadget that would deliver to him dominion over the entire world, but nothing they showed him ever held his interest. His occasional — infrequent if he was honest — tours of their playground were entirely for the sake of appearance.

Only through the Elsewhere could he attain the power he yearned for.

Entering through the kitchen at the rear of the House, Severin frowned.

All the power he needed was already banked in a white-hot slab of rock drifting in the Elsewhere.

What it needed was a conduit. At the merest touch from the right person all that energy would pour out, stunning the Collective Id and

allowing Severin to assume control. Willow had been intended for that purpose. Her absence at the critical moment was how the slab was lost.

Not lost, Severin reminded himself with a glance at his left arm. Moved. He trudged up the steps toward the attic.

Willow was no longer a viable conduit, so there was no reason to pursue her. She would never be made to cooperate voluntarily, even through trickery, and now with the slab adrift in the Elsewhere he couldn't forcibly apply her to it.

Melissa would make an excellent conduit. Like her twin, Melissa would be adept with his table, able to tune in to the Elsewhere effortlessly. Able to reach the slab. She just needed coaching, a bit of practice.

Which led to the frustration.

Severin hated the thought that Melissa might discover her aptitude, because along with proficiency at the table itself she would gain insights into her own sizable power. Power that terrified her, power that expressed itself in misshapen ways and made her miserable. If she understood how it worked, her fear and misery would dissolve.

The very fear and misery Severin relied upon to control her.

She would leave in a heartbeat. Threats would be useless. She might hate him, but she didn't fear him. She was only afraid of herself.

Even if he could deceive her into looking for the slab, there was no telling how long the search might take. Doubtless much longer than for her to discover mastery of her visions.

He reached the third floor and paused, still mulling.

The only avenue toward his ambitions was training Melissa to use the table. Otherwise the energy he'd spent a dozen years collecting could never be discharged. But by the time she could reach the slab, she would be transformed into a hideously potent rival.

Damn. Same answer every time.

Severin started up the final flight of stairs. Until some aspect of the game changed, he did not have a winning move. He would need to be patient. Watch for the correct opportunity.

He'd waited twelve years with Willow. He clenched his hand into a fist. No sense succumbing to impatience now.

When he reached the attic, Melissa lay in the hammock with a book, as always. She didn't acknowledge him, but her contempt was palpable.

Patience had hardly been easy with Willow. Wise, but not easy.

The Melissa situation differed in some striking respects. Most obviously, Melissa was physically unrestrained. She might change the game if her own patience wore thin enough. A subtler but perhaps more worrisome difference was Gale. Severin could admit, inwardly, that he'd depended on his sister. He didn't know the full import of her removal, how it might influence his own state.

Patience and wisdom need not always travel in company. To hesitate is lost.

"I have something different in mind for your next lesson."

Melissa rolled her eyes. "Unless you plan to bring livestock into the equation, I fail to see what else there is to try."

Severin smiled before he could catch himself. "Nothing like that." He walked to the table. She laid her book down and watched him skeptically.

"You've seen me use this, and you know how powerful it is." Severin pointed at the table with his stump. "Your lessons will now involve the table and how to use it."

Melissa's look turned downcast, but she rose from the hammock and took a few steps toward him.

"Some," Severin added. "Some of your lessons." He meant to allay her anxieties about approaching the table. "Of course," he continued in a lower tone, "you must never, under any circumstances, touch it without supervision."

Melissa stopped. "Hell with that. I don't want to touch it, under any circumstances, period." She returned to the hammock and collected her book.

Severin closed his eyes for a moment, and took a deep breath.

He tried another tack. "I'm trying to help you. Don't you want to

know more about your power? Isn't that why you stayed?"

Melissa didn't look up from her book. "I didn't 'stay.' I just haven't left yet."

Severin scowled at the book obscuring her face. His mouth stretched into a sneer. "I should have trusted my first instincts. I knew you weren't ready to move to the next stage, but I allowed my judgement to be colored by the wish that you be healed as soon as possible. I suppose it makes more sense to stick to the lessons you're used to."

Melissa turned a page.

"Put down the book."

*** *** ***

Both the murky lighting and the buzzing sound were familiar, but they didn't go together.

Rook recognized the bite of the tattoo needle on her thigh and knew it as the source of the buzz. Peering into the crimson gloom she saw the curved metal walls of the bomb shelter. Vesuvius on the kitchen table provided the faint light. Rook relaxed back onto the bunk.

The stabbing fire on her inner thigh continued, making her horny. Tattooing sessions with Marcus were always foreplay, or sex games outright. The erotic Pavlovian response was difficult to shake.

Rook could tell by the way the needle moved it wasn't Marcus tattooing her. She lolled her head and saw Fin holding the tattoo gun, lost in concentration, injecting emerald ink into her skin. As he paused to dip the needle into the ink cap, Rook shifted her leg to see her new art.

"Divided Seed shall a Divided Child Beget who shall grow into a Divided Man," repeated over and over like Jack Nicholson's rant in The Shining, circling around and around her thigh from knee to hip.

Why would Fin choose to give her those words? And why in a typewriter font?

He was almost done. Then they could fuck.

Everything suddenly smelled like pheromones and black licorice.

Fin was using his right hand, and the eclipse tattoo was missing

from his forearm. She looked at him more closely and saw he also lacked his other body art.

She picked up another tattoo gun and added the jagged eclipse while he continued to work on her thigh. Rook added the willow tree to his chest, then twisted around to reach his back and give him the double faces of Janus between his shoulder blades. This position put her thigh out of Fin's reach. She wrapped her legs around his waist while she inked him, allowing him to add more prophecy below her knee. She rocked her hips, grinding her sopping sex into him.

She was so horny!

Finally two-faced Janus was done. Rook added the circular border, noticing for the first time how it made the god resemble a coin.

"Come here," Fin said. Only it didn't quite sound like Fin. Rook climbed around and straddled him, bobbing on his cock. It felt so damn good!

When they kissed she realized it wasn't Fin at all, but Kyle.

Relishing the thrill of him inside her again, Rook picked up her tattoo gun and started working on his left arm. While she puzzled out the interlocking outlines of the Escher horsemen, Kyle distracted her by sucking on her nipples and scrawling the Divided Man Prophecy across her tits in a brilliant green stain. She wished he would stop, and wished he would never stop.

A dazzling viridescent light shone from all the tattoos, chasing away Vesuvius's dim illumination, reflecting in Kyle's ethereal eyes as he watched her finish the cuff around his biceps.

Almost done.

His right hand still held the vibrating needle, adding further reverberations of the prophecy to the tender skin around her bellybutton. It was his left she wanted anyway. He needed one more tattoo.

When she married him in the cathedral he did not take a wedding band, but he would now. And it would match her own.

Rook leaned back, deliciously shifting Kyle's angle of penetration

and granting him easier access to her abdomen. At the same time she pulled his left hand between them where she could see better in the eerie green light. With her own wedding ring as a guide she set needle to flesh, etching their bond permanently in place.

If she did a good job on the ring, Kyle would be Complete.

Rook raced to finish the tattoo before she came.

A shadow fell over their gyrations as soon as she added the last line. Rook traced the darkness back to Bramble, who stood naked beside the bed, watching them hungrily. Kyle handed Bramble his tattoo gun and grabbed Rook's ass, taking over the rhythm of their fucking. Rook handed her tattoo gun to Brook.

Sandy ash covered the mattress. The grit got everywhere and added texture to their coupling. It felt fantastic.

Bramble and Brook climbed onto the bed of volcanic ash, coaxing Kyle to sit up and hold Rook tighter. The twins dipped their needles into deep green ink and, working together, tattooed another of Reverend Shaw's prophecies around Rook and Kyle's torsos, the words flowing from one to the other and back again, binding them.

A Completer, an Unknowing angel with Shadowed Wings, Shall heal the Divided Man and restore Light upon the Earth.

Where the words passed from Rook to Kyle their flesh melded, providing an unbroken canvas. Rook could feel the needles biting into Kyle's smooth skin as well as her own. It drove her wild. She threw her head back and groaned out her impending orgasm.

Rook woke drenched in sweat, in bed with Fin, shaking and swampy with desire for his brother.

***   ***   ***

The spiders celebrated their success in manipulating Rook's dream. They had refined their technique considerably from the crude initial gambit of literally graffitiing her dreamworld with the Divided Man Prophecy. Tiny edits now sufficed to steer her toward the basic message of Completing Kyle. All they did was erase Fin's tattoos, and Rook's mind swapped Kyle in. The prophecy appeared spontaneously this time,

filling the spiders with joyous pride in their accomplishment.

They had trained her subconscious to invoke Kyle and the prophecy in response to stress.

The entries in her journal indicated this conditioning had not yet shown up in her conscious decisions, but that was only a matter of time. Each session with her dreaming mind moved her closer to heeding their call.

There was a 63% probability she would lapse back into sleep tonight. And dream.

***   ***   ***

Floating.

Bubbles of light drift around him as he drifts among them.

Kyle is slowly, so slowly, diffusing in the gelatinous atmosphere. His gritty essence is caught in ancient, torpid currents. If this dispersion continues, will he be diluted to the point of nothingness, or will he become omniscient?

The bubbles yammer incessantly. Their tinking, plinking voices overlap, creating a mass of carbonated static as they try to tell him important things. Vital things.

He gathers that the bubbles are lonely. The luminous green ones congregating near him say they want him to stay. They say he is Family.

The notion of family means little to Kyle. He desires only one other, his deceitful wife. With her he tasted Completeness, and he hungers for it again.

Amid the bubbles and their knowledge he floats and waits.

***   ***   ***

Marsh took the stairs two at a time all the way to the third floor where he found Rainbow in their shared room.

She saw Marsh's expression, and concern drew a frown on her lovely face.

Marsh shut the door. "The jewelry is gone. All of it."

Rainbow gasped.

The two of them were using the jewelry, or more specifically the

nanotechnology concealed within it, to perfect the dream visualizer. Its official name was 'neural-net modulator' but neither of them called it that anymore. Marsh refined the hardware while Rainbow wrote enhanced software. Without the jewelry as a resource, their progress would be torpedoed.

Rainbow accompanied Marsh back to the lab. The metal briefcase used to store the jewelry was missing, along with its keys. Nothing else had been disturbed. Experiments and prototypes covered the benchtops with the customary bazaar of electromechanical esoterica. The door and trapdoor showed no signs of damage.

"Inside job," Rainbow muttered. "We'll have to search all the rooms."

"Don't you already know who it was?" Marsh asked. Leaf and his little wad of alien fetishists were the only other people at the House who still showed much interest in the jewelry.

"Of course. We can start with his room. But he's clever, and so are his comrades, so I don't expect it to be that easy."

Marsh saw her point. "We should change all the locks out here, and the access codes."

"Good idea."

Rainbow reached up to squeeze his shoulder before they climbed the ladder into the garage and walked back to the House.

When they got to Leaf's room and found it deserted, they exchanged a glance and went to Flint's door without saying a word. No one answered their knock, so Rainbow opened the door. This room also was empty of personal items.

"She's gone, too."

Marsh rubbed his temples. "Who are the others in their group?"

"Sand, Worth, and Reed."

The story repeated. Five members gone without a word.

"Maybe the aliens finally checked their answering machine," Rainbow suggested.

Marsh smiled thinly. They were back in their own room, sitting on

the bed. "Are we jumping to conclusions?"

"I don't really think the alien theory is all that likely," Rainbow clarified.

Marsh smiled more warmly. "No, I mean by blaming them for taking the jewelry. Maybe there was foul play."

"You want to think the best about everyone."

"Even Severin," Marsh said sheepishly.

"Wow," Rainbow scolded. "That wasn't what I meant at all."

For months, Severin's leadership had been erratic or outright negligent. Plus, his hand disappeared one day, along with Gale. Gale had been replaced. The hand had not. Now even Marsh doubted the eccentric recluse's wisdom.

"Nobody knows what they're supposed to be doing anymore," Marsh muttered. "They look to me, and I say, 'Keep your eyes on the horizon,' or some other Severinish bullshit. They think he still tells me things, so they think I know what I'm saying."

Rainbow rubbed his shoulders.

He continued, "I love the fact that I can focus on my work, that no one is going to arbitrarily rearrange my priorities. But now all the pressure is on me to have answers like his. And people are starting to leave. It's all falling apart."

"Hey, it's good those people left. They were bad news."

"Thieves," Marsh added.

"Exactly."

"I let them make off with the jewelry."

Rainbow gave his shoulders a hard squeeze. "You didn't 'let' anybody do anything. Look at me." She leaned around so she could see his face. "This isn't your fault. And it's not your fault the lunatic in the attic is off his game." She kissed him on the cheek. "You need an action plan to keep your mind focused."

Marsh sighed and nodded, feeling crappy for putting his responsibilities onto her. But his mind still wasn't focusing.

Rainbow saved him. "We definitely need to change the locks out at the garage. And I'll reconfigure the firewall personally."

Marsh nodded with a grim smile. "I'll take care of the hardware side and cut new keys."

Chapter Seven

No More Secrets

Setting: arcade — loud, dim, smoky
Fin is using the claw machine, trying to get a job. I want to play
the New Revelations pinball machine, but I drop my quarter. It's
spinning and I can't catch it. The floor is a green checkerboard
except underneath the air hockey table where someone knocked
over the ashtray. My coin gets stuck upright in the ashy sand. I
crawl under to get it but Kyle won't give it back unless I fuck him,
so I do, standing up while we play pinball. He has his own set of
flipper buttons.
     Rook Tanner's dream journal

Behind the wheel of the Steel Shark, Bishop's ancient, enormous
station wagon, Fin waited for his wife to come out of the library. They
were going over to Mom and Brad's house to celebrate Solstice.

To his great surprise, Fin was looking forward to the gathering.
Mom was back, and he had Rook. Having something to celebrate put
Fin in a good mood. He even felt up to being around Brad and the baby.
For whatever reason, Brad made Mom happy, and Fin wanted his mom
to be happy.

Obviously all Bishop's coaching was sinking in.

After the big trust fund blow-up, Fin took a dishwashing job at the
Vagabond, a restaurant with a world-travel theme and an eclectic menu.
It paid minimum wage, but he could take home dinner for Rook most
nights. The two of them got along pretty well now that she didn't feel
like he was taking advantage of her by making her work while he sat on
$108,520 and did nothing. She still had trouble sleeping, though, and in
his more morbid moments Fin suspected she regretted marrying him.

Often after sex when he was ready to spoon their way into slumber with their mental vibrations as entwined as their bodies, she would apologize and grab her laptop. In the middle of the night he'd wake to find her in the recliner, typing away.

The insomnia made Rook absentminded and distracted, and Fin missed her sharp-witted banter. With the library on restricted hours over term break, maybe she could catch up on her sleep.

The glass front doors swung open and Rook walked out, carrying her skateboard and talking with her friend Lara. They stopped at the bottom of the broad entry stairs, their breath gusting out in miniature fog banks. Rook stamped her patent-leather boots, the thick soles accentuating the lines of her legs.

The women hugged and Rook hurried to the Steel Shark waiting at the curb.

Once buckled in she laid her skateboard wheels-up between them on the bench seat, and gave Fin a perfunctory kiss. "Lara gave me a few of her shifts next week. I'll be working open to close, but that's only 9:00 to 5:00."

So much for her catching up on her sleep.

"Great."

Fin pulled out and pointed the Shark toward his mother's house.

"Do you have the presents?" Rook asked.

"They're in the back seat. Bishop wants us to stay out of the way-back. He wouldn't let me borrow the Shark until I swore a solemn oath on Vesuvius."

Rook laughed. "Okay."

Once they arrived and Rook took her jacket off, Fin felt like he'd already gotten his present, but one he'd have to wait to unwrap. Her multi-buckled boots were just the start. A gunmetal suede miniskirt hugged her ass daringly. The combination of upswept hair and scoop-necked purple sweater exposed the tattoo on the back of her neck, the flaming tower from a tarot deck. Fin nuzzled her ear and whispered, "You look hot."

She smiled.

The cottage was now fully stocked with furniture. After dinner Fin and Rook curled up together on a comfy love seat by the crackling fire. Rook sat between Fin's legs and leaned against his chest until Brad walked over with Zen in her pink velour stretchy suit.

Fin was still unsure about his baby sister, but it looked like he was expected to hold her again. Rook moved, so he had little choice. He cuddled Zen the way he'd been taught, and she gurgled at him. He smiled. She waved her fist around until she found a grip on the shiny fabric of his shirt. She tried to put the pocket in her mouth.

Rook laughed.

"You want to hold her?" Fin asked.

"She's good where she is."

Willow came in bearing a tray laden with steaming cups of cocoa. Zen began to fuss and suck on her fist.

"She's hungry." Willow retrieved the infant and settled onto the sofa. They were directly across from Fin. He didn't avert his eyes quickly enough when she lifted her sweater, and caught a mortifying flash of boob flesh. After that he looked studiously everywhere but at his mother.

Brad added more logs to the fire, then it was time to open presents.

Fin and Rook got his parents photo paper and an album to go with their new camera. It didn't feel like enough, but Mom seemed pleased.

With minimal fanfare, Brad presented Fin and Rook with a gift certificate for Amadoro, an upscale restaurant downtown. Rook's eyes lit up, so Fin was happy even if it meant he'd have to get dressed up.

Willow gave them a framed copy of the photo from Thanksgiving. In it Rook sat on his knee, both of them smiling. They made a damn handsome couple, if he did say so himself. The indigo of Rook's dress brought out the sapphire mischief in her eyes. Fin looked to see if she liked the picture as much as he did, and noticed the deep circles under those blue eyes now. The month of insomnia had taken its toll. Fin pulled her in for a kiss, trying to put his worry away until they got

home.

Handing over Zen's present, Rook apologized, "Neither of us has any experience with babies. I hope this is okay."

"I'm sure it will be," said Brad as Willow opened the box.

On top was a tiny pink t-shirt with the message 'If you think I'm cute you should see my big brother' printed across it in primary colors.

Willow and Brad laughed and held the shirt up for Zen, who ignored it.

A layer of tissue paper hid Fin's old stuffed monkey. This was the part Fin was unsure of. Maurice was pretty much his only memento from his childhood, but he lived in a cardboard box in the closet. Why not let Zen borrow him for a few years?

"Maurice!" said Willow with delight when she pulled the monkey out of the box.

Brad teared up. "I didn't think you'd kept him." He beamed at Fin and joked, "You probably wouldn't have if you'd known I bought him for you."

Fin felt an unaccustomed stir of emotion in his chest. When Brad turned away to dangle Maurice in front of Zen, Fin wiped his eyes surreptitiously and handed Rook her gift.

This was a risky move. She was humoring him about the trust fund, so money was tight, and this gift moderately extravagant.

When she saw the new Doc Martens, she froze, blinked, and looked up at him.

"I know how much you missed them," he said. Her old pair was abandoned in Donner, in the penthouse she shared with Kyle. Gone forever.

Without a word she threw her arms around him and buried her face in his chest. She was crying, hopefully the good kind of tears. Stroking her back Fin said, "I had to sell the chess set because I didn't have quite enough. We'll pick up another. It's the same game whether the pieces are marble or plastic." Fin felt a pang. He would miss that chess set, but not as much as he would miss Rook if she left him.

"They're perfect," she said into his chest, and he knew it was worth it. She kissed him, deep and hard and joyful.

"They're even the greasy leather!" she enthused. "It's just what I would have picked. Thank you."

She stood. "I need the key to the Shark so I can get your present."

"I brought them all in," Fin said, handing over the key anyway.

"Yours is in the way-back," she said with a wink. "Bishop was helping me hide it."

She practically skipped outside. A minute later she stuck her head back in and told Fin to close his eyes.

When she told him he could look, he saw a long, beat-up, rectangular case with a festive bow stuck to it. His fingers tingling, he fumbled open the clasps, and was delighted to find, sure enough, a bass. And not just any bass: a sunburst Fender with a maple fretboard.

"I hope it's okay," Rook said. "It's used, and I don't know about the color…"

"I love it," Fin said. The happy tingle rose along his arms and up into his face. He kissed her on the cheek, then lifted the instrument out of the case. It felt good in his hands. It was cold from sitting in the car and he was impatient for it to warm up so he could try it out.

Rook looked at him, searching for reassurance.

"It's great," he promised. "It just needs to warm up."

"I sold my stuff to Kip, the piercer at InkWell," Rook said. "He gave me a pretty good price. I hope it plays okay."

Willow and Brad exchanged their gifts, things for around the house which Fin found dull, but they enjoyed. Seeing them, Mom in her goofy sweater with the moose parading around the chest, and Brad in a turtleneck, cuddling Zen, Fin was struck by how happy and normal they looked. He hoped he and Rook would be that happy together, if not quite so boring, and decided such thoughts must be signs of growth.

Even that didn't spoil his mood.

By the time Willow and Brad finished with their sappiness, Fin's new bass was warm enough to take for a spin. It had a rich voice, even

unamplified. Fin liked the feel of it, smooth and precise. Smiling, he nodded to keep time. He played for about two minutes, and received heartfelt applause from everyone except Zen.

Rook put her new boots on, and pronounced them perfect. Fin pulled her into his lap and kissed her. Swept up in the moment, he let his hand slide down to her ass.

"Fin Chester Tanner!" Mom scolded.

Rook pulled away, laughing. "Chester?"

Fin shrugged.

"Your middle name's Chester?"

"'Fraid so. What's yours?"

She thought for a second. "When I was Brook, it was Bramble, but I don't think I have one now."

"Bramble's cool," Fin said with a pang of jealousy.

"No she's not." Rook looked away.

She?

"Well, it's better than Chester. Why on Earth did you name me that, Mom?"

"Finally something I don't get blamed for," said Brad with a smile. "You were going to tell them, anyway, right?"

Willow took a deep breath and said, "Beacon told you my name was Liz. I called myself that when I first came to Webster, but it wasn't my real name." She paused. "My real name is Ester Elizabeth Finch."

Fin didn't know what to say.

"You must admit it's a little more likely than Willow Charm," she said. "When you were born, I wanted to acknowledge my roots in a subtle, safe way. Ester Finch equals 'Finch, comma, Ester' which I turned into Fin Chester."

"I was named after you?" Fin suddenly liked Chester a lot more.

"Does this mean you want us to call you Ester?" Rook asked.

Willow shook her head. "No, I like Willow."

"Me, too," said Brad. "I love Willow." He kissed her.

Fin had to make them stop. "But why did you change your name?"

"The nature cult," said Rook. "My mom was Cloud, your mom was Willow. What was your name Brad?"

"Brad," said Brad.

"The Following provided a convenient excuse," Willow said, "but I was already using an alias. I was on the run, hiding from the military. Still am, really."

Willow turned to Brad, who gave her a reassuring smile.

As Fin listened with increasing consternation, his mother told of growing up in a secret military psychic program and how she'd run away. She explained how she kept her past secret, even from Brad, and how she never felt entitled to ask anything of him since she couldn't be honest herself. It was novel and uncomfortable for Fin to see Brad as a victim in his parents' relationship. He always assumed Brad was a philandering asshole.

"It's scary to talk about this, terrifying to think what they would do if they found me." She looked at the baby in Brad's lap. "Or my children."

Brad took her hand.

"I had to be ready to run again if they came for me. So I never let Brad get close to you. I regret that."

Was she really taking the blame for Brad being a shitty father? Because secret agents were after her?

"Now for the weird part."

"It gets weirder?" Fin hugged Rook closer.

"You've heard about Severin, right?"

Fin nodded.

"He was the leader of the Following. The nature cult, as Rook calls it. He's very bad news, but I didn't realize that at first. He helped me establish the Willow Charm identity, and he paid my tuition at Buckminster."

Willow gazed through the wall for a moment, tugging on her hair. "He's something of a wizard. There's a magic table that's a portal into a dimension he calls the Elsewhere. He conjures objects through it and

uses them in a sort of fortune-telling way. I know this sounds ridiculous, but it's real. I used the table myself. It's not a trick."

"As my lovely wife keeps reminding me," Fin said, "I've experienced some rather impossible things myself."

Rook squeezed his hand.

Willow went on to describe her search for her mother using the magic table. She told how Severin kidnapped her.

Fin's fists clenched at the image of his mother in danger.

"I'm okay now, Fin," she reassured.

Brad put his arm around her. "It's hard for us to hear, Wil," he said. "It confirms our worst fears from back then."

"But I'm okay now." She looked at Fin. "I spent twelve years floating in the Elsewhere. It didn't feel like twelve years." She looked down at Zen. "It didn't even feel like six months. It felt timeless. A truly zen experience." Her eyes drifted to a horizon only she could see and her words came in a murmur. "It's like the air was thick, gelatinous. These bubbles of light floated around me and talked to me." Her fingers fluttered in the air around her head. "They told me so much. It comes to me sometimes like I'm remembering a dream."

"Elsewhere." Fin was curious. "I wonder what it really is."

"It seems to be a giant mind, like the world's mind." She was more focused now. "Not Mother Nature, or Gaia, or anything like that. More like a collective mind made of all the living things on Earth."

Fin sucked in a breath. This sounded like the Collective Id the spiders loved to talk about.

Willow waited for him to say something, and when he didn't she went on. "That wasn't my first visit to the Elsewhere. Back before you were born, Fin, before I even met Brad, I visited during a drug trip."

Fin laughed. "You dropped acid?"

"Some kind of mushroom juice. Injected."

"What the fuck, Mom?"

She shrugged. "Don't give in to peer pressure, son. Severin pushed it on me. As soon as my head straightened out enough, I got the hell out

of there, hitchhiking, and your dad gave me a lift."

"Hitchhiking!" Fin had never heard this story. "You met Brad when you were high?"

That might explain what she saw in him, actually.

Fin looked back and forth between his parents to see if either of them would let on they were joking. They smiled benignly. He turned to Rook, who looked politely interested, not scandalized in the least to learn her husband was the result of the 70s in microcosm.

"Anyway," said Willow, "if you're done being a prude, that first time it was all green tie-dye fire, and I astral projected, or whatever, right in the middle of it. Terrifying. I had to hide from the All Seeing Eye…"

"I think you're getting a little off topic, Wil," Brad interjected.

"So I am. Long story short, the green fire and the bubbles of light are the same place. The same colossal mind. It wants a companion. It keeps trying to make one, but loses track of its projects. It's also obsessed with twins."

She stopped talking and looked to Brad. He nodded.

"I feel like you need to know this because it might have a direct impact on you."

"Me?" asked Fin. "How? Why?"

"Webster is a nexus. The weird stuff the Elsewhere influences is drawn to its own kind. The Elsewhere created Severin's table as a portal. It created Severin and his twin, my mother, out of whole cloth as infants."

"Your mother was *created?* What does that mean?"

"It means the bloodline starts with her. The Elsewhere doesn't seem to remember why it created her and Severin. Once they were separated, it lost interest."

"But you weren't *created*, were you? You had a father." Fin didn't know why he was taking this seriously.

Willow raised her eyebrows. "Have you ever heard of a TV preacher named Brian Shaw?"

Fin nodded, wary.

"He was my father, according to the bubbles."

Fin shook his head violently. "Shaw? My grandfather?"

Rook looked horrified.

Willow wasn't done. "My twin and I were also separated, but we both ended up here in Webster, and we both got involved with the same man." She paused. "And we both got pregnant."

"Wait," said Fin. "Melissa? Are you saying Melissa is your sister?"

Willow and Brad both nodded.

"I suspected, but had no way to prove it," said Brad. "I never said anything." He sounded ashamed.

Fin's anger and resentment flared, but then he remembered he'd known Melissa for twelve years and never suspected. Now with their images placed side-by-side in his mind, the resemblance was eerie. Then he felt baffled.

"You told me, eventually," Willow said to Brad. "We both kept too much hidden, but now we know better."

Thinking back over what he'd witnessed of Brad and Melissa's married life, Fin was unable to recall a single warm moment between them, a sharp contrast to how Brad and Willow behaved, how they were handling this awkwardness.

"Twins aren't always the same," said Rook quietly, voicing Fin's thoughts. She looked at Brad. "Fin and Kyle are twins, in a way. Half-twins. And they're very different. I can see how you would be unsure."

"Do you know Kyle well?" Brad asked.

Rook squirmed. "He made a pass at me."

At least she didn't go into the whole 'I married him, too' thing. Talk about awkward.

"It's the twin obsession," said Willow. "The Elsewhere has meddled in human affairs, and especially this family, for decades, in an attempt to make more twins. Like I said, it can't keep track of everything and its projects get away from it. Webster became a magnet for our kind. It drew Severin here, and my mother. It drew me and my twin. The Elsewhere saw to it that Brad got involved with both me and Melissa.

He didn't have a choice."

It wasn't Rook's choice to be attracted to Kyle. Fin truly believed that. If he could make allowances for his wife, why wasn't he willing to do the same for his father?

"Why twins?" said Rook. "What exactly is it trying to do?"

Willow said, "It feels incomplete. It wants to make a twin for itself so it can be completed."

Rook stiffened at the use of the word 'completed.'

Oblivious, Willow went on, "The Elsewhere is made of everybody's thoughts. That leaves nothing leftover to form a companion. If everyone had a twin, it would have one, too, or so is reasons. There would be two identical subsets, Group A made of all the firstborn twins, Group B made of the secondborns."

"I've heard that twins are becoming more common," Fin said. "But it'll take centuries for this plan to work."

Willow shook her head. "It's the idea of twins, not literal biological twins. All it cares about is what we're all thinking."

"Oh, is that all," Fin said.

Willow smiled. "When everyone is thinking their own thing, the Elsewhere gets scatterbrained because it's pulled in so many directions. When large numbers of people obsess about the same thing, it can focus. That's where fads and religions come from: the Elsewhere trying to encourage lock-step thought. If it can get Group A and Group B to each have their own fixation, a second Elsewhere should be created. Then it wouldn't be alone."

This shit had the whiff of Shaw's New Revelations about it. But Shaw got it backwards, trying to make the Divided Man into one whole. The Elsewhere, this Id the spiders talked about, wanted two.

"Is it winning?" Rook asked.

Willow cocked her head.

"Well," Rook said, "Severin and Gale are reunited, right? And you and your sister are both here in Webster…"

"I don't think it works like that," Willow said. "Our generation is

played out. It's you kids that interest it now. Besides, Gale is dead. The Elsewhere reclaimed her."

"Severin's alone," Fin said. "Aren't you worried he'll try to kidnap you again?"

Willow looked at Brad, who shifted uncomfortably.

"Melissa is with him now," Brad mumbled.

"What?"

Brad took a deep breath. "I used her as a distraction the night I rescued Willow. I guess she likes Severin, though. She moved in. From what I understand she talks to Kyle's doctor sometimes, checks her voicemail." He shrugged.

"My guess is she's drawn to the power," said Willow. "Severin's table is a fascinating thing. I was able to use it. She probably can, too."

"Did you ever meet your father?" Rook asked Willow.

"No," Willow said, looking at Zen in Brad's lap. "He died a few months ago. I don't think I would have wanted to meet him, though." Fixing Rook with her gaze, she added, "Some people are best avoided."

Rook nodded. "I met him once. He kidnapped me."

Brad and Willow looked at Rook sharply.

"Me too," Fin said. "The reverend wanted to, ah, interview me. I don't think he knew we were related."

Brad and Willow both looked anxious and baffled.

"There was some body jewelry with miniature electronics in it," Rook explained. "I didn't know about the electronics when I pierced people with it. Shaw wanted to use the stuff to control people's minds. I guess he was doing the Elsewhere's bidding."

"I'm glad he's dead," Willow said.

Everyone sat quietly for several minutes, pondering how crazy the world had become.

"I hope I was right to share this with you," said Willow. "I couldn't stand the thought of more secrets. They only lead to trouble."

∗∗∗   ∗∗∗   ∗∗∗

After waving goodnight and shutting the front door, Willow

accepted the baby from Brad, who started gathering up wrapping paper. He located a bow and stuck it to Zen's fuzzy head. Willow smiled, but something weighed down her eyes, holding her gaze to the floor.

"Brad, there's something else I need to tell you about."

He motioned to the sofa and they both sat.

"I know about that electronic jewelry Rook was talking about." Willow's mouth felt dry. "I know a whole lot about it."

"What are you saying?"

"I designed it. My last freelance job." Willow traced the green satin bow Zen wore, her brow knitted. "I didn't know what it was at the time. I never knew anything more than the bare essentials. I never stopped to wonder where any of my work would end up. God knows how Shaw got hold of it, no pun intended."

Brad chuckled, but Willow winced. She cuddled Zen to her cheek.

"You need to tell Fin about this," Brad suggested.

Willow shook her head.

Brad gave her a gentle kiss on the temple. Her head drooped, pressing out a sigh.

"Why did you tell me?" Brad asked.

Willow studied him sidelong. "Secrets only lead to trouble."

"But did telling me make you feel any better?"

Willow pictured Fin's reactions to different ways she might explain this, toying with the bow until it tumbled to the floor. She shook her head. "It's all in the past. Shaw is dead, and everyone is safe. If I tell Fin, it will put a new barrier between us."

Brad gave her a squeeze. "Whatever you think is right." He held her shoulders, held her gaze. "Just remember what you said about secrets."

Chapter Eight

THE AFFECTED AREA

The id is an essential element of the mind, a fountain of drives to guarantee survival. Other beings do not exist for the id: there are only food-bringers, back-scratchers, playthings. It is a heap of urges and reactions. Consciousness, the ego, takes root and blossoms in the id's dark, fertile soil. Like a potted plant on a windowsill, that consciousness will bend toward the light of the superego.

Inside every individual human skull this tiny drama plays out as if for the first time.

On a grander scale, meanwhile, the Collective Ego's frail stem has hardly breached the surface of the vast Id, and no light shines to guide and nourish it. If someone could bring the dawn to that twilight garden, he would be the Collective Superego, bending the Ego and thereby all of humanity to his will.
          Severin Tenpenny's journal

At seven in the morning on New Year's Day, Fin had already been at work for an hour. He was still drunk, having come straight from the party. Kevin, the new guy in Kyle's old room, sprang for a keg. Bishop furnished a bottle of tequila. Booth provided the weed, Max the vodka, Quent the pretzels and nachos, and Fin brought all the leftover sauerkraut and bratwurst from the Vagabond's New Year's menu. At Bishop's insistence, the crowd was kept small. They had a great time, the best Fin could remember. Rook even persuaded him to dance with her for a few songs.

Now that he was married, people expected less from him in the way of crazy antics. It felt good to let loose and have fun without the pressure of putting on a performance.

The party petered out by five a.m., and Fin took Rook to bed so they could start the new year with a bang. She was sleeping when he left, which was a relief. She slept so little. When he got off work, he'd take her some food and see if she'd be interested in coming back to bed so he could get some sleep himself.

Right now he was up to his elbows in plate-scrapings. Belgian waffles, blintzes, Eggs Benedict, half-masticated bagels with lox. All of it went down the disposal as Fin loaded the next tray for the washer. He told himself to take his time, that his judgment was impaired and his reflexes dulled by all he'd imbibed the night before.

Out in the dining room, the music was some weird zydeco/world beat hybrid. Here in the kitchen it was Travesties of the 70s. The two were battling it out for the title of Most Annoying Music Ever until Fin's sozzled synapses misfired and they became one song, infinitely better than the original components.

Nodding to the beat of this imaginary new song, Fin didn't even dread the prospect of scrubbing the soufflé pans. It was that good.

Staying tuned in to the mash-up meant Fin had to shift his brain into approximately the same gear that once enabled him to converse with the Floating Wisdom.

Babble washed in from the dining room whenever the door swung open. He caught snippets of conversations, mingled with the global-village music and random clinks. These miscellaneous words and sound effects found a place in the surreal symphony inside Fin's head, interleaving with each other and the corny lyrics.

The random overlapping remarks produced a new thought cutting across them. Fin heard it as if it had been spoken by a single voice instead of a dozen.

I gotta be home by dinnertime.
I'll come up with something
That's the funniest thing I've ever heard!
it's just a joke.
Got an A in history last semester.
Hash browns, or a muffin?"
Bob's desk is the dirtiest in the office.
This is clearly not what I ordered.
Find out what it will involve.
Their fruit salad even has kumquats and
Either way, be sure to let me know

Fin heard, "Gotta come up with the funniest joke in history. Or the dirtiest. Clearly it will involve kumquats either way."

He laughed, and could tell by the glares of the line cooks that he was quite loud. With an inward note to suppress any further guffaws, Fin kept his ears unfocused just right.

The next one sounded even more distinct, incorporating lyrics from the song on the kitchen radio.

Now it seems so simple, but at the time
would never work to just have one car.
It's hard having everybody count on you.
I was off by two.
Seriously, what are the odds of that happening?
know when to hold 'em
Strider is Aragorn, and the Evenstar is Arwen.
know when to fold 'em
I hate parallel parking.
If Buck U ever processes my application
Don't make a big scene.
The cure for that is cutting the apron strings.
lot of freshmen experience loneliness at first.

All of which, in Fin's head, produced the phrase, "It seems so simple, to just have everybody count off by two. The odds know when to hold 'em and the evens know when to fold 'em. Parallel processes make a cure for loneliness."

"Most stupid ideas sound simple," Fin said under his breath.

"You got a better plan?"

Fin nearly dropped a glass, which he couldn't afford. It would come out of his pay.

Stephen, the biggest prima-donna on the waitstaff, was arguing with Jill, and his sarcastic whine had cut through the sonic undergrowth at just the right moment.

When his hands steadied, Fin loaded a rack of glassware into the machine. In his present condition, it was stupid to take anything he heard at face value. However freaky, the way the words lined up could be a mere coincidence, or an illusion manufactured by his compromised awareness.

Fin didn't believe any of that. He suspected it was the Elsewhere, the Collective Id the spiders had been so pleased to tell him about.

I should test it.

"Loneliness doesn't have to be viewed as a disease," Fin muttered.

A swirl of sound from the dining room, like verbal jigsaw pieces, replied, "How would you know what it's like for an only child? You have a twin."

Shit. It knows who I am.

"His company is a lot worse than being alone, believe me."

The response this time was built from the conversations among the cooks and waiters. "Being alone by choice is different. You don't understand, there is no one else."

What am I, your imaginary friend?

Fin didn't give this question voice. Better to terminate this conversation before he got in any deeper. His experience with the Floating Wisdom was a strong lesson about the perils of talking to collective minds.

"Admit it," the eddy of voices said. "You can't imagine being altogether alone, forever."

Fin turned his attention to the pots and pans that had piled up while he tried to keep up with the table service items.

The kitchen staff's chatter stopped. The radio station miscued a commercial, producing several seconds of dead air. The dining room

seemed suddenly somber as well. Fin concentrated on his work, aware the Id was fuming over his unresponsiveness.

With a crash like a bomb going off, Stephen dropped a tray of seven meals. The destruction of all the food for a large table disrupted the cooks' lives for the foreseeable future, which led to a volley of profanity to rival anything ever uttered at sea.

No coherent remark emerged amid all the swearing, but Fin took it as a comment about himself.

He drew a steadying breath as he soaped a particularly filthy saucepan. He glanced around, knowing it made him look paranoid. How far would things escalate?

The disaster with the dropped tray restored cacophonous life to the kitchen, even waking up the radio. Fin picked up another comment from the Id.

I don't want to know the sex of the baby.
Trig is the course that's killing me.
I have the ticket in my wallet.
What are blintzes?
A chef salad with ranch on the side.
and everyone already had theirs on!
You are being so stupid, Gary.
He's so preoccupied with football, I want to scream.
Man, it sucks being on call.
I can't remember the words most of the time.
Just leave a quarter, the service sucked.
There's no need to make that face, young man.
In the old days, you had to crank it.
get home and straighten up a little before your aunt arrives.

Relief washed the tension from Fin's head. New topic, and it was back to talking to itself.

For the remainder of his shift, Fin tried to tune out the Id's muttering. Now that he knew it was there, it was difficult to ignore.

***   ***   ***

Severin felt refreshed, his mind awakened by an infusion of tantric power. He stared at his table, while Melissa lounged in the hammock after her lesson.

He couldn't persuade her to reach under the sheet, but she laid on the table for sex without protest. This struck Severin as an irrational contradiction, but Melissa insisted it was perfectly logical.

"The first time you fucked me was on that table," she said. "I survived. However, when you reached under the sheet, you lost your hand. I have no wish to lose mine."

From her ignorant point of view, that made sense. The true contradiction was Severin's quixotic tutelage in the table's use. While he wanted to keep her in the dark, he also wanted her to explore the Elsewhere and encounter the slab. Sometimes he superfluously admonished her to keep away from the table, and other times ineffectually cajoled her to give it a try.

Frustration had led him to try drugging her. While she was out, he carted her to the table and put her left hand under the sheet. An awkward enterprise, his left arm wrapped around to hold her upright, reaching across with his right hand to guide her left, bending at the knees to duck her hand under the edge of the sheet. After all that, her hand just lay on the table, not in the Elsewhere at all.

This felt like a game he should be better at.

Using the table himself right-handed failed most of the time, and generated only disappointing trinkets otherwise. The situation drove home how deeply he depended on its answers. Without them, he made no progress at all.

The solution was to get his hand back. He'd already tried reaching into the Elsewhere with his stump. It did nothing. No regrowth of tissue, and without a means of grasping objects he gathered no artifacts.

He'd used energy from Melissa to heal over the original burn, and subsequently tried to further regenerate his flesh. So far he hadn't noticed any difference. But that first healing worked, so the power from her sex was the type he wanted. He had to get a stronger dose.

Apply it directly to the affected area.

"Melissa," he barked, "it's time for your next lesson."

Melissa put aside her trashy novel and exited the hammock, a feat

she had become far more adept at.

"On the table?" She undid the top button of her sweater, and let it slide off her emaciated frame. Her ribs and hips were more prominent than her breasts. Most of her caloric intake came from a vineyard.

"Yes." Severin disrobed. Melissa stretched out on the table.

"No," Severin said, "I need to be on the bottom." She made space for him, then straddled him and reached under to massage his genitals. Severin raised his stump and stroked the skin between her breasts, enjoying her attentions.

When she started guiding him toward her slit, he said, "Not like that." Melissa quirked an eyebrow. "Swing around."

Melissa rolled her eyes, but she pivoted atop Severin so her knees rested on either side of his head. He nuzzled her mons, gathering her heady aroma, and she gave his phallus a businesslike swipe with her tongue. Severin exhaled into Melissa's pubic hair and grasped her buttock. He caressed her thigh with his left forearm. She settled her hips lower, pressing herself against his mouth. He parted her labia with the tip of his tongue as she wrapped her lips around the head of his penis.

They indulged and teased each other until Severin sensed that she hovered at the threshold of orgasm. Without letting up in his oral stimulation, he shrugged his left arm free to achieve a better angle of attack. As she drew a deep breath and tensed, he pushed the stump firmly into her vagina.

The moment was complex.

Melissa's orgasm blossomed, even as she signaled quite clearly with her teeth that she disapproved. She bucked, and pumped her pelvis, trying to free herself and trying to get more leverage at the same time. Severin used his right arm to contain her, encircling her thigh and holding her in place as he imparted a gentle reciprocating movement to his stump.

It felt like the ecstatic bursting of ejaculation combined with the hard-edged warmth of plunging into a steaming bath. His abbreviated arm flooded with pulsating life, absorbing it from Melissa's womb.

Distantly, he knew she was still biting him.

Her climax subsided, and with it the throbbing vitality saturating Severin's stump. She lifted her head and snarled, "Let go of me!"

Severin maintained his grip, doggedly keeping himself lodged inside her. She wrenched free and lurched off the table, nearly upending it. She spat on him and stormed over to collect her sweater. She stomped down the stairs.

Severin lay panting on the table and gazed at his left arm. He almost expected to see his hand fully restored. It wasn't, but the shiny scar tissue of a few minutes ago was now pink, healthy skin.

***   ***   ***

Melissa got into the shower.

She felt revolted and violated by what Severin had done. She soaped herself all over, three times, then let the painfully hot water distract her from her mental anguish until it ran cold.

Still shaking with rage and nausea, Melissa toweled off and put the sweater back on.

Such a transgression would not be happening again.

Her uncle thought he could put her through anything, thought she had no choice but to stay with him if she wanted to avoid being dragged into madness by the patterns.

She could break his hold on her, if she had Kyle.

Melissa retrieved a bottle of wine from the back of the linen closet and uncorked it with her teeth. It took an hour before she was calm enough to go down to the kitchen, where she could rely on finding other residents of the House.

When she entered the kitchen, the two males in green sweaters leaning against the counter stopped talking. They looked in her direction, but didn't say hello. One of them gave a small nod. Melissa smiled, a little, not trusting her face not to distort it into a grimace.

"Good afternoon," she said. "I'm curious about the activities here. It's all very impressive. Does any of what you do involve medical technology?"

The young men glanced at each other, and the one who'd acknowledged Melissa said, "Yes, a little. It depends on how you define it, because there's monitoring associated with several of the projects, even though they're not strictly medical." The other man nervously looked out into the hall.

"You're Horn, right? And Free?" She hoped to put them more at ease. "I'm Melissa. I have a special request. More of a proposition really. My son is in a coma. He's at Webster General, but I'd be happier if he were closer. I'd like to bring him here. Would someone be able to maintain his care? You could do noninvasive experiments on him. He won't mind."

Horn and Free exchanged another look, and Melissa thought she'd played her card too quickly. With a shrug, the two turned back to her and said, "Sure," in perfect unison.

"Wonderful, thank you."

At the sink she ran herself a glass of water, drank it, and ran another, while thinking about how to accomplish the transfer. She would have to go along to sign him out. She'd need clothing, shoes at least, and she'd need to cope with the patterns on the ten-minute drive. Knowing the sanctuary of Kyle awaited should make it a survivable journey.

She turned to face the men, who had resumed their earlier conversation. They stopped again and looked at her.

"If one of you knows where there might be a pair of shoes I could borrow, we can go right now."

"I think we need time to set up a room for him," Free said, "and I'd like to run the idea past Marsh. Could we plan on doing this tomorrow, or early next week?"

"I think I can get you some shoes, though," Horn put in.

Melissa nodded. The trio agreed to firm up their plans the next day, and she set out for the stairs. Returning to her uncle's domain galled her, but she had no other option. She could loiter in the kitchen, or watch the enormous television in the living room, but she was in his

house no matter what.

Now that her shock had passed, Melissa could see today's incident was no more degrading than any of what she and Severin got up to on a typical day. It had been unexpected, and disturbing. The fact that he tricked her into it meant he knew she wouldn't comply willingly, which made it rape. All the same, she spent much of a typical day having drunken intercourse with her mother's brother, so who was she to pass judgment?

She focused her mind on the upcoming ordeal of leaving the House. She wouldn't be driving, so she could shut her eyes. Sounds and bumps in the road would be a problem, but by shutting out visual signals, she would remove the majority of troublesome sensory input. Messages could be carried in other kinds of sensation, though.

Severin had brought her another kind of sensation.

Memory of those cataclysmic moments flooded out the present, and Melissa stopped so she wouldn't tumble down the steps. A moan tried to force its way out, and she quaked with the strain of holding it back, of keeping her posture dignified as her loins again filled with electricity.

Even as she tried to fend off these recollections, she discovered a message buried within her erotic panic. Two lines of force crisscrossed under the House, energizing Severin's table as a portal into another dimension. Her uncle was only injured because of his own pride, his abuse of the table's power. She need have no fear of reaching under the sheet.

For once, Severin's habit of calling their assignation a 'lesson' hadn't been a lie.

Melissa took shelter in the small room next to the attic stairs to compose herself. She didn't want to learn more about her dark 'gift!' She wanted to rid herself of it completely. Instead, her only choices were to suffer in ignorance or let Severin defile her so she could attain understanding. She would never be free, either way.

Wiping her nose on her sleeve, she resolved to at least make sure all future incest was on her own terms. He would be keeping that stump to

himself.

*** *** ***

Both hands shoved in his pockets, Fin stared adoringly at the display of pens and mechanical pencils. Rook trusted his stationery lust to hold him spellbound long enough for her to accomplish her mission.

"Hey." She tried to sound casual. "I'm gonna find the bathroom. Don't run off with any Walmartians while I'm gone."

He gave her a kiss on the cheek. "I promise not to fall prey to the seductive wiles of anyone in a blue vest."

Rook gave him a second to become hypnotized by the office supplies again.

Health and Beauty was a quick walk away. The feminine products all clustered together in one aisle. Rook tossed a box of tampons into her basket along with KY, yeast infection cream, a pregnancy test, and a douche.

Wending her way through the store, Rook pocketed one of the items. She left her basket on a bench and entered the ladies' room.

Alone in the stall, Rook pulled the pregnancy test out of her pocket and stared at it. Her stomach clenched. The directions were absurdly simple, but Rook read them through twice.

Pee on the stick. Wait three minutes. I should be able to handle that.

She knew from experience this could be messy, so she wrapped her hand in a protective wad of toilet paper.

Once the stick was saturated, Rook stuck it back in the box and did her best to clean her hands. This would be a long three minutes.

An exhausted-sounding woman with three small children came into the bathroom. One of the kids was crying and the woman ignored it. She tried to get the one named Crystal to use the potty, which involved much haranguing. Rook squeezed her eyes closed and tried to banish the visions of her future.

One minute.

If she was pregnant, the only good news was it couldn't be Marcus's. She'd had her period right before her first date with Fin. It was actually

the main factor in the scheduling of said date.

Because she was apparently incapable of being anything other than an unfaithful slut.

She might not be pregnant. Her cycle was always erratic, which was why she tracked it on her Mac. She'd gone three months between periods before. With Kyle plaguing her dreams for the past 69 nights, she'd been super stressed. That could be the entire explanation.

Two minutes.

Probably wishful thinking.

She'd had a lot of unprotected sex. A whole fucking lot. For the entire fortnight in the bomb shelter when pretty much all she and Fin did was fuck, the thought of protection never entered her mind. Not even once. She'd been so fucking stupid.

Then there was Kyle. For over two weeks she was his prisoner and unwilling wife, and he fucked her even more than Fin had.

Birth control pills gave her migraines, but she used a diaphragm. She used it even when she made her boyfriends use condoms. This nigh-obsession deserted her just when she was getting her brains fucked out by both Fin and Kyle. Could she lay the blame on the Webster paranormal nexus twin obsession? That was more appealing than taking responsibility herself.

Three minutes.

Rook took the test out of the box.

"Fuck."

Chapter Nine

Buckminster University Library

The remaining structure of the Shaw Ministries Cathedral was demolished in late November, signaling the shift of investigative energies from the search for physical evidence to the analysis of intelligence data. To date, Reverend Declan Spitz and his followers have not been located, and are believed to be in hiding somewhere in Africa. While early reports suggested as many as 3,000 people were missing, that number was revised downward throughout the investigation. The final official tally is 415.
2000 in Review from *Webster Daily Press*

Both front wheels of the green metal book cart squeaked, a shrill duet that wore on Rook's nerves and eroded her tenuous grip on sanity. The students studying at their carrels glared as she passed.

Am I even on the right floor?

Last night she did not sleep at all. She laid awake beside Fin, trying to comprehend the fact of her pregnancy.

The mere idea was repugnant. She couldn't be a mother, couldn't be responsible for the care and feeding of another human. The boarding house was a laughably unsuitable home for adults, let alone a child.

Assuming Fin didn't kick her out, of course. He certainly didn't want to be a father.

Even if they stayed together and could find an affordable apartment, what the fuck did she know about babies? Fuck all, that's what.

Rook picked up the first book on her cart and wedged it onto a shelf without even looking at the call number.

Brook and Bramble taunted her with the certainty that the baby was Kyle's. Their schadenfreude laughter was as shrill as the squeaky wheels.

After dumping a stack of books on an empty carrel, Rook randomly shelved three more.

Abortion was the only answer. The question was how to accomplish it without Fin finding out. So far it seemed impossible.

Rook already knew where to get one and how much it cost. Her sister had started at Buckminster the previous summer and made a nuisance of herself, hanging out at Talisman until Rook told her to get lost. By August stupid little Junebug needed an abortion.

The nearest clinic was in Campbell, a two-hour drive. Rook borrowed Marcus's van. During the preliminary exam, she noticed a colorful beetle tattooed in the area exposed by her sister's Brazil wax.

Bug confirmed her suspicions. "Yeah, Marcus gave me a discount. Since I'm your sister."

Even with the sting of betrayal, Rook drove Junebug to the actual procedure. It seemed the sisterly thing to do. And how did the little bitch pay her back? By blabbing to Mom about Rook's marriage.

No, Rook would not be asking her sister for help. Bug would most certainly tattle again, to Mom and maybe even to Fin. And Fin could never know.

Rook had never loved Marcus, and even so it hurt to think of him fucking her sister. Imagining the same circumstances with Fin, whom she loved desperately, brought tears and an ache in her chest.

How had Fin ever forgiven her for what she did with Kyle?

The thought that she might lose him because of an accident of biology gutted her. Brook and Bramble cackled with malicious glee.

As if the Bug isn't bad enough, I had to invent sisters who are even worse.

Rook's bleary eyes focused on the call number of the book she held, then on the directional sign in front of her. Since she was close to the correct section, she made an effort to shelve this one properly.

It took all her concentration, but Rook put the next ten books away in approximately the right spots. She doubted she'd get the medal she deserved for her heroic effort.

The wheels sang their strident song as Rook trudged down the aisle.

Getting to the clinic was the first hurdle. She and Fin had no car, and she couldn't skateboard down the highway. Bishop might be willing to lend the Shark, but she would be in no shape to drive herself home afterwards.

There was a bus, but Rook couldn't afford a ticket.

Which brought up the second hurdle. If she didn't have $50 for the bus, she certainly didn't have $500 for the procedure.

The library keys on her stretchy spiral wristband clicked against the cart.

Well, technically she did. Brad gave them that much at Thanksgiving and it taunted her from their safe deposit box. All she needed was the key. A ridiculous little piece of metal was all that stood between her and her fondest desire.

The key was not on Fin's keyring. She tore the room apart and didn't find it. For all she knew, he swallowed it. The only way to get into the box without the key involved drilling, and cost $100.

If she had anything like a reasonable excuse, she could just ask for the key. But Fin could never know.

Fin's trust fund was fat enough to pay for any number of abortions. If only she'd followed through on gaining access instead of letting it drop once he got a job.

Stupid, stupid, stupid sang Bramble.

Slut, slut, slut sang Brook.

Rook shook her head in an attempt to silence the voices, and pushed her noisy cart around the corner to the service elevator. Down on the lowest level there wouldn't be as many judgmental students shooting her dirty looks. Rook's key opened the cage and she entered the tiny metal box, pulling her cart in with her as it shrieked in protest.

The quiet hum of the descending elevator lulled Rook. The wall she leaned on vibrated.

Rook's eyes snapped open. She had fallen asleep standing in the elevator. She opened the gate and got out, pulling her cart behind her.

It was deserted down here, and dark. Rook turned the dial on the nearest timer before closing the elevator. The fluorescent tube sputtered to sickly life. It would stay on for about ten minutes before turning itself back off.

The only sound was the bumblebee buzz of the timer. Rook moved down the rows of prehistoric doctoral theses in their olive drab bindings until she found a work desk. She sat in the old wooden chair and propped her feet up.

With a gentle click the lights went out.

Some time later a familiar voice spoke out of the darkness, "You have a lot of books to put away."

Rook sighed.

"I'll take care of it. You'll owe me." The squeaky cart rolled away and Rook heard the rattle of the service elevator gate.

That was nice of him.

After resting for a little longer in the dark, Rook went to the stairs. At the top she ran into Lara who had one of the big wooden carts, both levels packed with books.

"There you are." She shoved the cart at Rook. "You do these and I'll take care of the periodicals."

Rook pushed the books onto the elevator. She went back down to the bottom and started to try to find her way in the dark.

"You're exhausted. Let me help. You'll owe me."

Rook sat in the wooden chair and waited. When the voice didn't come back, she went upstairs. This time Lara met her with a cart the size of a bookmobile.

Rook loaded the monstrous cart onto the elevator and went back to the basement. Staring at the overwhelming number of books, she started to cry.

"Hey, don't worry about it. I got it. But you owe me."

Rook sat. A little later she felt a hand on her shoulder, on her tower-of-birds tattoo.

"Time to pay up."

The lights crackled on, dim and greenish. Kyle stood beside her, his hand on her shoulder. Rook's belly was enormous. Something inside writhed, and she felt a stabbing pain.

"A deal's a deal." Kyle put pressure on her shoulder, lowering her to the floor.

"No!"

"You knew what you were getting into." He pinned her shoulders to the green-speckled linoleum.

Hot fluid gushed out of Rook's vagina, acidic and bloody, and she screamed again.

"This is gonna be great!" Kyle smothered her next scream with a kiss.

Hands grabbed Rook's legs and pried them apart. They pushed her skirt out of the way, leaving her naked from the waist down. Kyle moved, and Rook saw the hands belonged to Brook and Bramble.

"Breathe!" they sang.

A terrible pain tore through Rook as whatever was inside her started to claw its way out.

"I always wanted a son," said Kyle, grinning as he pinned her to the floor. "You're doing great, honey!"

Rook wailed.

A snake with black scales and chartreuse eyes began to slither out of her womb, mouth wide, fangs dripping venom. It was immense, its girth painful.

Brook and Bramble laughed, spreading Rook's legs wider.

The snake stretched its head up, hissing.

A talon erupted through Rook's abdomen with a gout of blood, and tore a ragged gash toward her pubic bone.

Through the gory opening, Rook caught a glimpse of an eye, golden and unblinking, its pupil a stark black minus sign.

"Push!" cried Brook and Bramble.

Rook screamed again, waking herself.

Her heart raced. She was sheathed in sweat. It was dark. Rook ran a

hand over her stomach, lurched to her feet, and turned on a light.

She was in the basement of the library with her squeaky book cart.

*** *** ***

The spiders were initially pleased to see Kyle appear spontaneously in Rook's dream, as it indicated she was dwelling on him as they intended. However, the horrifying images and sensations seemed like something of a setback.

On the other hand, her pregnancy was valuable intelligence. Kyle claimed credit, and the situation distressed Rook.

Based on what the spiders observed, it was equally likely Fin impregnated Rook. Guilt distorted the facts in her mind until she could only conceive of the worst outcome.

Either way, the spiders now knew about a whole new set of buttons to push in Rook's dreams.

*** *** ***

Melissa was astride her uncle on top of his 'magic' table, sweaty with the effort of their coupling despite the icy breeze creeping in around the ancient windows. His thumb was in her mouth, massaging her tongue, his stump nudging incessantly at her vulva. She was propped on one hand, her arm quivering with the effort, but she couldn't switch because her other hand's thumb was trying not to be swallowed by Severin.

In the two weeks following the 'stump incident,' Melissa had taken a few steps to assert her rights. The first was bringing Kyle to the House. He lay inert on his hospital bed in the smallest of the third-floor bedrooms, directly beneath her.

Next, she took over the management of her mystical education. She set the lesson schedule and dictated the mechanical details. Her uncle voiced no objection, probably because now they fucked more than ever.

Beneath her, Severin clamped his teeth into her thumb. That meant he wanted her to slow down. She did, grinding her pelvis more with each thrust, and noting the subtle shift in the vibrations coming from the table.

Melissa kept careful notes, in her head, looking for clues about her

gift. Severin became more decisive and alert after each encounter. From this, she traced his technique of draining power from her, eventually identifying the actual sensation. It happened while she came, making it a challenge to focus on and learn to control. She often got wrapped up in the moment, making her despise herself.

Once she caught one thread, Melissa made further observations about the upwelling of energy that accompanied her orgasms.

She could feel it building now.

Intense physical pleasure was tied to the source of her patterns. She learned to guide and shape these waves of force to deprive her uncle of them. When she drank from her own well, Severin's spells of post-coital alertness became shorter. Once a day, about a quarter of their trysts, Melissa indulged his thumb-sucking fetish. Those sessions gave him the most significant mental lift.

She opened her eyes and looked down into the fierce blue of his.

Her other important discovery was that sex on the table produced a bigger wave. So, even though it frightened her, she chose the table as the venue for most of her experiments. The reason was only partly pragmatic. Her orgasm grew in proportion to the strange energy. She could feel how the waves emanating from her loins resonated with the unreality on the other side of the table. It felt dangerous, which added to her excitement, which added to her self-loathing.

All of that progress happened in the first few days. Since then, Melissa varied the lesson plan in an assortment of creative ways. Her theory, based on the 'stump incident,' was that the more degrading the sex, the more intense the surge of power. But no matter what kind of depraved gratification she gave Severin, her understanding of her dark gift did not increase.

The only thing off-limits was the stump. She remained adamant about that, and Severin's gambits to try to evade her defenses were feeble and predictable. Now she wondered, glumly, if that appendage might be the key to making further progress in her education.

Sweat trickled down her torso. She was so, so close to coming.

Melissa rocked her hips and clamped down. Severin's thumb squirmed in her mouth. His stump ground against her. He grunted, sucking furiously on her thumb. The raging torrent of pleasure swept her over the falls and she was tumbling, all attempt at rational thought obliterated on the rocks below.

Her heart pounded. She was freezing. Severin had taken control, pulling her into a deep kiss that robbed her of all the vital energy she'd accumulated.

He rolled them so that he was on top, broke the kiss, and dismounted. Whistling, he carried Melissa to the hammock, dressed, and went downstairs without saying a word.

For several minutes Melissa lay still, staring at her thumb. It was white and wrinkled like a drowned body.

Melissa took a sip from the open bottle she kept nearby, and slunk from the hammock over to the table. If she ever wanted to be free of Severin, she had to understand these mystical forces. Another pull on the bottle, then she set it aside on the worn floorboards.

She hugged herself and stared at the sheet, crisp and brilliant white. How was that possible in such a dusty environment, with all the activity that took place on it? Severin never took it away to clean it. Melissa felt her gorge rising and staggered back to the hammock to lay down.

As it swung back and forth, she lamented not simply collapsing on the floor.

After a few minutes of berating herself for cowardice, she made her way back to the table. She cracked her knuckles. She plucked a corner of the sheet with her right hand, remembering Severin's insistence that it was the proper way. Biting her lip and whimpering, she sent her left hand under and felt around on the table.

A tingling permeated her fingers, like the table was electrified. Melissa resisted the urge to yank her hand clear. The tingle dipped and swirled across her nerve endings, trying to tell her something. In that, it was almost familiar. Instead of meaning impinging on her mind, this time she couldn't make out the message. It was like a tactile version of

one of those trick pictures, where you're supposed to see the old lady and the young one in the same image.

Melissa made a policy of avoiding those kinds of pictures. Now she felt that if she'd practiced with them, she would be better prepared for this.

She pulled back her hand and let the sheet drop, frustrated.

Before returning to the hammock to drink herself to sleep, she smoothed the sheet so her attempt would stay a secret from Severin.

*** *** ***

Fin's strong arms held Rook in a tight embrace. He was fully clothed, she was naked. In the back of her skull, his vibration hummed gently. She inhaled the warmth of him, the savory tobacco and top-shelf rum smell of him, wanting to stay like that forever. He kissed the top of her head. "I'm gonna be late."

Reluctantly Rook released him, then tilted her face up for a real kiss. "I love you, Fin."

"I love you, Rook." He kissed her again and shrugged into his trench coat. "See you tonight."

Once he'd gone, Rook showered and began a search of their room for clean clothes.

In the two weeks since she discovered she was pregnant, her nightmares had grown worse, both the Kyle sex ones and the monster-baby ones. Her dream journal told her it had been 85 days since she'd slept through the night. No wonder she was exhausted.

"Rook," Vesuvius said, "are you okay?"

Rook blinked and shook her head. She had been standing in one place, staring at the wall. If she didn't get moving and find something to wear she would be late for work.

"Yeah, Suvi. Never better."

The lamp said something else, but Rook was too tired to pay attention. If she didn't go to work she wouldn't get paid and she would never be able to afford an abortion. The longer it went, the greater the chance Fin would find out, and she was certain he would leave her if he

knew she was pregnant by Kyle. He was the only good thing in her life and it made her physically ill to think of being without him.

That's what Brook wanted: to break Fin and Rook up so she could find a 'suitable' husband. Bramble didn't care who Rook was with as long as she didn't have a baby.

Semi-fresh panties would have to do. Rook slipped them on.

Even though she tried to act normal around Fin, she knew he worried about her and it made her feel guilty.

The first stockings she came across were black fishnets, and she wrestled her way into them, then stepped into her saddle shoes.

Feeling guilty about worrying Fin made it that much harder to act like nothing was wrong.

Her bras were all AWOL, so she just pulled on a snug thermal shirt.

It would be easier if she weren't around Fin, but she wanted to be. He was her bright spot at the same time he was the unwitting cause of so much stress.

Under a heap of Fin's shirts she found her harlequin miniskirt. It was a bit tight.

You're starting to show! Brook and Bramble teased.

Rook examined her reflection in the bathroom mirror, relieved to see she didn't look pregnant yet. There was still time.

January held Webster in its frigid grip. Rook donned her leather jacket, gloves, and a cozy knit hat, and picked up her skateboard. It would get her to work faster, and if she was lucky maybe she'd fall off and have a miscarriage.

The evil princesses in her head continued their chorus of doom as Rook skated toward the library. She closed her eyes and told them to shut the fuck up.

HONK!

Rook slammed to the pavement.

"Oh my god! Are you all right?" A woman helped Rook to her feet.

"I think so." Rook looked down. Her knees were scraped.

The driver who hit her wanted her to go to the hospital, but Rook

refused. They would tell Fin she was pregnant.

Brushing off the offers of assistance, Rook picked up her skateboard and rushed to work. After clocking in, she hurried to the basement.

The pink tile ladies' room was empty. Rook locked herself in. Her stockings were ruined, both knees bloody. Rock salt and gravel peppered the scrapes.

With a damp paper towel, Rook tried to clean the wounds, but her hands shook and tears stung her eyes. She could have been killed!

Isn't that what you wanted?

"No!"

Laughter filled her head.

Rook glared at herself in the mirror above the sink as blackness crept in at the edges of her world, constricting her field of vision until all she could see were her own furious blue eyes.

Growing up, perfect Princess Brook and perfectly naughty Princess Bramble were Rook's way of coping with her fucked up life. Her mother called them her invisible friends, but it went deeper. Way deeper. They were aspects of Rook's personality she saw as separate people. Brook embodied everything she thought she ought to be, Bramble everything she feared she was.

When she was good she was very very good, and when she was bad she was horrid.

As a little girl, when she was still called Brook, Rook often felt like she was watching herself speak and act. Her world was hazy, distant. Poking her finger with a needle or burning her palm with a match helped her concentrate and feel in control. Real. After more than a year of therapy, she symbolically locked the princesses away. They remained dormant for a long time. Until Kyle.

Now they ran loose inside her head. Neither of them approved of Rook's life, and they were intent on making her miserable. Rook agreed that she'd made a mess of things, but the incident with the car was uncalled for.

She stared hard into the icy blue depths of her reflected eyes and thought about Brook's prison, an orchid-scented crystal coffin on a bed of smooth, white stones, under briskly flowing water.

And she was there.

Chapter Ten

In the Tower

Setting: Shaw cathedral altar — technicolor bright, quiet, cold The pews are full and the cameras are running. My backpack is really heavy. I'm in a hurry to deliver whatever's in it, but I'm sinking in green quicksand. Kyle is there. He's missing one leg from the knee down. Brook and Bramble will get me out of the quicksand if I'll help Kyle. I agree. They pull me out, then undress me and help me mount Kyle backwards cowgirl style. I get the missing part of his leg out of my backpack and fit it into place as I come.
Rook Tanner's dream journal

Standing on the bank of the tiny river inside her mind, Rook saw the shattered remains of Brook's cut-glass coffin littering the stony white riverbed. The cloying smell of overripe fruit hung in the air. Across waist-deep water, a wall of thorny vines studded with ghostly white berries obscured the altar stone where Bramble had been bound.

Both princesses were gone.

They were abroad in her inner world, wrecking her life from the inside. She had to rid herself of their royal corruption.

Apart from the rushing water there was no sound. The immense pine forest loomed out of a thick fog that tasted like exhaustion. Rook parted two branches and entered the gloom.

The fog enveloped her in a damp cloud of weariness. Underfoot the blanket of pine needles and black feathers was treacherously slick. The shadow-green trees were dense, making every movement a struggle.

An aching fatigue settled into Rook's bones and mind, leaching into her from the fog.

Maybe it would be easier to give up.

Something half-buried under dead pine needles glinted in the oppressive murk. Rook picked it up and an overwhelming wave of shame washed her exhaustion away. On her palm sat a fist-sized crystal, greenish-black and iridescent like an oil slick, reeking of musky bodily secretions. A crystal of pure shame, born of her time with Kyle.

Rook's cheeks flushed and she dropped it.

Where were the princesses? Rook had to find them and end this.

She moved on, smothering in caustic exhaustion. When she encountered a shame crystal she touched it to drive the weariness away. Rook continued for what felt like hours, until she encountered the first signpost.

PUT IT BACK ON ROOK, the same message inscribed on the wedding band Kyle gave her. Rook shuddered and kept walking. The sign meant she was getting close to her tower.

Several times she encountered things resembling buildings, rotting facades abandoned long ago.

It can't be healthy to have so many false structures.

Pressing past the next knot of trees, Rook entered a clearing. In the center loomed a tower, but not the one she expected.

This tower was constructed of shame crystals.

It was tall and spindly and ominous. The malevolent sheen of the crystals kept the fog at bay.

Is this my new core structure?

That couldn't be good.

She circled it and located a narrow opening, not quite a doorway. Above it hung a sign reading The Tanners.

Rook moved to the fissure and peered inside. The interior was lit by a cluster of glowing green shards jutting from the wall. Kyle shrapnel. The glow pulsed like a heartbeat, each throb accompanied by an oscillation in the vibration Rook felt all around her, drowning out Fin's reassuring hum.

In the center of the room hung a rope ladder fashioned from thigh

bones and long skeins of black hair, grotesque in the extreme. Rook knew she had to climb it. The princesses would be upstairs.

As she entered the tower, a deluge of negative emotion engulfed Rook, drowning her in guilt and shame, sorrow and regret. Pheromones and the pungent funk of sex filled the space like a cloud of horny incense. She sobbed. It made no difference that she'd thought Fin dead, she should have resisted Kyle, should never have taken carnal pleasure with him, and certainly not so much of it.

The ladder's bone-rungs were icy cold, and slimy. When Rook reached the top she was dismayed not to find her quarry. The small room was also lit by the glow of Kyle, and it held three things: a cradle, a spinning wheel, and a large pile of black feathers. The rough wood cradle was crowned with a black stone gargoyle of some horrible mythic beast with both lion and goat heads, and a snake for a tail. Rook lacked the courage to see what the cradle held.

The spinning wheel looked innocuous enough, but come on. The bitch princesses expected her to prick her finger and fall into an enchanted slumber on the bed of rook feathers. They wanted to imprison her so they could be in charge.

The idea was tempting. Why not abdicate and let the two of them deal with the consequences of all their unsafe sex?

Rook reached toward the spinning wheel, index finger extended.

But she couldn't pin all the blame on their royal horninesses. She'd been screwing Fin bareback in the bomb shelter before they came back. There was a chance, however slight, that the baby was his. Did that make any difference?

The difference is I love Fin.

The thought of Brook and Bramble hurting him infuriated her. She lowered her arm. Had her duplicitous sisters left anything she could use against them? Rook sifted through the feathers, looking for anything hidden among them.

The feathers themselves made her feel stronger. They combated the crushing guilt. The big black birds they came from represented her self

and her chosen name. In this place they carried power.

She thought of making a crown of feathers, but it felt too much like a Marcus idea. Could she make arrows and use the feathers in the fletching? The idea was both too impractical and too practical at the same time.

Rook again looked at the spinning wheel, thinking of a different fairy tale now. Instead of spinning straw into gold, could she spin the feathers into… something? The dream logic of the idea appealed and she scooped up a handful of feathers.

She stepped on the foot pedal and the wheel began to spin. She kept pumping the pedal and watched how the thing worked, trying to figure out how the hell you'd use it to make yarn. She poked a feather at it, but nothing happened.

Would you like some help?

Rook couldn't tell where the voice came from, or whether she really heard it. Maybe someone was talking to her body in the library bathroom.

Why won't you talk to me?

Something about the voice reminded Rook of Vesuvius, only this voice was not monotone. It seemed to be all pitches at once.

Fine.

"No, wait," said Rook. "I don't know how to make this work."

The voice chuckled. *Any way you think it should work, it will work.*

Rook frowned. "Bullshit."

You're the one who's so into fairy tales. Let's do it that way. If I help, you will owe me a favor.

"What do you want?"

Slide the feathers in beside the bobbin one at a time. The bobbin's the small part that spins.

Rook tried it. The feather fed in and transformed into a length of tarnished silver chain. Each link was about a quarter-inch.

Don't forget our deal.

Rook fed more feathers into the bobbin, creating more chain.

When all the feathers in the little room were gone she'd spun a chain ten feet long. Enough to bind Brook and Bramble. Rook ran it through her fingers. The links were etched with images of rooks both chess and avian, and emanated an inner strength that lessened the self-loathing caused by the tower. She looped it around her neck several times and tucked the loose ends inside her shirt.

Rook climbed down and exited the tower. She studied the gray sky above the pines, but saw only unremitting dreariness. Parting the branches of two trees, Rook reentered the forest.

For what felt like days she walked on, inadvertently circling back again and again to the tower of shame. She passed PUT IT BACK ON ROOK over and over.

"I should leave a trail of breadcrumbs." Her voice sounded flat and dead.

Bone-tired, she shut her eyes and trudged forward with her hands held in front of her face to shield it from branches. In this somnambulistic manner she carried on for hours until she found no more trees to shoulder past.

Finally, finally! the clearing with her tower. The proper red brick one. Sleeping rooks blanketed the pointed roof, heads tucked under their wings, victims of the exhaustion fog.

Rook saw no movement in the single window. The doorway she'd created wasn't nearly as large as before. The rough edges were closing in toward the center, like a wound healing. Some of the new bricks were green-black shame crystals, the others a flat milky-gray.

Rook sighed. *I'm closing myself off again.*

Inside, the skeletons that had once been slumped along the walls and strewn across the floor were gone. She ducked through the constricted opening.

The only way to get upstairs was to stand in the old bucket and haul herself up with the rope. It was awkward as hell and Rook wished her worse half had built a rope ladder for this tower, too, even a macabre one.

The trapdoor was closed. Rook shoved it open and hoisted herself up onto the wooden floor.

Brook and Bramble were not here now, but they had been. The trunk was shoved against the wall, doll and dress-up clothes spilling onto the floor. An anatomically correct Barbie and Ken orgy was set up on the table amid the dainty china tea set. Scattered around the room and hanging from the rafters were dozens of masks: fancy beaded Mardi Gras masks, cheap rubber Halloween masks, wooden tribal masks, elegant porcelain masks. A television on the floor played the shaky hand-held video Kyle made of him and Rook fucking, specifically the part where she gave him head.

Her alter egos were taking over. Soon there wouldn't be room for Rook anywhere but in the shame tower.

That was unacceptable.

Rook stooped to switch off the TV, but it lacked knobs. And a cord. The thing seemed to have grown out of the floor.

"Oh, yeah, Rook. Suck me," Kyle said from the tinny speaker.

Her stomach clenched. She kicked the screen. Her foot throbbed, but the TV was undamaged.

"Fuck!"

"Oh, yes!" Kyle moaned.

Rook turned her back.

One of the princesses had pieced the broken mirror back together. Rook studied her shattered reflection. No wonder this place wouldn't listen to her. She was dressed for the world outside.

After running her fingers over the etched surfaces of the silver necklace she'd made, Rook undressed. The wet noises coming from the television aroused her, even as she tried to ignore them.

In the trunk she found a black and white gown of cheap velveteen and satin. A child's costume, but she tugged it on. As she zipped it, the skirt stretched down to the floor and she felt more at home. The little puff sleevelets made her feel like a princess.

She set about straightening up Brook and Bramble's mess,

periodically checking to see if the TV would respond to her. The video moved on from fellatio to the part with her on top. Kyle kept changing focus from a wide shot showing her face and torso to a tight close-up of their crotches.

"You don't belong here," two voices said in unison.

Brook and Bramble stood together beside the trapdoor. Brook wore a version of Rook's wedding dress, this one with acres of frothy skirting. Bramble was in a trashy interpretation of the wedding lingerie, with extra expanses of creamy skin on display. Both looked just like Rook, except Brook lacked tattoos and Bramble had a few extra. They each wore a rhinestone tiara and a necklace with a jagged, green Kyle splinter pendant.

"You're the ones who don't belong," said Rook.

Bramble's blue eyes flashed. Brook said, "Let's see if we can work this out."

She approached the table and made tut-tut noises about the orgiastic dolls. Bramble gathered them up and tossed them over her shoulder. Three child-sized chairs encircled the table. Rook sat in the one that kept her back to the porn video. Bramble draped herself into the one on Rook's left, leg flung over the armrest. Brook busied herself pouring everyone tea, then sat primly on the remaining chair. Her voluminous skirts pouffed up around her, threatening to engulf her.

"Cream?" Brook asked. "Honey?"

Rook declined. Brook served herself both. Bramble pulled a silver flask from her cleavage and poured a few drops into her dainty teacup.

This was like the tea parties Rook imagined as a child. It was so tempting to slip back into that old mode, to enjoy her tea and her friends.

Only these two weren't her friends. They were responsible for her current misery. Dr Wymbol taught her how to cope without them, but they lingered for years in the depths of her psyche. Now they wanted to take over.

Rook made this journey to reclaim full control of her mind, but

now, confronted with her foes, she lacked any real idea what to do.

"Please pass the cucumber sandwiches," she said.

"Certainly." Brook passed a doily-clad plate of rather questionable bread triangles with the crusts cut off. Rook took one and passed the plate to Bramble, who set it on the floor.

"The weather is so dreary," Brook said.

"Yes. So much fog," Rook replied.

"I'm horny," Bramble said, and turned up the volume on the television.

"I know," said Rook.

Rook struggled to keep two simultaneous conversations going with her enemies while deciding how to be rid of them forever.

"We're far too clever to be doing menial work at the library," said Brook.

"I like the library."

"Ooh, this is my favorite part!" Bramble slipped her hand into her panties as Rook heard herself pant and groan her way toward orgasm in the video.

I have to kill them.

"Bramble, that's rude," said Brook. "Our guest can't see the movie." From the folds of her skirt she produced a laptop playing the homemade porn and placed it in the middle of the table. Rook tried to close the lid, but it wouldn't budge. The onscreen Rook threw back her head and screamed in ecstasy. Bramble did the same. Brook smiled benevolently.

"Roll over," Kyle said. "And hold the camera."

Rook stood. This shit had to stop.

"I don't need you," she said, the way Dr Wymbol taught her.

Brook and Bramble looked at each other and laughed.

"You don't really mean it," said Bramble. "That's why it doesn't work." She pulled her fingers out of her panties and wiped them on the linen tablecloth.

"You need us to look out for your interests," Brook explained.

"You're not good at doing it on your own."

"Stop talking like Mom," Rook snapped. In the video, Kyle held her ankles near his shoulders, spreading her legs wide as he plowed her.

Brook sipped her tea to hide a smirk.

Bramble got down on the floor and crawled to the TV behind Rook.

"You know you can't kill us," said Brook. "We're part of you. If you kill us, you'll kill yourself."

"Maybe it would be worth it."

Bramble's hot fingers wrapped around Rook's throat and squeezed, trapping a gasp in her voice box. Sharp nails bit her neck.

Rook jabbed back with an elbow, smashing Bramble's ribs.

"You bitch!" Bramble squeezed tighter and threw her weight into Rook, knocking her to the floor. She landed on Rook's back, still squeezing.

Rook's eyes bulged. A terrifying ache built in her chest. Bramble's fingers sank into her flesh. Rook couldn't pry them loose. She got her knees under herself and thrust, slamming backwards onto Bramble. The grip on her throat released. Rook gasped and coughed.

Shrieking, Bramble raked at Rook's hair.

Fear igniting into fury, Rook scrambled to her feet. Bramble leapt up and came at Rook's face with her fingernails.

Rook lunged and tore Bramble's hair. Both of them screamed, fists and claws flying.

Brook pounced from behind and pulled Rook off Bramble. Working together, her evil twins subdued the kicking, flailing, cursing Rook and shackled her to the wall. There had been no shackles before, but that made them no easier to escape.

"We can't kill her," Brook told Bramble. "That would kill us, too."

Bramble pouted.

"You can't keep me here," Rook said.

"Someone does need to be in charge," Brook agreed.

"I'll do it," said Bramble. She picked up the clothes Rook discarded when she put on her princess gown.

"No!"

Bramble removed her bustier and pulled the thermal shirt over her head. "How do I look?"

"Like Rook," Brook conceded.

Bramble donned Rook's miniskirt, ruined tights, and saddle shoes. "Something's missing."

Both women looked at Rook.

"She's wearing a necklace," Bramble said.

"No!" Rook said. "It's mine. I made it!" What would happen to her if they took away the chain?

Bramble snickered and grabbed the necklace. "Ouch!" She let go and yanked her hand back.

Simultaneously, Rook's left shackle weakened. She strained against it before Bramble could regain herself. The cuff crumbled. Rook snatched the rhinestone tiara from Bramble's head, along with some hair.

Bramble screeched and fell to her knees.

Rook slapped the tiara on her own head and felt an infusion of power. Now *she* was the princess of the tower. She snapped the chain of her right shackle and lunged at Brook. They crashed to the floor. Rook punched Brook in the nose and grabbed her tiara too.

Brook lay whimpering in a ball, tangled in her ridiculous fluffy dress. Bramble howled and clutched her head.

Panting, Rook added Brook's tiara to her own head.

On the TV, Kyle grunted his orgasm and the video looped back to the beginning with them going at it doggy-style in front of the bathroom's full-length mirror.

With a roar of fury and disgust, Rook kicked the TV. This time it erupted in the most satisfying plume of smoke and sparks. On the table the laptop screen was blank.

Rook was in charge again. She felt a glow in her chest and clarity in her thoughts.

Before the twins could regroup, Rook bound them together with the

chain she'd spun from rook feathers, the chain that was purely her. They sat together on the floor, weeping like children.

What to do with them? They were probably right that killing them would be bad for herself, if not outright suicide. Now that she had reclaimed control, that option held no appeal. She wanted to live happily ever after with the prince of her choosing, Fin.

Wymbol would tell her she should absorb these aspects of her personality. Looking at them, pathetic yet dangerous, Rook knew she was better off without them.

If she procrastinated for too long her tower might seal itself up again, trapping her with her nemeses.

It had been so fucking hard to make that opening in the first place. She'd done it to aid Fin, so he could use her blocks to rebuild himself.

Rook had transported material out of her mind once. She should be able to do it again.

"What are *you* looking at?" Bramble sneered, then sniffled.

"I think I know how to get rid of you," Rook said. "Both of you."

Excitement brought a smile, until she realized she had no place to transport them to. What would happen if she ported them out, with no destination? Would they be free in the real world?

"You wouldn't dare get rid of us," said Brook.

"I would," said Rook. "I just need a place to send you."

I could help.

The voice from the shame tower, the one who helped spin the chain. Rook trusted that voice.

"How?"

You could give them to me.

"No!" cried Brook and Bramble, struggling against their bonds.

"They're dangerous."

I am vast. They would have no power here.

"Are you sure?"

They will be lost in the immensity of me.

Rook had an inkling her new friend might be the colossal mind

Focus on body.

Willow spoke of. If so, it might make a good repository for her wayward imaginary friends.

"Okay. You can have them."

Bramble wailed.

Brook spoke quickly. "If you get rid of us, you'll be responsible for *all* your own decisions. We won't be your scapegoats anymore."

"That's what I'm hoping for." She waited for them to disappear.

Nothing happened except their continued histrionics.

"Well?"

You must give them to me.

Previously her rooks did the ferrying, but they were all sleeping. Looking through the single window, Rook confirmed the exhaustion fog still shrouded her forest. The birds could not help this time. She would have to do it herself.

"I don't know how," she admitted.

The voice sighed. *Open a doorway in your psyche. It might hurt.*

Rook settled herself on the floor and tried to relax, slowing her breath and her heartbeat. Recalling the vision quests Marcus coached her through, Rook tried to experience their sensations without benefit of the actual psychotropic compounds.

Being inside her own head made such mental gymnastics easier, and Rook soon felt the rushing flood of insight. She directed it outward in a beam, battering a hole through her mental defenses in much the same way she'd punched the hole in her tower.

The pain was excruciating, more like tearing than cutting. Rook panted, her control slipping as the portal dilated.

Through this ragged doorway in her soul, Rook glimpsed roiling seas of green fire.

"Is that you?" she gasped.

Yes. Give them to me now.

Rook grasped the silver chain that bound Brook to Bramble, ignoring their panicked screams. Closing her eyes, Rook tightened the chain, binding and compressing the princesses into a single composite

entity and shoving it through the portal. The searing pain doubled, trebled, as the opening stretched to accommodate their passage.

The agony built in waves until it burst, showering Rook in a nigh-orgasmic rush of catharsis.

Don't forget our deal.

★★★ ★★★ ★★★

Excitement permeates the bubbles of light in electric yellow-green pulsations.

Someone new has arrived.

Kyle can sense it, a low purple vibration. He is drawn toward the source. The granules of his psyche feel its erotic, magnetic pull. Slowly, so slowly, his aimless direction through the dense atmosphere begins to reverse.

The first molecule of him encounters the source and he knows it is Rook. His bitch-goddess has come to him. Where he touches her they fuse in an act more intimate than sex. Shivers of pleasure roil the bubbles of light, sending shock-waves of lust throughout this place.

Rook's need for him elicits its own gravity.

She is insoluble among the bubbles of light. They are drawn to her, caress her.

Another molecule of Kyle electroplates onto his wife's essence and he begins to know the truth. This is not Rook. It is an imitation made of cast-off aspects of her personality, but it is bound together with a chain of pure Rookness, and somewhere in its heart it contains fragments of Kyle's own being.

It will do.

Chapter Eleven

THRESHOLD HOUSE INFIRMARY

Progress toward useful deployment of the microtransceivers is stalled owing to the unavailability of staff having prior contact with the technology. Based on intel collected at the Shaw compound, we know of an organization called TEF whose personnel would fill the gap. They've worked with the devices before. Recruitment is an absolute priority. Irregularities are anticipated with background checks, so maximal leeway will be necessary in granting clearances.
Operation Lullaby internal communication, 2-5-2001

Melissa lay gasping on the table beside Severin's sweaty bulk. Her uncle was drifting off to sleep, which he never did after a lesson. She kept all the energies for herself this time, not letting him steal a drop. She had in fact siphoned vitality from him. For the first time her control was total.

Over the past week, she'd been encouraging him to use the stump. The change in her attitude pleased him, and he showed no suspicion about it.

The first few times, she was helpless. The energies flowed so differently in that kind of lesson, none of what she'd learned about their manipulation applied. She worried this ploy would backfire, that it would rebuild Severin's power at her own expense.

She worried she might surrender to that fate. The abhorrent touch of Severin's unnatural arm, and the debilitating intensity of the climax such violation produced, threatened to drown her will.

On the third day she found her metaphysical footing. What felt like a sea-change was something much subtler. Once she tuned to this

wavelength, everything fit what she had already taught herself about shaping and guiding the power.

Then, it was just a matter of practice.

She practiced with the table, too. Usually she did it after he left the room. This time that didn't seem necessary.

While Severin snored, Melissa lifted a corner of the sheet and reached under him with her left hand. It was as if he wasn't there. She ran her palm over the wooden surface, trying again to decode the strange hum on her skin.

As she groped under the sheet, she asked herself if this life was the 'normal' existence she thought she'd been yearning for her whole life. Maybe she'd only ever felt like a freak because she hadn't been surrounded by them. *Is this where I belong?*

Her hand bumped into an object, something resting on the table's surface, brazenly occupying nonexistent space.

The buzzing in her fingers was gone. Melissa laughed. She had deciphered the message. A shape, squarish, cool to the touch.

Melissa pulled her hand free and saw the tiny house resting on her palm for only a second before it faded and vanished. A Christmas ornament, detailed down to the white picket fence and the shutters flanking its glistening windows. All the imitation comforts of home.

Her face brightened into a mischievous smirk at her unconscious uncle. Now she could do what he could do. Plus, she had Kyle stowed on the third floor.

She didn't need Severin for anything.

*** *** ***

Marsh wheeled a cart into the former storeroom on the third floor, where they had set up a bed for their guest. It was a nice enough space, the same size as the other singles, with a view of the neighbor's property line pines. Marsh ducked under the attic stairs impinging on the doorway, which were why no one normally used this room. Kyle didn't object.

Kyle had been in a coma for four months. When he'd first arrived

three weeks ago his body exhibited considerable atrophy. Melissa approved nearly any form of experimental therapy, so Kyle received daily skeletomuscular electrostimulation treatments through a rig Wind designed, along with simulated load and range-of-motion exercises for his surgically repaired knee. His intravenous nutrition underwent fine tuning based on Horn's biochemical assay. Consequently, he regained twenty pounds and his complexion lost its pasty pallor.

Today, they were adding a new study to Kyle's regimen. Rainbow joined Marsh and closed the door.

Ever since Leaf's theft of the remaining jewelry specimens, work on the dream visualizer had stalled. While talking to Wind and Horn about their patient's impressive progress it dawned on both Rainbow and Marsh they now had available a different angle for their research.

Kyle's EEG was misread at both hospitals, which was not hard to understand. The doctors fixated on what was missing, and saw a brain that didn't work. But those at the House who studied it saw brainwaves in slow motion, their frequencies deepened as they stretched over longer spans of time. Speeded up a hundredfold, Kyle's EEG data looked perfectly normal.

There was something going on in there.

Kyle's head was physically undamaged, giving every reason to expect cerebral activity. Something had altered it, resulting in his coma. Marsh leaned across Kyle to attach electrodes to his forehead and temples.

This latest version of the dream visualizer was theoretically capable of rudimentary video. Trials on himself disappointed Marsh, however. The imager, although fifty times as fast as the last one, was still too slow, producing a series of incomplete images overlaid and blended. If Kyle's attenuated EEG trace meant his mental processes were slowed down, perhaps they were sluggish enough for the imager to keep up and produce intelligible video.

"All set?" Rainbow asked.

Marsh nodded, backing up to get a view of the monitor. Rainbow

started the machine.

It took several seconds to obtain an image, and Marsh's hopes withered when it appeared. A tangled, indistinct mess, worse than the previous trials.

Rainbow said, "Hang on, that's with the autocalibration settings. Let me noodle around."

"It won't make any difference."

Rainbow spoke while she made adjustments. "I know you're frustrated, but this is the first run with a new subject. A subject whose condition could affect things in ways we didn't anticipate. Don't jump to conclusions. You're a better scientist than that."

Marsh sighed. "I agree completely. Thank you for not letting me fall apart."

"We can't afford to have that happen," Rainbow muttered. Then she added, louder, "I'm starting the next imaging pass now."

Marsh knew why she was trying to change the subject. Attrition had become a real issue at the House as Severin continued to abdicate responsibility. Although Rainbow told Marsh over and over it wasn't his problem, even she came to think of him as the de facto leader.

The imager was barfing on the monitor again, so Marsh had something to distract him from the dilemma of being in charge with no authority.

Rainbow's noodling made a difference. This tangled mess more clearly gave the impression of multiple, overlaid images than the first one.

"That's looking better," Marsh offered, but he felt they had seen enough. The same fundamental problem remained: multiple images smearing together.

Rainbow heard the defeatism in his voice and shot him a cagey look. "I don't think this is the same overlay problem we saw on your trials."

This project was instantly interesting to Marsh again. "What do you mean?"

Rainbow traced some vague forms on the screen, where the image

had updated to the next frame, indistinguishable from the first.

"This shape is echoed all over the screen, but the scale and perspective are changed. It's probably the same object. I don't think the various overlays are chronologically organized. I think they're views from different angles."

Marsh brought his brows together. "What does that mean?"

"Maybe he's trying to look at an issue from both sides. Maybe he has multiple personalities." Rainbow shrugged. "Lemme tinker with the settings. We might get a clearer view of this object that has Kyle so preoccupied."

Marsh watched as Rainbow tweaked the machine's configuration. He wondered if it was normal to find someone's typing unendurably erotic.

The next frame came up, much more organized. "Dropped out a bunch of channels," Rainbow explained. "Hoping to get it down to one point of view."

Her modifications worked perfectly on the first try, which made Marsh envious. Over the next five minutes, the images on the screen shed more and more clutter, until Marsh and Rainbow agreed on what they were looking at.

"It's a chain," Marsh said. "Great big links."

They viewed the chains in Kyle's mind from ten different vantage points. The frame rate was fast enough to capture clear, sequential images from any one of them at one time. If they stayed with one view for a few minutes, they could perceive a gradual drifting motion. Always converging with the chains.

"Go back to seven," Marsh suggested. Once Rainbow pressed the key, he said, "There's something different about this one."

At the extreme right side of the screen they could see a sliver of some other object.

"Is there any way to steer?" Marsh asked, knowing Rainbow would shake her head.

"There are a lot more viewpoints, though," she offered. "One of

them would probably show more of that thing. I could hack something together in a couple hours, to get around the limit of ten."

The next frame loaded as she spoke, with a perfect circle of white in the lower-left quadrant.

They stared in silence. A few seconds later, the next frame contained a portion of the same circle, cropped by the upper edge of the screen.

Rainbow said, "What did we just see?"

"It moved vertically, whatever it was. Rising. We had it for one-and-a-half frames. If the imager was faster... but I need more than a couple of hours to hack that."

"Well, let's take this gear back to the shop and get to work!"

*** *** ***

Propped up on his elbow, Fin watched Rook sleeping in Vesuvius's perpetual crimson twilight. Her eyes fluttered open.

"Morning," she mumbled.

"That's two nights in a row you slept right through," Fin said with a smile. He kissed both eyelids and her nose.

Rook yawned and snuggled into his chest. "What time is it?"

Fin fumbled around on the floor by the head of the bed until he located the alarm clock. "A little after 11:00."

"A.m. or p.m.?"

He checked again. "A.m."

"I'm pregnant."

For the first second, Fin thought she must be joking.

The realization that she was serious set loose a blizzard in his head, burying him under images of a future he wasn't ready for. The whole boarding house was an inappropriate place for children. They'd have to move, a repellent idea. Drinking and playing their music too loud, fucking whenever and wherever they chose, staying out until the next morning, he wasn't done with those things yet. Now he was going to lose them. They'd have to buy a car. They'd have to behave like respectable adults, like role models.

That was all in the next second.

Then came the guilt, sweeping all of that aside. She must be furious at him for being so careless.

"I'm sorry," Fin blurted.

Rook stared at him with her magical blue eyes, then she blinked. "*You're* sorry? Oh, I thought…"

"What?"

"I thought you would be angry."

"Why would I be angry?" Fin stroked her hair and gathered her into his arms. "It's not like you did this to yourself. I should have been more careful."

"I just thought… I was scared to tell you."

Fin rocked them back and forth. He wanted to tell her she was being silly, but that felt like the wrong thing to say. He could see how she might have been unsure what sort of reaction to expect, but it disturbed him she'd been afraid.

"I don't want you to ever be scared to tell me something. I'm so sorry." He kissed her freckled nose. "You can tell me anything. I want you to know that. And I am sorry."

Rook nodded, and sniffed. "You need to stop apologizing now."

Fin nodded too, and they leaned back and looked at each other.

"What do you want to do?" Fin asked.

Rook drew a deep breath. "For the past few weeks I've been trying to figure out how to get an abortion."

She'd kept this to herself for weeks, plural, and he'd suspected nothing. Was their communication that bad? She'd told him to quit saying he was sorry, so he didn't say anything for a moment. Then, "An abortion, is that what you want to do?"

"I was sure before, but now I'm not. It seemed obvious and necessary, and I was so afraid of losing you."

"That's impossible."

She smiled, but her eyes showed unhappiness. "I wasn't thinking clearly for a while, so now I'm not sure about anything I decided. Now that I can think, it seems like I should do that. Think."

Cold dread gripped Fin's gut. Their marriage was accomplished so quickly, could that be something she felt she didn't think clearly about? Now he'd made her pregnant, something else she wasn't ready for. She was the best thing in his life and he felt like he was losing her.

"What do you mean about not thinking clearly?"

Rook squeezed her eyes shut.

"You don't have to be afraid to tell me," Fin reassured. *Please still trust me.*

"I got myself psyched up to tell you I'm pregnant, but I should tell you this, too." She took another deep breath and Fin braced for the worst. "When I was little, I had these imaginary friends. Really, it was closer to multiple personalities, two extra people living inside my head."

Bewildered by the conversational turn, Fin held her as she told him about Princess Brook and Princess Bramble and how she'd gone through therapy to deal with them. It was unusual for her to open up about her past, and Fin was gaining a deeper understanding of why. Her childhood rivaled his in dysfunction, surpassed it when you took the mental illness into account.

"Not too long ago, the princesses got loose. They're how I coped while I was… away. Once I didn't need them anymore, they wouldn't leave. They screwed with my dreams, poisoning me against you."

Fin's brow furrowed, but with Rook nestled into his chest she didn't see. He'd been partially right. Part of her didn't want to be married to him. What on Earth was he supposed to say?

Rook continued, saving him from saying the wrong thing. "When I found out I'm pregnant, they got me convinced you would kick me out. They enjoyed making me miserable. I didn't know what to do. I wanted to ignore them, but they made me skate into traffic."

"What!" Fin clutched her hands, holding onto her in a reflexive reaction to the thought that he could have lost her so totally. She glanced down at the scabs on her knees.

"I didn't fall off my board. A car knocked me down. But I'm okay. Really. That's what convinced me I had to get rid of them."

"How does that work?"

She shrugged. "It'll sound crazy, but I guess we're past the point of crazy already. I went in there, inside my mind. They'd taken over my tower, so I confronted them, had a very uncomfortable tea party, and kicked their asses. I threw them out, and I feel so much better."

"Threw them out? Out where?"

"I'm not sure," she admitted. "There was this voice — *not* one of mine…" She trailed off, looking confused.

Fin felt there was more to the story, but he didn't doubt the basic truth of it. He had a nagging sense of worry about her mental stability, and a heavy load of guilt. He vowed to keep a much closer eye on her.

Especially in her delicate condition.

"What do we do next?" He rested his left hand on her still-flat abdomen.

"I have an appointment next Monday. I'd like you to come along."

"Absolutely."

They hugged, skin on skin.

"I love you, Fin."

Fin burrowed into her hair, holding her tighter. "I love you too. I love you so much. I'm so sorry I didn't help you. I knew you were struggling, but I thought it was because you didn't want to be married." Tears stung his eyes and squeezed his throat. "You were so frustrated with me, and you stopped sleeping. I was afraid to talk to you about it because I thought I'd lose you sooner."

Rook brushed her hair off his face and made him look at her. "We're not too good at this communication thing yet, but we both have to work at it, okay? 'Cause I'm not going anywhere."

Gazing into his wife's fathomless eyes, Fin saw she meant it, and the relief made him giddy. He smiled a huge, dopey grin. She grinned back.

Their future was more complicated than he might like, but it thrilled Fin that they had one.

He gave Rook a deep kiss, which she devoured. She wrapped her arms and legs around him and pulled him on top of her.

What the hell, she was already pregnant.

*** *** ***

Severin descended the main staircase, feeling like he was waking from a dream. It appeared to be late afternoon, but of what day he couldn't recall. The dream almost escaped, but he grasped it and recognized it as a real memory, not a dream at all. He'd spent the past few hours having tantric sex with Melissa.

Resuming his descent, Severin remembered many previous afternoons spent in similar pursuits with his sister, Gale.

She's never coming back.

He and his twin were created as a pair, counterbalancing each other. If Gale was dead, he no longer had a counterbalance, and would grow ever more destabilized.

He realized this was not the first time he made that connection. His mind was falling to pieces.

Melissa had turned the tables on him. He must have allowed her to understand too much of what he did during intercourse, and now instead of serving as his energy source she stole power from him. She'd done it moments ago, he felt sure, but she had to reflect some of the energy back to him or the whole enterprise would be pointless. He was too far gone to even serve as a slave. Too far gone to understand his predicament.

Except in these few moments after she'd used him. Carrying the secondary recharge she grudgingly provided, he could think for a little while. He would have to make good use of his time. Lay a trap to set things back as they should be.

Severin started down the final flight of stairs.

Her weakness was drink, Severin remembered. He should create a notebook to keep these ideas in, so he wouldn't have to rediscover all the same information anew each time. With a scowl, it occurred to him he might already have any number of such notebooks hidden away.

Reaching the bottom of the steps, Severin glanced at the smooth pink stump of his left arm and found a reason to smile. The slab drifting

loose in the Elsewhere held the real prize: a mammoth store of power.

Never mind trying to gain control of Melissa, or use her as a surrogate twin. Her job was to deliver that jolt to the Collective Id. While it was stunned, Severin would achieve his goal of becoming the Collective Superego, and he wouldn't need her, or Gale, or anyone.

All he need do was trick her into touching the slab. The power would arc to her, drawn to such a superb conductor. If she survived at all, she'd be far easier to manage.

Before his wits deserted him again, Severin needed a plan. Something simple, something Melissa wouldn't object to. Perhaps it could be as simple as encouraging her to experiment with the table. Or rather, reminding her he didn't want her to.

He turned around, intent on getting back upstairs while he could still form coherent thoughts and Melissa was intoxicated with appropriated power.

"Severin," Marsh called from the office, "I need to talk to you. It'll only take a moment." He came out to the foot of the steps carrying an armload of bank statements.

"I haven't got time," Severin muttered.

"This is crucial. Cliff always did the bookkeeping, and since he's been gone it kind of piled up. Some of the utilities are past due, and needless to say it would be catastrophic for us to lose electricity. Plus, the only names on the accounts are yours, and... Gale. I strongly advise we change that."

Severin glared at Marsh, who swallowed but didn't back down. He was right, of course. Severin nodded, and Marsh released a gust of tension.

"We will go to the bank this afternoon," Severin decided aloud. "Since you'll be doing the books, Marsh, you'll be signatory on the accounts."

The relief in Marsh's eyes turned to alarm. "Maybe we should discuss the assignment of the financial duties, to make sure we get the best person for the job."

"You're the obvious choice. Thank you for bringing this to my attention."

Marsh blinked and nodded uncertainly.

Severin looked up the stairs, certain he'd just come down them a moment ago.

That's right, he thought, I was on my way to the kitchen.

Chapter Twelve

GRAINY SQUIGGLY CONFUSION

When two possible fathers are related (brothers, half-brothers, father/son) they may share many DNA markers. This complicates paternity testing and necessitates the use of more extensive analysis. We are happy to provide this service at an additional cost.
           excerpt from DNAnswers Labs brochure

"Both of you can watch the screen," suggested Betty the sonogram technician. She smeared cold blue gel on Rook's belly and positioned the sensor against her skin. Grainy shapes panned across the machine's display. Rook looked at the screen with interest, if not eagerness, and Fin squeezed her hand and looked too. So far, none of the images resembled anything Rook could identify.

"How long have you two been married?"

"Four months," both Rook and Fin answered. They smiled at each other.

Betty nodded, pressing keys on her machine and surveying Rook's tummy with the sensor. On the screen, Rook thought she saw something that could be a face, but it vanished. Betty ignored it, so Rook decided she must be imagining things.

"Alright, here we go," Betty announced.

Fin leaned in and said, "Oh, I think I see it."

Rook got another glimpse of a face, in profile, but it looked all wrong for a fetus. None of the mess on the screen made any sense, but Betty was now using keys on the machine to mark specific places on the image, and Fin was absorbed by whatever he thought he saw. The face

flashed by again, then again.

Betty pressed another button and a whooshing, pulsating sound came from the machine.

The rapid rhythm corresponded to the way the face kept coming into view, and soon Rook recognized a circular shape enclosing it. She saw a spinning coin, heads on both sides, turning in time to the baby's heartbeat coming through the speakers.

Rook watched the spinning coin on the monitor as her memory filled with an unwelcome vision of a desolate lakeside, herself in a black and white gown. The inlaid table beside her, and the inimical chill of the two-headed coin that she had to keep spinning.

"Would you look at that," Betty said. "We have a honeymoon baby! You're almost exactly four months along."

Tears stung Rook's eyes. She had started to let herself believe it would be a more recent conception, that the ultrasound would leave no doubt Fin was the father. This was the worst possible news.

Fin dropped her hand and left the room without a word.

***   ***   ***

Fin stalked to the waiting room, looking for something to break.

After pacing back and forth five times in the small room, he slumped into one of the uncomfortable chairs and held his head in his hands.

Fuck!

He'd been kind of weirdly happy thinking about Rook having his baby, and looking at the ultrasound was exciting. Until, confronted with evidence it could be Kyle's baby, he instantly felt like a moron for not thinking of it before.

Kyle was supposed to be done fucking things up.

Accepting the idea of fatherhood was difficult, and Fin still hadn't fully accomplished it. This hit him low and hard.

He guessed he deserved a kick in the nuts for letting his guard down.

No wonder Rook thought he would be angry. *She didn't mention*

this possibility.

Fin hung his head. It had been just that, a possibility. She hoped it would turn out differently and they could ignore this issue. That's why she didn't bring it up.

For that matter, it remained entirely possible the baby was his. Kyle hadn't been ruled out, but that didn't prove anything.

Rook didn't want to be reminded of Kyle any more than he did.

She needed his support, and that was all that mattered.

He got up from the shit-colored chair, and took a steadying breath.

*** *** ***

"Are you two women still fussing over that baby?"

Fin came back into the room and gave Rook a smooch on her cheek. She cried happily then, a little, and he mumbled "sorry" in her ear before seating himself on a stool and taking her left hand in both of his.

"I told you to stop saying that," Rook reminded him.

"Then I guess I'll have to stop being such an ass."

"Are we almost done?" Rook asked Betty.

"Pretty nearly. I just need to get a few more pictures for the doctor."

Rook looked back at the screen.

The coin was there, but less distinct. As it revolved, more slowly now, she could see past it when it turned edgewise. A small twitch in her abdomen coincided with a leg giving a tiny kick on the screen.

Suddenly, the grainy, squiggly confusion on the monitor contained a baby. With each turn of the coin, Rook's view cleared for a moment and she found the outline of the fetus's head, arms, legs, and spine. It was beautiful, and she was thrilled she hadn't missed it. That she saw, eventually, what the others saw.

Fin squeezed her hand, and she planted a kiss on the back of his.

*** *** ***

On the walk home from the ultrasound, Fin and Rook held hands. The sun was bright, the air cold. Rook looked cute with her fuzzy wool cap pulled all the way down, but her legs must be freezing. Fin couldn't understand why she didn't buy some pants. He'd made a standing offer

to let her borrow a pair of his anytime.

"Thanks for coming back." She looked up at him, her entrancing eyes red-rimmed and a little teary. "I know how hard that was to hear. I didn't…" She wiped her eyes on her glove, then cleared her throat and went on, "I didn't want there to be any chance it was his."

Fin squeezed her hand, glad she could talk about the issue directly. "Yeah. It's not good news. But I know you didn't mean for it to happen."

They walked on in silence along the quiet, snowy sidewalk.

"I don't know yet what I want to do," Rook said.

"Me neither."

"There's one thing I do know. I love you and I want to be with you, but I don't want you to feel trapped."

"I don't."

"You don't right now." She smiled grimly. "I know what it's like to have your dad leave because you're not really his. I won't do that to a child. I won't." Her eyes threw emphatic sparks. "So if we have this kid together you're stuck with both of us forever. That's a huge deal, I know. I'm not asking for an answer right now. I don't even know yet if I want to have it. I just want you to know where I stand on that."

They'd stopped walking at some point during her speech and she stared, unflinching, into his eyes. He stared back, hoping he measured up to her standards.

"I understand," he said.

After a few moments, they resumed walking.

"We need to make this decision soon."

Fin nodded. Sometimes being a grownup sucked.

*** *** ***

"You wore that on our first date," Fin said, appraising Rook.

Valentine's Day and they were going out to dinner. How sickeningly normal could you get? Fin was in a hokey mood and insisted they both wear red, so while she donned her satin dress with the embroidered dragon, he put on a shiny bowling shirt with his black jeans.

"Can I come too?" asked Vesuvius. "I'm red."

"Valentine's Day is for lovers," Fin said. "If you want, I'll put on some Barry White and you can try to seduce Rook's Mac."

"You don't have any Barry White."

Rook ran her hands down over the dress, pressing her belly flat. In the four days since the ultrasound she spent a lot of time thinking about the images she saw on the screen, both the baby and the spinning coin, and she still didn't know what she wanted to do. "Does this make me look pregnant?"

Fin shook his head. "It makes you look sexy. I remember peeling it off you and dropping it on the floor." He added coyly, "And then I fucked you."

Rook felt herself blush.

A car horn tooted outside.

"That's probably the cab," said Fin. "I'll have it wait while you finish up." He left the room.

Rook picked up her eyeliner and makeup mirror, intent on making her eyes so flawless no one would notice she even had a stomach.

When she finished she said goodbye to Vesuvius and hurried down to the waiting cab.

During the short drive, Fin nibbled on her neck and made her giggle. The cab stopped in a residential neighborhood. Fin paid and then they stood in the driveway of a dark and abandoned Chez Tanner. Rook looked at him quizzically.

Fin offered his elbow. He led her down the sidewalk away from the house, scooped her up, and carried her across the snow and into the trees. He stood her on her high heels beside the bomb shelter.

He opened the hatch. "Ladies first."

Rook shook her head and started down the ladder. What in the world was he planning? When she got to the bottom her mouth fell open.

The entire shelter was neat and tidy, the bunks made, the garbage all cleared away. The table was set for dinner. A single red rose lay across

one of the plates. She could smell chicken roasting. Red and white crepe paper streamers adorned the ceiling and trailed along the walls in long spirals. Inflatable Sally in her housedress sat demurely in the corner holding a heart-shaped box undoubtedly containing chocolates.

Fin closed the hatch and climbed down to stand beside Rook.

"Happy Valentine's Day," he whispered.

Rook knew she was grinning like an idiot.

Fin pulled out his lighter and lit the two candles on the table. He made a circuit of the shelter, lighting a dozen tea-lights.

"It's amazing," Rook said, and turned off the overhead light.

They took off their coats and Fin swept her into a kiss.

"I wanted to give you the honeymoon we never had," he said. "This seemed like the right place."

Down here she and Fin first felt their mental connection, the biggest factor in convincing them to marry so quickly. That alone made it the perfect place. Rook closed her eyes and enjoyed his hum, all but unsullied by traces of Kyle.

"Can we spend the night?"

"Better. I have a few days off. And I talked Lara into covering your shift tomorrow. We have the whole weekend."

"Can we be naked the whole time?" Rook asked, her desire hot enough to melt her panties.

"After dinner." He kissed her, then went to the small oven. "I'd be afraid of burning myself otherwise."

Over dinner they flirted shamelessly, but after the meal Fin turned serious.

"I've been thinking a lot about our situation." His deep green eyes searched her face. "I don't want to be just another man who lets you down."

Rook smiled tentatively.

Maintaining eye contact Fin went on, "I love you, Rook. I'll support you no matter what you choose. If you want an abortion, I'll help you through that. If you want to have the baby, I'll be its father. No matter

what."

Rook's smile broadened. "Are you sure?"

He nodded. With a shrug he said, "It's not like you'll be able to tell by looking who the father is."

"Very pragmatic," she said in mock-seriousness.

"Thank you."

"I love you Fin. Will you take me to bed now?"

He kissed her for a long time before peeling her dress off and dropping it on the floor.

*** *** ***

Willow asked Brad what he wanted for lunch, and the question had most of his circuits occupied when the doorbell rang.

"It's Fin and Rook!" he exclaimed. He opened the door and waved them in.

"Hello, kids," Willow said as she came into the living room.

"Hi, Mom," Fin said, intercepting her to give her a warm hug. Rook gave Brad a quick hug and a peck on the cheek.

Everyone stood around awkwardly for a moment or two. Brad detected the awkwardness after it was pretty well established, busy as he was puzzling over the handsome young couple.

"Why don't we all go to the kitchen," he suggested. "Wil and I were discussing lunch."

A few minutes later, they sat in the breakfast nook with peanut butter sandwiches.

Rook gazed up at the ceiling, then nudged Fin, who nodded and poked at his sandwich. She stared at him for a few seconds and nudged him again. Fin sighed.

"We came over to ask for your help," he began. Brad thought he must have misheard, the idea of Fin admitting he needed anything from anyone was so farfetched. "We did a lot of talking recently. And we decided some stuff. But, well, we don't know where to start."

"Just start at the beginning," Willow coaxed.

Fin smiled. "No, what I mean is, we don't know how to get started,

which is why we need help." Rook nudged him again. "Brad, we need your help. To buy a house."

Brad felt pride and shock in equal doses.

Fin hastened to clarify. "We don't expect you to buy it for us, we'll pay for it."

Brad nodded, but he wondered if they knew what they were getting into. Did Fin think they could live for free if they found a place he could pay for outright from his trust fund? His initial surprise was replaced by worry about the depth of the hole they might dig for themselves.

"Thing is, like I said, we don't know where to start. Who to talk to. Who to trust. We hoped you could introduce us to a real estate person, or someone at the bank who can help us." Fin looked Brad in the eye, for a second. Then he studied his intact PBJ with great care.

"I can put you in touch with the right agent," Brad said. *Someone I hope won't give you enough rope to hang yourself.*

"We kinda need a car, too," Fin told his sandwich.

Brad thought that sounded like a much better place to start. Fin's expression darkened, so he must have seen Brad's look of relief. "Okay, sure. I can give you some advice there," Brad assured in his most serious voice.

"Thank you," Fin said, momentarily making eye contact again to convey his sincerity.

"This seems like a lot of growing up to do all at once," Brad observed.

"Well, um, yeah."

Fin turned to Rook, who wore a peculiar look made from most of a smile and part of a frown. She furtively wiped her cheek, and Fin laid his arm around her shoulders. They kissed, paused, kissed some more. Brad wondered where he was supposed to look while his semi-estranged son and stunning daughter-in-law made out in the breakfast nook. After a few seconds they stopped, and Rook nodded.

"We're having a baby," Fin announced.

For a moment all was stunned silence. Willow exclaimed,

"Wonderful!" Everyone laughed except Zen, who bawled in her crib. Willow jumped up, saying, "Wait until I get back. I want to hear everything."

While Willow was out of the room, Brad smiled at Fin and Rook in nervous silence.

The two of them put up a buoyant front, but Brad suspected that was all it was. Underneath their happy bravado he detected cold terror. Nothing about their current lifestyle was compatible with parenthood. At least they recognized that, but were they ready for so much change?

Like father, like son. Racing into a relationship, escalating it to marriage and parenthood without giving themselves a chance to grow together. At least when Brad did all this, he was completing a graduate degree and starting a stable career. On the other hand, Fin knocked up only one young lady. And married her first.

Brad hoped for the best, because it was all he could do.

Zen's shrill protests stopped, and Willow's voice preceded her return, soothing the infant. "You should be sleeping, I think, but you want Mommy. Since Mommy wants to talk to these people, Zen needs to wake up. Or, maybe she can cuddle up on Mommy's lap and sleep some more? How would that be?" Willow resumed her seat beside Brad, bouncing Zen on her knee. To the adults, she said, "Tell us everything! Well, not everything, but you know what I mean."

Fin shrugged nervously. "Well, Rook thought she might be pregnant, and we got an appointment and found out how far along we are. Four months." A strange, fleeting look passed between them.

"I'm due July 7." Rook didn't look like she believed it yet.

"It was unexpected," Fin admitted, and they exchanged another mysterious glance.

Brad felt relieved to hear it was unplanned. Anything else would suggest these two might be idiots. He held out hope that they were merely crazy. Rook didn't give off what Brad would call a maternal vibe, but she had proved to be a good influence on Fin.

"Here," Willow chirped, producing a possibly sleeping baby from

her lap like something from a magic act and holding her out toward Rook.

Rook looked at Zen the way she might a rattlesnake. "Oh, but I don't know about..."

Willow swung around the end of the table and bestowed the tiny girl into Rook's arms, too suddenly for any response other than holding the baby. Rook's eyes were twice their normal size.

"You're a natural." Willow said as she sat back down. She winked at Brad.

"I have a question for you, though," Brad said to Fin, startling him. "How do you plan to support your beautiful family?"

The answer would certainly involve his band, at which point the conversation would turn awkward.

"I have a job interview tomorrow," Fin said. His tone added, "Sir."

Brad nodded. "Outstanding! What sort of work?"

"It's at a new place that does web design. I know someone there, he used to work at *Sycamore*. I think I have a good shot."

"Well, good luck with it." Brad wanted Fin to have more than luck. He had to give this new family a chance, even if it meant burning his own capital. "Let me know if you need references."

"Thanks, that might come in handy as a matter of fact."

Rook was still staring at the baby she held, but the panic had departed her eyes. Now she was fascinated.

This news from Fin and Rook was both worrying and welcome. Brad missed his visits with Kyle, now that Melissa had discharged him. The chance to help these kids made Brad feel needed again.

He caught Willow's gaze and they raised their eyebrows at each other. Their world would soon be full of babies. He couldn't quite shake the thought that he and Willow might end up raising Fin's.

∗∗∗   ∗∗∗   ∗∗∗

One by one the gritty molecules of Kyle wend their way through the gelatinous atmosphere to fuse, with a rapturous jolt, to Rook. Given enough time, her sensual gravity of need will collect enough grains to

heal him.

The bubbles of light frolic in excitement, casting prismatic shadows. Their movement hinders Kyle's progress, but every time a piece of him touches one, it imparts knowledge.

Rook is pregnant.

Not this Rook, but the real one.

Kyle is suddenly drowning in the awareness his wife is pregnant by another man, his nemesis, his brother.

Their enormous sense of pride lends the bubbles a golden tint.

The Divided Man is now truly Complete.

The realization that this mind knows his name, his function, fills Kyle with renewed self-importance. When he is healed, he will find the Completer and Complete himself upon her.

For the Completer to carry out her function, both halves of the Divided Man must be Complete. They are.

Confusion ripples through Kyle's dispersed psyche.

The trickiest part was arranging for the Completer to mate with both halves of the Divided Man in the space of just a few hours.

Is it twins?

A rosy pink wave of nostalgic pleasure washes through the bubbles at the thought of twins.

Better. Two fathers. One mother. One child. Twins in one body. The chimera child is the culmination of generations of work.

Both he and Fin are the father of Rook's baby. Consternation pricks at Kyle.

Neither half alone could have accomplished this task.

This assertion angers Kyle.

The bubbles of light continue their giddy dance, oblivious.

With the Completer's sisters removed, there is no danger of the chimera child being lost.

The colossal mind's plan will move forward.

Another molecule of Kyle's scattered being fuses with Rook. His plan will move forward, too.

Part Two

Chapter Thirteen

MID-CENTURY MODERN

2 Bedroom ranch on half acre in Hemlock Heights neighborhood.
This mid-century charmer has a lot of potential and is the perfect
starter home for a handyman family! Two cozy bedrooms and
two baths feature tons of retro charm.
from *Webster Daily Press* real estate supplement

At Goodwill, the chess table didn't seem heavy, but after lugging it six blocks through the mid-April damp Fin regretted not going back for it with the car.

Another block-and-a-half and he'd be home.

Home these days was an actual single-family house. For over a week he and Rook had been homeowners. The search was disheartening at first, with an endless parade of cookie-cutter townhouses and uninspiring ranch boxes in 'young-family' neighborhoods. Once Fin took the job at Binary Images, they were able to raise their budget.

Their diamond in the rough was a small mid-century modern with a flat roof, drafty floor-to-ceiling windows, two bedrooms, a tiny office that might have once been a large closet, flagstone flooring in the open living area, a stone fireplace wall, and a carport. The landscaping long ago went feral, but that was okay. The overgrowth gave them privacy.

Much of the mid-century charm was hidden under a disastrously thorough 70s decorating scheme, but the lack of updating allowed Fin and Rook to afford it.

As housewarming gifts, Brad and Willow gave them a microwave and Zen gave them a lawnmower. Fin and Brad did some father/son bonding over ripping the aqua and avocado shag carpeting out of the

bedrooms.

Other than a new king-size bed and a sofa from the thrift store, they made do with furniture from Fin's room at the boarding house and scavenged from the bomb shelter. That gave them four gorgeous Eames bentwood dining chairs, but no table. For now the chairs were lined up forlornly along the wall like nerds at a school dance.

The house felt empty. Every day this week on his lunch hour Fin visited thrift shops, scouting for things to surprise Rook with. Mostly kitchenwares so far, along with a few baby things, so the chess table today was a welcome change. Fin lusted after it the minute he saw it. He missed playing chess with Rook.

Apart from being really goddamn heavy, the thing was a gorgeously tacky piece of art. Fin kept reminding himself of that as he made his way the last half block, the copper legs biting into his fingers.

Inside their entry courtyard, Fin stood the table beside the stagnant koi pond and flexed his hands a few times before letting himself into the house. It would be an hour before Rook got home from the library. Plenty of time to clean up the table and start dinner.

Fin placed his prize in the dining room beside the cafe table where the lava lamp lived. "Hey, Vesuvius, look what I got."

"Please tell me that thing's not for me."

Vesuvius's dismissive attitude stung. "Do you think Rook will like it?"

"Hard to say."

"Why's that?"

"Well... You want her to like it, right?"

"Of course."

"Then I think she'll like it."

"You're not much help today. What's gotten into you?"

"Sorry."

Fin concluded Vesuvius was jealous of the new arrival.

From the narrow kitchen he retrieved a roll of paper towels, cleanser, and a bucket of warm water, and began to wipe down his

treasure.

Waist-high, with six verdigris copper legs and an oval ebony top, the table was also filthy. Through the generous application of elbow grease, Fin removed years of neglect and uncovered a deep green undertone to the finish. He took special care with the reversible top. The plain side had a band of mother of pearl inside the lipped edge, with small patches missing.

The chess side was what made Fin buy it before anyone could snake him. The board was inlaid stone, cool and slick. The greenish tint made Fin think it was jade. The borders of the playing field were bowed to mimic the oval shape of the table, creating an optical illusion that twisted the brain just right. It would be so fucking fun to play chess on.

Concealed under the top was a storage compartment for the playing pieces, upholstered with cracked green leather. It held a threadbare velvet bag. At Goodwill, Fin peeked inside to make sure it went with the table, and saw chess pieces. Now it was time to find out if he had a full set.

Damp paper towel in hand, Fin pulled pieces out of the bag and cleaned them as he placed them on the board.

He shook his head and smiled.

"I don't remember your other set having a metal top hat," deadpanned Vesuvius.

"That's from a different game. The iron, too," Fin explained as he lifted them off the board and put them back in the bag.

It was like someone scavenged yard sales, culling loose game tokens from the crap left at the end of the day.

The only pieces matching the table were black: a bishop, a rook, four pawns, and the king. They were wonderfully detailed figures, the pawns two inches tall, the rest about three. The remainder of the black army consisted of a wooden queen, two glass knights, a marble rook, a plastic bishop, three plastic pawns, and three pawns from a Civil War chess set, for a total of 10 pawns.

The white army was even worse, having no pieces that were original

to the board. The plastic king stood a good inch shorter than the pewter queen, there were two glass lumps Fin took to be bishops, three mismatched wooden knights, a plastic rook and a marble one, and nine pawns, none of which matched.

In addition to that mess and the Monopoly pieces, he had five checkers, a domino, three dice, a submarine from Battleship, and a dime.

To keep the chessboard aspect a surprise, Fin put the pieces inside and turned the top plain side up.

While debating the relative merits of buying a uniform set versus using the mongrel horde, perhaps even constructing a new game that included all the other detritus from the velvet bag, Fin put the cleaning supplies away, and began cooking dinner.

Having been taught to cook by hippies, many of the recipes he knew were vegetarian. Rook didn't mind. His wife was fantastically resourceful and competent in many areas of life, the culinary arena just wasn't one of them. She was happy with whatever Fin chose to make, as long as it involved no seafood, and Fin enjoyed cooking for her. It felt comfortingly domestic, a phrase he never expected to use in a nonironic way.

He'd been domesticated, and didn't mind at all.

The new job was much more interesting than *Sycamore*. He got to stretch his artistic muscles at the same time he learned some programming skills. His coworkers didn't suck, his schedule was moderately flexible, his pay astronomically better.

It felt strange not to have anything to complain about.

Rook was still shelving books at the library, a job she mostly enjoyed. She planned to look for a 'real' job once the baby came, since it would hamper her chances if she waddled hugely pregnant into an interview.

Not that she was hugely pregnant. She was six months along and sexy as ever. Maternity clothes vexed her. According to her, they sucked. It amused Fin to imagine her in a shirt festooned with teddy

bears or storks, largely because he knew he'd never see it.

Apart from the sartorial suckiness, and occasional worries about her tattoos distorting, or losing her figure, Rook was happy. They had both been spending extra time with Zen. Turned out babies weren't so bad after all. Except when they were awake all night kicking you.

With Rook on her feet all day the baby slept, which meant it spent all night flexing its muscles and pummeling its dad. Boy or girl, the kid was going to be a kung-fu master.

As Fin stirred a pinch more basil into the spaghetti sauce, he heard the car pull into the carport. Moments later Rook came in through the back door, her vinyl leopard-print raincoat hanging stiffly around her.

"Oh, Muffin, that smells good!" she said.

Fin smiled at the pet name, how it had mysteriously stopped sounding like an insult, and greeted her with a kiss and a hug that made her coat squeak in protest.

"It can be ready any time, Cookie," he said. "I just need to boil the noodles."

"Do that now, please. I'm starved." She slipped her coat off and tossed it into the booth at the end of the kitchen. She wore a sleeveless minidress in an eye-bending acid green paisley. The top fit nicely, but the lower portion stretched taut across her belly.

Fin placed his hands on either side of the protrusion, which was a little bigger than half a basketball. "How you doing today, Thumper?"

The baby kicked his right hand. Fin smiled.

Rook laughed.

After filling the big pot and putting it on the stove, Fin said, "I found the world's coolest thing today at Goodwill."

"Another colander?"

Fin rolled his eyes and started toward the living room. "Even cooler."

"That remains to be seen."

*** *** ***

Rook experienced a long moment of both excitement and dread.

She knew that table.

Instead of passing, the feelings intensified and sent a shudder through her. Thumper shoved and wriggled.

Rook's brows furrowed.

Fin's grin quickly devolved into a frown of concern. "What's wrong?" He put a steadying arm around her.

Shaking her head, Rook said, "Deja vu. I'm okay."

"No you're not. Come sit down."

He led her to the retro-futuristic sofa, then hurried off to get a glass of water.

Rook closed her eyes as Thumper jabbed her ribcage from inside. In her mind she stood on the shore of a still, gray lake, regarding a table, twin to this one.

It couldn't be the same table. The one she remembered only existed inside her head.

Fin sat beside her and rested a hand on her belly. Rook sipped her water and stared at the table.

"I think I'm just hungry," she said. "Low blood sugar."

"The pot's not boiling yet," Fin said. "Do you want a snack? I think we have some pretzels."

Rook nodded. Fin got the bag of pretzels, then carried his new treasure over and placed it in front of her.

"I know it's a little beat up," he said, "but what do you think?"

"It's, umm…" She didn't want to say 'creepy.' Stalling for time, she popped a pretzel in her mouth.

"Archaic?" Vesuvius suggested.

"He doesn't like it either, but let me show you the best part." Fin lifted the top off and pulled out a velvet bag, black on one side, white on the other, and drawn with a black and white cord. Exactly like her destiny vision. This one bulged with something larger and lumpier than a single coin.

Fin flipped the top over and put it back in place. The table was now a crazy, warped chessboard, and a bit less menacing.

Rook smiled hesitantly.

"I hope you like it." Fin pulled a series of ridiculously mismatched pieces out of the bag and lined them up along the curved rim of the board like the cast in an amateur production of *Camelot* taking their curtain call.

It was obvious why this bizarre relic appealed to Fin. Rook chuckled at his enthusiasm.

He added the last two pieces, a white pawn and a black rook. "Is that my pendant?" Rook asked.

"Hmm?" Fin fiddled with the pieces, making sure they all faced straight at her.

Rook reached across and picked up the miniature tower. Definitely her pendant.

"I guess it matches the board, but I'd rather keep it as a necklace," she said.

"What?"

"Where'd you put the cord?"

"What are you talking about?" Fin asked, clearly playing dumb.

Rook held the pendant out.

"Oh, that's cool. It does look like your necklace."

"It *is* my necklace."

"No."

Rook sighed, and went into the bedroom. She located the shoebox where she kept her jewelry and brought it back out to the living room. She handed it to Fin.

"Prove it."

He quirked his eyebrow at her and opened the box. After a few seconds he pulled her rook pendant out and dangled it by the black string.

Rook opened her hand and compared the rook to her pendant. They were identical, down to the block pattern and the placement of the tiny windows.

Fin whistled.

A fascinating mixture of dread and wonder seeped down Rook's spine. Her left hand crept up and covered her gaping mouth. Her right closed into a fist around the rook.

Fin put her necklace back in the box and took her hands in his. "Hey, it's okay, Cookie."

"I dreamed about this table, Fin. The night we got married I had a vision — a destiny vision, dumb as that sounds. This table tried to make me choose, tried to make me Be the Completer."

"You did choose." He smiled and gave her hands a reassuring squeeze. "You married me. Completed me."

Rook was grateful he accepted her wing-nut assertions, and wasn't questioning her sanity. Ever since she told him about Brook and Bramble he'd been very attentive to her mental well-being. It would be frustrating if that caused friction now.

"Where did you get your necklace?" he asked.

"My grandma. I found it at her house and I liked it, so I stole it and made it into a necklace. It was just a little castle statue in a box of junk in the attic. She had lots of junk. Salt and pepper shakers, porcelain figurines, silverware, rhinestone jewelry. All family treasures you understand."

Fin nodded. "I bet this was her table, too. You saw it at her house and that's why it showed up in your dream."

Rook shook her head. "First of all, she lived in DC before she moved out to Arizona to live with Uncle Phil, so why would it turn up in Webster? And second, I spent more time with my grandparents than with Mom when I was young. I would know it if this was their table."

"Maybe it was in the attic?" Fin sounded doubtful.

"The attic was my domain. I was up there all the time to get away from Bay."

"And Junebug?" Fin liked to collect information about her family, like she was a jigsaw puzzle he kept finding pieces for.

"The Bug wasn't around as much. Unlike with Bay and me, Mom knew who her father was. Her other grandparents took her a lot."

"I never met my grandparents." He smiled a wry smile. "Except for Shaw."

Rook placed Fin's large hands on her belly. "This poor kid is going to have the most sordid family tree in history."

In the kitchen the pot lid started rattling. Fin leaned down and kissed Rook's protruding navel, then went to add the pasta to the pot. Rook placed the rook on the chess table and followed him.

"Remember what Willow said about Webster being a nexus?"

"I was thinking about that." Fin gave the pot a stir with a wooden spoon. "I guess this is another example. Weird and unusual things are drawn here. I suppose the Id likes synchronicity."

"It is a good album," Rook joked.

Fin groaned. "I'm almost afraid to ask if we can keep it," he said. "The table I mean, not your sense of humor. But if that's up for debate…"

Rook swatted him and walked back into the living room to look at the table. Fin put his arm around her and stood there bouncing on his heels. Clearly he adored his find.

Oh what the hell.

Rook fished her necklace out of the shoebox and untied the cord. She looked Fin in the eye and handed him the rook. "Promise me we can get rid of it if it creeps me out too much."

"I promise," said Fin, then he pulled her to him. As they kissed he set the rook on the table and Thumper started auditioning for Riverdance.

*** *** ***

While Fin and Rook ate spaghetti in the kitchen, Vesuvius regarded his new roommate.

Fin thought Vesuvius disliked the chess table, but that wasn't the case. Vesuvius had many questions about it, and wasn't sure it was safe to have around. With Fin too much in love with the table to give such considerations any attention, Vesuvius had to handle those details.

It did make him a little jealous, watching Fin fuss over this gaudy

thing.

Where had the table come from, prior to Goodwill? An awkward familiarity about it made Vesuvius uncomfortable. Knowing the table's past would probably tell him things about himself.

Did the table originate when it appeared in Rook's mind? Or was it as old as it looked?

One sure thing was the table had no consciousness of its own. So, it had no agenda. That didn't mean it didn't have a purpose, perhaps even a destiny.

As Rook and Fin entered the room, she said, "Okay one game."

Fin said, "You bring the chairs. I'll set up the pieces."

Rook put her hands on her hips and huffed. "In my delicate condition?"

"The chairs are light."

"We'll see if you even get one."

Fin began arranging the two armies. Vesuvius watched with interest, noting that the bowed lines of the board seemed to acquire greater curvature as more pieces went into place. Rook came back with one of the bomb shelter chairs and sat with her arms folded. After several seconds, both she and Fin cracked up and she stood to go get another one.

The board was ready, and Fin turned the white army toward Rook's seat. She returned with Fin's chair, but didn't give it to him. She stood pouting. Fin quirked his eyebrow at her with all his might, until she picked up her old pendant.

"I want to use black this time."

Fin looked ready to debate, but came to his senses quickly. He moved to the other chair while Rook replaced her rook.

As he usually did, Fin first moved one of his knights.

Rook advanced a pawn, one of the minority of pieces original to the set.

As she made her move, Vesuvius experienced a form of double vision. On one level, he saw the event in an ordinary sense, but on

another he saw the spaces of the board realigning. On that channel the board didn't have ranks and files, but concentric rings. The ring with Rook's pawn turned to keep pace with the motion of her hand.

This was too startling and fascinating for Vesuvius to respond to. He watched Fin counter by bringing out his other knight, expecting a repeat of the bizarre phenomenon, but it didn't happen. Vesuvius wondered if he had let his mistrust of a new piece of furniture escalate into hallucinations.

Rook advanced a bishop, which convinced Vesuvius he wasn't imagining things. He got another dose of the dual-reality view of the board, and again the movement of the piece caused corresponding rotation of the ring it rode. The bishop's diagonal travel created added complexity. Two adjoining rings moved in unison, then the inner one carried on for an extra space. A sensation of vertigo accompanied Vesuvius's augmented view of the game.

This was exactly the type of danger Fin's infatuation blinded him to, and Vesuvius wondered if he should interrupt before anything weirder happened. Fin, uncharacteristically, made his move without stalling, so Vesuvius had no time to speak up. A pawn this time. Again, his move didn't produce the effect. It seemed to be Rook.

Vesuvius braced as she reached for her next piece. Best to be sure, before saying something that might upset them. She moved one of her knights, and nothing unusual happened. Vesuvius felt warily relieved and decided to let them keep playing so he could observe the strange properties of the table.

The overlaid vision did not return for the next four moves, and Vesuvius wondered if it was gone for good. Then it happened again as Rook moved another of her pawns. He still didn't feel he had enough data to say anything.

Over the next ten moves, the effect reappeared twice. Both times on Rook's turn, but otherwise no pattern was obvious.

With a savage little chuckle Rook said, "This is what I've been waiting for," and pushed out her pendant-turned-chess-piece. The

board became a writing nest, as multiple rings moved in different directions. At least one made a complete revolution. Somehow all of this only affected the position of the rook.

As the rings found their new configuration, the image that settled in Vesuvius's mind was of a puzzle, or a combination lock. His earlier anxiety forgotten, he waited for Rook to make another move and spin the dial. He had some guesses about how the mechanism would behave and wanted to see if he was right. The flow of the actual game eluded him, as he spent the time between spins concentrating on solving the puzzle.

The gaps between spins seemed to be lengthening, or was it just his impatience?

When the wait became irritating, Vesuvius noticed Fin wasn't in his chair anymore. He was kneeling in front of Rook, between her knees, and they were kissing. Chess was a reliable aphrodisiac, and this game had run its course for tonight. Vesuvius now wanted to persuade them to keep playing.

As Fin scooped her up, one of Rook's boots bumped the table and toppled a few of the pieces, dissipating the energy Vesuvius felt building throughout the game. He didn't know if he was relieved or disappointed.

*** *** ***

Sunlight bathed the sidewalk, scarcely hindered by boughs putting forth tiny green buds. Those limbs chopped the light into a crazed mosaic with their shadows. The air was clear and clean on Melissa's face, and chilly on her bare legs.

She was two blocks from the House, practicing. These jaunts were supposed to help her gain independence from Severin. As the weather improved, perhaps she would make them more frequent, as they at least gave her a change of scene.

Melissa felt heavy certainty that her stamina for the outside world would never progress beyond the one-hour mark. Some traitorous part of her was not on board with the quest for independence, and invariably

after 60 minutes the patterns would invade the edges of her perceptions.

Then it was time to go back, straight to the attic for a round with Severin.

Birds called to each other across the quiet street.

A few weeks ago Melissa had turned one of her strolls into an experiment. By the time her world began caving in, she had already seduced a stranger.

The most difficult part that day had been deciding where to look for her energy donor. Her first, obvious idea was any of the innumerable student bars, but she found it too nauseating to even contemplate the type of 'man' she'd find there. Plus, she'd be competing with all the trashy coeds. She'd sooner let madness claim her.

A hotel bar was perfect. Lonely business travelers, and private rooms upstairs. Someone from out of town would be an ideal test subject.

At the Best Western, she'd set her sights on a tall, slim man nearing 50, hunched at the bar. He reminded her of Brad, which might have bothered her, but she chose to focus on how the familiarity would simplify things when they got to his room. His name was Ron, and it took some nudging to get him to buy the second drink. Melissa allowed him to notice she wore nothing underneath the sweater dress. After that, it was only a matter of minutes until he suggested they head upstairs. Melissa agreed demurely, although by then she was impatient to fuck. The patterns muttered in the wings, triggering a Pavlovian response.

The room was smallish and dingy. Melissa sank to her knees as soon the door shut, undoing Ron's fly. The bed was a few toddling steps away, and Ron soon sprawled across it on his back. Melissa quickly mounted him, watching his face as she undid her sweater buttons one at a time. By the time she opened them all, she'd begun draining his energy.

Ron was no match for her, and he was no Severin. His eyes rolled back in his head. Frustrated with the meager amount of power she'd

collected, Melissa dug into him for more, pumping her hips to relieve a different frustration. She didn't discover he was dead until about thirty seconds before her climax.

What little power she obtained was already fading. Her peripheral vision crawled with portents, like centipedes on the walls, rekindling her libido.

The floral bedspread presented a list of size and color variations for Lands' End mock turtlenecks. A nearly inaudible hum from the clock radio whispered disgusting statistics about the fluid and tissue makeup of biomedical waste from all of the hospitals in California.

Melissa had buttoned her sweater and raced back to the House, straight to the attic.

Her experiment that day hadn't been a total failure. She now knew that ordinary folk couldn't give her what she needed. Even a roomful of Rons wouldn't suffice.

More birdsong floated past, tentative in these early days of spring.

Melissa turned right at the corner, her course winding through the secondary streets without ever extending more than three blocks from the House. If she needed to retreat, it would take only minutes.

In addition to these excursions to practice controlling her patterns, Melissa also practiced with the table. The objects she found nearly always lasted long enough to get a look, especially if she'd recently taken a big gulp of her uncle's power. Not that the random items from under the sheet bore any significance for her: shoelaces, a tarnished silver butter knife, a crushed Matchbox car, a whistle.

She kept her table experiments secret from Uncle Severin, but sometimes she wanted to ask him to explain what the big deal was. She watched when he used the table, and from what she could tell it worked just as well for her. He seemed to think the odds and ends he got were so profound. He would pace for half an hour brooding over a cork, or chuckle about an empty plastic bag like it was the punchline to a joke Melissa didn't get.

Hoping to pick up some clue to what it all meant was a major factor

in her policy change about their intercourse. Once she'd learned how to control the power, she'd drained Severin every time. He went into rapid decline, and she worried she would use him up. He hardly got out of the hammock, much less performed supernatural feats. Now, once a day Melissa gave him all the power. Surrendering control never came naturally for her, but a sweet sinking oblivion on the giving end of their twisted power equation promised an escape. The feeling she might sink so deep she'd never have to come back up.

But that was only once per day. The other two or three sessions, Melissa drained as much as she could. She would indulge Severin's repulsive thumb-sucking fetish, even encouraged the use of the stump, but she took all the power for herself.

Except sometimes he surprised her.

It didn't take much to allow herself to slip, to sink. In spite of losing the upper hand to Melissa, and literally losing his hand to the table, Severin remained smug. He acted like he was winning, no matter what happened. Whereas Melissa felt lost, even when she beat him at his own game. With no joy in winning, sometimes losing offered a kind of solace.

Sometimes Melissa had to talk herself out of going out to another hotel bar.

She turned right again, continuing her erratic orbit of the House. She wondered if she would last the full hour today.

A car rolled past, the shushing chorus of its tires and engine saying how many new area codes would be added to US cities over the next fifteen years, and listing them by time zone. Melissa turned toward home, quickening her stride.

*** *** ***

Marsh glanced back at the door, as if showing the visitors out might somehow not have worked. He joined Rainbow in the living room.

"New clients?" she asked.

"Not exactly." He hesitated, superstitious that they would know if he spoke their name aloud. "Feds."

Rainbow bit her lip. "I'm confident we're in full compliance with environmental protection measures, but shit, Marsh, any number of financial rules could have tripped us up." She looked worried. "Is it bad?"

Marsh took a seat beside her on the sofa. He sighed, rubbing his temples.

"They're recruiting. Our reputation is sterling in tech circles, and the government is prepared to make handsome offers to everyone here." He snorted. "They really missed their chance."

Over the past several weeks, departures had taken the TEF's number down to ten.

"Why aren't you happier? That's so much better than I expected." Rainbow smiled, but her eyebrows weren't buying it. "Did you give them names?"

He shook his head. "I don't trust them."

"The deserters, or the headhunters?"

"Any of them." He stopped talking and looked at his hands.

"What?" Rainbow put her arm over his shoulders. "What's wrong?"

"I don't want to tell the others. I don't trust them, either."

Rainbow sat up. "What's going on?" she asked. "What did they want, really? If they want to offer people jobs, now of all times that seems like a good thing."

Marsh looked at her, sidelong.

She sighed. "A little too good."

"They have a special project," Marsh confirmed. "Something our expertise is especially suited to. They didn't ask about anybody's credentials, just laid out a blanket deal for anyone who's interested."

"The jewelry."

"It has to be. They have it, and now they don't know what to do with it."

"Maybe not, though. Maybe they're trying to start from scratch."

Marsh frowned optimistically. "Well, in any case. We can't help them with it."

"You're doing the right thing," Rainbow told him, patting his back. "I know it feels dishonest to hide this from the others, but it's how it has to be."

"I wish I knew whether they have it. I assumed they did, but I'd feel better thinking they didn't."

"So, let's think that. Easy."

Marsh chuckled and shook his head. "Not easy. What if we're wrong."

Rainbow shrugged. "First time for everything."

Marsh chuckled again, and this time it felt good. "They must have it."

"Like you said, we don't help them either way."

Marsh nodded, but his mind was preoccupied with a shimmering distant ideal. "Too bad we can't ask Kyle Tanner. He's the last known owner and he's right upstairs. We even have a window into his head, but all he ever thinks about is that damn chain."

"There's someone else we could ask," Rainbow said hesitantly. "Of course she knows me as an air-head hippie, so I'll need to get into character."

Chapter Fourteen

INTO THE STORM

The only local source of the microtransceivers is Talisman Tattoo. Using Guidebook sample collection protocol 2c I obtained our first specimen today (1 μΩ). In accordance with protocol 2c, I left my uniform at home and dressed as a hippie girl. I also acted the part, dumbing down my vocabulary and behaving in a stereotypical druggy fashion. May I add here that a tongue piercing hurts like hell and I will be expecting a large bonus to reward my dedication.
        TEF progress report M00427

In the library lobby, a vaguely familiar voice called Rook's name. She looked both ways as she put on her leopard-spotted raincoat, and soon found the smiling face of one of her regulars from Talisman, the blonde hippie.

Rook gave a polite smile and waved. The woman intercepted her at the ponderous revolving doors.

"Remember me? It's Rainbow." She had to practically shout over the roar of rain on the broad concrete steps outside. "Like, wow, is it ever raining."

"Yes," Rook agreed, content to stall before braving the elements.

"I'm totally glad to see you. Can you give me a ride? I'm really sorry about, like, imposing. But wow. That's a lot of rain." Rainbow stared out into the downpour, mesmerized by the mist kicked up as the drops pelted down. Mesmerized by something, anyway.

"Okay," Rook said. "But my car's nowhere near here. You're gonna get wet."

"For sure."

Rook raised her hood and Rainbow hitched her windbreaker up over her head. The rain pounding on her hood drowned all other noise, so Rook didn't know whether Rainbow said anything during the trek to the small blue sedan. It took about five minutes, and by the time they reached the car Rook felt soggy. Her coat protected her from the rain on its way down, but not so well from the backspray. Rainbow was drenched.

Inside the car, the noise was less obnoxious. The moisture they brought in condensed on the windows, and when Rainbow used her sleeve to clear hers it fogged again in seconds. Rook started the engine and turned on the defogger and the wipers, and Rainbow sought among the meager assortment of adjectives at her disposal for a way to describe the weather and how wet it had made her.

When the rain diminished to merely cats and dogs, Rook could see well enough to get underway. "You'll want to go left out of the parking lot," Rainbow instructed.

Rainbow's directions kept them on narrow alleys and back streets. Rook knew generally where they were, but seen from this angle it was an unfamiliar part of town.

"Okay," Rainbow suddenly announced, "you can just park, like, right in front of that garage door." She smiled warmly. "Cool. Thanks for the ride."

"No problem."

"You should totally come in for a minute. I can make us some herbal tea?"

Rook didn't have to rush to get to Brad and Willow's for dinner. She switched off the engine. "I can't stay too long."

They hurried to a doorway beside the large garage door, and Rainbow unlocked it so they could dart inside.

Rook expected to find a beat up car, or an efficiency apartment with lots of tie-dyed tapestries. Instead the well-lit space was an electronics workshop, cluttered but clean. Two long workbenches filled most of the floor, and shelving lined the walls.

Rainbow faced Rook and gave a vague spread-armed gesture and a lopsided sad kind of smile. Rook stayed near the door, her surprise sliding toward distrust. After several seconds she asked, "Weren't you going to make us tea?"

"Of course, right." Rainbow moved to a cabinet with a microwave. She worked with her back to Rook, running water into a pair of mugs and placing them in the microwave. Something about the way Rainbow moved seemed odd. "While this warms up," she added hesitantly, "I need to tell you something."

Rook reached behind herself and placed her hand on the doorknob.

Rainbow's voice seemed different as well.

For a moment she leaned on the sink as if exhausted, then she straightened. Rook heard her draw a deep breath as she turned around. Rook looked her in the eye, and saw a stranger.

"Please," Rainbow said, with perfect diction, "stay for one minute and hear me out."

Rook shook her head and began to turn the knob.

"I'm so sorry," Rainbow pleaded. "It was an act. It seems so stupid now, but we didn't know you and I thought I should have a persona, someone who'd be in a piercing parlor all the time."

"Why."

Rainbow looked at the floor. She said something as the microwave's beep interrupted, and put her hand over her face until it fell silent. "I'm sorry," she repeated.

Rook felt queasy and furious. She took a closer look at the sophisticated bits and pieces on the nearest workbench, and knew why this woman had deceived her.

"The jewelry," Rook spat. "You used me to get at it."

Rainbow nodded, still staring at the floor.

"You knew about it! You knew, and you let me keep handing it out."

"I'm sorry. We didn't know enough about you to share our information. We couldn't lose our source."

"You admit you used me."

"I said I'm sorry. I truly am, and I'm coming clean now. You know how important that jewelry is. Dealing with it took priority over everything. And it's not dealt with yet. We need your help, again."

"Who's 'we'?" Rook demanded.

"We're called the TEF. It's pretty complicated."

Rook recalled the name from Shaw's files. This outfit was one of the bidders in the black-market auction. "Why should I help you?"

"We think someone plans to set up another program. It's going to start all over again. We're trying to find out who has the main lode of jewelry, and where it is. We want to stop them, but we need more information."

"Well, I'm afraid all your soul-searching was for nothing. I don't know anything about any of that."

Rainbow shrugged. "We can still have our tea. I'll talk about the few things we know, and rattle off our wild guesses about what it might mean, and maybe it'll turn out something you know can help us after all."

"I'm not convinced I even want to help you," Rook reminded her.

"I understand. That doesn't mean you can't hear me out, right? I'll just talk, and if you don't want to respond then that's fine. I don't blame you for being wary."

Rook didn't want to give an admitted liar more chances to mess with her head, but this proposition felt pretty safe. But she wouldn't drink the tea. Or the Kool-Aid.

"Okay."

Rainbow sighed in relief. As she dropped teabags into their mugs, a door across from Rook opened and two men came in. The first, startlingly tall, wearing a snot green cardigan, collapsed his yellow umbrella and deposited it in a stand by the door. The second man was older and squatly built, with scruffy gray hair and beard. He wore all black, and the instant he came in from the rain his icy blue eyes locked onto Rook.

Rainbow hurried to make introductions. "This is my boyfriend

Marsh, and that's Severin. Marsh, Severin, this is my friend Rook. She was kind enough to give me a lift home."

Severin! Rook tried to maintain an outward calm as her mind and heart raced. This man kidnapped Willow.

"I'm most pleased to make your acquaintance, young lady," Severin said. He never broke eye contact as he navigated around the workbenches. Rook couldn't drop her gaze either. He grasped her hand eagerly. His skin was cold, clammy with rainwater. A shiver grabbed Rook by the spine.

Now that he'd come closer, she saw the smooth pink stump of his left wrist.

Keeping Severin's eyes under careful surveillance, Rook said, "Never mind the tea. I have to go." She tore herself loose from Severin's grip and bolted into the storm.

*** *** ***

"Ba ba ba ba ba," Zen babbled as she drooled all over the bunny on her purple sweatshirt.

"That's right," Willow said, "Fin and Rook *will* be here soon. Zen is such a smart girl."

"Ba! Ba ba ba ba," Zen agreed.

Willow carried her mug to the kitchen and loaded it into the dishwasher. The meatloaf smelled delicious.

The back door opened in the laundry room, letting in the loud rushing hiss of the rain along with Brad and Fin.

"Look who I found," Brad said cheerfully.

"Hi Mom." Fin gave her a kiss on the cheek. His trench coat was soaked, as was his hair.

"Why didn't you call for a ride?" Willow asked.

"I had an umbrella," Fin explained. "The wind took that as a challenge."

"It's a good thing your mother needed her beer," Brad joked, "or you'd still be out there drowning."

"Oh, yes. *My* beer." Willow took Brad's six-pack and put it in the

refrigerator.

"Is Rook here?" Fin asked.

"Not yet," Willow said.

The three adults moved to the living room where Zen sat on a yellow blanket, babbling.

Fin scooped his sister off the floor so she could drool on his black shirt.

"Ba ba ba ba ba," Zen said emphatically.

"You don't say," said Fin.

Willow watched with a grin as her two children carried on their nonsensical conversation. These weekly parenting practice sessions had been a great success. Both Fin and Rook were quite comfortable with Zen, and, more important, they realized it. Impending parenthood frightened them much less. Willow thought about suggesting they take Zen overnight now that they were in their new house. It would be good practice for them, and it would be an opportunity for Brad and herself to be alone together.

Date night. Willow sighed at the thought.

Headlights cut across the wall signaling Rook's arrival.

"Guess who's here, Zen," said Fin.

"Ba!"

"That's right!"

He crossed to the door and opened it.

"Ba!" said Zen.

"Ba," said Rook. She wore another of her signature bizarre outfits. This one paired a leopard raincoat with plaid stockings and her beloved boots. She shrugged off the jacket and hung it in the closet. Her red stretch velvet skirt was quite short, as usual. The t-shirt with the Nicotine logo had been Fin's. It fit snugly over her rounded belly.

Rook closed the closet door and stood staring at it, smoothing her shirt several times. Turning abruptly to face everyone, she plastered on a too-wide smile and ran her hands through her wild, damp hair.

"Boy, that weather's something!"

Fin handed Zen off to Brad on his way to embrace Rook. "Everything okay?"

She blinked rapidly at him and nodded.

Willow was unconvinced, and it seemed Fin was too.

He cocked his head and looked down at Rook, resting one hand on her abdomen.

"Everything's fine," she insisted. "Really." A tear trickled down her cheek.

"Rook," Fin said. He cupped her face in his hands.

"I just had a fright. I'm okay." She stood in front of the fire. "Did I ever mention Rainbow?"

Fin thought for a second, shook his head.

"One of my piercing customers. Sort of a wifty hippie. She was at the library today and asked for a ride. You'd think with a name like Rainbow she'd like the rain… Anyway, I took her home."

"Did she make a pass at you?" Fin asked.

"Fin!" Willow admonished.

"What?" He shrugged. "Lesbians like her."

"No," Rook said. "Well, I guess some do. But that's not what happened. We went inside this sort of garage workshop. For a second I thought maybe her boyfriend built pirate cable boxes or something, but she started asking me about the jewelry, asking if I knew where it was. And she didn't sound like a wifty hippie anymore."

"Oh, shit," Fin said.

"Yeah," Rook agreed. "Then her really tall boyfriend walks in wearing a green cardigan."

"The Sweaterguys!" said Fin.

Beside Willow on the couch, Brad sat up straighter. Willow put her hand on his knee to keep him quiet so Rook could finish her story.

"And with Rainbow's boyfriend was this short guy with a gray beard, dressed all in black." Rook paused.

Willow gasped. "Oh no."

"Rainbow introduced him as Severin."

"Did he hurt you?" Fin demanded.

"No. He stared at me and shook my hand and I got the hell out of there. His eyes were creepy and so blue." She shivered and inched closer to the fire.

Willow stood. "Rook, you must never go back there. Ever."

"I wasn't planning to."

"Severin is dangerous. Especially to you."

"Me?"

"I think he recognized you." Willow wished she didn't have to deliver this news.

"What do you mean?"

Willow glanced at Brad and Zen, then at Fin, and finally looked at Rook.

"Severin is your father."

Rook's brows tried to converge, but her widening eyes forced them apart.

"I thought it safer if you didn't know. I was afraid you might want to meet him."

"My father?" Rook shuddered and pressed against Fin, who enfolded her in his arms.

"I got the story from your mother when she left the Following."

Rook looked ill. "I don't want my father to be a kidnapping bastard."

"It's no reflection on you," Brad assured.

"Isn't Severin your uncle?" Fin asked Willow.

Willow had hoped this part wouldn't come up. "Yes."

"But that means…"

"Rook is my cousin," Willow confirmed.

Rook's sharp blue eyes, a vibrant echo of her father's, darted around as if searching for a way out of this situation. She stepped away from Fin.

"But—" She looked down at her belly.

"Everything's fine," Fin blurted. "We saw the ultrasound. It's fine."

"Remember I told you the Elsewhere created Severin and Gale?" Willow said. "There are no bad genes to pass along."

"How can you be sure?" Rook asked.

"The bubbles told me," Willow said. "Not in so many words, but that information is there. Beyond that, though, we have physical proof. I'm healthy. Fin and Zen are healthy. You are healthy. The Elsewhere's plans might be inscrutable, but it does have them. It made sure its offspring are genetically sound."

Rook allowed Fin to put his arm around her again. "What about Severin's hand?"

"What about it?"

"He only has one," Rook stated like it should be obvious.

Willow's eyebrows drew together and she looked to Brad. "The last time I saw him he had two hands."

"Same here," Brad said. "Maybe Gale did something to him. They had quite a battle. Green lightning flying around."

"That's reassuring," scoffed Rook. "Everybody in the family tree has the right number of hands, but they're also evil and have magic powers!"

"We're not all evil," Fin reassured.

"Some of us like to see ourselves as somewhat heroic," Brad added with a smile. "You and Fin will be great parents and your child will be perfectly ordinary. And I mean 'ordinary' in the best possible sense. Now who's ready for meatloaf?"

"Ba!"

***   ***   ***

Severin returned to the attic immediately.

The lovely visitor in the workshop was his kin, he felt it the instant he saw her. The daughter he'd sired with Cloud. He hadn't thought of his offspring since first learning of its inconvenient presence in his lover's abdomen.

Severin glanced at Melissa slumbering in the hammock. They'd devoted much of the afternoon to physical gratification, most of it

revolving around his stump, and she was spent in direct contrast to Severin's invigoration. He'd kept control this time, and pushed things as hard as he could.

No matter how much vitality his niece's loins held he was unable to use her as anything but the crudest conduit to the Elsewhere. Given enough sessions he would succeed in regrowing his lost hand, but her 'elsewhere' never yielded objects for interpretation, nor answers to his queries. She was no substitute for his table. In addition, Melissa had grown quite devious and strong. She was dangerous, and Severin was running out of time to remove the threat.

Severin shook his head and brushed his fingers across the sheet, chastising himself. He must stop making excuses for keeping her around. Melissa would kill him eventually, or he would be forced to kill her.

If he could replace her with someone else, he had to seize the chance.

But first came confirmation of the girl's identity, which meant using the table right-handed. He drew a slow, deep breath and let it out. His batteries were well charged, and he held a clear question in his mind. The table would cooperate.

Ducking his truncated left arm under a corner of the sheet, Severin lifted it so his right hand could probe for answers.

His confidence was rewarded, as his fingers closed around a slender, nearly weightless object. Even before drawing it out, Severin knew it would be a gleaming black feather, and that he had indeed just been introduced to his daughter.

Rook.

Severin smiled his approval. Everything about the young woman was perfect. Being family, her reserves of mystical energy would be boundless. Being young, all the more so, and she would be far easier to control than Melissa.

*** *** ***

Fin drove them home, less out of gallantry than concern that Rook

was too preoccupied to operate the vehicle safely. Where he usually felt her comforting mental hum he now felt tension. They reached the house without talking.

Rook sat on the sofa, and as he joined her Fin expected her to curl up into a ball or lean on him. Instead she leaned forward, poised for action and staring into the distance.

"Listen," Fin began, the tension too much to bear, "you don't have to worry about the baby. I mean, closer cousins than us have perfectly healthy kids, and like Mom said, this family is a kind of special case. It'll be okay, I promise."

Rook gave him a tired smile and patted his knee, which made him feel foolish.

"Thank you," she added, "but Thumper's not what has me worried. I don't know if there's any sane reason to expect it to be fine, but I know it will be. We will be."

"Then what's wrong?" Fin asked, somehow more worried than before.

"The jewelry."

Fin took her hands in his, and shook his head. "Cookie, let someone else deal with it."

Rook shook her head, too. "I was part of the problem. I can't let it just exist out there in the world. It's dangerous. And I'm responsible."

"No, you're not. You're really not."

Rook looked at her boots.

"You don't owe anybody anything," Fin assured her.

"I know," Rook said in a tiny voice, still looking down.

Fin lifted her chin and tried to look into her eyes, but she kept her gaze averted. He felt tears threatening, although Rook's features remained composed. He swallowed, and she finally met his eyes. She looked sorry but resolute.

"Why?" Fin asked. *Why does it have to be you?* Just because the Sweaterguys thought Rook had information didn't obligate her to anything.

Rook shrugged. Fin clenched his jaw and blinked to clear his sight. Was that the only answer he was going to get?

"I have to do this," she said, "have to help destroy it. Severin can't be allowed to have access to it, and Rainbow can't stop him." Fin shook his head, but Rook continued. "When Kyle took over, you knew you had to stop him. You didn't let me talk you out of it."

Fin dropped his gaze. He tried to say that was different, but the words wouldn't cooperate. Tears ran down his cheeks.

"I would like to ask you to help," Rook said, and Fin's tears ran faster. She threw her arms around him. Fin held her tight.

"We have to be careful," Fin said eventually. Rook gave him a long squeeze. Fin sniffed and sat up straight.

Rook nodded, saying, "We can't go rushing in."

"Damn right. Let the Sweaters do the heavy lifting this time."

Rook smiled. "Okay, that's the plan. But I have to give them something to get them started."

"They asked for the location, right?"

"Yup. Unfortunately, I know less than they do."

Fin had a flash of inspiration. "The aliens know all kinds of useful things. Let me see what I can get out of them."

"Great idea. They'll be so happy to hear from you after all this time, they'll tell you anything."

He eased back on the couch and put out a call on the space spiders' channel.

"Hey, fellas. You still out there?"

It is always a pleasure to converse with you.

"Bullshit, but it's nice of you to say."

What prompts this exchange?

"I need a small favor."

Our curiosity is aroused. Please elaborate.

"It's just a quick question. Where is the jewelry, right now?"

You refer, presumably, to the microtransceivers with which some humans adorned themselves?

"Presumably. I need to know where the main pile of it is."

As you speculated, we can provide this information quite easily. However, its value arises not from the effort it requires, but rather from how badly it is needed. It must be a matter of considerable importance, or else you would not have asked us.

"It is, and I don't have time for games."

We won't waste your time, then, but explain the terms directly.

"Terms? You scuttling bastards have a lot of nerve."

There's not much point debating about that. In return for the answer to your question, we require your commitment to help us gain control of the human collective mind.

"You have got to be kidding me! I don't think I can make myself any clearer on that topic."

Did you expect us to abandon the idea? Is it any less reasonable for us to expect you to open your mind to our vision?

"Look, you said your whole take-over-the-collective thing was supposed to help my species, right? I think the plan's for shit, but your goal is noble."

We never got as far as discussing details of a plan. But yes, our aim is to help your people.

"This jewelry is a big problem for my people, and you can help by giving us its location. Prove to me you're on the level, and maybe we can have some deep discussions about the best way to help humanity."

In our estimation the location of the microtransceivers is of almost no consequence to the welfare of humanity, but this information represents our only leverage. We can't part with it casually.

"We're negotiating here. I'm counter-offering."

Your offer is to commit to 'deep discussion'?

"Isn't that a step in the right direction?"

You must commit to something substantive. Discussion, however deep, is inadequate.

"At least I'd be talking to you. Take it or leave it."

It will be interesting to see whether you are resourceful enough to

locate the devices on your own. If not, you can always speak with us again.

"You're telling me to fuck off?"

That wouldn't be very original. We're simply declining to do business at this time.

Fin rubbed his temples and opened his eyes.

Rook said, "You don't look like somebody who just talked a bunch of extraterrestrial arachnids into revealing the location of illicit technological marvels."

He smiled ruefully. "Some idiot taught them to play hardball."

Rook smoothed his hair back from his forehead. "I guess that means we're stuck."

"Hey, we'll think of something. Tomorrow. Let's sleep on it."

Rook's brow showed momentary doubt, but she nodded. "You're right. That jewelry's been out there for a long time. What's one more night?"

***   ***   ***

Rook lay beside her husband, both of them breathing slowly and deeply, monitored by the alien spiders.

Her mind loitered at the edge of alertness, drifting toward sleep. She was thinking about the jewelry.

Her grip on consciousness relaxed, and her mind entered an early stage of sleep. The aliens waited for her to reach REM stage before conveying their message.

She dreamed of a typical day at Talisman Tattoo. Someone shouted her name, disturbing her nap on the parlor's green velour sofa.

Rook sat up and rubbed her eyes to discover Fin standing before her.

"I suppose you're here for a piercing."

Fin smiled and said nothing.

"Come on, then." Rook led him to the back room. Fin sat on the table. Rook donned her gloves and searched for the hoop to insert into his eyebrow. She was anxious to get this part over with so they could get

to the kissing.

All of her inventory was gone.

Kyle smirked in the corner, wearing a familiar green cardigan.

Rook ransacked the place, shooting occasional dirty looks at Kyle, who remained smug. When she'd torn open every drawer and dumped out every box, she faced him, hands on hips.

"You have it, don't you?"

Kyle shrugged, and his grin enlarged maddeningly.

On the table Fin checked his watch. If she didn't pierce his eyebrow soon he would leave and they wouldn't live happily ever after.

Panicking she turned back to Kyle. "You know where it is, I know you do."

Kyle nodded, still smiling. He strode from the piercing room, and Rook followed right behind him. When she reached the outer room, no one was there.

Rook tried to look for Kyle, but she was too tired. She stretched out on the sofa to rest.

The spiders ran the same dream through her subconscious over and over all night. Kyle knew where the jewelry was, and finding it was key to Rook's future with Fin.

By morning the message was deeply rooted. They hoped it wouldn't take her long to act.

*** *** ***

Rook slipped off both go-go boots and wiggled her toes in the spring air. Yesterday's rain had passed and today was sunny and cool. Everything was budding, granting the trees and bushes pale green halos.

Having spent the morning in the perpetually murky depths of the stacks, Rook happily agreed when Lara suggested they eat lunch in the courtyard. Dimness and solitude had eroded the optimism she'd woken with. It left her brooding about the jewelry, her father, and, of all people, Kyle.

The sun on her bare shoulders and legs, and arguing musical tastes with Lara, afforded a welcome distraction from her obsessions. While

savoring the last bite of a Snickers, Rook slid an errant spaghetti strap back into place. Another dress she wouldn't be able to wear much longer. The blue and purple satin concoction used to hang from the straps and flutter around flirtily, but now her expanded bust barely fit into it. The empire waist provided room for Thumper, but if she got any rounder it would raise the hemline to obscene proportions. Rook sighed and peeled a banana.

Lara stood and crushed her cigarette as she drained the last swig from her can of Red Bull. "Well, I gotta get back in there."

Rook swallowed a mouthful of banana and said, "Have fun."

"Nothing but."

Rook pulled her boots on. She should get back to work herself, but dreaded it. Alone for these few seconds and her mind already returned to plotting micro-technology jewelry destruction.

If the government had it, she would need to accept there was nothing she could do. But if there was a stash of the stuff she could disable or destroy, she had to do it.

Kyle is the last known owner of the devices.

Either he sold them or he hid them in the Ministries compound. Having spent two weeks there with him, Rook thought she should have some idea where. She could rule out the penthouse, but nothing else.

Some investigative reporter I turned out to be.

The location of the jewelry was locked inside Kyle's comatose skull.

And I have a key.

Since evicting the twin princesses, Rook had been untroubled by dreams of Kyle, and once she and Fin committed to having Thumper she'd scarcely given him a thought.

Until today.

Today he popped up whenever she contemplated the jewelry. The mental connection she shared with him would allow her to access his knowledge. She just had to be near him. It would be like doing research in a very unusual library.

Rook's stomach knotted.

He was in a coma. He couldn't hurt her. All she had to do was slip into his mind and find the information she needed to buy herself some absolution.

Rook gathered the remainder of her lunch and stuffed it into the garbage can. She went to the sorting room to collect the next cart of books to be shelved.

Her supervisor looked worried. He had been overly solicitous ever since learning of her pregnancy, always trying to talk her into switching to the circulation desk so she could work sitting down.

"Rook, you don't look so good."

"I think my lunch didn't agree with me, Darryl." Today might be a good day to take that job at the desk. Let the public distract her at the same time it annoyed the hell out of her.

"Then I want you to go home," Darryl said.

"What? No, I—"

"I can't be responsible for the health of your baby, Rook. Go home and rest."

What the hell. "Okay. Thanks Darryl."

While walking to her car, Rook contemplated her unexpected afternoon off. Maybe she would drop by Binary Images and surprise Fin. But then what? She couldn't hang out all day. He had work to do.

And so do I.

How would they ever find the jewelry unless she could get the location from Kyle?

Maybe she and Fin could drive to Donner and search the compound. She dreaded the idea of going back there, even knowing that Kyle wouldn't be around. Besides, the place was enormous. The main building was seven or eight stories high, plus the seminary building which she'd never been in, and Fin talked about an entire underground complex. It would take days to cover everything, assuming they could even get in. There were all sorts of electronic locks and alarms.

Rook groaned. It was hopeless.

Except it wasn't. All the security codes were in Kyle's brain. The

layout of the facility, and the location of the stash, too. Everything they needed.

She didn't know where Kyle was, making all of this irrelevant. Rook brightened. Her ignorance, in this case, was bliss. Melissa checked him out of the hospital and left no forwarding address.

Rook's freshly minted smile faltered. Melissa probably moved him in with her at Severin's house. Rook could picture Kyle in one of the ugly green sweaters Rainbow and her friends were so fond of, and knew she was right.

Half an hour later Rook sat behind the wheel of the Nissan, chewing the black polish off her thumbnail, and staring at the hulking three-story house where her reputed father lived with his cult of technology fetishists, her comatose ex-husband, and Fin's wicked stepmother.

Walking into that house would be inviting trouble. *Kyle probably isn't even there.*

He probably was, though. Webster, nexus for strange occurrences, drew all Id-spawn together.

From the spacious porch she read the sign beside the entry: Threshold Electronics Fabrication, Consultation by Appointment. The door hardware was vintage, probably original to the house's construction in a previous century. She picked the lock in thirty seconds.

Rook eased the door open. The cool air inside smelled antiseptic. Not like a hospital, but like a laboratory. Rook stepped through and closed the door, but kept her hand on the brass knob, ready to bolt.

In her skull a low vibration joined in with Fin's signal. Rook's eyebrows drew together as she tried to place it. With a jolt it came to her: Kyle's signal, made almost unrecognizable by the lack of unpleasant emotions. It wasn't proprietary or erotic anymore, nor was it comforting like Fin's. It was just there. A palpable sign Kyle was nearby. Rook would follow it to its source, accomplish her mission, and leave this place.

She crept up the broad, wooden stairs. Kyle's signal strengthened as

she climbed. She paused and listened for movement on the second floor.

Someone was snoring behind one of the closed doors. Staying on tiptoe, Rook hurried around to the next flight of stairs.

Now each step brought a noticeable increase in Kyle's vibration. He was definitely up here.

Is this really such a good idea?

It would be easy. All she had to do was get close enough.

On the third floor a row of closed green doors presented themselves. Rook snuck past them until she reached the correct one. The second-to-last door before the corner.

Rook pressed her ear against it but heard nothing.

Her hand shook as she reached out to turn the knob.

The door swung outward revealing a small, sunny room. Kyle lay on his back in a hospital bed with his torso slightly elevated, his eyes closed. He didn't stir.

Rook's lungs froze and her heart thudded painfully. A thin veil of sweat glazed her body.

Kyle inhaled.

Blinking away tears, Rook eased into the room and closed the door. With her back pressed against it she stood and stared at the man who tried so hard to possess her.

His hair was longer, almost to his shoulders, and darker. On his left arm, the sleeve of his blue cotton pajamas obscured a single IV line. A heart-rate monitor clipped to his finger drew a jagged line on a screen beside the bed. Rook expected all sorts of equipment, and for him to look frail and wasted. Apart from being somewhat paler, though, he looked quite robust.

A white blanket covered him from the waist down, so Rook couldn't tell what sort of shape his knee might be in. She hoped it was bad. He'd earned the gruesome injury when he told Rook Fin was dead, when he tampered with her mind. When he raped her.

For many minutes Rook stood and watched him. Apart from

breathing, Kyle didn't move.

"Kyle," she whispered.

No reaction.

Rook cleared her throat and said, louder, "Kyle."

Nothing.

Reassured, Rook approached the foot of the bed and said his name again. When he still did not respond she swatted one of his feet.

What now?

The information that would allow her to locate the damned jewelry was right there in his head, floating tantalizingly close. She would need to find a way into his thoughts.

Biting back panic, Rook stepped to the head of the bed. She watched Kyle's eyelids for the darting movements that would signify REM sleep. They were utterly still.

The vibration in her head felt quite strong now, but unfocused. Rook couldn't get a handle on it to trace back to its source.

She would have to use his eyes as a doorway like she had with Fin. Once inside she would know everything immediately. No reason for him to hide this knowledge inside his mind. She wouldn't even have to rummage, would leave no trace. Assuming he ever woke up, Kyle would never even know she'd been there.

Rook perched on the edge of the bed and fought to control her breathing. Hyperventilating would not help. She reminded herself he couldn't do anything to her. He was in a coma. With a little sabotage from the inside, she could guarantee he stayed that way.

She leaned forward, her right hand outstretched and poised to open Kyle's eyes.

"One," she muttered.

"Two." Her fingers shook.

"Three."

Rook pried Kyle's eyelids apart and yanked her hand back.

Thumper kicked hard at her bladder.

Rook whimpered.

Kyle's green eyes stared, the pupils constricted to pinpricks.

Rook waved her hand in front of Kyle's face. His eyes didn't track it. She very nearly poked him in the eye and he didn't flinch.

With her eyes closed, Rook turned Kyle's face and repositioned herself. She took three quick breaths and opened her eyes.

And plummeted into the bottomless green.

Chapter Fifteen

THE UPSTAIRS ROOM

REVIEW OF SOCIAL HISTORY
Patient is 10 years old and lives with her mother, older half-brother, younger half-sister, and third step-father. Contact with father ceased at age 3 months. Patient has spent little time in a family unit. She has lived sporadically with her mother, and maternal grandparents, often without siblings. Patient reports infrequent alcohol use. Details — beer and wine. Denies cigarette and drug use. Denies history of physical or sexual abuse.

HISTORY
Patient's mother and teachers report delusional ideation in the form of sisters named Princess Brook and Princess Bramble. Patient displays symptoms of depersonalization disorder (watching herself in the third person, haziness of surroundings and sensations, anxiety, not feeling in control of her speech and actions) comorbid with symptoms of Subjective Doubles Delusion and Clonal Pluralization of the Self (the 'princesses' are aspects of her personality she sees as separate). Patient has begun engaging in self-harm.
        Dr Gerald Wymbol's case notes on Brook Bramble Parker

The instant she felt herself falling into the wasteland of Kyle's ruined mind Rook tried to backpedal and escape. There was nothing to grab onto, nothing to push off from, nothing except onrushing waves of vertigo and buffeting currents of Kyle.

This was a terrible, terrible mistake.

Under ominous, leaden skies a forbidding jungle landscape

stretched out in all directions. Patches of dense metallic fog hung in the stagnant air. Foliage of the deepest, darkest green grew in tangles around glowing shards of emerald glass, the same glass Rook had seen inside her own head.

Around her in the vast emptiness Rook could hear a faint crackling sound, as if the glass splinters were breathing.

The shards were wickedly sharp, and Rook was not dressed for exploration of such a hostile environment.

As she picked her way through the devastated landscape, Rook remembered venturing into Fin's mental desert in order to heal him. Fin's mind had retained a very few elemental building blocks with which she began his healing. Perhaps Kyle had something similar. It might contain the information she needed about the jewelry.

Behind her the clinking crackle intensified. Rook turned as quickly as she dared.

A few yards away a big black bird circled. It wanted her to follow.

The bird waited for Rook to make her careful way through the dense undergrowth and needles of glass. The leaves and vines were the same deep, oily green as her shame crystals. There was no emotion in the plants, just a trace of clinginess. The bright green splinters, on the other hand, were suffused with Kyle's essence. Every time she scratched or poked herself she got a jolt of his cocky self-assurance.

The rook flew in a tight circle and cawed. As Rook approached the indicated spot, it rose higher and soared in a wide arc, keeping a beady black eye on her.

Rook squatted and began to peel away layers of vegetation in search of whatever the bird wanted her to find.

Under several inches of glossy, evil-looking foliage Rook uncovered a human skull encased in a brittle helmet of green glass razors. After staring at the unsettling thing for a while, Rook searched the surrounding area and found seven more skulls, each sheathed in jagged splinters. Each vibrated at an inaudible pitch, something Rook felt in her sternum but could not hear.

They felt familiar.

She could not bring herself to touch them.

Rook stood and massaged the small of her back. This was futile. Nothing here would answer her questions. She should go.

With growing horror, she discovered she didn't know how.

Would she be stuck forever in this treacherous hellscape?

A rustle of feathers swooped in from above and blotted out everything.

*** *** ***

Severin took his time tucking in his shirt, surreptitiously monitoring the baleful expression on Melissa's face. Her fuming amused him. They'd just copulated, and it was a tie. This pleased Severin well enough, but Melissa was more competitive.

Once presentable, Severin went down the steps. Something drew him, a mystical vibration like the scent of blackberries and cinnamon.

It was in Melissa's son's room. Severin licked his lips and turned the knob.

On the bed lay the invalid. Beside him, with her back to Severin, sat a young woman in a flimsy purple dress and tall white boots. His daughter, Rook. Severin eased into the room and closed the door. With her potential escape route covered, he called softly, "I am happy to see you again."

The girl didn't stir. Severin stepped closer, until he could touch her black hair. He stroked it, and she remained still. He moved around to face her, and saw her commanding blue eyes locked onto the comatose boy's unseeing green.

Severin stroked her hair again. He traced her jawline and her delicate throat with his index finger. His hand trailed down onto the slippery fabric of the dress, tracing her cleavage. He leaned close, resting his stump on her bare thigh for balance. His hand slid lower, over her abdomen.

He stopped. A distinct bulge in her belly was apparent to his touch, although the drape of her garment concealed it from view.

Damn! Always too late!

Severin stepped back from the bed, snarling. His breath seethed through his bared teeth. His hand closed into a fist.

No. Not this time. He wouldn't wait his turn. It wasn't fair.

Severin stormed out of the room, slamming the door and executing a u-turn to go back to the attic.

Melissa huffed at his abrupt return, but didn't look up from her magazine.

Severin approached his table. It felt potent, invigorated by his daughter's proximity. Feeling this wave of power, Severin knew Rook would be of much greater utility in regenerating his left hand.

He raised a corner of the sheet with his stump and reached in with his hand, immediately finding a few small objects. Dice, three of them. Closer examination showed they didn't have the traditional spots, but letters. One had only Xs, while the other two bore both Xs and Ys. Turning them over in his palm and contemplating the possible combinations, Severin pondered the identity of the man responsible for Rook's gravid state. Was he the one laying in the bed? Did that account for her visit to the House? The presence of a third die held salacious implications.

Ultimately it didn't matter. Her womb must be readied to accept his seed. Waiting for nature, settling for second-hand power, proved unsatisfactory with Willow. Severin learned from that miscalculation, and this time he had a clever and elegant solution.

He cupped his hand and rattled the dice, then cast them under the sheet, transferring the inconvenient child to the Elsewhere.

As he let the sheet fall back into place a wave of spatial distortion rolled out from the table, warping the floor like the surface of a pond. Severin felt himself carried up one side and down the other. The wave reached the hammock, prompting a yelp from Melissa. The hammock swayed in the wake of the surge, probably due to the way Melissa tensed and kicked her legs in the air. Severin laughed, a booming thing altogether unfamiliar to his own ears.

He couldn't remember when he'd been so alive, and he had only greater fulfillment to look forward to with Rook.

*** *** ***

Kyle is dispersed, flecks spread throughout the drowsy world of the bubbles of light. He has no center. The bubbles swirl and drift and he mingles with them.

One thing in this strange realm draws him, and he deposits there in a thin layer.

Rook. He is with her, a little. Enshrouding her.

The bubbles know it's not really Rook. They know because they brought the dark sisters here in chains, bartered for them. They try to remind Kyle of the facts.

But Kyle only wants Rook, so it's Rook who wears him like a second skin.

It's Rook.

A word resounds through the bubbles, and they swarm and cavort. Kyle is caught in their giddy currents and jostled into joining their dance, although he tries to focus inward, to dwell on Rook.

Chimera! Chimera!

The word passes through schools of bubbles.

Chimera!

The word grows, and echoes, and twists. It races to the highest and lowest extents of this place, and everywhere its touch brings a glittering radiance.

Chimera! Chimera!

The word means nothing to Kyle. He wants only Rook, but the bubbles give him knowledge.

The chimera child, twins in one body. Here, like the dark sisters, but so much better.

Kyle understands that they mean Rook's baby. His baby.

The bubbles' exultant bacchanal froths around and through Kyle. They tell him the good news again and again, whenever one of his particles contacts a bubble of light.

He can't make them stop.

*** *** ***

The bird transported Rook to her own mind. Once both feet were firmly on the ground, she looked around. Tall evergreens surrounded the small clearing.

A foul wind kicked up and swept through her forest. The twilight sky disappeared behind a sudden flood of screaming black birds as all the rooks took flight from their roosts. Laughter more unhinged than any Rook ever heard resounded and surrounded her. With a frightening surge that electrified every muscle, she knew Severin had found her.

Her real body was vulnerable and she had no idea what her father might do.

The triumphant laughter slithered over her, fondling and molesting, before folding in on itself and leaving behind a terrifying stillness.

Tears stung Rook's eyes. She had no recollection of how she'd exited before, only the certainty she wouldn't be free to leave until her job was done.

"Fuck. I've got no choice, do I? I have to Complete him."

Rook blinked burning tears from her eyes, and swallowed hard. Far away in the sky above her she could see her namesake birds circling. She tried to tell them it was alright, the danger passed, but they did not heed her. This defiance enraged Rook. She was the boss in this place.

The queen.

After so many years of sharing her personality, emotions, memories, mind, her *self*; after so much time suppressing the undesirable parts; after all that time hiding and protecting herself from herself, Rook was unused to being solely responsible for her thoughts and feelings. With wonder she realized there was no authority but Rook.

Gathering a sense of self-assurance she never before possessed, Rook yelled up at the soaring, panicked birds, "Enough!"

One by one, then in small flocks, the rooks dipped down and settled in the dark pines. Soon hundreds of shiny black eyes were trained on her.

Even without Brook and Bramble to influence her, knowing she would finally Complete Kyle felt right. She would fulfill her destined role and be off the cosmic hook.

To the closest rook she said, "Take me to the shame tower." *Kyle could use a good, strong dose of shame.* "The rest of you gather whatever's left of Brook and Bramble's prisons."

The other birds flew away. Rook followed her guide through the trees to another clearing. In the center lay a small ring of glossy, deep green crystals, merely the foundation of the tower that had been.

The tower of shame was gone. While that was good news from a mental health perspective, it left her with little building material. The rest of the birds returned bearing meager shards of Brook's crystal coffin and thorny tendrils from Bramble's thicket.

"Fuck." The birds gave no response. Rook sighed. "Quoth the raven, 'Don't look at me, lady. This was your brilliant idea.'"

Rook had no time to dwell on her disappointment.

"Right then. Bring all of this, and take me to my core tower."

Through the lonely, empty silence the birds led her to her tall, brick tower. The scab of shame crystals around the fractured opening had finished its transmutation into a dull, gray metal scar. The improvised doorway was only half its original size.

Rook gripped the edge of the cold metal and yanked. Nothing moved. She tried jerking it, hoping to force a chunk out of place. When that failed, she aimed a kick at a lower chunk, but again had no success.

The scar tissue was too resilient.

On the ground inside the tower Rook found the baseball bat she used to batter the half-closed archway. When she picked it up, an unwelcome knowledge crept through her.

She had to make another opening.

Gritting her teeth, she stalked through the empty skeleton chamber to the wall opposite the half-healed doorway, and swung the bat with all her strength. The bricks shifted under her barrage and some mortar crumbled out.

Grimly and efficiently, Rook pummeled the wall. Each blow kicked off sparks, showing flashbulb impressions of her life. Some were fragmentary memories, some like scenes from a movie. A buzzing ache built with each thud of the bat. The stroboscopic slideshow was laced with discordant emotions, now aloof and bemused, now lonely and frightened. Seeing, feeling, a succession of abandonments filled her with hopelessness.

Rook faltered, longing to drop the bat and fall down beside it.

She thought of Severin finding her in his house, of what he might do to her.

One last swing, and a brick fell.

Seeing this first indication of progress, this proof it wasn't hopeless, pulled her out of her despair. Rook assaulted the wall with renewed spirit. The task still dredged up uncomfortable memories and feelings, but gradually more bricks came free until a narrow hole opened from shoulder height to the ground.

"That better fucking be enough."

She ordered the birds to transport all the rubble to Kyle's mind. If she worked fast, she wouldn't have time to be afraid.

*** *** ***

Melissa twisted her neck to see what Severin was up to. He'd gone to his precious table to screw around, then the top almost came off the building, and now he stood there braying like a psychotic donkey.

Melissa was punch-drunk from the aftereffects of whatever he did, quivering with unnameable panic and rage.

"What in hell do you think you're doing?" she demanded in a constricted voice. Severin's laughter reached the foot of whatever perverted defile it was tumbling down, but the way his eyes wandered the dusty recesses of the attic suggested he hadn't heard her question.

"Uncle," she barked, and he darted a dismissive glance at her. Melissa drew a sharp breath, feeling her nostrils flare. Severin grinned savagely, and she felt hot color flush her face and neck. She stood, meaning to shoo him out, but her nudity robbed her of any authority.

Severin appraised her, his dementia receding until it was only an exaggerated species of smugness. It seemed to Melissa she had his attention at last.

"What's going on here?"

"Here? Nothing," Severin said. "The interesting news is directly beneath our feet." This cryptic statement contained a hilarity Melissa couldn't grasp but Severin could barely hang onto. His shoulders bounced with stifled laughter. "She's right downstairs. I could have tracked her down, but now it's unnecessary."

"Who?" Melissa tried to sound impatient rather than alarmed. "Who is downstairs?"

Severin had to chuckle for a moment before he could respond. "My daughter."

Melissa's innards froze solid. *He has a daughter?*

"I'm quite pleased to see how she's turned out. It's very pleasing indeed. We have so much to catch up on. I look forward to... bonding."

Melissa's knees wobbled as the import of this announcement resonated with the residue of the malaise induced by Severin's mischief with the table. The sympathetic vibrations stacked up inside her skull, and she knew his table stunt was connected with this female.

Her heart raced and tears boiled. To be thrown over for another woman — again — was intolerable. She looked at Severin through narrowed eyes, but he wistfully surveyed his drafty little kingdom as he headed for the stairs.

He was on his way to her. Right now.

He passed Melissa without sparing a glance.

Melissa took a step after him, intent on pushing him as he stepped off the top tread.

In the next instant she rejected that plan as too unreliable. She needed something final, the most potent weapon imaginable.

And it was here in the attic.

"Uncle," she purred, and he hesitated with his hand on the railing. "I felt something when you used your table a minute ago. It caught me

off guard, but it was an impressive demonstration."

Severin quirked one eyebrow at her.

"It felt... Well, I can't describe it. But it made me excited." She backed up a step, in the direction of the table. "Very excited. I'd like you to give me a lesson. Right now."

Severin sneered. "You're pathetic. Am I meant to be flattered by your phony arousal, or irresistibly drawn to your bony nakedness? My prize downstairs is far more beguiling than you ever were."

Melissa trembled with rage. She passed it off plausibly, she thought, as a shiver of desire. "I don't care what hateful things you say to me," she simpered. "And I don't care where you go after. I just know I need my lesson."

She considered pouting, but feared it would be too much. The resulting indecision apparently came across as something her uncle enjoyed seeing on her face.

"That is in fact an excellent idea," he said. "I'll give you your final lesson. I will consume what little remains of you, and you will cease to be. But," he paused to chuckle and unsnap his fly, "I'll make sure you enjoy it."

Melissa nodded and slunk backwards, holding him with her eyes. She slithered onto the table and rolled herself up in the sheet.

This was a ploy Melissa contemplated hundreds of times, but she'd conceived of it as a means of suicide. Fucking underneath the sheet, agitating the mysterious powers with the heat of their bodies until she was taken away, or incinerated.

Her sex tingled.

Severin shed his clothes and joined her under the sheet.

Immediately, they were copulating in direct contact with the surface of the table. Melissa felt the tide going out, her uncle draining her. She could let go, let him take it all and see what happened. She could...

No! She couldn't. She couldn't let the bastard win.

Melissa reoriented herself with the stump inside her. Severin increased his pull, demanding power from her. With effort she

maintained her equilibrium.

The table responded to their passion. Melissa felt ecstatic tension building all around them, swelling toward release. Her own pleasure was a torrent sweeping her along. The sheet caressed and enfolded their flesh. The table, both lovenest and lover, rounded out their trio.

Severin too seemed overwhelmed, but strove to assert dominance over Melissa. He devoted all of his attention to conquering her, ignoring the table and how their gyrations charged it up. His voraciousness held the allure of oblivion, but Melissa refused to surrender.

The tidal wave building in the table couldn't remain stable much longer. Melissa channeled her tantric vibrations toward it, favoring both of her lovers. Controlling Severin through his hunger, and the table through her pleasure.

She knew, but didn't care, that if she missed the wave by the barest margin she would be destroyed.

Melissa let go, dumping all of her power into Severin, giving him everything. He took it, gorging himself and draining her to the verge of annihilation.

His thrusting, truncated limb erupted in a white-hot surge, a sudden writhing fullness in her loins.

Severin howled in triumph and gave a wriggling tug. As he replaced his arm with his penis, he displayed his reformed left hand to Melissa's dazzled eyes for a moment before shoving the new thumb into her mouth.

The tidal wave crested and crashed at the same instant, and she drank the whole surge. It refilled her as Severin sucked away her life. It flowed in a million times faster than what he took out. It was not only more energy, it was different. Better, lighter, sweeter.

She was a goddess in a reeling universe of erotic bliss.

Severin, his power at an all-time high, glowed feebly between her legs. He hardly mattered.

In the eternity of a heartbeat, Melissa passed from the glory of orgasm into afterglow, and began to regain some sense of proportion.

The power from the table washed through her, leaking back to its source. It couldn't be grasped and held. She considered Severin again, drunk with her essence. That stolen power would remain with him for hours or days, not fade in moments like what she'd imbibed. In another few seconds, they might be evenly matched.

Melissa reclaimed her own energies. Then, casually, almost thoughtlessly, she consumed Severin and his energy, too.

His body, regenerated hand and all, transmuted into swirling green fuel for her furnace.

There were no remains.

The last of the sweet, ecstatic glow from the table ebbed back to its source, but Melissa didn't mind. She owned her uncle's power now. It was power she looked forward to employing.

She donned her sweater and went looking for this interfering minx he'd claimed was his 'daughter.'

Chapter Sixteen

GREEN GLASS PYRAMID

This letter is to inform whomever it concerns of my resignation, effective immediately. My departure has been prompted by the general deterioration of morale here, as well as getting a better deal elsewhere. I am taking copies of all my own work, plus related data, but unlike some people I'm not stealing the originals or any equipment. I guess I want credit for not being sleazy.
Cordially, Aaron Hapner (formerly 'Acorn')
TEF internal communication

Back in Kyle's head, Rook finally understood her connection to the Divided Man. Both halves had incorporated some part of her essence into themselves. She had helped Fin willingly, providing blocks to rebuild him, enmeshing herself with him eternally. That was why she could always sense him, why their casual fling turned so quickly into a lifelong bond. She'd brought some of Fin's volcanic ash into herself as well. They truly were a part of each other.

The same could be said of her and Kyle, she now knew. That their connection was not her choice made it no less real. These awful skulls were hers, forgotten remnants of discarded Brooks and Rooks and Brambles. The hum they emitted was her own. It excited the vibrant green splinters like a magnet would iron filings. Kyle invaded her mind and stole them, brought her secret pasts into himself, cementing their connection. The glass shards in her mind were his parting gift, a connection she had been ignorant of and could not break. Now she was going to add even more of herself to him, to rebuild him like she rebuilt Fin.

Would that strengthen her ties to her enemy?

Their original connection was unpleasant. It was based on thievery and something akin to rape. This time she would be helping him, if not voluntarily, at least on purpose. Would that change the nature of her feelings? By healing Kyle would she feel for him the way she did for Fin?

The thought nearly paralyzed her.

But there was another possibility. She had liked Fin quite a lot when she went into his head, and she'd come out the other side with her feelings magnified. She already hated Kyle. Where would things go from there?

The skulls were arranged in a rough square, so the structure she built from them would be, too. The thought of touching them…

Being here inside his mind was terribly intimate. It brought back awful memories. Rook worried about the influence they would have on his reshaped psyche. As she added remnants of Bramble and Brook she wove in the knowledge that it was these parts, not the true Rook, who responded to Kyle, so he would not be deluded into thinking she cared for him.

When adding bricks from her tower she cemented them in place with an understanding of the bond she and Fin shared so he would not want to break it again.

As she laid all the various parts of herself into place, Rook concentrated on building a better, gentler, less evil Kyle. It was exhausting.

Rook didn't want to waste time scavenging more bricks, so she made the second row smaller than the first. She hoped it wasn't cheating.

How long will it take for him to take over the healing?

When she started the third row, inset to mimic the sloping walls of a pyramid, the blocks began snapping into place as she moved them near.

Dull flickers of lightning blossomed on the horizon, and the air filled with the smell of ozone and black licorice.

The blocks fitted into place greedily. The lightning spread across the

entire sky in a blanketing web. Brilliant green shards of glass flew out of the black vegetation and with sickening crunching and crashing sounds added themselves to what was now clearly a pyramid.

Rook was terrified of being slashed or impaled. She worked in a frenzy as the glittering knives flew around her. Not a single one touched her.

Kyle's pyramid took shape quickly. The skulls anchored it. The slanted walls were a motley mixture of emerald glass, deep green shame crystals, prismatic shards of Brook's coffin, and Rook's red core bricks, all entwined with creeping thorny vines from Bramble's thicket.

The vines grew and encircled the walls, blossoming in strange luminous flowers as the lightning scrawled warnings across the sky.

The last few bricks from Rook's core tower lifted off the ground and flew toward the apex of the pyramid amidst a hail of green razors. Rook stifled a shriek and cowered in a low square doorway at the base.

Millions of glass splinters rose from the dense underbrush and sped toward the pyramid.

Rook shrank further into the recess. Behind her she could sense a large open area. As much as she didn't want to enter Kyle's core structure, she wanted to escape the serrated chaos outside more.

In here the walls were smooth plaster, the floor carpeted in astroturf. Stadium benches were arrayed like church pews, facing a pulpit with a huge bible and a TV. Wall niches held trophies and guns.

The pulpit drew Rook's attention. It had a different feel from the rest of the collection.

As she approached, Rook realized it embodied the knowledge Kyle stole from Reverend Shaw. It was what allowed him to take over Shaw Ministries.

All this junk represented information.

Somewhere in here was what she came looking for: the location of the jewelry and knowledge of the security measures guarding it.

Rook stood behind the pulpit and examined the bible. White leather, with gold accents. The last thing she had any interest in was

reading from Kyle's enormous tacky bible, but it felt like the place to look for what she sought.

Rook flipped open the front cover to find a rumpled diagram pasted to the inside. Passing her fingers over it, she knew it was not about the jewelry. But she was getting close. She perused the massive tome, turning the pages faster as her impatience grew. Halfway through she discovered something meaningful.

Of course Kyle's bible has a centerfold.

The image was animated, like a banner ad for a porn site. The page felt charged, as if it wanted to tell her something, but all she saw was a naked bimbo, a version of herself with a fake tan and fake boobs.

Disgusted, she folded the page closed. The spark of meaning crackled when her gaze fell on Miss Deuteronomy's turn-ons and turn-offs. One of the things that really got her going was all that body jewelry hidden away in the subterranean vault at the Shaw Ministries compound, and she got a major thrill just thinking about the tunnel system, with its concealed entrances and miles of buried passageways. But hottest of all were the secret access codes.

Rook sighed with relief. She had what she came in here for. A rash undertaking, but worth it. She and Fin would go to Donner, easily locate the cache of jewelry with its nefarious electronics, and destroy every last piece. By wiping it out she would make amends for her unwitting collusion in distributing it.

Around her, tendrils of green electricity crawled over every surface, sizzling like static, causing the fine hairs on her arms to stand up. Her blood felt alive, her heart pumping a warm glow that suffused her with pride and satisfaction.

The Completer's task was fulfilled.

The Divided Man was Complete, both halves healed through her actions. Rook enjoyed the feeling for a fleeting moment, but then realized she did her job too well.

Kyle was waking up.

The exit from Kyle's pyramid would serve as her exit from his mind

as well.

Rook took one last look at Kyle's secret knowledge, committing it to memory. She walked through the doorway.

A brief tug of vertigo and she was sitting on the edge of the bed, staring down at Kyle. His eyelids twitched.

Rook stood, smiling. She knew what she and Fin needed to find the jewelry and destroy it.

Her smile faded. Something was wrong. Horribly wrong.

Her baby was gone.

Rook clutched her abdomen. Flat.

Empty.

Thumper was gone. Severin had done something unspeakable.

There was a horrible silence in her mind. Alongside Fin's and Kyle's vibrations was an empty spot where the baby's signal should have been. She had never been conscious of it, but now the silence was deafening.

Kyle sat up.

*** *** ***

At last! The months of effort to reprogram Rook paid off!

This moment thrust the prophecy nearer than ever to fulfillment, the Collective Id nearer than ever to awakening.

Kyle Tanner was healed, the Divided Man twice Completed.

The awestruck spiders watched to see what he would do first.

*** *** ***

Melissa glided down the narrow attic steps. The enormous influx of power from the Elsewhere faded away to nothing, but what she'd taken from Severin was still with her. She felt bright and hard as emerald, more in command of her world than ever before.

She went to Kyle's room.

The blue-eyed creature standing beside Kyle's bed stared back at her in blind panic as Melissa opened the door. Severin's offspring. Melissa felt a wicked grin begin to take shape, until she saw movement behind the girl.

Kyle lifted a hand to rub his eyes, sitting up in bed. He gave his IV a

disapproving look.

Melissa's grin stretched into a savage grimace and she swept into the room, screaming.

"This is ALL your fault! I killed Severin because he wouldn't shut up about you. The fucking bastard is gone! Gone! GONE!" Melissa advanced on the cowering raven-haired female. Kyle blinked. How would she keep him near, now that he'd awoken? "You won't take my son! YOU WON'T!"

Melissa's arm moved so swiftly even she didn't see it, a backhand blow sending the interloper crashing against the wall. The wicked grin invited itself back to Melissa's face as she pivoted to keep her prey in her sights. The young woman's arctic eyes — her father's eyes — remained riveted to Melissa as her limbs scrabbled uselessly at the wall and floor. Melissa raised her arm and extended her index finger accusingly, feeling her rage coalesce into a weapon.

The room turned a vivid, swirling green and the girl on the floor shrieked. Melissa saw the flames flowing over her own arm. She was bathed in green fire, and though she could feel its heat she wasn't burned.

Melissa threw back her head to laugh, but it never came. Pain encircled her throat, blocking her air. She staggered as the constriction increased, yanking her off balance. Blood roared in her ears and throbbed in her neck and face.

Her vision dimmed, but she saw a hand as it wound another pass of tubing around her neck. She pitched backwards against her attacker. Against Kyle.

The green fire vanished. *Mustn't burn Kyle.* Melissa's world grew darker. Crushing agony filled her chest. The tubing, stretched thin, dug into her flesh. Each throb in her head pushed everything else farther away, blurring and softening the sensations.

Need to tell Kyle it's okay to be out of bed.

The world backs away slowly, quietly.

Need to tell Kyle.

Pain fades, and time softens.
Need.
Kyle.

*** *** ***

Kyle Tanner looked down at Rook, cowering on the floor with her eyes clamped shut. In his head her signal was stronger than ever, a terrified whine. He let his arms droop, but kept a grip on the tubing wound around his mother's neck. She slumped to her knees in a puddle of urine.

"Run," he said, his voice hoarse and dry. Rook's eyes opened and met Kyle's. She glanced to Melissa's face, and the fear in those eyes was alloyed with shock. She didn't move.

"Run!"

Rook shrieked and jumped to her feet. She darted from the room, and Kyle heard her on the stairs. She took days to reach the bottom. Her mental hum faded along with her footsteps, but didn't disappear.

He relaxed his fingers, and the body at his feet tipped sideways with a thud as the plastic tubing slithered out of his hands. It remained embedded in the throat. There was no blood. The color of the face was dark and blotchy, and the eyes and tongue bulged from their accustomed homes.

Kyle walked to the door and used the shirttail of his blue pajamas to polish the knobs on both sides. He looked at the numerous doors ringing the central stairs, and leaned over the railing to see how far down they went. The view confirmed his impression from listening to Rook's flight. There were a lot of damn steps.

Getting clear of this place had a lot to recommend it, but he couldn't work up any interest in heading down all those stairs. He opened the door beside his room, already knowing it would lead him even higher.

The same place in his head telling him he wanted to go up, not down, also knew things about Rook. About her chimera baby. Replaying her panicked retreat, Kyle contemplated her shape and concluded she wasn't pregnant anymore. The bubbles were on the level.

They had her baby now.

Reaching the attic, Kyle homed in on the sheet-covered object on the far side of the cluttered space. He felt its pull like a physical force, knew that it was a gateway back to the bubbles of light.

Kyle raised a corner of the sheet and reached under. At first his fingers groped about on the blank surface of the table, but soon he reached through and into the other place. Eyes closed, he held in his mind the image of his goal. He searched patiently for several minutes, until he felt smooth, warm skin.

Gently, Kyle took hold of the hand and pulled its owner back into the world. In a few seconds she lay naked on the table, partially covered by the sheet. The silver chain that bound her to herself was gone, its purpose served. A faint green line winding around her torso was the only reminder of its former presence. She sat up, her movements fluid and sensuous. Her shimmering black hair spilled over her shoulder and outlined her right breast. Her fiery blue eyes raced over him.

She pulled Kyle into a desperate kiss. He returned the passion, their tongues entwining. She ran her hands over his back, and under the waistband of his pajama pants, slipping them down. She perched herself at the edge of the table, knees parted eagerly, and Kyle entered her.

As they crashed against one another, Kyle compared her to his memory, searching for flaws, imperfections, tell-tale signs she was not who she seemed. When he first tried to possess her he'd made the mistake of changing her hair and her clothing, as if by doing so he could tame her. This time would be different. She was physical perfection and absolute lust. Her mental purr filled his head, drowning out every trace of the other. She was as he'd always wanted her to be. His Rook.

"I am," she panted, eyes lidded, "I'm, I'm Brook. I am Bramble..." Her chant followed the rhythm of their coupling. "I am... Brandy... Moon... I am..."

"Shhh," Kyle said. "You are Rook."

Her eyes opened. Kyle nodded and kissed her again.

She whispered, "I am Rook. I am Rook. I am Rook." The mantra

grew from a whisper to a throaty murmur. "I am Rook..." Her voice descended to a growling moan of delight, and her legs wound around Kyle's waist.

Kyle kissed her breasts and her neck, inhaled her spicy smell, tasted her silky perfection. All traces of the chain's green echo faded away, leaving her marked only by her stark black body art. They clasped hands, interlocking fingers as her movements gained forcefulness. Kyle kissed her fingers, first on her right hand then the left. Her urgency kept building, and Kyle matched her pace as he studied the intricate tattoo on her ring finger.

Rook's wedding ring, signifying her bond with his brother.

Without breaking stride, Kyle guided her hand under the sheet. He caressed her palm with his thumb. Thrusting harder, he gripped her ring finger. He held it between his own thumb and forefinger as she bucked against him. Her back arched, he pulled, and her finger parted from her hand.

He let it go.

As her orgasm crested, Kyle saw double, two Rooks overlapping. Their cries of pleasure harmonized eerily.

Rook's faces showed pain, then she became a single being once more. She smiled, and Kyle came.

He kissed her, lifting her from the table to set her down a few feet away. He stroked her hair. She was still smiling, and breathtakingly nude.

"Here." Kyle took off his shirt. "Wear this." He put his pants back on, and began searching the room.

"What are you doing?" Rook asked, but he didn't answer. She would see in a minute.

A makeshift shelf in the exposed framework held some lumpy old candles and a lighter. Kyle took them to the table. He balled up the sheet and tucked the candles in among its folds before lighting them. He applied the lighter to the fabric in several places as well.

The candles melted and ran, the wax soaking into the sheet which

became an enormous wick. The fire grew rapidly.

Rook leaned against him. Kyle held her hand and looked at it while she admired the leaping flames. Her ring finger was absent, leaving a perfect gap between middle and pinky, with perfect unscarred skin.

"We have to go," Kyle told her, and they walked down the steps. By the time he shut the attic door, Kyle could hear the fire roaring.

*** *** ***

Mid-afternoon, the mental connection Fin shared with Rook went haywire. He tried phoning, but got no answer. Now he was hurrying to her, her anguished signal a homing beacon.

Rounding the corner he spotted the Nissan in the carport, parked crooked. She was here. But what was wrong with her?

He wiped tears from his cheeks. The tall narrow windows of their house looked like funhouse mirrors, distorting the sky, the trees, and Fin's own image as he staggered up the walk and across the small courtyard to the front door.

Fin heard Rook's sobs the moment he turned the knob, felt her despair through their shared connection. She huddled on the sofa, her face buried in her hands. Fin got down on his knees, putting his arms around his wife. She clutched at his shirt and pulled herself against his chest, wailing. Fin embraced her and rocked back and forth.

Thumper was gone. He knew it from the sound of Rook's anguish, by the change in her body quaking in his arms.

It could be wrong, somehow. Somehow! The more clear the fact became, the stronger his rejection. He didn't know how Thumper could be okay, but he needed there to be some chance all of this was wrong. Wrong.

Fin wept, holding Rook as she wept.

It was true.

Wailing gave way to sobbing. Exhaustion quieted their grief, but did not diminish it.

Rook drew two deep, shuddering breaths and gave a keening cry. Fin squeezed her closer, and she repeated it. She was trying to speak.

"Shh," he said, but she shook her head and sat up.

"I did something really stupid," she said in a high, quavering voice. The right side of her face was swollen and pink. "Please forgive me," she pleaded.

Fin blinked tears away, nodding. Her words and the vicious slap mark twisted his insides. What had she done? The images that tried to fit the nauseating question were abhorrent, he shoved them away.

"I was trying to help," she began.

In a fragmentary recounting she told him what happened to her at her father's house.

Fin pressed a cool washcloth to her cheek. He'd never liked Melissa, but never suspected her capable of such violence.

"We can't make Severin undo it. She killed him. We can't make him give Thumper back." She broke down in sobs again.

*** *** ***

Even though it was a beautiful spring day, it wasn't nice enough to be shirtless. Kyle shivered and turned up the heat in the minivan he'd stolen from the TEF garage.

In the passenger seat Rook alternately watched him, fiddled with the radio, and stared out the window. She looked sexy as hell in his pajama shirt, the blue accentuating her eyes, and the hem riding up to reveal she wore nothing underneath.

Kyle turned on the heated seats.

When they exited the highway and turned onto Ministry Road, Rook said, "Let's fuck in the cathedral, right where you married me."

A throb of want coursed through Kyle. "Absolutely."

Five minutes later they reached the compound's gate.

Brown bouquets of desiccated flowers, waterlogged bibles, candle stubs, stuffed animals, deflated mylar balloons, and half-rotted tribute posters and cards lay in drifts against the closed barrier and empty gatehouse.

Kyle snorted. What a ridiculous way to be memorialized. Nothing had been placed recently either, so not only did his fans have

questionable taste, they also had short memories.

The security keypad was on the side of the gatehouse. Kyle put his window down and typed his code. The wrought iron gate swung inward, causing a small avalanche of tchotchkes which Kyle happily drove over.

He stopped and watched in the rearview mirror to make sure the gate would close again. It did, scraping most of the dilapidated tributes back into place. On the off chance anyone came around to check on things, Kyle got out to straighten up. Rook came with him.

As Kyle shoved a mildewed bible back between the bars, Rook tossed a dead bouquet tied with a black ribbon over her shoulder into the woods, laughing. Her laughter stopped as quickly as it started, and she looked bored. She scooped up a formerly white teddy bear with a golden tinsel halo and got back into the van. With his bare feet, Kyle scooted a few things under the gate, then joined her.

His right knee ached.

The two-lane asphalt drive wound through the trees toward the enormous glass cathedral. The closer he got, the more disappointed Kyle became. The grounds had not been tended in months. Ratty weeds abounded, and dead branches lay where they fell. He had planned to oversee the demise of the Ministries and run it into the ground, toasting marshmallows with Rook over the flaming wreckage.

Rounding the last bend, the road emerged from the forest. The neglect was more apparent here: overgrown lawns, litter, flowerbeds full of dead stalks, drifts of last fall's leaves, and, most important, the cathedral.

The last time Kyle saw it, it was intact and gleaming in the sunlight, almost too bright to look at.

More specifically, the last time he saw it from the outside.

Kyle recalled the spire-shattering battle fought there with his brother over their wife. Nothing he remembered, though, accounted for the cathedral's utter destruction.

Sure, he and Fin broke a couple of windows and maybe started a few

fires, but there was nothing left at all. Someone razed the place, leaving only a gaping hole full of twisted iron and golden glass, ringed with yellow hazard tape.

"Kyle," Rook purred, "let's go home."

Kyle tore his eyes away from the cold ruins of his empire and looked at his lover. Her attention was on the beige stone and blue glass Ministries headquarters, the remaining fingers of her left hand pressed against the van's window.

Apart from being dark, the building looked untouched. Kyle saw no reason they couldn't go up to the penthouse and celebrate their wedding night all over again.

He smiled and put the van in gear.

***   ***   ***

At the sink in Fin's kitchen, Willow kept glancing over to the living room at the kids, trying not to get caught at it, while Brad kept glancing at her and trying not to get caught at it. Brad chopped the carrots slowly, but Willow had no urge to hurry him. His attention wasn't on the knife.

Rook and Fin huddled together on the sofa. Their new house, purchased to start their family in, loomed empty around them.

"Don't stare," Brad said. Willow added some freshly rinsed celery to his cutting board to keep him busy.

Brad chopped the celery slowly. Willow gathered the carrot pieces, picking up each one individually.

"I guess I'm happy about one thing, at least," Brad said, frowning.

"Kyle?"

Brad nodded, still frowning, then his head wobbled side to side. "I mean about him waking up, sure. That's good news." He stopped chopping and took a few slow breaths. Willow laid her hand on his shoulder.

"But, Melissa..." she said softly.

Brad nodded without wobbling. "I mean, not her, per se. What happened. What he did."

Willow nodded. "He was protecting Rook."

Brad kept nodding, torment showing on his face. He grimly resumed chopping. The noise helped cover the sobs filtering in from the living room.

"I guess Severin went soft in the twelve years he had you trapped." He chopped another stalk. "Fitting that one of his intended victims was his undoing."

"I wish it could have been me," Willow said.

"No." Brad set the knife aside. "I wish he'd never taken you away, or I'd found you sooner, but you don't want his blood on your hands."

"He was utterly evil," Willow declared. "I hate that he had control over me. I hate that I never got to confront him." *I hate that I let this happen.*

Brad wrapped his arms around her. "It's better to just be rid of someone like that. We should be grateful, however it came about. You don't have to prove anything."

Willow returned the embrace, and whispered, "I know, I know." She relaxed her arms, but Brad wasn't ready to let go.

He squeezed her and said, "You're going to do it, aren't you? You're going to use Severin's table."

Whatever Severin did with the baby, Willow knew it had to be related to the suspended animation he'd inflicted on her. Which meant Thumper was floating safely with the bubbles of light. All she had to do was break into Threshold House and use that table to get Thumper back.

"I have to try."

"I know." Brad sighed, still holding her. "I know you have to try, but Wil, it's dangerous."

Willow hugged him. "This is all Severin's doing. He stashed me and Zen there until you saved us, and now he's stashed Thumper there. I have to try to rescue our grandchild. I promise I will be as careful as I can be, but I have to try."

"I wish I could do it instead."

The remainder of the cooking didn't take long. Brad withdrew again into his own darkness.

They set the plates on the kitchen table before calling for Rook and Fin. The meal proceeded in gloomy silence.

Rook pushed the food around on her plate. Fin took an occasional bite, too preoccupied with Rook's sorrow to make much progress toward feeding himself. Willow watched them, aching to make it better, and forgetting to eat. Brad was quiet, lost in thought, as he polished off his second helping.

"Severin's table," Willow blurted. "I can use it, a little. I know enough to have a good idea what he did with the baby and how I could use the table to bring it back."

Rook set down her fork and beamed at Fin. His glance flicked between Rook and Willow before locking onto Willow's eyes and demanding to know that she was sure. She tried to throw him a confident look but only managed the tiniest, grimaced smile. He nodded slowly. Gradually his own smile grew to match Rook's.

Rook jumped up and flung her arms around Willow's neck, tears flowing down her cheeks.

*** *** ***

"This day could not suck more," said Marsh, hoping he was right.

Rainbow massaged his shoulders. "Sure, it could. The whole House could have burned." She climbed up to sit on the back of the sofa where his shoulders were easier to reach. She resumed kneading.

The two of them were alone in the media room with the TV muted. The police were upstairs talking to the loyal few who remained with the TEF after the mass defections of the past months.

"How could Severin do this?" asked Marsh.

It was a question they'd been over many times since the discovery of Melissa's body.

After breakfast, Rainbow and Marsh spent the day in the garage workshop, tweaking the neural net modulator. The other six TEF members were there too. At 5:00, Wind went into the House to change

Kyle's IV and take a reading of his vitals.

That's when everything went to hell.

Melissa lay dead on the floor. Long dead. Cold. No reviving her, even with the advanced equipment at the TEF's disposal. She'd been strangled with Kyle's IV cord, and Kyle was gone.

While waiting for the police, Marsh and Rainbow went to the attic to tell Severin his girlfriend was dead. Perhaps unsurprisingly, Severin wasn't there. Just evidence of his inept attempt at arson.

"I can't wrap my head around the attic," Rainbow said. "I always assumed it was finished space, that Severin had some sort of disgustingly tacky love den, all faux fur and waterbeds and lava lamps."

"Nope." Marsh shook his head in wonder. "Just a dusty, drafty attic full of boxes."

Rainbow shuddered.

"You okay, sweetie?" Marsh asked.

She slid down off the back of the sofa and curled up under his arm. "I was thinking about Gale and how she disappeared when Melissa showed up. I always assumed Severin dumped her, but now I'm not so sure."

Marsh sighed and nodded. "You don't suppose he buried her in the basement, do you?"

"Oh, I hope not. We should mention it to the cops though."

They sat in silence.

"At least Severin's gone now," Rainbow said, looking for the bright side.

"Why did he take Kyle?"

The question of the hour.

"Maybe Severin didn't like having a competitor for Melissa's affections."

Marsh snorted. "She ignored Kyle!"

"Maybe she talked about him a lot or something. Who knows."

"So Severin gets pissed and strangles her, but what did he do with Kyle?"

"I have a theory, but it's gross."

Marsh raised his eyebrows.

"I think he wanted to torture Kyle and take his time about it. He set the fire to cover up Melissa's murder."

"Why did he have to kill her?" Marsh asked. "And why did he have to do it here? I feel like a terrible person for thinking this, Rain, but on top of everything else, he fucked up our research!"

A tight, humorless smile played at Rainbow's lips.

Marsh blushed. "It's tragic that a life was taken, of course it is. And had Melissa ever engaged anyone in conversation, we'd no doubt be more affected by her murder. But without Kyle, the Dream Machine is done. And I'm a dick for thinking this way."

"Make room in that handbasket for me." Rainbow sat up and kissed Marsh on the nose. "We shouldn't have to worry about funding, right? Severin put your name on the accounts?"

Marsh nodded. "I can make sure everyone gets paid. Keep the lights on. Buy beer and microprocessors."

"Great! And if we're smart — which we are — we ought to be able to use our new security clearances to further our private research." Their new jobs with the Office of Communication Technology would start as soon as their clearances came through.

"You don't think the Dream Machine's totally dead?"

"I think it's been dealt a stunning blow, but just might recover."

Marsh pulled her into his lap and hugged her tight. "I love you, Rain."

"I love you, too."

The three uniformed cops left through the front door. Detective Avebury followed them down the stairs, but came into the media room. In a plastic bag he held a handgun.

"Either of you see this before?"

"No," they both said.

"We found it in Mrs Tanner's purse. It's probably hers, but we'll run the serial number to be sure."

Once more through the facts with Detective Avebury: Melissa and Severin got along well enough, but were rarely seen together. Nobody ever heard them argue. Melissa never mentioned being afraid, didn't act scared. They'd never seen her taking drugs, prescription or street, but she drank. A lot. Severin never showed the least bit of interest in Kyle, and neither did Melissa once she'd brought him to the house. While in the workshop that afternoon, Marsh heard one of the vans leave, but attached no significance to it. He couldn't pin down the time.

Not wanting to bring any further disruption to the house, but wanting even less to potentially cover up a murder, Marsh brought up Gale's sudden departure.

Detective Avebury asked some questions and made some notes. Marsh showed him to the basement, but he returned quickly.

"There's no evidence of digging," said the detective. "I'll see about bringing in a cadaver dog or some sonar equipment tomorrow, but I don't think she's buried down there."

Rainbow sighed, relieved.

"I know this is a long shot, given how secretive Mrs Tanner was, but do either of you know anything about her family? We need to contact someone, but the number associated with the address on her license is disconnected."

"I heard her say she'd left her husband," said Marsh.

Detective Avebury nodded.

"I can't remember what she said his name was," Marsh continued. "I think she was talking to her mother. On the phone. We could look at the long distance records…"

"That would be excellent, Mr Marshall."

Chapter Seventeen

GARDEN OF EDEN

WEBSTER — A woman is dead and her invalid son missing in an apparent murder-kidnapping yesterday at a downtown home. The female victim was found strangled in an upper story room at the house on Oak Avenue at around 5:00 p.m. yesterday. She was pronounced dead at the scene.

Police say the prime suspect in both crimes is Severin Tenpenny, age approximately 60. "We believe that, after killing the female, he fled with the comatose young man," said Detective Paul Avebury.
Webster Daily Press, 4-21-2001

In the chilly bedroom, Rook Tanner clung to her husband's warmth, absorbing it along with his mental vibrations. It was glorious to be with him, skin on skin. She kissed him, long and wet and urgent, their souls entwining along with their tongues. She ran her fingers through his shaggy hair, pulling him deeper into the kiss, until she had to come up for air.

"Rook," he breathed, his deep green eyes alive with longing.

She knelt on the bed and coaxed him down beside her. Beginning with his throat, she kissed her way down his torso, sometimes licking, sometimes nibbling, inhaling his wild, dark aroma, exulting in every element of him. It was all familiar, but also brand new. She had never touched him with these fingers, never tasted him with this mouth, never taken him inside this body before today. In the past she experienced him at one remove. Now she was in control and the power was intoxicating.

She moved lower.

This act would be more romantic with the lights out, but her eyes were new and had not yet had enough of seeing him. Every detail meshed with her memory, but was more intense, more real, more Kyle, and Rook became giddy from sensory overload.

There were two discrepancies between this flesh-and-bone Kyle and the one already fading from her memory.

He had a scar on his right shoulder where Marcus shot him, and the thought of him taking a bullet for her broke her heart and revved her libido at the same time. She kissed the puckered flesh.

The other difference was his right knee which carried fresh scars crisscrossing the faded ones in a complex map of pain. Rook didn't like to think about her role in authoring that pain.

Kyle rolled them over. Erotic deja vu overwhelmed Rook as he slid inside her.

The discomfort of the cold, damp sheets contrasted wildly with the joyous heat of Kyle, and Rook struggled to reconcile the two disparate sensations. How could one body contain such extremes?

Like magnets repelling each other, the halves of her psyche drifted apart. This delicious agony persisted long after the bed warmed up and the dueling sensations passed. Concentration was required to keep the rift from growing, and it also delayed her orgasm. Rook wrapped her legs around Kyle's ass and bucked her hips to meet his thrusts.

Kyle smiled mischievously. He pinned Rook's wrists to the bed above her head and slowed, teasing her. She stared into his eyes, floating in their warm green ocean and drawing strength from him to hold herself together.

Funny to think that the Completer needed a Completer of her own.

Rook did not doubt Kyle was the only man for the job. He'd stood on the Threshold of Elsewhere and enfleshed her, bringing her forth from the vast, roiling nothingness to be his bride. Her life and body created by and for him.

Her oh-so-recent birth was overtaken by their first, frantic fuck as

quickly in memory as it had been in actuality, there in her father's attic lair on the edge of Elsewhere, and it threatened to unmoor her.

That first fuck had been as necessary as breathing. The moment she opened her eyes she'd needed him. Without him inside her she'd feared she would slip back into the Elsewhere and be lost amongst the bubbles of light.

As she focused on that chaotic memory her orgasm began to build again. Kyle shifted his grip from her wrists to her hands, lacing their fingers, reminding Rook forcefully that she was not whole.

The amputation site did not hurt, but it left her with a void both physical and ethereal, deeper and more dangerous than mere flesh. It felt like her tether had snapped. She had to fight to not be washed out to sea, and that terrible drowning sensation was rooted in her missing finger.

Kyle's desire was manifest in her very existence, so why remove the digit where she wore her wedding ring? Rook pictured the perfect golden circle, and saw its inky shadow, the tattoo connecting her to Fin. Covering that tattoo with the ring of their own bond hadn't been enough to counteract it, leaving Kyle no choice but to disfigure her so they could be together always.

"I love you," she murmured.

"I love you, too."

Eyes locked, their pace increased, each striving for release.

What if the tattoo had been the force keeping her integrated? How ironic that by breaking that connection to Fin, she and Kyle might lose each other.

It's not fair!

The first wave of her orgasm crashed and her mind was riven. Pain and pleasure mingled and she cried out. Her climax triggered Kyle's in a storm surge of bliss that left them both exhausted and soaked with sweat.

*** *** ***

Kyle lay on his side and watched Rook sleep. He had dozed after

their housewarming fuck, their bodies pressed together against the chill in the apartment. The room was warmer now, almost comfortable.

He got up and went to the kitchen. Before he fired up the generator on their way in, the place had been without electricity for ages, but lots of edible material could be in the cupboards.

He was surprised by the diversity of the salvageable items, even though not much of it went together in any appealing way.

The glasses in the cabinet were free of dust, cleanliness verging on the surreal amid so much decay. Kyle ran himself a drink of water, then another, his thirst far stronger than the flat metallic taste of the tap water. Fluids replenished, he spooned up a large glob of peanut butter. There was also honey, which he thought would be more enjoyable in the bedroom. Thus preoccupied, he stood naked mouthing peanut butter off the spoon.

Kyle Tanner, greetings and felicitations.

The voice occurred inside his head, feeling almost like a memory, but all the same Kyle glanced around to find the speaker. Its tone was cordial, perhaps even awestruck if Kyle wasn't reading too much into so few words.

"Yeah, what?" he said, his own voice sticky.

We are pleased to see you restored to health. It is good to have an opportunity to speak with you.

Kyle ate more peanut butter. He had not been wrong about the gushiness.

We need your help with our mission. Now, when we at last understand what we must do, our power to effect such changes is diminished almost to nothing. It is fitting that we be helped by one of your kind. That you, Kyle, will help lead your race into the next phase of its evolution.

Kyle swallowed and asked, "And what phase is that?"

A glorious unity transcending anything you ever imagined. A wholeness like our own, but far greater! We, singly, are but lowly automata, while you are already marvels each on your own. In your

united form, you will be such a flowering as even we cannot comprehend.

"How am I involved?"

You are a marvel among marvels. We have vision, and we have power, but the task is too great for us. Your power is vast, more than you have even begun to suspect. You honor us by listening, and you will glorify all your kind by partnering in our mission.

These must be Fin's alien friends, his allies from the battle at the cathedral. They sounded ambitious, and evidently Fin was no longer in the picture.

"Go on."

The aliens, thrilled to have this encouragement, explained how they'd been inspired by the Divided Man Prophecy, making sure to illuminate Kyle's own privileged treatment in that tale. Kyle listened as they spelled out his destiny, as they described the miraculous future he would usher in.

He forgot all about his peanut butter.

***   ***   ***

Fin parked on a side street where they could watch the big, green house. The place looked deserted. Willow fidgeted in the back seat while Rook sat up front in a loose billowy dress. "So there'll be room for Thumper," she had explained.

A miscarriage would be hard enough to accept. Their situation was made so much worse by the fact that Thumper was out there, alone and unprotected, stranded in the Collective Id. Rescuing the baby was a good reason to take some risks, and thanks to Willow they had a plan. A crazy plan, but that's what such insane circumstances demanded. The sensible voice inside Fin's head, urging caution, would have to go fuck itself.

They ventured onto the porch. The front door was locked. Rook produced a paperclip and a safety pin from her jacket pocket and picked the lock with impressive ease.

She crept in, followed by Willow. Fin stepped through the door and closed it quietly, then hurried to the stairs after the women. By the time

the trio got to the third-floor landing it was obvious they had the house to themselves.

Rook stepped wide as she passed the door with the yellow police tape, sneaking past like it was a sleeping tiger.

Willow opened the door to the attic steps, revealing more police tape. She shrugged and ducked under, and Rook and Fin followed. The ancient wooden stairs creaked in their claustrophobic space. Fin's heart thudded against his sternum. Entering this lair felt like the worst possible mistake, and he was powerless to put a halt to it from his position in the rear. Willow reached the top and disappeared. He crowded behind Rook as they took the final steps, so she couldn't perform a similar feat.

He wrapped one arm around her waist while surveying the attic for imminent threats. The most interesting thing he spotted was a hammock suspended from the beams. Otherwise it was just dim and dusty, its recesses crammed with boxes and crates. Stuffy, with a charred undertone. It made his old room at the boarding house look homey.

Willow sank to her knees, whimpering, "No, no... how?"

Rook knelt beside her while Fin acted as lookout, wariness returning.

"What's the matter?" Rook asked.

"It's gone." Willow pointed across the broad room to a neat gray heap.

The stale woodsmoke aroma grew as Fin neared the pile of ashes. Nothing else bore any sign of scorching, although everything about the attic suggested great flammability.

"Someone burned it." He looked back and saw Rook look pleadingly at Willow, who shook her head.

Rook stood and walked stiffly to the center of the room. She paced within a small space there, a little room only she could enter. Her eyes hunted the attic, their intensity reminding Fin again how combustible the place seemed.

He held out his arms, but she didn't even slow her fitful marching.

He went to Willow's side and rested his hand on her shoulder as she cried silently.

Rook burst from her invisible cage and strode to a corner where she took a small wooden box from an exposed beam. She yanked it open and rattled it, pawed through its contents, then slapped it shut and tossed it back before stooping to rifle the old clothes in a steamer trunk. Fin took a step toward her, but in seconds she proceeded to a stack of cardboard crates and began the same rough search. He watched for several minutes as her explorations took her halfway around the large space. In her wake she left things disheveled, but not upended.

Fin yearned to show her how to ransack the place.

Eventually she just stopped, facing away with her head bowed and one hand resting on a beam.

Fin crossed the room as Rook furtively shoved her fist in her coat pocket. He wanted to tell her she didn't have to be sneaky, that no one would care if she stole something from this drafty hole, but instead he enfolded her in his arms, and she sobbed. They held each other, and she burrowed into him to muffle her screams of frustration.

They'd stoked their courage to come here, and now the mundane, desolate place mocked them.

*** *** ***

Shivering and in pain, Rook woke and discovered herself alone in the bed. An erotic, comforting hum in the base of her skull told her Kyle was nearby. No need to worry, at least not about that. Worry about the pain instead. Pain like biting down on a loose tooth, the sharp stab fading to an insistent echoing throb, pain for which the cure is more pain, if only for an instant.

This misery ran throughout her body and the cure would mean splitting herself in two.

Rook groaned and hugged herself, wallowing in self-pity for a short while before getting up to look for something to wear. The penthouse was warming up, but she was cold.

Dresses filled half of the walk-in closet. Rook tried to remember

which Kyle liked her in best as she shuffled through the choices. Something blue, maybe, to bring out her eyes.

Something blue.

Something old, something new…

Her wedding dress! He always liked her in that.

Chosen by Kyle, worn during their wedding, it was a powerful thing. Maybe even powerful enough to fuse her fragmented psyche.

A few minutes later she stood in front of the full-length mirror in the bathroom, struggling with the zipper. Under the frothy layers of tulle she wore the bustier and garter belt, the white silk stockings and the satin heels.

She donned relief along with each piece of her trousseau, every garment bringing its own narcotic to the party.

Once zippered she pulled the pale blue garter into place on her thigh and pinned the veil into her hair.

The pain was blissfully deadened.

Rook smiled, twirling in front of the mirror. Her virginal cocoon fluttered and floated. So much better than an ugly ring tattoo!

Passing back through the bedroom, Rook scooped up the teddy bear angel and held it in place of a bouquet.

Recognition flirted with her as she walked through the dim penthouse.

Usually at night the wall of windows into the atrium acted as a mirror, reflecting the tastefully decorated rooms like a cut-rate Versailles. Tonight the lights were all but out, and with the bright moon shining through the glass roof Rook could see a ghostly image of herself superimposed over the remains of Shaw's Garden of Eden.

The view over the balcony railing revealed dead palm trees, a few desiccated brown fronds hanging like skeletonized rib cages. Curious to see the extent of the neglect, Rook passed through the french doors and out into the cold, still atrium.

Eerie silence greeted her. Before, this place was never quiet. During the day it teemed with ministry employees and visitors. At night it was

full of the crash of the waterfall and the calls of the birds. Not anymore.

Shadows blanketed much of the ground, but in the sporadic pockets of chill moonlight Rook saw withered plant stalks and a dry column of stained boulders where the waterfall should be. The pool at its bottom held a mass of algae.

What happened to the birds? Had someone rescued them or, come daylight, would she see their fragile skeletons on the flagstones and in the flower beds?

Rook couldn't stop smiling. Life was perfect now, she and Kyle together with no distractions. Their empire had fallen, their kingdom was dead. Together they would rule over the wasteland. It was desperately romantic and unspeakably sexy. Rook hurried inside to find her husband.

He was in the kitchen, naked, holding a spoonful of peanut butter and staring vacantly in the direction of the sink.

"Kyle," she purred.

He blinked several times and regained himself. She clutched the angel bear in a parody of sweetness and fluttered her eyelashes.

A lascivious smile crept onto his lips.

"You seemed a million miles away," she cooed.

"More or less."

Holding his left hand in her right, whole hand, she guided the spoon to her mouth and licked the peanut butter.

"Are you hungry?" he asked.

She was famished, but eager to see whether her nuptial attire was powerful enough to prevent her dissolution during orgasm.

"A little," she fibbed. "I'm hungry for you."

"I'm not going anywhere," he reassured, "but if I don't eat I won't be good for much."

Rook pouted for about a second, then got herself a spoon and scooped out a big blob of Jif.

For a few minutes they munched in companionable silence, maintaining a low-level flirtation. When she moved to the fridge for a

cold drink Kyle stopped her with a shake of his head.

"Power's been off for months." He opened the pantry and brought out a bottle of champagne. When he popped the cork the bottle erupted and foam slid down over his hand to splatter on the floor.

He raised the bottle, said, "To us," and took a swig before handing it to Rook.

"To us," she agreed, and took a long drink. A pleasant fuzzy feeling spread through her body. They each took another quaff before Kyle wrapped his arms around her from behind, nuzzling her neck through the veil.

He bent her forward over the granite counter and raised the back of her skirt, running his hands up her thighs.

"No panties," he whispered with approval and parted her legs.

It felt so damn good, and Rook was desperate to have him inside her again, but she managed to say, "Wait."

"Why?" he asked, his fingers stroking and prodding.

"Not here," she gasped. "Balcony."

Kyle chuckled. "Bring the champagne."

*** *** ***

Kyle smirked at memories of his debauched wedding night with the other Rook. That one participated enthusiastically enough, and she didn't even like him. Not really. Not like this one did. All he'd done to overcome the other Rook's reluctance was enter her mind and tweak a few factory settings. This one had no reluctance, but it could still be fun to see what her mental landscape looked like, maybe make a few modifications.

He lifted her onto the rosewood railing and she clung to his neck as he cleared her voluminous skirts out of the way and thrust himself into her mind as well as her body.

At first it looked like the other Rook's. Same starry sky, same dense pines. Her core tower stood in a clearing, rising from the blanket of pine needles and raven feathers like the one he remembered, but this structure was a composite entity, just like his Rook. Half was rough,

black rock, the other half opalescent glass, shimmering with rainbows even in the starlight. The two materials zippered together in a jagged seam that ran diagonally from the base to the roof, bleeding together in a disconcerting ombré. Both halves were studded with luminous green shards. He smiled to know he was incorporated into the very fiber of her being.

Encircling the tower, binding the two halves into one perfect whole, were silver chains like metallic ivy. The links clinked against the tower in the breeze.

At the base, a warm light glowed through folds of deep pink curtains in a peaked archway. As Kyle approached he felt Rook's desire more strongly and knew the root of her arousal waited inside. He pushed through the warm, clinging draperies and into a pleasure grotto.

The walls were marble in undulating reds and flushed pinks, slick with moisture running down their faces to pool on the ground. The sultry air smelled like sex. In the center of the circular chamber stood a round bed, obscured by a canopy of vines draped with flowers so voluptuous they would make Georgia O'Keeffe blush. A ring of candles lit the space.

Kyle parted the floral canopy, releasing a burst of pheromonal pollen.

On the balcony, Rook moaned.

Atop red satin sheets Kyle found his prize. Surrounded by white flower petals and wispy black feathers, two Rooks sprawled, the two halves that together made the exciting woman in his arms.

The Brook half lazed against black fur pillows wearing a white bustier and frilly panties, looking radiantly innocent. The Bramble half lay beside her, masturbating. She wore only a leather collar, silver rings in both nipples, and her tattoos. A length of chain snaked from her collar down off the bed.

Both women looked at Kyle with half-lidded blue eyes.

Kyle joined them on the bed, slipping straight into Bramble's ready wetness as he gathered Brook into a deep kiss.

Rook's response was immediate and overwhelming, and for a giddy second Kyle feared she might topple backwards off the railing. Instead she clung to him as she spasmed through a shattering orgasm. It was beautiful to watch her enjoy herself without ripping herself apart. Kyle congratulated himself on healing her while she leaned on him, trying to catch her breath.

He lifted her down, turned her around, and bent her over the railing. As he took her from behind he focused again on her libidinous internal twins.

Gentle persistence and the untying of many satin bows coaxed away Brook's lingerie until she lay upon the red satin wearing nothing but her shy blush. Kyle pulled out of Bramble and positioned himself to deflower his virgin bride. With his thrust her eyes flew open and she gasped.

Kyle kissed Brook as he fucked her, then kissed Bramble, fingering her nipple rings. He brought the two women together to kiss. Brook was hesitant but Bramble knew what she liked and they were soon making out in a slippery, sweaty, wet dream come to life.

It went on for what felt like hours. He alternated between the women, leaving no orifice unexplored. Some light bondage and plenty of girl-on-girl kept his interest riveted and kept Rook in near-constant climax. Choreographing the moves of their sensual ballet, Kyle lived out every fantasy, and in doing so strengthened his hold on Rook. Both halves of her wanted nothing but him, now and forever.

And he wanted nothing but her.

As his last act, Kyle gathered up the chain dangling from Bramble's collar and tied the loose end around Brook's neck. They were bound together, like the tower they inhabited, so Rook could stay whole.

*** *** ***

After the anticlimax in Severin's attic, Rook withdrew deeper than ever. Fin wished they hadn't gone, that he hadn't been complicit in feeding her false hope. When they got home, he steered her to the sofa and eased her onto it, where she sat staring into the middle distance.

His mother, by contrast, didn't stop moving at all. Willow stalked the flagstones of the living and dining rooms, over and over, her hands busy scolding, clutching and strangling an endless bazaar of invisible items.

Brad laid Zen down for her nap in Thumper's nursery and sat at the other end of Fin's couch, sadly tracing Willow's movements with his eyes. His mournful gaze paused on Fin for a few seconds, drifted to Rook, then resumed its pursuit of Willow.

Suddenly Fin heard his own voice, human speech alarming to his ears.

"I have an idea."

Willow froze in mid-stride, and Rook's head turned toward him. Fin jumped to his feet. He went to the radio and turned it on, then seized the TV remote and turned that on too. Every face in the room wore a baffled look, but he couldn't slow down to compose an explanation. When he grabbed Rook's laptop and started playing a CD to add to the jumble of noise, Brad threw up his hands.

"What the hell are you doing?" Brad asked in a level and reasonable tone.

"I'm going to talk to something," Fin said. "And I need your help. All three of you." Mild panic on Brad's face, calm interest on the women's. He presented the laptop to his wife. "Keep flicking from track to track, just randomize it. Mom, play with the tuning dial on the radio. I don't care what kind of station it is, music, talk, commercials, just keep hunting around, and don't settle on anything for more than a couple seconds. Dad, you do the same with this," tossing Brad the remote. "There's no way to do this wrong."

Fin caught himself about to clarify that it would be wrong if they went too slow, or if there was too much dead air. He could tell Brad picked up on the presence of unspoken qualifiers, so he smiled encouragingly as he sat down on the floor.

"Okay, go!" The already head-spinning noise went through some hellish kitchen device and came out shredded, chopped, and diced. The

disorienting effect multiplied, throwing together tiny snatches from dozens of sources. He closed his eyes and tried to let his auditory channels unfocus, like listening to a Magic Eye puzzle.

Fin muttered under his breath, "We're looking for our baby, do you have it?"

A blast of canned laughter from a sitcom coincided with lulls from the radio and laptop. Nothing else felt like the personality Fin conversed with before. Everything was too disjointed to set up a flow he could access.

Keeping his eyes squeezed shut, he gestured 'slow it down' with both hands. This felt like a good step, bringing things closer to the desired flavor.

He repeated his question and picked up in reply, "All is well with the baby, baby, baby." The voice, combining lyrics from three different songs, sounded blissful, frantically happy, and Fin trembled with mingled hope and outrage.

After a deep breath, he whispered, "We love the baby. Can you please return it to us?"

The pop-diva-of-the-moment exclaimed, "Oh, no! Couldn't let go!" which blended into a random anchorman's, "… assure the public that everything is under control."

Fin ground his teeth. He had expected indifference and was prepared to go to some lengths explaining how much it mattered. To find the thing so gleefully stonewalling placed him off balance.

"Fin?"

Fin shot Vesuvius a quizzical glance.

"You need to play more chess. With the new table."

Fin and Rook both turned their heads to glare at Vesuvius, then shared a momentary look of bewilderment.

"Please," Fin addressed the Id.

"The first ten callers will get—" then a second of dead air, followed by, "Nothing!" capped off raucously with, "All day and all of the night."

"You have no right!" Fin declared in a constricted whisper. "Give

our baby back now."

To this Fin got no distinct reply.

"Don't make me come in there," he muttered.

"I hear you knockin' but you can't come in."

Fin put his hands over his face and wept, his rage extinguished by a flood of grief. He had failed. There was no way to make a start against something so big and heartless.

*** *** ***

Willow watched Rook gather Fin up to console him, and her heart went to them.

She glanced at the radio. While she'd played her part in Fin's orchestra of chaos, she'd felt it tuning in more than electromagnetic signals. Without knowing the whole pattern, she nevertheless knew instinctually what she should do with the tuning knob. When to pause, when to go down the dial and when to go up, like she was cracking a combination lock.

It felt, more than anything, like watching Severin use the table that first time.

The difference was, there was nothing special about this radio, or about the television or the computer for that matter. The way Fin brought them together connected him to a massive font of energy, something staggeringly huge.

And he talked to it like it was completely natural. Pride and awe at her offspring's audacity were tempered by a frisson of motherly concern, and a faint, petulant whiff of obsolescence.

Fin's disappointment and frustration were understandable, but the longer she thought about it the more Willow saw a renewed source of hope. Her despair at finding Severin's table destroyed now seemed silly. There were other ways to go about this.

All she needed was a means to open a portal into the Elsewhere. Fin evidently had an ability to channel messages using found objects, but for Willow's talents to serve she would need items that were themselves special.

"Fin, Rook," she called, "I have an idea. It's going to be tricky, but I'm sure I can do it if I can get hold of what I need."

The kids looked at her guardedly, waiting for her to nail things down. She took a deep breath.

"You know about the jewelry with the listening devices embedded in it?"

Their faces darkened. This wasn't going to be fun.

"Well, I know quite a bit about it. I'm the world's greatest authority, I guess." Dubious looks, now, still wary. "Because... because I invented it."

Fin looked away, his neck and ears reddening. Rook stared, a stare that made Willow nervous. Willow put her hand over her mouth, giving herself time to think before blurting out anything more.

"You what?" came Fin's voice, with forced calm.

Willow sighed. "My last freelance gig. I guess it's dishonest to say 'invented,' because someone else came up with the basic premise. All I did was get it working after they couldn't. I was more midwife than mother. The blueprints just appeared under my pencil, like someone else — or something else — guided my hand. I know that doesn't matter, and neither does this, but I had no idea what its purpose was. I'm sorry." She paused, but not long enough for anyone to interject. "The reason I raise this painful subject is, that jewelry is what I need. I can use it instead of the table. The jewelry's nanotechnology will let me open a portal to the Elsewhere, because that's where it came from in the first place."

Fin turned to face her again, his color returning to normal but his eyes shining. Rook now looked hurt and confused.

"I'm sorry," Willow repeated.

"I think we all understand you wish it never happened," Brad said.

"Okay," Rook announced. "Okay. Let's do it. At least once that stuff ought to be used for something good."

"Do we want to think about it a little longer?" Fin asked.

"No!" Rook said. "We can't sit around. This is our plan, and we're

going to make it work and we're not taking any fucking shit from anybody!"

Willow for one wouldn't be trying to give her any shit.

Fin looked at Willow. "How many pieces do you need?"

Willow considered the question. "The more the better. Do you have any?"

Fin shook his head. "Rook thinks she knows where it is. We should be able to get as many as you need."

Chapter Eighteen

Affront to Reason

In addition to the standard genetic tests offered by other labs, DNAnswers is proud to offer testing for less common disorders and traits. We are the only lab in the US testing for genetic chimerism, a rare condition in which fertilized eggs fuse together but retain their own characters, resulting in offspring that is a mixture of tissues.
excerpt from DNAnswers Labs brochure

Rook and Fin were both quiet for much of the drive to Donner to collect the jewelry for Willow. Rook spent the time going over the knowledge she stole from Kyle's mind about Shaw Ministries' clandestine wing. As Fin navigated the winding drive up to the compound, Rook felt she should say something to break the ice, to get them ready to face this. But she didn't have anything to say.

They reached the gate and saw the heaped-up debris of Kyle's memorial shrine.

"That's fucking disgusting," Rook said, happy to have a topic.

"Amen." Fin rolled down his window. "Here's the keypad."

Rook recited the nine-digit code she learned from Kyle, and the gate swung open. Fin rolled forward over the soggy mementos and proceeded into the complex.

As Fin drove, Rook surveyed the unkempt grounds. When they rounded the last bend she caught sight of the rubble where the cathedral once stood. Yellow police tape, strummed by the breeze, encircled the twisted, shattered mess. The surrounding area showed the tracks of bulldozers.

It was a visceral thrill to see the site in ruins. Rook had been in the cathedral twice, and neither time was pleasant.

"There's a parking garage by the seminary school." She pointed to a short, white brick building.

They followed the corkscrew ramps all the way to the bottom of the empty garage, four levels below the surface. Fin parked in a space, which Rook found amusing. She went to a light switch at the foot of the stairs and pressed on the metal plate. It flipped open, revealing a small keypad where she tapped in the code again. A section of the wall swung inward.

Fin said, "Let me go first."

Rook shook her head. "I'll recognize the mercenaries, and some of them would know me, too." Fin looked like he wanted to say any number of objectionable things, but they all tried to get said at once and logjammed. He grumbled and fell into step behind Rook.

She headed down the long white passageway toward the secure storage area, trying to walk quietly without looking like she was sneaking. Fin clomped behind her, clearly counting on her ability to sweet-talk the guards.

The place seemed abandoned, the air still and smelling faintly of mildew. Their route took them past the armory, which stood open and empty.

When Rook told Fin what used to be on the racks he said, "Well this is good. The soldier-boys left and took their toys with them."

"Let's keep this quick, all the same." They moved on.

The vault also stood open, cleaned out.

"Shit!" Rook yelled.

Fin sagged against the wall. When Rook met his eyes, he smiled sadly and shook his head. "I don't know why we're surprised. There must have been lots of people who knew about this cache."

"They moved it."

"Where?"

"I don't know," Rook replied in an irritated tone. She gave herself a

chance to take a deep breath before going on. "They hid it. Let's look around."

Fin didn't move at first, but he shrugged and tagged along after Rook.

"I'll take the right side," she said, "you take the left. Check every room."

The system of tunnels was large, but not complicated. Barracks holding skeletal cots with no bedding, mess halls with ranks of spotless empty tables, training rooms devoid of free weights and heavy bags, offices with the desk drawers all hanging open, and most intriguing and most frustrating, labs and control rooms stripped of anything that hadn't been bolted down and much that had.

Rook knew Fin was going through the motions, but he didn't complain. It took them an hour to scout the whole warren.

"Long way back to the car," Fin said. "At least I think so. You have a better idea of the layout."

Rook nodded, but she wasn't thinking about leaving yet. She said, "Right around the corner there's a tunnel into the main building."

Fin shrugged.

"That's where Shaw's old office, or Kyle's... both I guess. Anyway, that's where the office is. I want to check it out."

"I don't think the jewelry is up there."

"Probably not, but we've come this far," Rook said. "There were files, paper files, detailing who had interest in the stuff. I went through all of it, but I couldn't take notes. I'm sure it's still there."

Fin looked unconvinced.

"We came this far," Rook reiterated.

Fin nodded wearily. "Lead on."

It was about 100 yards to the end of the line, then up a steel staircase and through another hidden door to a landing where an elevator door greeted them. Rook pushed the button and a few seconds later the panel slid open. She pushed Private and it closed again. Now, confined in the tiny metal box, Rook started to feel nervous. This place awakened an

echo of Kyle's vibration in her head.

Fin was more alert now than during their subterranean explorations. Maybe it made him nervous, too.

The elevator stopped and opened, and they passed through the vestibule into the once-sumptuous penthouse. Sun angled in from the atrium, casting long shadows. An aroma of stale neglect made the starkly lit room gloomy. Rook flipped the light switch, which chased the shadows back and revealed a littering of styrofoam cups and burger wrappers on the coffee table, but did little to make the place appealing.

Fin held up a hand for her to wait, and started some form of perimeter sweep. His stealth was impressive, now that he felt motivated to be quiet. "What are you up to?" she asked.

Fin paused and gave her a discouraged look. "I don't like this," he said. "Someone has been here."

"Yeah, months ago," Rook agreed. Fin gestured again for her to stay put and carried on his explorations. Rook took in more details of the dusty room while awaiting the all-clear.

To her left stood the credenza with the chessboard she remembered from her stint as a preacher's wife. The glass case on the wall above it held an incomplete set — only white pieces, and not all of those. She was struck by a resemblance to the men that came with Fin's table.

Rook stepped closer to get a better look.

*** *** ***

Kyle's eyes opened. All was still in the bedroom, and Rook slept securely under his arm. A low, throaty sound through the walls told him the elevator was moving, and his head suddenly contained twin hums.

Kyle slunk from the bed and into a pair of boxers. He got his gun from the nightstand and padded over to listen at the door. The elevator opened.

When he heard their voices, his brow furrowed. *What are they doing here?*

Kyle advanced a few steps into the hallway. Fin moved farther into the living room, out of view, and when Rook also started heading off

without looking his way, Kyle cleared his throat.

Rook gasped and froze in place, then Fin was there shielding her and looking almost as flummoxed.

Kyle set the pistol on the credenza and took another step.

"What are you doing here?" He kept his voice low to not awaken Rook. "Go away. I'm retired from evil now, so whatever it is it's no concern of mine. I just want to be left alone."

Rook peered around Fin's shoulder and said, "We need the jewelry. Where is it?"

Kyle studied her, and she shrank back. *The jewelry? Why would they think it was up here?*

Obviously they hadn't expected to run into him, so they didn't really think he would know. They must have already checked the vault, so someone beat them to it. Kyle's first guess would be the sweater nutjobs. Of course, Rook had the run of their house and she was out looking for it, so scratch that. Who would that leave?

"The mercs handed it over to the government, in exchange for the cathedral coverup," Kyle said. "Probably took black-ops jobs, or got double-crossed. I don't know. I don't care. Please go away now."

Fin reacted stonily, but Rook wailed. Despite his irritation that the noise might wake his Rook, Kyle felt bad for her.

"Look," he offered, "I wish you luck getting the baby back. Especially since it's your only chance to have a kid."

Their faces told him they weren't aware of that.

Fin demanded, "How do you even know about the baby in the first place?"

Kyle sighed and rubbed the back of his neck. "While I was… away, I had company. Like a voice all around me, like floating in it. It told me things, lots of things. And the baby was exciting news for it. It wouldn't shut up. More prophecy garbage. Sorry."

Rook sniffled. "What did you mean, we won't have another chance?"

Kyle knew the next part would upset her.

"Divided Man stuff. Both me and Fin are the father, and that's the only way you could have ever gotten pregnant by either of us. One or the other can't make it happen. It has to be both."

Rook hugged herself and studied the floor.

Fin looked skeptical. "Two fathers? I seriously don't think it works that way."

Kyle gave him a pitying look. "Yeah, I forgot. None of this is ever weird."

Both Rook and Fin were nonplussed.

"That voice went on nonstop about all this shit. It's got some big plan, except I think this is not the original version of the plan."

Fin tried to usher Rook toward the elevator, but she resisted.

"What do you mean, a plan? It told you about this?"

"It was just muttering to itself most of the time. Prophecy stuff, like I said."

Rook's eyes grew wide. "Junebug?"

Kyle turned and saw his Rook at the bedroom door in her white dress, blinking at her own radiance after the dimness of the bedroom.

"Who are our visitors?" she asked sleepily. Kyle smiled and extended his hand.

Her own smile as she took it turned to an angry sneer when her eyes accommodated and she saw who was there. Kyle could feel her trembling with rage.

"What's *she* doing here!" his Rook hissed.

The other Rook sucked in a breath. "What. The. Fuck." She got louder. "That's not my sister, Fin," she said with mounting alarm. "That's not Bug."

"I'm not the fucking Bug, but I am your sister," Kyle's Rook shouted. "Don't deny it!"

Kyle held onto her hand, and blocked the hallway as much as possible. Inside his mind, the signals from both women, nearly identical, amplified, their slight anomalies clashing against each other. His Rook was ready to start a fight, and he didn't know what would

happen if the two of them touched. He was near panic at the thought she might disappear.

"My… my sister?" the other Rook stammered. "No! No!"

"What the hell is going on?" Fin asked.

"Can you see her, Fin? Can you see her there with Kyle?" She was sobbing now. "Is she real?"

"I see her." Fin reached for his wife. "It's okay, Rook, I see her. Who is she?"

"That's Brook, or maybe Bramble," said the Rook in the living room with a shudder.

"No," Kyle asserted, "She's Rook. She's *my* Rook." Fin looked about to express his disapproval, so Kyle continued, "There are two rooks on a chessboard anyway, so you should be fine with this."

"Actually, there are four," Fin said.

Kyle felt his face grow hot. Always such a wiseass!

A dissonant keening noise drew his attention back to his Rook. He thought her trembling had become a convulsion, but this was something worse. She grimaced in agony, vibrating into a double-exposure of herself. Only her hand, in his, remained stable and fixed.

Kyle flung his arms around her, to hold her together in one piece. He squeezed her tight, squeezing tears from his eyes at the same time. Fucking damn his interloping brother and that doppelgänger woman! He scowled over his shoulder at them and yelled, "Get the fuck out!"

"Let's go! Now! Let's GO!" the Rook behind Fin screamed, tearing at his jacket, dragging him bodily to the elevator vestibule and thrashing at the button. The doors slid open and they piled in, Rook still screaming until the doors closed again.

Kyle looked at his Rook, now whole again, weeping in his arms. He took a steadying breath and caressed her cheek.

"They're gone, they're gone," he whispered. "It's okay now."

Rook clung to him savagely, and suddenly she devoured him in kisses. Kyle pulled her hair, tipping her head back so they could both get some oxygen. He kissed her throat and carried her back to the bed.

*** *** ***

Fin slapped the button for the lower level, and thumbed Door Close. Rook scrambled to one of the back corners of the car. She hyperventilated for the whole ride down, while Fin worked on prying her loose from her corner. When they reached the bottom, he opted for hiking to the parking structure in daylight rather than retracing their steps through the passageways.

"She was never real before," Rook said shakily. "They. She. Whatever. They were just in my head. They weren't real. Now they are. They're her. I'm not losing my mind, am I Fin?"

"I saw her, too," Fin reassured. "Is there any chance you had a twin? Like a separated at birth thing?"

Rook looked at him with undisguised disdain, which was a whole hell of a lot better than the incipient insanity she'd been displaying moments ago.

"You're talking shit," she said, and Fin nodded in agreement. "The only twins I ever had were a product of depersonalization disorder comorbid with subjective doubles delusion. They were delusional ideations."

Fin made note of those terms so he could look them up later.

"They weren't real, Fin," Rook said, her eyes closed. "They weren't real. I know they weren't. But they are now." Her brows pulled together. "She is now."

Fin drew her in and hugged her.

"I know what she's like," Rook said. "What she's capable of."

"I believe you."

She looked up at him, her blue eyes bright with fear. "You do?"

"Of course."

With a half-smile she broke into tears and hugged him. "Thank you."

They were about halfway to the garage, breaking trail through knee-high grass. There was a paved walkway, but this was more direct.

Rook recuperated on their hike. "What the fuck is happening up

there?" she asked, and Fin wasn't sure which particular affront to reason she wanted to discuss. "I got away from him, but he can't let me go. And how the fuck did he do that? He has a living, breathing, creepy-in-so-many-ways creature in his bedroom. He even calls that thing Rook. That is not me. He has no claim on me."

Fin wore a grim mask of solidarity, but his thoughts were not as unambiguous as Rook's. The state of affairs upstairs was indeed odd, but from where he stood it looked like Kyle would be content to leave them alone from here out.

"He's a knock-off of you, so he needs to have a knock-off of me. How original. They're mocking us. They are a parody. A grotesque, loathsome, foul, demented, twisted, slimy, hateful cruel joke at our expense!"

Fin put an arm around Rook's shoulders but said nothing. He felt that he should offer a more positive take, interject with a pragmatic point or two, but knew it would feel like an argument. He didn't disagree with her, so it would be starting an argument he didn't even want to win.

"At least they'll keep each other busy and leave us alone," Rook said, rendering moot the one salient point Fin might have offered aloud. But he was happy she was trying to find something to feel hopeful about.

Rook's quiet lasted until they were off the Shaw campus, at which point a whole new program of ills welled up and overflowed.

"I can understand if Kyle's miserable, but I hate the way he had to shit all over our lives. Even that I could let go, if you and I were wafting along without a care in the world. But we've had our child taken from us, and now he has to put the boot in by saying we can't have another one. I'd forgotten how much I hate him." Rook folded her arms over her chest and cooked the horizon with her stare.

"He's lost his mind," Fin said. "Not surprising when you think about what happened."

"He doesn't need you to stick up for him, right now."

Fin felt offended, but tried to keep that out of his voice. "I was

agreeing with you. He's cracked."

"He knows what he's saying! He knows how hard it was for us to cope with him possibly being the father. So he claims he is, because it will stir shit up between us."

Fin drove in silence, reliving that ugliness. Kyle certainly knew where to place his shots. Then again, how could he know the date of conception? Lucky guess? How could he even know about the baby? Rook didn't look pregnant now. Was it possible he'd been with the Id?

"I wish he was still in a coma," Rook said, and Fin nodded his agreement. A moment later she added, in a dead drone, "I wish I hadn't been such a moron. I should have stayed away from him. Then Severin couldn't have gotten to Thumper, and Kyle wouldn't be saying these horrible things, and we'd be wafting along without a care in the world." Her voice dropped almost to nothing as she spoke, and when Fin glanced over he saw tears on her cheeks.

Fin rested his hand on her arm. "You are not a moron, and I won't let anybody talk like that about my wife. Even Kyle knew better." He chanced a crooked grin there at the end, and thought he spotted a fleeting glimmer of amusement on Rook's face.

"Not to be disrespectful of your dad," he added, "but Severin was a total dick."

Rook chuckled darkly. "Yeah, what kind of grandpa banishes his unborn grandchild into another dimension? Of course," she added, "my treatment of my inner children wouldn't win me any mother-of-the-year awards. I never expected to run into them again, especially not merged into a clone of me, playing house with Kyle. It's too weird."

She seemed too fatigued to be upset anymore.

"You know what's really bothering me?" she asked.

"No, what?" Fin asked, baffled at the thought of choosing one thing from such an extensive list.

"So much of what Kyle told us lined up with what Willow said back at Solstice. The way he described his coma was a lot like her story.

"So it bothers me," Rook concluded, "because it makes me believe

him."

Fin refused to accept that, but couldn't think of any way to refute it. Having a spotlight shone on the similarities between Kyle's and Willow's accounts made him angry, his mind balking at any attempt to put those two individuals into a shared category. There had to be another explanation for how Kyle knew what Willow knew, and he was exploiting that information, playing them.

Fin wanted to say something like 'everything will be okay,' because he wanted to make Rook feel better and had nothing of substance to offer. He knew he wouldn't sound convincing, so he clenched his jaw instead. Miles passed without a word spoken.

Halfway home he pulled into a hectic truck stop to get gas. Other drivers loitered while their tanks filled, many on cellphones and others with their car doors standing open and music blaring.

"Will you talk to me?" Fin asked the tangled background noise.

I need some coffee
give my love to Grampa
I'll talk to you tomorrow

"Who is the father of the baby you stole from my wife?"

I'm not even kidding!
like a thief in the night, see the world by candlelight
don't forget the lottery ticket
baby, baby it's a wild world
that jacket was a gift, you asshole

Fin ground his teeth. "Who is the father?"

you little shit
which way are we supposed to turn when we get to the highway?
Mountain Dew and a pack of smokes
so is Ashley still pissed off?
I hate visiting your brother
We need at least two bottles
sweetie, Daddies aren't allowed in the girls' room
getcha getcha one way or another
Mom! Jason put his finger up his nose!
and one night only
Even white boys got to shout baby got back

You are, and so is your brother. Two daddies, one mom, one baby.

While he pumped gas, Fin muttered more incredulous inquiries. The answers were smug.

Yes, the baby was a chimera. Yes, it represented tangible fulfillment of the prophecy.

No, Fin and Rook could not get pregnant without Kyle's participation.

Fin had been counting on being able to contradict Rook's fatalistic take on Kyle's allegations. He'd hoped for evidence that Kyle lied, but instead he now had verification of everything.

He rejoined Rook in the car and started the engine.

"I checked in with the Id," he said. "Kyle told us the truth."

"I thought so."

"You always were smarter than me," Fin said with a warm smile. "But, we got so distracted over Kyle we both forgot what he told us."

Rook blinked, not looking like the smarter member of any duo.

"What we went there for," Fin said. "We found the jewelry, so we're on track to make a portal into the Id. Alright, it's true we didn't find the exact location, but we know who has it."

*** *** ***

Rook lay in the protective circle of Kyle's arms, pressed against his bare chest. The bodice of her wedding dress was pushed down, exposing her nipples and acting as a crude push-up bra. The layers and layers of net skirts were bunched up around her hips in front, pinned between her ass and the bed underneath. Her legs were free and she wrapped them around Kyle. Her breaths came in ragged gasps, now more from their frenzied coupling than her earlier excruciating dissociation. That was the worst episode yet, the sickening, shredding full-body migraine too strong for even the wedding dress to counter.

Kyle knew just how to help her reintegrate.

Both of her component halves craved him. Where he touched her skin they swarmed together, eager to experience him, and he melded and forged them with the heat of his body, creating an alloy he called

Rook. While he fucked her he eclipsed everything. Her warring polarities ceased their terrible rending and came into resonance, and she was whole again, even through her orgasm. And his.

Kyle squeezed her, kissed her flushed forehead, smoothed her wild hair back from her face, kissed her numb lips, stared into her eyes with his troubled green gaze. He repeated the process several times, murmuring reassurances.

"I'm okay now," she whispered when she felt strong enough.

He kissed her and she felt hot tears on his cheek.

"I have to keep you safe," he breathed into her ear, nuzzling her neck. "You Complete me." The anguish in his voice broke her heart.

"No," she said, stroking his hair. "Now you Complete me."

He sat with his back against the oak headboard and cradled her in his lap.

"I have an idea," he said, brightening. "A way to keep you safe. Let me think for a minute."

Rook relaxed into him, synching her breathing to his and listening to the steady beat of his heart.

Suddenly the world shifted, becoming slippery and weirdly stretchy. Rook thought she was coming apart again, utterly, but as the seconds passed and her situation didn't worsen she realized this was something else, something familiar. Kyle's arm tensed around her.

Then it was over.

Rook opened her eyes and knew immediately where she was: the web chamber on the asteroid. The rock-walled cavern held little she could see in the greenish light besides the glistening spiderweb. All of the creepy cocooned abductees were gone, and the spiders themselves were not in evidence.

Her slight movements were enough to break her free from Kyle's grasp and she began to float away from him in the low gravity, her dress billowing with a life of its own. She shot out her hand and grabbed his, pulling the two of them together in a comical bounce.

"So it is real," he said, smiling. "You'll be safe here. We'll be safe."

He kissed her and it was joyous. "Wait here. I need to find some clothes and talk to the aliens. Establish some ground rules."

***   ***   ***

Marsh considered not going to the door. He considered it very seriously, because whoever it was might simply go away. He would just send them off if he did go to the door, so there was a certain elegance about not getting involved.

The knock came again, and it sounded determined. Marsh headed into the front hall.

Every day since Melissa's death there had been at least one reporter on the porch. The persistent ones came back several times. Then there were the morbid tourists. Marsh could at least understand why journalists would turn up, why they might even presume they'd get in, but the amateurs disturbed and puzzled him.

He reached the door and looked out through the leaded glass, surprised to recognize the visitors. The woman was the piercer, Rook Brandymoon. With her was Fin Tanner, whose reverse-Houdini into the TEF's old listening post downtown became a minor legend. Marsh wondered if Fin would remember him.

"Rainbow," Marsh called over his shoulder, "we have company."

He opened the door. "Welcome to Threshold House. Please, come in."

Rook sidled through the doorway, lost and worn and a little afraid. Fin followed her closely, protectively. He glanced up at Marsh, and gave him the hairy eyeball.

He remembered.

"Why don't we have a seat in the living room." Marsh led the way. His guests sat on the edge of the sofa. Fin pointedly refused to make himself comfortable, and Rook looked like she might cry at any moment, not for the first time today.

Rainbow came into the room and said, "Oh!" with a happy chirp of recognition. She saw the grim mood of their guests and stopped short.

Fin said, "We want to talk to you two, alone."

"Well, we are," Marsh said. "Alone. Everybody else left."

Rook and Fin looked at each other in mild alarm, and Rainbow and Marsh sat quietly while the visitors sorted out how this news made them feel. Eventually they shrugged, and Fin took a large breath to speak.

"We have some information about the jewelry. We thought you should know the government has it."

Relief bathed Marsh in coolness, and now he and Rainbow gave each other a look, and a small shared smile. Their decision to accept jobs with the agency was the right course to follow. With access to the nanotechnology they could continue their work on the Dream Machine on their own time.

Fin continued. "Not that we know where it is, like to point at a map. Which is really why we're here."

"We need it. Some of it, anyway," Rook broke in. "We need you to steal as much as you can for us."

The bluntness and urgency of the request startled Marsh, and he struggled to find the right words to respond.

"Absolutely," Rainbow said in a firm voice.

"Thank you!" Rook gushed. Both women now looked ready to cry.

Marsh knew Rainbow's empathy was in overdrive because she wanted to make up for maintaining a deception, for using Rook to get at the jewelry before. The symmetry now was poetic, and he didn't blame Rainbow for lunging at the chance to atone. All the same, he would have preferred to talk things through before agreeing to break quite so many laws.

"Yes, thank you," Fin added. "You can't know how important this is." His eyes were moist. Marsh felt bad for not crying.

"Thank you," Rook repeated, and she and Fin got up.

The past few minutes began to feel unreal. Rainbow looked pleased as she came back from closing the door.

"What just happened?" Marsh asked.

"If we dragged our feet, they would try something crazy. It's not like what they're asking is any different from what we were planning

anyway, and it's not like we were going to not help them. Why play around at being unsure?"

"I am unsure," Marsh insisted. Rainbow quirked her eyebrow at him. "Well, I mean it's espionage. Yeah, we planned to abuse our clearances a bit, but this is different. This isn't in the gray area. I wanted to stay in the gray area for a while."

Rainbow smiled. "Those are all excuses, and you know it."

Marsh shook his head, but he smiled too. "Some of them sounded like pretty good excuses to me. You should know, normal people have to go through a process, with definite stages. You skipped right over the 'Scared Shitless' stage and I was waiting for you to be struck by lightning. Since it looks like that won't happen, okay. I'm on board."

*** *** ***

Fin and Rook shuffled into the house and sat next to each other on the black leather sofa.

Vesuvius wanted to ask if they found the bugged jewelry, but their subdued demeanor suggested they hadn't. He kept quiet.

A full minute passed without conversation. Vesuvius tried to gauge whether he should suggest a chess match.

"I wish we had another angle," Fin said. "Something we could do in the meantime. Or something we could just do, without needing to rely on anyone else at all."

Vesuvius wouldn't get a better cue.

"I keep telling you to play chess, but you won't listen." The two of them looked his way and Fin got an annoyed face.

"Explain," he said.

"Like you said," Vesuvius replied. "Something you don't need other people for. You can go right ahead." He knew they weren't seeing his real meaning, but he wasn't sure how to be more specific. "You should use the new table," he added.

Fin and Rook looked to each other and back to Vesuvius.

"Why?" Rook asked. "What does it do?"

"I don't know," Vesuvius said, "but there's something odd about it.

When you play, it behaves differently from Fin's other chessboard. It doesn't do it on every move. I haven't seen enough to understand it yet. You never play a full game because you always get distracted by sex."

"It didn't do anything odd, though," Fin argued. "We were there, playing the game. We were watching the board the whole time, at least at first."

"I could see it moving and changing shape. I could feel it, on a deeper level."

"And you want us to mess around with it some more?" Rook asked a bit crossly.

"Well, yes."

Rook and Fin went to the chess table.

"It's just a low-grade antique," Fin said. "It didn't even come with all the original pieces."

"Wait a second," Rook said. She went to her coat and reached into the pocket and returned to Fin with her prize. She opened her fist and displayed a pale green statuette of a warrior queen, a veritable Boadicea in a chainmail skirt, sword at her side, a spiky crown atop the long, wild hair that covered her bare breasts.

"I found this in Severin's attic." Rook held the slender figurine near the chess table, turning it from side to side. The grain and color matched the light squares on the board.

"Wow," Fin said.

Rook straightened and held the piece out toward Fin.

"Don't you think," she asked, "this looks like it belongs with the chessmen on display in Kyle's apartment?"

Chapter Nineteen

THEY'RE JUST HORSES

If there is a document, such as a family bible, showing the complete history of Shaw Oracle, Brian Prophet Shaw has it. And he's not sharing.
from *Brainwashed* by Julie Rome ©1998 Futhark Press

Seeing the aliens in person was not something Kyle was prepared for.

They didn't look like spiders at all. They looked like something out of a cheap sci-fi movie, little green men with oversized heads and huge eyes that never blinked. Their arms and legs were spindly, almost mechanical. Why did Fin think of them as spiders?

Not that this was much better. They were just so… alien. And far too numerous for casual conversation. Then again all of them were really just one… not person, exactly. One *thing* to talk to.

Kyle's adrenal glands weren't reading any of those memos. The cave smelled like waxy hydrocarbons, faint, but enough to make the whole place feel flammable. Floating felt like falling, which further unsettled him. His nakedness didn't matter to the aliens, but it made him acutely aware of the nightmare forms surrounding him.

A trio of aliens approached.

"Thank you for taking us in," he said to the one in the middle. He knew he didn't need to address any particular one, but felt ridiculous otherwise.

It is our honor, he heard in his mind. *We regret that our physical manifestation is making you uncomfortable.*

"I just need to get acclimated," Kyle insisted. "And I need to discuss

details of our arrangement with you."

After a brief pause, the aliens said, *We will do our best to live up to whatever you require.*

Kyle liked the sound of that.

We are eager to begin.

"I don't have a to-do list for you, yet."

The plan will take shape around the goal, as a crystal forms around a mote.

Now what the hell were they talking about?

"What the hell are you talking about?"

We are prepared to perform our duty. We will help you unite the mind of your race.

"Slow down," Kyle barked. "Slow way the fuck down." The three aliens in front of him startled, backing up a step in perfect unison. The sudden move split their arms and legs. They had not four limbs, but eight, and the staring 'eyes' weren't on their faces.

They were spiders after all, spiders who learned a trick to imitate bipedal form.

"Holy shit!" Kyle took a step back himself. The trio gave up their act and lowered themselves into a more comfortable posture, now matching the image from Fin's memories.

Kyle said, "Let's deal with my issues first, shall we? Then we can maybe have a chat about long-range goals."

Of course. Please tell us what you require.

"All right. Ground rules. No talking to my brother or his wife. No bringing anybody out to this rock, especially not my brother or his wife. You got that?"

Yes. We will not molest Fin, or the Rook who dwells with him on Earth.

Kyle's request hadn't sprung from any concern that Fin be free from molestation, but he was pleased to have their agreement regardless.

We will transport no other humans to the asteroid.

"Super. Get me some clothes."

As you wish.

"We'll need water, and food."

We have already established these things, in anticipation of guests. We are well versed in matters of human nutrition, respiration, and sanitation.

They'd given this a lot more thought than Kyle.

"Wonderful. Your hospitality is appreciated. One other request."

Certainly.

"Privacy. Don't come around unannounced." If at all.

The need for privacy, of course, vanishes once unity is attained.

"Knock it off," Kyle grumbled. "I said we're not talking about that right now."

This rebuke prompted a lengthy silence. Eventually Kyle realized they let him have the last word.

On the way back to Rook, a golden glint caught his eye. He changed course, and discovered the other Rook's wedding band resting against the rugged rock surface of the passage. She must have ditched it up here when she ran away from him. He read the inscription, PUT IT BACK ON, ROOK, and smiled.

"I have something for you," Kyle said as he glided over to Rook. She looked like a doll, floating with her arms by her sides and her feet sticking out comically from her skirt.

Kyle unrolled his hand, and the ring rose slowly from his palm. Her azure eyes sparkled as she watched it tumble. Kyle caught it in his fingertips and slid it into place between her left pinkie and middle finger, guiding it over the length of her missing digit. An invisible force akin to magnetism tugged it from his grasp and snapped it into place.

"I love you," Kyle said.

The ring moved with her hand as if the finger were there. Rook beamed at it, and at Kyle, and seized him in a passionate hug. She plastered his face with kisses, pausing every few seconds to look at the ring again and melt his heart with her smile.

***   ***   ***

A late night chess game had Vesuvius assuring both Rook and Fin that their chess table was behaving strangely, even if they couldn't see it. His descriptions were vague and confusing, and he seemed frustrated that the humans weren't more impressed. They cut the experiment short.

What they really needed, Rook decided, was more information about Shaw. He was Fin's grandfather, and the chessmen in his penthouse matched the queen she'd stolen from Severin. With Kyle and his concubine in residence, she and Fin couldn't just go collect those other pieces, so she opted for the next best thing. Research.

Driving to Barnes & Noble instead of walking downtown to the used bookstore spared her the likelihood of encountering someone she knew, someone who would notice she wasn't currently pregnant. They *were* getting Thumper back, and she wanted to be spared awkward explanations.

She bought a book entitled *Brainwashed*, and took it home to devour. It felt good to stretch her investigative muscles.

The cover featured a retro television with a gold cross glowing from its screen. The cross, the saintly TV, and its corona of beatific radiance were all printed with metallic ink. But it was the text under the title that piqued her interest.

The Bizarre Family History and Controversial Rise to Fame of Brian Shaw

When Fin returned from signing for his leave of absence at Binary Images, Rook was keeping four different places in the book with her fingers.

"Is it good?" he asked.

"Yes," Rook said without looking up. "A lot of it is about Shaw's career, which is boring, but there's also a whole history of his family, which is anything but."

"That's my family too, you know."

"Yeah, you might not want to start telling lots of people about that, Muffin."

Rook opened the book to the first spot she'd been saving. She read:

James and Adam Shaw brought their families together each Sunday after church. They were a religious family, and close-knit. James and Adam were twins, their wives were sisters.

Identical twins occur in the Shaw family with startling frequency, perhaps because of early generations' habit of pairing first cousins for marriage — twin brothers with twin sisters. The previous year, James's sons married Adam's daughters in a double wedding, and it was planned for Adam's sons to reciprocate and marry James's daughters once the girls got a little older.

On March 9, 1851, the extended Shaw family was gathered at Adam's house when something terrible happened, something which had an immediate and dramatic impact and changed the course of all future generations of the family. This event led directly to the enigma that is Brian Prophet Shaw.

In letters from the time, the family calls this event the Angelic Visitation (see Appendix I).

A bright, greenish light appeared inside the house, opening a window in the air too bright to look through, obviously a view of heaven. A voice "made of many voices" spoke. There was disagreement about its exact message, but all agreed it spoke of protection or safety. When this "angel" withdrew, it left behind a singular artifact: an ornate chess table. Arrayed across it were the armies, detailed figures carved from jade.

Everyone gathered to watch James and Adam finish the game in progress. The first several moves were uneventful, but when James moved his rook the squares on the board seemed to move. This remarkable behavior continued through several more turns, until a doorway opened in the air. The landscape on the other side was a terrifying "lake of green fire." Voices cried out, begging

and desperate. The Shaw family were convinced they faced the entrance to Hell. They heard Lucifer himself invite them to join him. When they refused, the fallen angel demanded, becoming increasingly agitated. The family fled the house in terror.

"The description of the voices reminds me of the conversations I've had with the Id," Fin said.

"I thought so," Rook said. "The green fire stuff sounds an awful lot like where I exiled Brook and Bramble, too."

"Our table opens a portal into the Collective Id."

"If you play the right game. There's nothing in here about how the board was set up when these Shaw idiots got it."

"We're good at chess, right Cookie?"

"Right Muffin."

"We'll figure it out. We'll solve the puzzle, open the portal, and sneak into the Elsewhere and save Thumper."

"You make it sound so easy," she sighed.

"Does the book say anything else helpful?"

The Shaws debated what should be done about the table. It was dangerous and should never be used again. At the same time it was a holy relic, given to them by an angel of God. The angel charged them with keeping it safe, so it could not be destroyed.

In order to assure that the chess set could never harm anyone, it needed to be divided, the parts separated. Abel and Seth Shaw were precipitously married to their young cousins who, at 13, were deemed old enough after all. Those two young couples were given charge of the white chessmen and sent away to find a safe place in which to guard them. The black pieces and the board would remain with David and John Shaw.

Abel and Seth and their child brides had the more difficult mission. After outfitting themselves as well as

possible, they set off to found a new home, far away from civilization. They ended up in a rocky, inhospitable valley in the Ozark mountains. Records show they passed through St Louis in May of 1851 (see Appendix III), but after that there is no documented contact with the outside world until the summer of 1949 when 14-year-old Brian Shaw walked out of the woods and into tiny Blessed, Missouri, and into history.

"And back here, in the appendices," Rook said, flipping to the spot held by her pinkie:

Appendix II

In 1980 I accompanied my mother to her grandmother's funeral and to ready her old farmhouse for sale. Among the generations of accumulated bric-a-brac in the attic I made an interesting find: a jade figurine, two inches high, depicting an armored warrior. It caught my eye because it was so unlike anything else in the house. In the small wooden chest along with the serene-looking little figure were several handwritten letters.

Those letters and that small piece of carved jade inspired the genealogical research that led to this book.

As you can see from the family tree, Brian Shaw and I are distant cousins. My great-great-great grandparents were Ruth and David Shaw, siblings of the four founders of Shaw Oracle. It's not possible to say exactly how Shaw and I are related since no public records are available for the 98 years his branch spent in Shaw Oracle.

David and Ruth Shaw took charge of half of the black chessmen and, upon their deaths, passed them on to their grandchildren along with the letter reproduced below. This is the source of my information about the Angelic Visitation.

The white army stayed in Shaw Oracle, more or less intact, until Brian (Prophet) Shaw left in 1949. During excavations of the site, I uncovered a shattered rook, a damaged knight, and an intact pawn. Pictures of those pieces are included in Photo Insert 3, along with a publicity photo of Brian Shaw, taken in his penthouse apartment at the Shaw Ministries Compound. In the background, slightly out of focus, you can make out a display case containing the remainder of the white army. Obviously it meant something to young Prophet Shaw for him to bring it with him to civilization.

"It was her great-grandma's attic where she found the pawn," Rook recapped, "and on the family tree her great-grandfather's name is Parnell Tanner. Ever heard of him?"

Fin shook his head.

"The pictures from her dig in Missouri are cool." She flipped to the spread. "The pieces she excavated definitely go with the ones we've seen."

Fin shook his head some more. "'Angelic visitation'?"

"We know something happened." Rook handed him the book. "The table is real."

"Well it must have been the Id. Where people now see aliens, then it was angels. It depends on the current state of the collective unconscious. That's how the Id operates."

He stopped speaking and stared at the open book.

Rook waited for several seconds. "What's up?"

"I have to ask Brad about great-great-grandpa," Fin answered. "The knight in the picture matches those horse figurines of his."

*** *** ***

Kyle was turning out to be something of a disappointment.

Agreeing to his terms without negotiation was an obvious blunder, in hindsight. It had seemed reasonable to suppose Kyle wanted to see humanity unified. His track record spoke for itself. Acquiescing to his

short-term demands served to help him establish a home here, and in that regard succeeded immensely.

Now it would mean breaking a promise to approach Fin again, meaning Kyle had made himself the sole option. And he was preoccupied with other matters. Copulating, principally. Like now, for instance.

"I thought you liked to keep the dress on."

"I don't need it so much anymore."

"Need it?"

"To keep from splitting apart. Ever since you gave me this ring, I'm cured. I'm whole."

"That's wonderful. Move your knee a little."

"Ohhhh!"

"Mmmmm."

This round of activity would last for hours. It happened several times per day, leaving little time for anything else. Kyle had no interest in anyone but the female, nor any goal other than more intercourse with her.

Could this possibly be the same Kyle Tanner?

Fin and his female, on the other hand, pursued several interests besides one another. They played a good deal of chess, albeit not many actual games in the conventional sense. They also maintained close contact with a tight circle of family and acquaintances.

Surveilling Fin was force of habit, with a twist of wistfulness. And it was not forbidden by the terms of their agreement with Kyle. Despite the fact that working with him had been arduous, and despite the ferocity of his refusal to help with the unification project, Fin remained an object of fascination. He too had evolved a great deal. Matured. Many signs pointed to him as the agent of destiny, which made it inscrutable that his attitude about completing the work was so enduringly hostile.

Logically, those signs must point to Kyle instead. A message speaking of one Tanner might be mistaken for the other.

Kyle at least never repudiated unity. Was working with him any worse than working with Fin?

Impossible to say, as working with Kyle was still in the realm of the hypothetical.

He was a different person than the impassioned orator and skillful general who, not so long ago, nearly brought about a form of mental unity for his species.

He needed a reminder of those heady times, of his power and what it felt like to wield it. He needed motivation.

When properly motivated, he showed the ruthlessness necessary to usher in such an enormous transformation. He sacrificed 3,000 human lives for the sake of a grand vision. It had not been Kyle's own vision, but one he appropriated from Shaw. That was the tragic thing, that he'd had to be stopped. Could his efforts have been redirected rather than counteracted, the great design might have even crystallized then.

Seeing Kyle fall, supplying the fire that burned him, had been confusing and distressful. Fin called those shots. He wasn't satisfied until Kyle lay broken. Kyle, now risen from the ashes, had a second chance if only he would see it.

He should be demanding action, atonement. When he called to be brought to the asteroid, hope flourished that Kyle would take command. Amends could be made!

His apathy was like being spat upon.

It was time to press the issue, rouse him even if it meant angering him. As soon as he had taken his fill of the clone woman, Kyle would part with a few moments of his undivided attention. It was a small price for room and board.

*** *** ***

Vesuvius worried about his humans.

Rook sat on the sofa, feet tucked under herself, flipping through her new book and marking pages with strips of newspaper. Her serious expression was at odds with the fanciful paisley pattern of her minidress.

Fin kept fidgeting with the chess table, frowning and sighing. The storm clouds in his eyes showed no signs of lifting.

The doorbell rang, filling the house with the oddly somber sound of *La Cucaracha* played on a xylophone.

"I hate that doorbell," Fin said as he crossed the room and opened the door.

Vesuvius was surprised. It seemed like something Fin would like.

Willow and Brad walked in, doing nothing to lighten the mood. Willow carried Zen in her car seat. Brad brought a shoebox.

"Mom, Brad. Thanks for coming."

"Ba!" Zen said, which brought a small smile to Fin.

"Ba yourself, Zen," he said and made a face at her.

"Did you bring them?" Rook asked. "The knights?"

Brad held up the shoebox. "They're just horses, but yes, I brought them. What's going on?"

Vesuvius listened with interest while Fin and Rook tag-teamed each other, telling Willow and Brad what they learned from their research into Brian Shaw.

"You think this is *the* chess table," Brad said, pointing. "The one from the angel?"

"Yes," Fin and Rook both said.

"We don't think it's really from an angel," Rook was quick to clarify.

Fin pointed out which pieces came with it.

"This rook," Rook said, picking hers up, "belonged to my grandmother. I used it as a pendant until Fin brought the table home. It matches this other one, see? Plus she had a twin sister, and my Uncle Wyatt and Uncle John are twins. My grandmother must be descended from those Shaws."

"Which means you are, too, Cookie," Fin chided.

"I do realize that, dumbass," Rook teased back. "That brings us to your knights, Brad."

Brad looked trepidatiously at the Nike box beside him on the floor. "They're just horses."

Rook flipped her book open to a page toward the back and held it up for Brad and Willow to see. "They look like this, don't they?"

Vesuvius took advantage of the opportunity to finally see what all the fuss was about. The pages each showed two color photos of damaged chess pieces made out of luminous, pale jade. The first was a lonely castle tower, shattered in some long-ago accident, the fragments fitted together like an incomplete puzzle and matching in every detail Rook's old pendant. Below it on the page was a warhorse figurine made of the same ghostly green jade, missing its right foreleg and ear, and its tail.

Brad nodded once, picked up his box, and handed it to Rook. Willow took possession of the book and began to leaf through it. Vesuvius couldn't tell what she was thinking.

"Just because they match, it doesn't mean it's the same set," Brad said. "I'm sure the manufacturer made tons."

Rook was busy with the newspaper-wrapped contents of the box, and didn't reply.

"I don't believe that," Fin said. "And I don't think you do either, Dad."

Brad sighed and watched Rook set the knights on the coffee table in front of her. Apart from being a darker shade, and intact, they were identical to the one in the book.

"I'm awfully tired of all this intrigue," Brad said. "I want our family to have a normal life, and if Rook's some relative of Shaw's, and your mother is his daughter, it would be nice if I wasn't also in the tree. But in fact the opposite is true. I have *both* knights."

"It's a distant relationship. Like fifth cousins, or something," Willow said.

"That's just it, though," Brad said. "I'm doubly related. One of those came from my mom and one from my dad. Mom always said that's one of the ways they knew they were meant to be together: they each inherited one of these horses. They saw it as romantic. And while we're talking about it, my dad had a twin brother, and so did my grandfather.

And on my mother's side, my Grandma Mirabelle had a twin sister. And her maiden name was Shaw." Brad looked queasy. "Shit. I hadn't thought about that."

***

Vesuvius tried to calculate how many generations of inbreeding could be crammed into 98 years.

All that genetic purification distilled into a single individual, Brian Shaw, who then impregnated Gale, the offspring of the Id itself. Vesuvius could not believe that was a coincidence, but he could also not believe the Id was capable of such long-range planning.

If you ignored the Shaw family after the Id's failed gambit with the chess table, the next bit of interference Vesuvius knew about was the creation of Gale and Severin. From everything Vesuvius heard, the twins in the family were always identical, but Gale and Severin were the shining exception. Being opposite genders made them unique in the Id's sphere of influence, so clearly it was important. The obvious conclusion was the Id intended for them to mate and produce children. To what purpose?

Perhaps what the Id intended didn't matter any longer. Gale and Severin were kept separate until it was too late for them to reproduce, at least together. With their *raison d'etre* out of reach, each was driven to procreate with Id-touched individuals. Gale entered into Brian Shaw's orbit and bore him twin daughters Willow and Melissa. Severin fathered Rook — and her no-longer-imaginary pseudo-twin — with a woman of the Shaw bloodline. The Id bided its time, the one thing it had in abundance.

Vesuvius had difficulty charting the Id's next move, but concluded it was Brad Tanner and his two wives. The machinations necessary to maneuver both of Gale's daughters into sexual relationships with yet another Shaw descendent probably stirred up the aether and planted the seeds of the Divided Man Prophecy in Brian Shaw's mind.

The births of half-twins Fin and Kyle fell in neatly with that prophecy. Severin's daughter Rook filled the role of their Completer.

The child who until recently grew in her womb united Gale's and Severin's bloodlines in the way they were unable to. Equally important, the child had two fathers; three strongly Id-tempered parents. Its chimeric genetics gave it unique potential. Thumper was the culmination of over 100 years of the Id's interference in human events.

No wonder the Id was so pleased to take possession.

What would it do now, and how could Vesuvius hope to help stop it? He thought the answer lay in the frustrating mystery of the chess table.

***

Later, after Willow and Brad took Zen home, Fin and Rook returned to the chess table. Brad left his knights behind, and Fin placed them on the board along with the queen from Severin's attic.

Adding each knight caused a minor rippling effect, subtle enough to be overlooked if you didn't know to watch for it.

The queen caused a far more pronounced disturbance, appearing from Vesuvius's vantage as a brief, bright glimmering of sparks accompanied by a deep thudding note like a bass drum full of laundry.

By the look in Fin's eyes, Vesuvius knew he felt something when he set her on her space. Rook nodded at him. She'd felt it without even touching the board.

"That was pretty intense," Fin said. "Vesuvius, did you see anything?"

"A flash of sparks. The vibration was more impressive, weighty."

Fin nodded. "Okay. Maybe now we're getting somewhere. I felt that too. We all did, when before it was just you, Vesuvius."

"That's the only original white piece we have," Rook said.

Fin frowned. "Why would only one side's pieces be special?"

"I don't think that's it," Rook clarified. "Both sides are important, but each is meaningless by itself. I think the set is reacting to becoming more complete."

Fin stroked his chin. "Okay. Let's start a game and see what happens."

Things were different from previous sessions. Both Rook and Fin could feel a mild tingling as they made the moves that caused the squares on the board to migrate. They could still not see the effect, so Vesuvius did his best to keep them posted.

After three more moves with Vesuvius reporting, Fin said, "It's the original pieces. Since most of them are black, that's when we see the effects. Well, Vesuvius does. My only piece that does it is the queen."

Rook nodded, looking glum. "We'll never get it to work."

"Hey now," Fin said in a gently scolding tone.

"I mean, it works by playing a game. And it only recognizes the original pieces. Which we don't have, not enough. If the replacements don't count, what we're doing can't ever create a valid game. No white king."

Fin stood and stretched. Vesuvius waited and wondered what unspoken conversation was taking place, as Rook gazed at Fin and he gave an almost imperceptible nod.

After a moment Fin said, "We don't even know what would happen. I mean, the story in the book is pretty vague. Maybe it's better we don't have all the pieces."

Rook sighed and nodded. "The jewelry is a better bet. It just sucks not knowing when they'll have it for us. Or how long it will take Willow to get the portal open. If we could make the table work, it would be something we could do instead of waiting, instead of sitting back while someone else does the hard part."

Fin settled beside her, rubbing her shoulders. "I think we got used to doing the hard part. But would it be so bad if we didn't have to?"

"It's all going to work out, right? It has to."

"It will. We won't give up. And we're badass."

Chapter Twenty

AN INCOMPLETE SET

WEBSTER — No new leads five days into the manhunt for
suspected killer and kidnapper Severin Tenpenny, and police
concede that's a bad sign for the young man taken at the time of
Melissa Tanner's murder.
Webster Daily Press, 4-24-2001

After a couple days of roughing it, Kyle and Rook were set up quite
well. They had a roomy chamber with the gravity augmented to nearly
normal levels, a large, comfy mattress, and a big TV. Rook was safe and
happy. It was a nice little nest, considering its location in a cave millions
of miles out in space.

But the spiders were a colossal pain in the ass. They seemed to think
Kyle should feel obligated to them for all the amenities. Well, maybe if
they gave him any time to enjoy the place he'd start to feel that way.

They had already interrupted four times today to demand a
conference. Yesterday he came out the first time they asked, hoping it
might appease them. After rolling his eyes through an hour of their
wheedling about how cool it would be to jam all of humanity's minds
together into one big gooey wad, then excusing himself politely, he still
had to put up with them barging in on his thoughts.

It wasn't that the spiders were rude, as such. Kyle would have
preferred it if they spoke more directly. They tried to butter him up by
going on about how mighty and special he was, as if their opinion
would matter to him for some reason. They were willfully stupid about
Rook, about how important she was. How much fun she could be in a
room with not-quite normal gravity.

He should have known any friends of Fin's would be annoying.

Fin: the slimy icing on the rancid cake. He was practically in the room whenever Kyle was among the spiders. They obsessed about him, and they spied on him. During the telepathic sermons they delivered, all their thoughts of Fin bled through into Kyle's mind. He saw and heard the surveillance feeds, blended with all the hot air about needing to unite his species, and he couldn't figure out a way to shut it off.

The bugs wished they had Fin instead, were disappointed the brothers weren't more alike.

Kyle told Rook he would be back soon, and told the spiders to shut the fuck up already because he was on his way. As he neared the web chamber, the Fin Channel started to come through. Kyle wrinkled his nose and tried to think about something else, tried to think about Rook waiting for his return, but it didn't help.

Fin and the other Rook were in their house, playing chess. Talking about it, too, snobby chess jargon about stuff named after dusty grandmasters. It did at least make Kyle glad he had the right Rook.

The spiders greeted him and thanked him at great length and made a big fuss. Yeah, yeah. Whatever. The same sales pitch started in again, with that same undercurrent of disapproval that they lacked the social awareness to hide.

Kyle mentally recited *99 Bottles of Beer on the Wall*, trying to guess how many bottles had to be taken down and passed around for this meeting to count so he could leave.

At 58 bottles of beer on the wall, Fin and Rook went to their door. Their visitors were a slender blonde and a distinctively tall man. Rook asked if they'd had any luck, and the girl handed over a small package.

"It's just two pieces," the man apologized as Rook accepted the foil-wrapped bundle. "Rainbow deleted their serial numbers from the databases. I made a false bottom for an Altoids box and we smuggled them out."

The spiders droned on at Kyle. Didn't they listen to their own surveillance?

"Thank you," Fin said. "We don't want you to take any big risks. Keep watching for an opportunity, I guess."

Rook folded back the foil and held the tiny silver objects in her palm. Earrings, or navel rings, or 'wherever you want them' rings. After a pointless ten seconds of staring in silence, Rook wrapped them securely once again.

"Hey," Fin said to Rook with a chuckle, "it might be quicker for you to track down your old clients and tell 'em there was a recall."

Fin and Rook had a line on the jewelry. That they might get their hands on it worried Kyle. He couldn't guess what they would want it for, but the stuff was too potent to wait and see.

The spiders asked a question, he had no idea what.

"I don't care about that," Kyle said in a firm but calm tone. "Here's what you must do next. Focus surveillance on the man and woman who just came to Fin's house. Deliver detailed summaries every eight hours, and report immediately if they deviate from their routine. Is that clear?"

The aliens seemed perplexed, but agreed and tried to apologize for not understanding he had a plan of his own all along. Kyle cut them off.

"Make it up to me by doing a good job on this stakeout."

He left the chamber and propelled himself through the rough stone tunnel, whistling.

*** *** ***

Willow's optimism about this venture was extremely low. It started out high, when she heard Fin's voice over the phone saying they had some pieces of the jewelry. "I'm on my way!" she'd said, almost forgetting to hang up.

At Fin's house she learned 'some pieces' meant 'two pieces,' at which news her outlook crashed and she nearly refused to try. But the kids spent a lot of time prepping the location by wallpapering their little office with foil to block the jewelry's signal. Plus, they were so buoyant, so encouraging, Willow started to feel it herself.

Then she had to figure out how to use these scant resources to accomplish a miracle. She'd had a vague picture in her head of

organizing all the pieces into a circle, reaching through it. The particulars would have come to her as she worked.

Two pieces.

Geometry gave her the finger if she tried to claim that counted as a circle. She had to improvise, but that was, Willow reminded herself, one of her more developed talents.

Inspiration struck, and jubilantly she told Fin she only needed one thing.

"Mom, we don't have one. Nobody does anymore."

No turntable, no vinyl records. A setback for their project, and a reminder of how old she really was. Fantastic. Back to the drawing board, to work out a means of sending the jewelry along a circular path.

Willow jingled the tiny silver objects in her palm, and could almost hear them speaking to her. She closed her eyes and thought back to the day — mere months ago by her personal timeline — when she designed their complicated innards, remembering some of the technical details but finding only smudges and nonsense in place of others.

These tiny transceivers were connected to the Elsewhere. In a limited way, each one was already a portal to it.

Also mere months ago she experimented with creating her own magical table. She had limited success, but enough to know she could do it. Using these electronic marvels as an antenna to gather the unnamed power of the weirdness, it would work even better this time.

"I need a washcloth," she said to Fin. "And dental floss. Do you have any?"

Fin looked puzzled, but nodded and trotted off to the bathroom.

While he was gone Willow picked up the lava lamp to move it off the round cafe table. Rook lurched into motion and intercepted her, looking concerned.

"I need to use the table," Willow explained.

Rook cradled the lamp to her bosom, then set it carefully in the middle of the chess table. A few seconds later she said, "Oh, yeah," and moved it to the floor.

Fin returned and took in the minor redecorating with a furrowed brow. He carried a spool of dental floss in one hand, a green washcloth in the other.

Willow took the items and directed Fin to move the cafe table into the office. There was barely room for the three of them to fit with it. She spread the washcloth on the stainless steel surface of the table, smoothing it carefully.

She pulled off a long strand of floss and tied each end around one of the earrings.

"Now, for the tricky part."

Willow pinched the floss at its center, adjusting her grip until both sides hung exactly even. She held it out over her improvised magic table.

Here goes nothing, she thought.

"Here goes," she announced.

Willow twirled the floss between her fingertips, first one way then the other. She paused a moment before reversing direction each time, letting momentum carry the silver hoops around a few extra times, putting in a few more twists with each pass. As it unwound, centrifugal force pulled the hoops out, and the more iterations she completed the faster they spun and the wider their course, drawing ever-growing circles in the air.

At first the span of the circle grew quickly, but progress leveled off at a foot in diameter. She needed to match the circumference of the table, which meant she was only about halfway.

Willow concentrated, varying her technique in subtle ways to increase the spin. Each inch was harder to gain than the last, and sometimes her timing was off at a crucial moment and she lost ground.

If the silver hoops were heavier her job would be easier. More mass would translate into more momentum to overcome drag, and more weight pulling on the floss would wind it tighter, storing up energy to accelerate things in the other direction. Of course, if they were too heavy this wouldn't work at all. As her fingers focused on building the

speed of the winding and unwinding, her mind focused on calculating the optimum jewelry mass and estimating how much it differed from the actual case.

With each spin, that difference felt less. Each pass, Willow refined her calculations. Each recalculated value was closer to the mass of the actual hoops, and the process again picked up steam.

In another three twists, the difference between real and ideal disappeared, and on the next pass the circle described by the whirling silver matched up with the outline of the tabletop. The floss vanished, but the jewelry maintained its orbit, a glinting blur of movement.

Willow reached down through this circle with her right hand and lifted one corner of the washcloth. Leaning forward, she reached under the washcloth with her left, and felt her fingers close around a metal object.

Withdrawing her hand, Willow held it out for Fin and Rook to see the antique baby rattle resting in her palm.

"It works!" Rook cried.

The rattle disappeared.

Willow nodded, sadly. The whirling circle lost altitude, and a second later crashed onto the tabletop.

"Not well enough," Willow sighed. "It couldn't transport a person, and even if it could it wouldn't last long enough for what you need."

"I'm sure we could find a turntable somewhere," Fin blurted.

Willow shook her head. "Now that I've seen how this worked, I doubt the turntable idea was viable. Not fast enough. Not big enough. I'm sorry."

She retrieved the jewelry. The hoops were ringing, not with actual sound. It was a resonance with the Elsewhere, a residual wave from their participation in making her tiny gateway. Willow squeezed her fist tight around them, straining to capture that mystical tone before it faded.

Rather than simply tapering off, the tone grew fainter then stronger again several times. Willow closed her eyes, listening to that signal, an

echo bouncing back from the main hoard of jewelry. The pieces were all attuned, and that energy affected them all.

Willow opened her eyes and pulled off another length of floss. She set to recreating the portal, ignoring the kids' questions. It went faster this time, because she had a feel for the physics of it and because this time she knew it would work. As she spun it up, she called to that distant cache, inviting all the jewelry to take part.

Although another portal opened, it was no more stable than the first. She felt all the jewelry resonating but there was no flow of power to bolster her efforts here.

"Dammit!" Willow hissed.

The kids were watching her, and when the silence grew awkward Willow said, "I had an idea, but it didn't pan out. Something like this could work, with a few modifications. And with a bunch more jewelry. It's the key, and this isn't enough."

Rook said, "We're hoping to get some more, but it might be hard."

"How much would you need?" Fin asked.

A reasonable question, and Willow started another set of calculations. To scale from the rattle to a person, to extend a few seconds of working time to hours, each of those was an increase of several hundredfold. "A lot. Like, crate-loads."

Rook was crushed. Fin looked sullenly at Willow, and wrapped his arms around his wife.

Tears stung Willow's eyes. "I'm sorry."

*** *** ***

Kyle found the key to his happiness in keeping the spiders busy. While occupied with a task he assigned them, they stayed out of his way and out of his thoughts. In addition to surveilling Fin and the other Rook, and the TEF couple, Kyle had them conducting sweeps of Webster, Donner, and other cities around the globe. Every eight hours, punctually, he had to make himself available for a status report, but the aliens' updates were much briefer and more concrete than their usual yammerings. Kyle could quickly issue new orders and return to the

warm, wet embrace of Rook's thighs.

He would need to devise an actual plan to get the spiders off his back permanently. Maybe it would be easiest just to unite humanity after all. As long as he and Rook weren't part of the new super-blob-mind, what did it matter?

Kyle, it is time for our update.

"I need to teach you how to knock," Kyle grumbled. Rook paused and looked down, but he smiled and grabbed her ass, easing her up and down, getting the rhythm going again, and told the spiders, "I'm busy."

It has been eight hours. It is time for your update.

"Fine," he said, fondling Rook's nipple. "Go ahead. I'm listening."

Rook increased her pace, making a bid for his undivided attention.

Jay Marshall and Rain Beauregard are at their place of employment.

Kyle saw the inside of a nondescript laboratory: white walls, glass-front cabinets, scarred black tabletops. The room lacked windows and looked old and utilitarian, like a high school chem lab. The equipment at the work stations was complex, but unfinished. Most lacked outer casings, their multi-colored wires and circuit boards exposed. Kyle was unimpressed.

The overly tall TEF scientist stood at a lab table, poking the insides of a particularly ugly machine with a voltage meter and making notes on a clipboard. His girlfriend approached, carrying a tray on which lay three barbell studs, each of a different metal.

"Where did she get those things on the tray?" Kyle asked, interested in spite of himself.

Rook dismounted in a huff and rolled to the other side of the bed.

The tracking jewelry came from the vault.

Kyle's head filled with a swish-pan away from the nerds over to an immense door like the one at Kyle's dad's bank. The motion disoriented Kyle and prevented him from going after Rook. He fell back on the bed and was inundated with a tsunami of technical information about the nanotech jewelry, and how the Floating Wisdom used it to track their experimental subjects before their discovery of the wonder that was Fin.

"Stop it!" Kyle croaked. "I don't need to know all that."

The flow of information slowed to a trickle, leaving Kyle with a view of the vault door, overlaid with interference from the Fin Channel.

"I want every single piece of jewelry in that vault. Bring it up here now. Put it in one of the small chambers. You can do your transporter thing through metal walls, right?"

Of course. Our transportation system utilizes dimensions beyond the three recognized by humans and—

"I don't need to know the details. Just do it."

It is done already.

Kyle thought the spiders sounded eager. That was only natural. They assumed he had a glorious plan for the unification of the human species and were excited to aid him. In reality he had no plan at all. It was important to possess the bugged jewelry so no one else could. It was an advantage, a potential weapon no one else should have. Accomplishing this coup felt like a good day's work and Kyle was anxious to get back to more pressing matters, namely the pleasures to be had with his female companion.

"Good work. Now, inventory the jewelry — by hand, or antenna, or whatever. Also maintain surveillance on those two, plus Fin and his wife. Got it? Report back in twelve hours."

Eight hours is the standard interval.

"Now that I have the electronics we're going to change that. Got it?" He tried to sound as stern as possible.

The alien presence retracted from his mind without reply.

Once again able to concentrate on his immediate surroundings, Kyle discovered Rook lying on her stomach, watching TV. He leaned over and placed a kiss on the curve of warm flesh where the underside of her ass met her thigh.

*** *** ***

The frightened looks on Rainbow's and Marsh's faces told Fin their news wasn't good, but he was unprepared for the totality of the badness. "I think we're lucky to be alive," Marsh said. It went downhill from

there. The jewelry was in the vault at the beginning of their shift, gone at the end. All of it. Security footage exonerated the scientists, barely. They were interrogated thoroughly and then fired.

Rook commiserated with the couple and thanked them as she ushered them out.

"Floating Wisdom," Fin swore. "I wonder when they were going to tell me. Dangle it like a carrot so I'd help them on their fucked up mission."

He fumed and stomped around the house. He called to the aliens. He kept it up until he was mentally hoarse and heard not so much as a peep.

"Why did they take it if they don't want to talk to me?" he asked.

"I hear some idiot taught them to play hardball."

Fin scowled.

"Since we have no intention of playing their game, we have no choice but to play our own." She rolled her eyes to the haunted chessboard of doom.

"To play the right game, we need the right pieces," Fin reminded her.

"We know where to get them."

"You up to facing Kyle and Her?"

"To get Thumper back? Fuck yeah!"

**

Fin slumped in the ratty recliner, exhausted. His eyes stung and his head felt too heavy, but not in the good way brought on by certain recreational pharmaceuticals. This was a bone-weary, desperate exhaustion brought on by who-knew-how-many hours sitting in this chair staring at the damn chess table, trying move after move, variation after variation, opening gambit after mid-game finesse.

At least the trip to Donner was uneventful. They'd spent the car ride psyching themselves up for another confrontation with Kyle and the other Rook, but the place was abandoned. Unchallenged they walked in, grabbed the glass display case, and walked back out.

In the car on the way home Rook said, "Ask me again why the aliens took the jewelry."

Fin played along. "Why did those fucking bugs steal the jewelry if they don't want to talk to me?"

"Kyle." Her single word reply hit him like a fist to the gut. Kyle and the aliens were in league now. To what purpose he had no idea, but it couldn't be good.

The rest of the trip home was silent, both of them pondering doomsday scenarios. The hours since their return were spent right here, taking chess advice from a talking lava lamp.

Across the table from Fin, Rook sat on the leather sofa. Apart from her bloodshot eyes she looked alert, and Fin was determined to keep going as long as she did.

The new chessmen definitely matched their table. They were the same eerie pale green. The bishops were little men in clerical robes and mitered hats, identical to the lone bishop in their possession down to the flowing beard. The five pawns also matched their own darker green warriors. Most important they now possessed the white king. They could play a legitimate game.

After cracking her knuckles, Rook made a face at the board and moved a knight out. An unusual first move for her, made all the more unusual by the fact the knight was a picture from Julie Rome's book.

"That shuffled things differently," Vesuvius said.

"Differently good, or differently bad?" Rook asked.

"Differently," Vesuvius said.

Since retrieving Shaw's partial white army they experienced a lot more movement from the board, or at least Vesuvius did. He was eager to help, but had difficulty explaining what he saw. It was like trying to pick a lock relying on someone else's verbal description of how the tumblers moved.

Fin advanced his opposing knight and waited for a reaction.

"Wow," Vesuvius said, and nothing more. The lamp spoke in a monotone, making it impossible to tell if he was genuinely impressed or

being sarcastic.

Rook raised her eyebrows at Fin. Maybe they were finally onto something. She moved her other picture-knight and the lamp said, "Hmm."

Another four moves convinced them they made a wrong move somewhere because, according to Vesuvius, things were now rotating backwards.

As Rook stood to reset the pieces she said, "I just had an awful thought."

"Hit me," Fin said.

"What if it matters which square each individual piece starts on. Like maybe this pawn," she waved one of the white warriors at him, "maybe he has to start on the second square from the left. If he starts on the edge, or in the third spot, or wherever, it doesn't count."

"Aw, fuck."

"I think the Id is catastrophically lonely," Vesuvius said.

Fin cocked his head and looked at the lamp. Where had that come from?

"Too fucking bad for it," Rook said. "It can't have our baby. Now, do you think we should mess around with specific square placements? See if 'Suvi can tell if one is better than the others?"

Fin shrugged, desperate for sleep.

Rook went on, "I wish we knew how the pieces were arranged when the table appeared. The game was supposed to be played from that point." She stopped talking and looked at Fin. "You look like shit, Muffin."

He smiled feebly. "Thanks, Cookie."

"Let's put you to bed. Maybe I'll stay up for a bit with Vesuvius and see if I have any luck with my latest brainstorm."

Fin lacked the energy to argue. He flopped down on the sofa. As his eyes closed he felt Rook pulling his boots off.

*** *** ***

Under their current arrangement, the spiders had a lot of time to

think.

Kyle evinced no desire to interact with them on any level. He had acclimated to their presence, as hoped. A warmer, more open climate did not result, however. Instead, he and the spiders settled into a state of brittle tolerance that would snap at any mention of uniting the mind of humanity. He was as far away now as when he'd lain comatose on Earth.

Their reports always focused on Fin and Rook, as per Kyle's standing orders, but during surveillance a secondary player held the spiders' attention.

It wasn't sentiment that made Willow so interesting, although she had been the first thing they ever saw. She spun them from her own imagination while journeying in the collective mind. Her more recent feats were just as impressive, despite her evident disappointment.

That never came across in the reports.

Her recent visit to Fin's home was related to Kyle as, "Willow visited and did some magic tricks."

Kyle didn't ask if the magic worked. It wasn't Willow who was under surveillance, so it would have been extraneous detail to describe her limited success.

Nor would Kyle have any interest in understanding the ramifications.

He owned the means to tap into the fabric of the collective human unconscious. Direct access. Willow contacted the Id using only two pieces of the jewelry. Thanks to Kyle's paranoia, the spiders now possessed a truckload. Because they continued to follow his directives, they'd witnessed how it could be used.

All because of Kyle's leadership. All kept secret from him.

It would be premature to bring any of it up with him at this stage anyway. Willow's performance was impressive and inspiring, but calculations showed that even with the prodigious quantity of jewelry at their disposal it would not be feasible to open a portal large enough and stable enough to be of any tactical use. Willow's method would not

scale.

If they could show him a working portal, surely Kyle would listen to them.

And they could! The key lay in constructing an emitter for a special carrier wave, adjusting the transceivers' output — a mere firmware update — and deploying the devices in the correct formation. With the carrier wave to supply raw energy they wouldn't need to boost the power of the individual pieces, just calibrate their resonance so the peaks of all their waves lined up. That, and configuring the array as an antenna to concentrate this augmented output rather than letting it disperse in all directions, would produce geometric signal increases.

It had to be ready for launch before Kyle could know about it. He would divert them if they let him find out too soon, dismiss their careful reasoning and detailed computations. They would need to prove it to him, to open his eyes.

The necessary tinkering was rudimentary for a mind like the spiders'.

Chapter Twenty-One

Crossing the Threshold

The investigation into the theft of the microtransceivers is
inconclusive. There remains no sign of the devices, nor any
indications of a foreign power or rival cell recently handling a
large covert delivery. All potential suspects have been ruled out,
including research staff on duty at the time of the disappearance.
Operation Lullaby internal communication, 4-26-2001

The bugs insisted on an audience, refusing to tell Kyle what it was about.

In the large chamber, they'd woven an opaque sheet of gauzy webbing. It hung from the main web like laundry on the line. They'd told him 'the demonstration' was ready and instructed him to lift one corner of this shimmery panel and reach through.

His reluctance prompted the spiders to think about Fin, and Kyle saw they believed Fin would go along with it, and they admired that. His face flushed with anger, and he felt stupid for being baited so easily by implied jeers of 'chicken!'

Kyle poked his head through an open space in the webbing to look at the underside. No foreign objects planted for his chance discovery. No clever pockets worked into the material. In the spiders' mind he read no deception.

He withdrew his head and reached under the gauze, immediately grasping a small hard object. When he opened his fist he saw a gray-green clump of old coins welded together by corrosion. It faded after a few seconds.

"What was that?"

The spiders were almost too excited to answer, their giddiness trying his patience.

The importance lies not in the item itself, but in how it came to you. You reached into the Collective Id, by way of the portal we generated for you.

This was like the table where he got Rook. The spiders built him one for some reason.

"Why do you think this is useful to me?"

This is a small demonstration! At full scale, this device will offer the power to invade the Collective Id, the chance to seize control.

Kyle blinked. "Go on."

The power lies in the jewelry you so foresightedly directed us to acquire. We built new hardware which enables the jewelry to function as a portal. A portal into the Collective Id, the source of the miraculous inner workings of the jewelry, the place where we were born.

Kyle made himself stop rolling his eyes and listen. At least until he knew why the bugs thought he would care.

Woven into this web, arrayed in careful geometry, are 169 pieces of jewelry. The aggregate result is a stable, persistent portal.

Kyle moved behind the sheet and floated close to inspect the underlying web structure. The intricate design held a shiny silver hoop or barbell at every junction.

He considered the many dozens of cases of the stuff stowed in a nearby chamber.

"That's going to be a big web."

In the final design there will be no web. Such a deployment would be static, whereas real-time adjustments are needed for full optimization. Additionally, by meshing the transceiver impulses with the natural electrochemical signals of the central nervous system there is a boost in—

"How will it be rigged, if not in a web?" Kyle cut in, his impatience returning.

They showed him. The jewelry would be installed in 10,201 human subjects, each transported to particular coordinates so the mob's overall

arrangement would form the array. The people could even be puppeted to fine tune the geometry and perform the necessary real-time adjustments.

We will initiate the carrier wave and position the devices. When the configuration is perfect, this wave will be relayed and amplified throughout the array, opening a glorious doorway into the Collective Id. It is told in the Divided Man Prophecy that you can enter and assume control. We will achieve our Great Work at last.

Kyle had assumed this obsession of theirs was purely theoretical, that however much they talked it wasn't something they'd ever be able to actually do. He'd been wrong. Bluffing wasn't their style, and it was unwise to bet against them on anything technical.

"You guys can really do this, can't you?"

Yes.

Well, that settled it. Kyle shrugged. He had Rook. Let the bugs do whatever they wanted with everyone else.

We can create the portal, but the next task is beyond us. It has to be someone special, per the prophecy.

Kyle scowled. "You're saying it has to be me?"

It has to be a Tanner.

Kyle's expression shifted to a sneer. They didn't have the balls to break the agreement, so they couldn't get Fin involved. His face clouded as he thought about potential loopholes. They wouldn't have to bring Fin here, hell they wouldn't even have to talk to him. They might set it all in motion and shanghai the bastard without violating the rules.

Shit. There was no way for it to play out that didn't suck. Fin had to stay out of it, period.

It had been perfect when he could blow them off, knowing it would never amount to anything. Now, he couldn't keep stringing them along.

It was unjust that these aliens were about to get everything they wanted by depriving Kyle of the only thing he wanted. He wished them dead, but then his floating love grotto would become a tomb for Rook as well. Dammit, they had him trapped!

You are troubled.

Wait! What trap? They were talking about making a magic doorway and holding it open for him. The Id wasn't such a bad place. He lived there for a long time. Rook also, in a way. This time they would be there together, physically. Very physically. They would never come back. All he had to do was say yes.

"No, not troubled. Impressed. I suppose you'll want Rook to do the piercings?"

When the spiders finished heaping thanks upon him, he went to tell Rook about the project. She was delighted at the idea of piercing unwilling strangers and watching them tromp around in formation like zombies.

"It'll be marching band mind control," she chuckled. "I'll need some equipment, and an assload of latex gloves."

*** *** ***

The initial giddy luster of surreptitiously puncturing hordes of strangers had worn off long ago, the illicit thrill replaced by grinding monotony and cramping, sweaty hands.

"I'll have to open a new box soon, babe," Kyle said. "Do you want barbells or more hoops?"

Rook tilted her head far to the right, stretching her neck and shoulders as she pondered her answer. "Barbells."

One of the smaller spiders scuttled forward with her next customer, an unconscious middle-aged man in green and gray Buck U sweats. Rook looked disdainfully at his receding hairline and flabby physique.

"Maybe I should pierce his love handles."

Kyle snorted. "Stick to ears."

Rook picked up the last hoop from the carton. There were 48 pieces per box and this was the 102nd box, she thought, so that made… a whole fucking lot of earlobes.

Initially she had fun randomizing which body parts to pierce and imagining the consternation of her customers when they regained consciousness and discovered a hoop in their nipple or a stud in their

dick. But that didn't last. It took too long to expose the really interesting sites, and when it became clear how many of these damn things there were she opted for simple earlobes and the occasional eyebrow or lip. Also falling victim to the assembly line rush-job mentality was any pretense of sterilization. Rook made sure her gloves were intact, with the left ring finger tucked inside-out to keep it from flopping around, and left it at that.

"I'd say we're about halfway done," Kyle said as Rook fastened the gold hoop in place.

Rook groaned. "My hands are cramping."

"We'll take a break." Kyle grinned and said, "Do you have any idea how pornographic you look wearing nothing but lingerie and rubber gloves?"

Rook surprised herself by blushing.

Kyle bobbed his eyebrows at her. "Let's find a clean pair of gloves and get you in bed."

*** *** ***

Headlights splashed across the living room wall as a car pulled into the driveway. Brad put his bookmark in place and stood to meet Willow as she came in. She looked distraught, a look she had been wearing for the past week. It hurt to see her so worried.

"No luck?" He pulled her into a hug and kissed the top of her head.

"No luck," she confirmed. "They're exhausted. I finally talked them into sleeping."

Fin and Rook had been banging their brains against their allegedly magic chessboard for three days and Willow was their babysitter, making sure they ate and got a modicum of rest.

"You look exhausted, too, Wil."

She nodded and went into Zen's room to say goodnight to the slumbering baby. Brad checked the doors and turned out the lights on his way to their room. As they lay on the bed together Brad began kneading the knots in Willow's shoulders.

"Tell me," he said.

She sighed and rolled over to look at him. "They're so close. Closer than I got."

"You said you reached in. Or through. Across?" Brad was uncomfortable with this topic but desperate to ease Willow's burden.

"What I did was a parlor trick compared with what they're doing. The potential they're working with is orders of magnitude stronger. It's like I've got a jar with a couple lightning bugs and they've got a klieg light. All they have to do is plug it in."

"Will they be able to?"

"I hope so." She looked glum. "I feel so helpless, Brad."

He squeezed her. "Me, too."

After a minute of uneasy silence Willow whispered, "There is one thing I can do."

"What's that?" Brad suspected he wasn't going to like the answer.

"I can destroy the jewelry before it's used to hurt anyone else."

"What if the kids need it?" Brad was proud of his calm tone.

"They don't. It wouldn't do them any good. Now that I see the real power they're tapping into I can tell my method would never work. Maybe I could have done it with Severin's table…" She blinked tears out of her eyes.

"I think you should do it." It was contrary to his every protective impulse, but he knew Willow needed to do something, anything, to ease her guilt.

She looked at him, disbelieving.

"I know, I know," he said. "I *will* worry while you do it, but I understand that you have to."

"Thank you." She kissed him and sat up. "Now I have to figure out how."

Brad watched in worried silence while she thought. He fought not to make suggestions or ask questions, and at the same time to keep from spinning doomsday scenarios of losing her again.

Finally she said, "I have a plan."

Brad rolled onto his side and looked at her. Despite his dread over

the risks, he was intrigued about this side of Willow. Given her long imprisonment by Severin, his fears were justified. Yet it was a part of her, one he knew of only through hearsay.

"I've never actually seen you do... this."

Willow glanced at him and gave a small smile. Brad fell silent so he wouldn't cause her to make any mistakes.

She lay still for several minutes wearing a look of intense concentration. Her hands began a series of erratic movements under the blankets. To Brad it looked like a pantomime of sorting laundry.

After a few minutes she blew out an irritated sigh and let her hands drop. She took a few slow, deep breaths and resumed.

This time, Brad could tell she was tracing out shapes with her fingertip, drawing something on the underside of the sheet. Her face looked more composed now. Brad started to feel a prickly excitement on the back of his neck, wondering what might happen when she connected with her power source.

What happened was she flung the blankets off and clutched her face, sobbing. Brad reached toward her, wondering if he should panic.

"I can't do it!" Willow wailed. "I'm useless!"

Brad rolled halfway onto her, enveloping her in his arms and cradling her head.

"No you're not," he said. "Shh, it's alright."

"It's NOT alright," Willow croaked, her voice thickened. "If I can't do this, what good am I?"

"You can try again in a little while."

"That's just it," Willow said with a sniffle. "I never have to *try*. Sometimes I need to explore, search out the right feeling. But it's always there, just *there*, and this time it's not. Why now? Why when it's actually important?"

"Maybe you're too keyed up, thinking too much. With most talents, the more you get out of your own way the better it will work." Brad swallowed. Now that Willow's distress had diminished, he had mixed feelings over providing such encouragement. "So," he finished, trying to

keep his voice bright, "be confident and it will come."

Willow wiped her eyes with her knuckles and gave him a warm, sad smile. "Thank you," she said. "I appreciate the pep talk, Coach, but I think I'm going to call it for tonight. You're probably right about psyching myself out. It's so odd, the missing feeling. It's like being blind, only I hadn't noticed because I was walking around with my eyes shut. When I opened them everything stayed dark."

Brad patted her shoulder and gave her a kiss. He had no idea what to say, and didn't trust himself not to beg her to never talk about this again.

"Maybe it's your fault," Willow said sleepily.

Brad tensed, and she gave him a squeeze. "No, I didn't mean," she said, groping for words. "All I meant was, I wanted to impress you. Maybe without an audience I wouldn't have seized up."

"You know it bothers me," Brad muttered.

Willow squeezed him tighter. "Even though it scares you, you told me to try."

Brad kissed her again, because he was unsure what he was supposed to be saying but mainly because she was gorgeous and he was out of his mind in love with her. And she called him brave, even though it was her doing the scary stuff.

Neither of them spoke for the next minute or two, their lips too busy at more primal tasks. Willow said, "I do feel tense. And you feel tense to me. I think we could both use some release."

Brad signaled his agreement by kissing her some more, on her lips and ears and down the side of her neck. She nipped at his collarbones, and what came perilously close to a tickle-fight turned into something much sweeter.

*** *** ***

"We're done," Kyle said. "Everyone's pierced and ready to go."

The web chamber is full and we are eager to begin.

Kyle sighed. "We need to sleep. Give us twelve hours."

Your biological functions will be sufficiently refreshed after eight.

"Give us twelve," Kyle growled. "Then we'll unite humanity." He floated moodily down the corridor and into the chamber he shared with his female.

The spiders maintained cursory oversight of the two humans as they copulated then slept. At the same time they recalculated all of the equations pertaining to the physical distribution of the mind control marching band, as Kyle called it. It was unnecessary, of course, because they did not make mathematical mistakes, but this was the closest they had ever come to the goal of regaining the vast assuredness they once knew with the Floating Wisdom. If anything went wrong, Kyle was unlikely to cooperate again.

At the ten-and-a-half-hour mark, Kyle and Rook awoke and began another session of coitus. The spiders took that as the cue to begin deployment.

In groups of varying sizes the tagged humans were transported to carefully targeted locations in the Shaw Ministries compound on Earth, a site Kyle assured them would remain undisturbed for the duration of their operation. To the aliens' supreme satisfaction the carrier wave functioned perfectly, and each tagged human responded to his or her individual instructions and moved into the required position.

*** *** ***

Brad was in the kitchen making batter, so breakfast was going to be either pancakes or waffles. The sounds of him scurrying and stirring, and the warm, happy baby at her breast, filled Willow with joy.

It made her think of Rook's anguish. She felt sadness and happiness together, then.

Soon she smelled waffles. She switched Zen to the other side and moved to the kitchen where Brad was setting out their plates.

"You are a god," Willow said.

Brad hoisted a prodigious forkload of waffle into his mouth and dedicated his attention to chewing for a few moments. He swallowed and said, "I thought I might look in on Fin and Rook. See if they need any errands run, maybe give them some moral support."

Willow nodded. "I think that's a great idea."

They finished eating, and Brad threw on jeans and a t-shirt, looking more like a college student than he ever had in college. He gave Zen a nuzzle, and kissed Willow. She helped Zen wave bye-bye as he went out the door.

Willow played peek-a-boo with her daughter, her thoughts turning to her failure of the night before. She couldn't sit still, worrying herself with questions about her powers. She paced with Zen, through the kitchen, dining room, and living room, trying to sort her feelings. On one hand she felt a certain level of relief. She knew the kind of trouble such weirdness could get her into. On the other hand, the thought of it being gone made her feel incomplete.

She remembered the exact sensation from last night, what she'd described to Brad as blindness. Now she was afraid to open her eyes again.

Thinking back to the stuck feeling when she created the jewelry in the first place helped her to calm down, because she'd succeeded in that task. She could succeed here too.

Destruction is never as complicated as creation.

She let her memory play back the moment of creation, more a moment of discovery because until she looked down at the paper she'd had no idea what would be there. Perhaps the same process that allowed her to make the stuff would work for the unmaking as well?

With Zen safe in her playpen, Willow tried several things. She doodled without looking at the page, as she had when the original design came into being. Nothing remotely similar to the specifications emerged. She recalled those specs well enough, so she tried a careful recreation which she then ritualistically erased. She went back to unsupervised drawing, devoting her thoughts to the puzzle of what would be the direct opposite of the transceivers, hoping to cancel them out of existence.

Some things don't have opposites. The opposite of a transmitter is a receiver. A transceiver is both, rendering Willow's riddle a koan. How

zen.

There was no progress to show for her efforts, yet the hopelessness from the night before did not accompany her frustration. This morning she could feel her connection to the weirdness. She could push the buttons and turn the knobs, while last night she couldn't even reach them.

Willow stretched her neck and shook out her fingers, cramped from all the sketching.

Not only could she feel the currents of the weirdness, she could also feel subtle filaments woven through it, connecting her to individual pieces of the jewelry. She started tracing some to see where they led her.

They all led to residents of the Webster area. She followed a couple dozen strands, and developed a rough idea of their total number. Maybe as few as 200. Those were all she could sense.

Where was the other 98% of it?

Willow went to the kitchen and refilled her coffee as she pondered the unmaking of those specimens she located. She absently plucked out a simple tune on an imaginary harp, playing her notes on the jewelry filaments. Certain strands held their vibrations longer, and Willow experimented with the effect. Soon she set aside her mug to use both hands to create the music.

She discovered the voice of each string could be adjusted by pulling it taut or letting it relax. And, each piercing hoop and barbell had a frequency that would overload it and burn it out, a death note. She created an eerie blend of bending harmonies, chamber music for whalesong and theremin. Anyone watching would have thought she was rehearsing to conduct a stormy symphony, not performing the piece.

Three minutes later she picked up her mug and took a well-earned sip. All the jewelry she'd tracked down was now defunct.

Which left her free to concentrate on the mystery of the missing remainder with renewed confidence. It also left her view that much less obstructed.

The missing specimens would all have their own tendrils connecting them back to her in some way. It shouldn't matter what kind of vault protected them, or how deep underground it was buried. The connections should still be there.

Suddenly a filament lit up, and another a few seconds later. She watched in bewilderment for a full minute as the shining strands accumulated.

Willow wanted to know why this was happening, but it wouldn't matter once she'd finished her job. She started warming up her new and growing orchestra.

Her previous technique didn't work.

She could slide the pitch up and down, but their voices were joined by a new overtone that drowned out her adjustments.

Thirty minutes of tugging and plucking at these new strands brought her no closer to finding the death note frequencies, and they kept appearing at a brisk rate. She estimated there were now nearly a thousand, and every one of them traced to the same general area outside of Donner.

Willow abandoned any pretense of musicality. She tried to yank the lines loose, to break them, kink them, tangle them. She exhausted herself trying to tear them out by the roots.

While she rested she studied the phenomenon. The people materialized out of nothingness, and as they did she could feel it.

Willow selected one filament and tried every way she could think of to break it. She twanged from it every tone it could produce, without results. She plucked out 'initiate self destruct sequence' in Morse code, followed by a stream of profanity. Meanwhile hundreds more joined the throng.

Whoever was using the devices knew as much about them as she did. Not only their technical specifications, but their supernatural specs as well. Willow reeled at the inescapable truth of it. They'd used this knowledge to engineer a companion wave that interacted with the jewelry's signal, stabilizing it and strengthening it. The result was

something new, something synergistic. Something beyond Willow.

She could not unmake it.

***   ***   ***

Fin wearily placed his bishop. "Check." He and Rook had played this same sequence at least five times already. Rook had the black army this time.

"Have I ever moved my rook at this point?"

Fin tried to remember but Vesuvius answered. "No."

"Okay. It's not a good move, but..." Rook slid her namesake tower ahead to foil Fin's attack and all the squares on the board slid with it, like an Escher-designed tile puzzle. Vesuvius's descriptions of such things had become routine, but this was the first time Fin saw it for himself.

"Whoa," Rook breathed.

"You saw it too?"

She nodded emphatically.

"That was a big one," Vesuvius confirmed from his perch on the cafe table. "The most movement I've seen so far."

Rook picked up her notes and scribbled down the move. "We must be getting close."

"What should I move?" Fin asked as he studied the game. He had several options, but none of them looked promising. He wiped his palms on his jeans.

Rook drew her bare feet up and rested her chin on her knees while she studied the board. "You can take my rook with your pawn."

Hand trembling, Fin did just that. The table seemed to sigh and subside into something less than it had been.

"Shit," said Fin and Rook at the same time.

"Reset them, quick," Rook said. "We'll start over."

Consulting Rook's notes, it didn't take long to reconstruct the game to the fatal point. This time Fin advanced his knight, placing it alongside the rook. The table became a veritable kaleidoscope of twirling patterns.

Wide-eyed, Rook wrote the move down. "I'm still in check," she

said. Fin heard a spark of excitement in her voice that kindled in him something like optimism. They might actually make this work.

He held his breath.

Rook reached for her queen to take his knight, but changed her mind and shifted her king to the right instead.

The board erupted into complicated gyrations, the layout becoming an ever-widening circle of interlocking puzzle pieces. Fin clambered over the back of his chair to avoid the growing chaos and saw Rook scramble off the sofa, too. He ran to her and held her.

Rook squeezed him painfully and stared into the expanding ring. It was full of undulating green fire and overlapping voices.

Terror gripped Fin. Their baby was in there. He looked at Rook and saw determination on her face. With one hand she clutched at her abdomen where Thumper should be.

The chess table kept unfolding, the squares shifting and clattering like an endless Jacob's ladder. All the game pieces hovered on heat shimmers before tumbling to the floor. Every hair on Fin's body felt the currents of energy pouring from the Elsewhere.

The portal tipped upright, a gaping hole in the wall between reality and madness. It was oval, bowed like the chessboard it once was, and rimmed with the chessboard's alternating dark and light squares. The chess table opened itself entirely, blossoming into their entry to a vivid green hellscape.

"I have to go in there," Rook whispered.

"*We* have to," Fin corrected gently. He kissed her for what he hoped was not the last time.

Holding hands they stepped forward together and crossed the threshold.

*** *** ***

When only 100 subjects remained, the spiders contacted Kyle, happy to catch him between coitus sessions.

It has been twelve hours, Kyle Tanner.

"Are you ready?" Kyle asked.

The final humans are being positioned now.

"I wasn't talking to you. Rook, are you ready?"

She smiled and said, "Yeah."

"Put on your wedding dress."

The aliens began the fine adjustments necessary to bring the portal into alignment by directing specific humans to shift their position.

"They look like they're drunk," Kyle commented.

It is more akin to somnambulation.

"Whatever."

The thousands of pieces came into perfect alignment and the long-anticipated moment arrived.

We are ready, Kyle Tanner. Unite us with all of humanity in the glorious oneness!

"Rook and I will go do that."

We will follow you!

"No!"

Kyle radiated anger the likes of which the spiders had not felt since his brother destroyed their previous unity. They cowered.

"You will wait here," he ordered, "until I call you. Do you understand?"

Yes! Yes!

"Start it up."

Ripples like ultra-violet heat shimmers lit the sky above Kyle's mind control marching band. As the formations shifted and spelled words in secret alphabets, the glow coalesced into a burning green landscape of electricity and fire.

Rook gasped. "I know that place!"

Kyle lifted her into his arms. "Send us through. And Do. NOT. Follow."

The terrified spiders rushed to comply. Kyle held Rook and kissed her as the transporter whisked them from the asteroid and into the maw of the writhing green storm.

Chapter Twenty-Two

TIE-DYE FIRE

A Completer, an Unknowing angel with Shadowed Wings,
Shall heal the Divided Man and restore Light upon the Earth.
from *New Revelations*, by Rev Brian Shaw, unpublished

A babble of voices washed over Kyle and the air felt greasy and overly familiar.

He set Rook down beside him and took in the landscape of green fire. During his coma, the bubbles of light told him so much he didn't want to know. He couldn't see the bubbles now, but he could feel them clamoring like gnats, suffocating him with their eagerness to be his friend, crowding his brain with their ceaseless yammering.

Definitely the same place. It looked different when you had actual eyes.

Rook clutched his shirt and he kept his arms around her, resting his chin on top of her head.

On the periphery of his vision, massive, indistinct shapes loomed out of the rolling green waves and sank again without leaving a ripple. Crop circles flowed over the surface of the undulating landscape like alien hieroglyphics. Everything anybody thought was in here somewhere.

"Rook, we're home."

She looked up at him, her eyes all the bluer in contrast to the green, green world.

Kyle brushed his lips against her ear and whispered, "We're going to kick the Id out of here. Send it to the asteroid with the spiders so they can annoy each other forever. We'll close the portal and live here, in the

empty shell. We'll take over. And," he kissed her earlobe, "you'll be safe."

Her smile was bright enough to scatter the cloying bubble-voices. For a few blissful moments he felt and heard only her, felt her erotic thrum inside his mind.

"That's so romantic!" she breathed.

Kyle turned and saw an enormous shape breaching the surface of the waves of fire. A dollar-bill pyramid, complete with its creepy floating eye. It was glowing white-hot, a massive stone chunk adrift in this place, radiating a warhead's worth of unspent energy.

Panic froze Kyle. His heart pounded, pumping fear throughout his body. They could never outrun it! He brought Rook here to keep her safe and instead they would be incinerated, turned to ash and scattered through the Collective Id forever.

Baking heat like an iron foundry slammed into them, the slanted pyramid wall just a yard away. Kyle could see the texture of the stone, the mortar lines between the massive slabs, and an incongruous patch of black.

A charred handprint.

*** *** ***

Fin expected something momentous to signify the crossing of such an important barrier, but there was no outcry, no fireworks, no alarm bells. One moment he stood with his wife in the retro decor of their suburban home, and a moment later they inhabited a viridescent landscape of liquid flame. A cold knot of fear oozed from his brainstem and down his spine.

Rook looked around with wide blue eyes, her grip on his hand tightening past the point of pain.

Thumper was in here somewhere, lost in this tie-dye ocean of endless green fire. Rook was counting on him to find the baby, but he didn't have his sea legs yet. The babble of voices drowned him in meaninglessness. He found no handholds and was in danger of being washed away on a tsunami of crowd noise, his self eroded and mingled

with the rest of humanity.

"Fin?" The terror in Rook's voice galvanized him, driving his own fear and confusion back. He snapped his head around to look at her, tried to project confidence.

"It's a lot to take in," he said.

"Fin, I don't feel Thumper." Panic rose in her voice and made her mental signal shrill. "I thought I would, but I don't. I can't feel my baby."

"Our baby's in here, somewhere," Fin said in the most reassuring tone he could. "We should move around and see if we can get a fix."

Rook's eyes showed panic. "We'll get lost. What good is it to find Thumper if we can't get home?"

Fin didn't like the idea of being trapped here, either. The terrain shifted and surged like a rough sea. There were no stable landmarks. Moments ago they stood in a tiny valley, but now it was a hilltop.

"I think we'll be okay," he said. "We can look for the portal whenever we're on high ground. It stands out, what with Vesuvius's color coming through."

"Follow my voice," Vesuvius said. "You can hear me, right?"

Fin looked at Rook before answering. She nodded. "Yes, buddy. We hear you."

"Then you can use me to home in. Go now, find the baby."

Fin said, "I think we should listen to him."

Rook tried to smile. "He's never steered us wrong before. Which way?"

Every way looked pretty much the same, except a nearby gully where the green flames had taken the shapes of trees, reminding him of the firs that made up so much of Rook's interior world. He was about to point that way when he spied movement, a huge apelike creature sidling deeper into the woods.

"This way." He pointed in the opposite direction. Fin kept one ear out for Vesuvius, who commenced a spoken-word rendition of *Hush Little Baby* at a stately pace.

*** *** ***

Visitors!

Oh, this is indeed excellent, like fried cheese. Fried cheese is the most popular appetizer at Mama Leone's Pizzeria in Hoboken, New Jersey, but is among the five least popular nail polish colors at Bambi's 'Quality' European Nail Salon in St Paul, Minnesota. St Paul is one of the Twin Cities, the other is Minneapolis. Twins are best because two is better than one. One is the loneliest number. Who ever heard of tea for one? Two by two the visitors came. Two couples, and a couple is two. Two's company. Two heads are better than one, and two hearts beat as one. Two heads and two hearts means two babies. Divide the chimera? No! Division is less. A divided chimera is just two children. Multiply! Multiply the chimera. Two perfect chimera babies. Like looking in a mirror. But not reversed, no. Never reversed. The same, always. Always the same. Identical. But raised apart, one in Minneapolis, one in St Paul. Apart, apart, apart. Identical and apart. Separate but equal. Two! Two is better than one. One chimera is good because it is two in one. But two chimeras is better because it is two in one twice. But if one is good and two is better, what is three? Or four? Or six billion? Too much! Noise, confusion, no peace.

Two.

The Texas Two-step can be danced to tempos between 130 and 200 beats per minute.

*** *** ***

Brad parked behind the small blue car in the driveway of the retro-modern house, but no one came to the door when he knocked. He knew Fin didn't care for the doorbell, but after knocking again and waiting, he pressed the button. Still no answer.

The door was unlocked. He said "Hello?" as he stepped inside, trying to tell himself he shouldn't panic.

Another few steps gave him a view into the living room.

In the middle of the room hovered an oval-shaped hole filled with seething green fire. Fin's cherished lava lamp burbled away nearby. The

lamp's red-gold tone seemed all the more intense beside the hot green glow.

Brad stared at it stupidly for a few seconds, then darted back around the corner.

The kids did it.

Brad edged up to the corner, unable to go any nearer the thing. He knew the only way to help them was to go through. Also he knew he'd already spent too much time thinking about it, and more thinking would only make his legs more rubbery.

He walked up to it, meaning to stride right through. He stopped. Were those flames actually hot? What if the portal closed behind him? What if it closed *on* him? Cut him in half? He felt sweat on his scalp, on his torso. His heart beat too fast. He thought about having a heart attack in that weird green place, where no ambulance could find him.

Brad reached up with one hand. He wanted to reach through, to prove to himself that it worked, but even there he hesitated.

Someone had glued his feet down.

Just step through, already, Brad thought he heard someone say, but it was clearly his own frustration with himself for stalling.

He clenched his eyes shut, constricted his held breath.

He stepped through.

The green fire didn't burn.

It was everything, it was the ground he somehow stood on. The air seemed to be made of voices, a raucous blather of conversations and screams and laughter, and someone droning *Camptown Races*.

Spinning around, he saw Fin's living room through the oval hole. The portal looked even more out of place from this side, which Brad found staggering.

He scanned the horizon and the nearby waves for any idea of which way was the right way.

The landscape moved like swells on the open sea, but its surface shimmered like wind-teased grass. He watched as the random dappling on the flank of a hill organized itself into a Starbucks logo.

***   ***   ***

Off to their right Rook heard a raucous din composed of thousands of tweedling ringtones. She and Fin both ducked as the swarm of cellphones buzzed overhead, antennas lashing to propel them like sperm racing to fertilize the world's unluckiest egg.

Fin tripped over a hula hoop that rose from the glowing swirls. Soon they were popping up everywhere. They wafted above the waves and spewed immense, crystalline orbs, like the bubble wands Rook loved as a child.

All of the bubbles drifted away, except for one. It was smallish and emitted a golden-green glow.

"Look out," Fin warned, tugging on Rook's arm. She shook him off.

The bubble was not empty. Inside the glow, a fetus, tiny and peaceful. Her baby. For only a second Rook drank in the sight of the perfect little fists, the bald head, the closed eyes. She reached out to the bubble and it disappeared.

The emptiness she'd felt for an entire week turned inside out, replaced by a comforting, familiar fullness and a tickling vibration. Inside her womb a tiny, fluid movement told her Thumper was home.

Fin grinned and rested his hand on her belly where it peeked out between her zebra-stripe tank top and the waistband of her miniskirt. Thumper gave his hand a kick.

"Let's get the hell out of here," Fin said, turning toward Vesuvius's comforting intonation of *Camptown Races*.

"Wait." Rook furrowed her brow and concentrated.

"What's wrong?" Fin asked.

"I don't know." Rook looked at Fin, pleading with him to understand. "Something's missing. Thumper's vibration is off. Incomplete. Fin, we can't leave yet."

***   ***   ***

The massive, glowing pyramid bobbed on the surface of the green sea for a long second before toppling backwards into the trough between waves and beginning to subside.

Rook laughed with relief. Kyle looked down at her, his eyes a swirling green like their new home. He kissed her hungrily and she responded in kind, the adrenaline surge from their near incineration feeding her libido.

A slow, warm breeze ruffled her hair and carried a cloud of enormous soap bubbles overhead. One by one the bubbles popped, chiming out *Bicycle Built for Two* like a music box, and raining soapy mist that smelled of baby powder. A single golden bubble, smaller than the others, sank straight toward Rook like a helium balloon in reverse.

Kyle pulled her aside, but the infernal orb swooped down and pain shot through Rook's belly like she'd been punched. Her beautiful wedding dress cut off her breath, suffocating her.

Kyle looked alarmed.

The side seams on her dress split with a terrible ripping sound and Rook could finally scream. Her hands flew to her stomach and confirmed the truth. She was pregnant, huge and swollen and filled with something battering against her from the inside, trying to escape.

"No!"

Rook felt herself fracturing. The agony of her soul rending in two brought fiery tears and incoherent screams, but then Kyle was there. He held her tight, pressing the jagged edges of her psyche back together, forcing her to stay whole.

"You can't go," he told her. "I need you."

Painfully Rook felt her disparate personas coming together in uneasy alliance. "I can't have this baby," she said.

"We'll figure something out, Rook. Just stay with me."

*** *** ***

Willow felt like giving up. It was devastating to have the jewelry within reach but be unable to affect it.

By now there were thousands upon thousands of glowing filaments, each linking Willow to one transceiver worn by someone standing out in a field outside of Donner. The mass of tendrils was enough to blot out everything else. She sought a clear vantage, rising up within her own

thoughts until she could survey the pulsing skein in its entirety.

The strands swayed and undulated with gentle waves, intertwining like ribbons on a möbius maypole. Their green-gold glow rose like steam to form tall, shimmering curtains, northern lights reaching into the infinite distance.

Well, not infinite, but mind-bendingly far.

Odd such soft energy should be organized into such a cohesive beam. Willow sighted along it. She soared up, racing into the stratosphere and beyond in the blink of an eye.

In a moment that might have been a second or a day, she reached the terminus of the auroral beam at a lumpy chunk of stone far past the orbit of Mars.

The asteroid was riddled with passageways and chambers, many lined with equipment far more sophisticated than Willow could grasp. The beam reached through the thick rock to a chamber holding dozens of huge, pseudosentient spiders.

Willow recognized them instantly, despite all the years since she created them during her first visit to the realm of swirling green fire.

She hadn't expected them to persist, much less grow to such gargantuan size.

Their involvement with the jewelry was less of a surprise. Like them, it was something Willow called into being, and they were responsible for the interfering signal that prevented her from reversing the process, from rendering the nanotech inert.

The spiders upgraded the transceivers, but no one upgraded the spiders.

Willow touched her left thumb and right forefinger, then pivoted her hands, walking the itsy-bitsy spider up the water spout.

She felt tension building with each step. The spiders felt it too, but they didn't know what to do about it.

The longer Willow kept up the ritual, the more discordant the arachnids' thinking became. The mass intellect crumbled, and when the individuation was complete Willow brought down the rain to wash the

spiders out.

One moment they were there, the next they were gone, sent back to the nothingness that spawned them.

Unmade.

Willow leaned on the table, lightheaded. She took several deep breaths. A quick peek in the playpen confirmed that Zen was playing happily. Only then did Willow check on the jewelry again.

It was there, still indicated by myriad silky strands, but the color and intensity of their glow had changed. The towering aurora was gone.

Willow selected one filament and plucked a few notes. In seconds she located the key frequency and burned out the hoop. By erasing the spiders, she also erased their signal generator. The transceivers were again within her grasp.

One down, 10,000 to go.

*** *** ***

While Rook wept in his arms, Kyle struggled to formulate a plan. Something simple and elegant, something that would evict the Id from its realm and simultaneously evict the fetus from Rook's body, solving both problems at once.

Kyle could feel the spiders lurking around the edges of his thoughts, too scared to disobey him, at least for now. Soon they would overcome their fear and come charging in, and he'd be stuck with them forever.

Fuck elegance and simplicity.

Flexing mental muscles he hadn't used in a long time, Kyle reached out to locate the Id's core. He would choke it into submission and toss it back through the portal to the asteroid.

Kyle sought the seat of power, taking inventory of the abstract landscape of the Collective Id along the way. Then things changed.

First the aliens' oversight ceased, which Kyle didn't consider a problem. Then the portal slammed closed.

"Kyle!" Rook wailed.

He hugged her and whispered, "It'll be okay, Rook, I promise."

Kyle's thoughts raced and Rook leaned against him, weeping.

Another portal popped open near where they stood. Through it Kyle saw a grassy expanse under a blue sky. It could be anywhere.

Go now.

The voice came from all around and reminded Kyle of the bubbles of light.

Go now.

Kyle spoke loudly, not sure where to direct his words. "Give us a minute."

I have returned your child to you and your chosen mate. Go now.

"We don't want it!" Rook cried.

Kyle tried to think of a way to trick the Id into passing through its own doorway.

Around him a whirlwind of songs surged up, all tangled together, threatening to drive Kyle mad until he caught a single coherent thought spiraling through the vortex, repeating and repeating.

from both sides now

girls just wanna have fun

everything that rises must converge

since I don't have you

five to one baby, one in five

The swirl of voices raged, kicking up a rush of wind that tore Rook from Kyle's arms and buffeted her toward the portal.

"No!" Kyle yelled.

Rook screamed.

Kyle lunged forward and snagged her hands, hauling her back from the brink. For one wonderful second he felt her warm fingers in his grip and saw a flicker of a smile on her beautiful face, then an unseen force took hold of her and pulled. She screamed again, as much in pain as terror now. Kyle braced himself and held on, refusing to let her go.

Rook's body wrenched violently in the Id's grip. Her hands tore from Kyle's and he was left holding her wedding ring.

"Rook!"

As Kyle watched in heartbroken horror, Rook split into two shadows of herself. Her agonized scream shattered into a million pieces

and the shadow-Rooks did too. The instability she fought since her rebirth finally, irrevocably, won. Like cobwebs in a gale, she disintegrated and disappeared into the vastness of the Id, leaving the fetus behind in its green-gold bubble.

Clutching the ring, Kyle collapsed and sobbed.

*** *** ***

Rook loved Fin for listening to her about staying in here when she couldn't really give him a reason.

It was Thumper in her womb, she was certain, but the baby's signal was wrong somehow.

Go now.

The booming voice came from everywhere. Rook said, "Wait, please! Something isn't right!"

Go now.

Fin looked at Rook, but she shook her head, tears brimming.

I have returned your child to you and your chosen mate. Go now.

Fin ran both hands back through his hair and blew out a frantic kind of sigh. He bellowed, "We're working on it."

A throaty tremor rattled their fillings. It sounded like distant thunder and felt like an earthquake, and the sinuous fires all around them dimmed as it rolled past.

"What the hell was that?" Rook asked, although she knew from his face Fin had no more idea than she did.

"We need to get out of here," Fin said.

"I know, but... no," Rook replied miserably. A UFO glided over their heads and vanished among the dunes of chemical green fire.

*** *** ***

Brad slogged ahead, trying to pace himself. The swirling surface dragged at his feet, and even downhill portions were hard work. The chattering roar of voices was like a continual headwind.

Everything about this place felt soggy and heavy. He didn't belong, wasn't compatible with its laws of motion. He scooped up a double handful of the bizarre green material. The moment he collected it the

color dulled and it transmuted from liquid emerald to used cat litter, as if something about Brad negated its very essence. He wiped his hands on his jeans.

A square flying saucer buzzed him. He recognized it as a wrapped condom as it crashed and sank.

Judging his progress was impossible. All he could do was keep slogging and hope he'd been right to come in here.

Ahead of him, some distance away, sat a young man. He looked like Fin, but he was alone.

Brad raced toward him, the strain almost unbearable.

It was Kyle.

And he wasn't alone after all. A bubble of brilliant green-gold light hovered beside him, enclosing a tiny baby, far too small and unfinished to be outside the womb. Brad pushed to get there before some wave or obstacle separated them.

"Kyle!" he shouted.

Finally he made it, and placed a hand on his son's shoulder.

"Kyle," Brad said again. "What are you doing here?"

Kyle looked morosely up into Brad's face.

"Hey, Tiger." Brad hugged him, his heart full. "How did you get here?"

No answer.

Brad said, "I came through the portal. Is that how you got in, too?" Kyle's eyebrows twitched. Brad nodded. "At Fin's house. I came through looking for them, but I found you." Kyle stood. Brad hugged him again, and even though Kyle still didn't hug back it felt nice.

"I see you found the baby," Brad said.

Kyle's face darkened.

"Rook and Fin will be overjoyed!" Brad declared.

Kyle glanced at the fetus.

"Let's find them." Brad wondered if the coma left Kyle with impaired speech.

Kyle nodded, his expression relaxing. He gazed out into the distance

and looked back at Brad. He finally spoke. "Which way?"

Brad shrugged. "I took a wild guess at a direction, and it led me to you. Maybe I can do it again."

The infant's bubble bobbed alongside Kyle like a balloon on an invisible string. Brad huffed and strained to keep his feet moving, but Kyle skated along. None of the clinging, buffeting friction affected him. Meanwhile, Brad had no breath to spare for conversation.

When Brad thought he would have to ask for a break, their wave lifted them high enough to see over the next few rises. Two figures stood on a crest, outside of shouting range but close enough for Brad to be sure they were Fin and Rook.

Brad smiled. "Let's rest a minute."

"I don't think so."

The last thing Brad saw was Kyle's fist.

*** *** ***

Rook cradled her belly with both hands and drove out everything else to listen to Thumper's vibration, trying to isolate what was wrong.

It was like hearing a familiar tune over shoddy speakers, like the betrayal of hearing a recording of your own voice. Something was elusively incomplete about it.

A new complementary tone formed in her mind, filling in the thin spots. The stronger Rook's sense of recognition grew, the more she could hear this new tone, until it was almost like she was really hearing it, the melody to complement the harmony.

Rook opened her eyes and scanned the waves. She wasn't imagining the new vibration, it was coming from somewhere close, and getting closer! A second later she pinpointed the direction, and watched ecstatically for the source to appear.

She reeled when Kyle stepped into view, felt panic sinking its claws into her mind.

In the same moment, she spotted Kyle's curious companion. Floating through the air beside him, enclosed in a luminous amnion, was another tiny, curled up fetus, all spindly arms and oversized head.

She didn't understand how it could be, or what the Id had done, but she needed that baby, too. It was the source of the complementary vibration. It was what she was missing.

She made only one step toward Kyle before the world exploded into chaos.

The fiery waves surged, doubling in height, their gentle fluid motion turned to violent collisions. Rook staggered on the heaving surface, fell. She rolled to her feet and pushed toward the baby. Furnace winds howled, pushing her back down the slope. Lightning seared the sky.

THIEF!

Rook wailed in fright at the concussive shout, but kept straining to reach her baby.

Two doesn't work like that! Two means divided! Two with one mother is too much like one.

The towering waves began to topple like dominoes, creating a circular current that strengthened into a whirlpool. Fin scrambled to the lip, hauling Rook up with him, and they were carried around, away from the baby.

Tried two together. Tried it twice! Broken apart! And two minus twoness was nothing. This time each one is two, times twice in space and once in time.

Rook and Fin ran to keep from being pulled into the vortex, as its rotation now swept them back in the fetus's direction. Rook's legs ached, and her bare feet could get little purchase in the writhing green energy. Kyle stood beside the baby, neither of them appearing to feel the heat or wind, both unfazed by the violent heaving of the ground.

The voice of the Id crushed down, drowning out the thunderous cacophony.

You can't have both, that's too together. Two tied together. Tried together! Tried it! You can't do together now! NO! Now is two! Now is two! Two! TWO!

With a desperate lunge Rook flung herself beyond the rim of the whirlpool and raced toward the baby. Fin cried out as the current bore

him away.

Rook fought on. The wind robbed her of nearly all progress.

You could have had both the last time. You could have had both the first time. Not my fault you're too late. This time you can't. You can't. You don't understand two! TWO!

"I do understand!" Rook screamed, although her mind held nothing but her need to reach the baby.

Not both with you. The two are alike, too alike. Melting, blurring, blending into just another One. One can't be, One is nothing, without another. One with no company but chaos, the billions' babble. No company, no one else, means One can't. Just can't.

Mournful loneliness poured over Rook from all sides. It was the fire, it was the wind. It was the Id, and now she truly did understand. Its tirade made sudden sense as hollow emotion threatened to overwhelm her faculties. The obsession with twins all came down to a need for companionship. The whole game, all the prophecy and conspiracy, and especially the kidnapping of her unborn child, a scheme to make of itself someone to talk to.

So split it up. Yes! YES! Split it up, and cast a shadow. Cast a twin.

Rook had reached the peaceful enclave where her baby waited with Kyle. She looked up, looked at Kyle smiling and extending a hand to help her the last couple of feet.

"Rook!" came Fin's voice, this time near. Kyle snatched at her hand, and Rook saw his scowl rearrange itself into that sardonic expression from a moment ago.

"Stay back!" Fin yelled, as Kyle offered his hand again. She sidestepped, hoping to get around him to reach the baby. Kyle pivoted. When she retreated a step, his eyes flashed. She took another step back before she risked turning away, and found Fin at her side.

*** *** ***

Kyle concentrated on making his smile warm, contrary to everything he felt. In his left hand, behind his back, he held the wedding ring. Before him stood Rook, the only Rook now, and he seethed with

need. She was a perfect fit for the ragged hole in his psyche, the only thing that could make up for his loss.

She was drawn to the fetus as he'd known she would be.

Rook became wary, hanging back out of reach. Her need for the baby was every bit as primal as Kyle's need for her. If not for Fin, interfering as always, it would be a simple matter of waiting her out.

She glanced into his eyes, and Kyle held her gaze. She edged nearer, unaware she was doing it. Fin pulled her back, and at his touch she shivered and began to cry.

Fin stepped between Rook and Kyle. He rested his hand on her protruding belly. He looked toward the fetus and addressed Kyle without looking him in the eye, "I can guess what happened."

An image scorched Kyle's vision, how she didn't even have time to smile. Her scream flooded his head.

"No, you can't."

"I can guess it was bad. I won't claim I understand how it feels. But I'm sad for you, and I wish there was a way I could help."

"You want to help? Get out of the way."

"I said I wish there was a way. There isn't."

"I don't need your pity," Kyle spat. "If you can't help me, why are you still here?"

"For Rook."

Kyle laughed, bitterly and mirthlessly at first, then savagely, and then furiously until it was an animal howl. He tackled Fin and they rolled down the slope away from the whirlpool, past Rook and out into the blazing tempest.

*** *** ***

Rook dodged as the men careened by. She had an impulse to aid Fin, but a far stronger one to go to her baby now that the way was clear.

Of course. It had to be both.

Both babies needed her, and she needed both of them.

When she touched the cocoon of energy surrounding it, the fetus vanished and she felt its harmonious arrival in her womb. Her belly

stretched a few more inches, straining to contain such a sudden increase in population. Despite the discomfort and heavy fullness, she felt complete for the first time in a week.

The waves all around stopped crashing, the swirling current ebbed and the vortex dissipated. The tumultuous gale subsided, replaced by ominous, brooding calm.

*** *** ***

Fin drove his knee into Kyle's gut. He bucked and kicked and twisted to get free of Kyle's grip on his throat.

Kyle's only tactic was strangulation, which did make him predictable. But he was manic and tenacious, and gave little reaction to Fin's punches.

Fin got his legs under himself, at last pulling free as he stood. He took heaving breaths as he backpedaled, fending Kyle off with his fists.

Kyle charged, both hands reaching for Fin's windpipe. Fin kicked him in the stomach. It halted Kyle in his tracks. He slumped forward but didn't fold.

Fin landed a haymaker that dropped Kyle to one knee. Fin backed off, and Kyle began to rise.

"Wait," Fin said. "Wait. We don't have to do this. We should be helping each other."

Kyle went for Fin's throat again, and Fin blocked. Kyle grabbed him by the wrists and shoved, and Fin shoved back. He had to keep Kyle off his neck, but also had to keep them from getting spun around, keep Kyle from spotting Rook. So he gave ground, and Kyle kept pushing.

Heat roasted Fin's back, intense enough to make the horrible wind feel refreshing. He fought to get his retreat under control, and Kyle's inchoate snarl became a sneer.

Fin risked a glance over his shoulder. A huge pyramid bobbed like an iceberg a few feet behind him, glowing white hot.

Kyle laughed and Fin lost a step.

The pyramid rocked away, and Fin saw a charred handprint on the bottom before it rocked back toward him.

Kyle's laughter reached hysteria as he poured on more strength and Fin skidded closer to the blistering rock wall.

He couldn't get traction against Kyle's relentless pressure. He lost ground a millimeter at a time.

Mania distorted Kyle's face almost beyond recognition.

In desperation, Fin yanked his left hand back. The sudden reversal pitched Kyle forward as Fin pivoted and melted aside.

Kyle landed back-first on the glowing face of the pyramid, still clutching Fin's wrists.

Fin felt the heat through Kyle's hands.

Kyle went rigid as green flames outlined him. His laughter decayed into a descending cry that might have been a sigh or a moan.

His grip didn't weaken. Straining, Fin tore loose and staggered back a step from the blowtorch heat. The emerald corona around Kyle advanced outward from the wall, engulfing him further.

"Kyle!" Fin seized Kyle's wrists, and they hissed. He held on and pulled. He kept pulling as the desolate sound faded from Kyle's throat and the green fires closed over his face.

The flames enveloped Kyle's torso and climbed out along his arms, and Fin pulled desperately until he was knocked down.

Brad lay atop him, sobbing, and Fin wept as well.

Where Kyle had been was a black stain.

Chapter Twenty-Three

Rook of Rooks

DONNER — Authorities are investigating how over 10,000 individuals from the tri-county area came to be on the grounds of the former Shaw Ministries compound last night, with fresh body piercings. "It's like they were dropped here by aliens," said Detective Althea Smalls.
The Donner Observer, 4-28-2001

The pyramid coasted nearer. Fin rolled, dumping Brad off, then stood and pulled him to his feet. They backed away from the incandescent stone monster.

The whirlpool and maelstrom had stopped. An ominous dark form towered over the horizon. The peculiar optics of this place made it impossible to be sure what it was, but the shape suggested a volcano.

Fin couldn't find Rook. A few seconds of panic followed, until her tingly vibration registered, soothing his mind. She hadn't been mowed down by the glowing pyramid.

He looked at his father and said, "I have to find Rook."

Brad scanned all around, like maybe she just sat down somewhere to read a book. His face looked far older, lined with hopelessness and blanched by the eerie light of this place.

Fin put his hand on Brad's shoulder, and Brad wiped away tears.

"Rook's okay, I think," Fin said. "I can feel her. I have to go to her."

Brad clasped his own hand over Fin's. "I'm coming along. I just lost one son, and I'm not going to lose the other one, too."

After a quick embrace, and Fin wiping his own eyes, he reoriented on Rook's signal. Unsurprisingly it aligned with the looming shadow in

the distance. Whatever it was.

They set off at a run.

Soon Brad panted, "Don't wait for me. I'm slowing you down."

Fin looked around at the bizarre, surging environment, and at the huge white-hot pyramid again heading their way. "Dad," he said, "I can't run off and leave you here!"

Brad chuckled. "Who saved whose ass a minute ago? I'll be fine." When Fin stood there dithering, Brad yelled, "Go!"

Fin ran. Each rolling wave lifted him for a glimpse of the distant, dark shape. He couldn't decide if it looked any closer. It seemed bigger, but not more distinct. If anything, the hazy shimmer around it increased.

His destination's true nature wasn't clear until he topped the final ridge.

What he'd thought might be a mountain was a chaotic, shifting city. Structures of every conceivable type all heaped together and in constant motion, like a mosh pit made of buildings. Around the edges, whole districts calved off like icebergs from a glacier, only to sink and disappear. Other zones crumbled, or melted, or folded in on themselves. New neighborhoods grew like mineral crystals, elbowing existing structures aside.

That churning shape embodied the personality of the Collective Id, everyone's core structures piled up in one place.

Thunder echoed around the smooth, crater-shaped zone surrounding the construct. Fin looked for signs of an impending storm, but the booming noise wasn't thunder. It was the Id bellowing "Two! Two!" over and over.

He now knew without doubt where he had to go.

*** *** ***

Rook was back inside her tower, the structure at the core of her mind, with no idea how she got there. From where she lay in a nest of black feathers, she saw the trunk with its round top and the table with the tea set. She saw also that the trapdoor was padlocked and the sole

window blocked by iron bars as thick as her wrist. A low, chaotic rumble was the only sound.

An ache stretched her abdomen, the skin taut as a drum, ready to split.

Two babies, she remembered. Two babies inside her now in a space accustomed to one. She hoped her body would adjust quickly. They would only get bigger before they were born.

Inside her head, and in her heart, Rook felt their twin vibrations coming together in a single clear tone. They were both Thumper.

Rook could feel Fin, too, distant but strong as ever. He was safe. Kyle's hum was gone, which suggested he was too. Good.

She rolled onto all fours to get up, then waddled to the window like a drunk. She grasped the bars. Outside, where she expected a moonlit forest, she instead saw a grand ballroom, all gilt molded ceiling and crystal chandeliers. The breathtaking beauty shuddered, becoming the interior of an immense, empty sports arena. That spectacle lasted a few seconds before warping like a funhouse mirror to show Rook that, in fact, her tower overlooked a rat-infested alley in an anonymous city with a swirling green sky.

The scenery lurched again as her tower sank like an elevator, dropping toward someplace new. Rook couldn't tell if she was moving or if the world slipped and whirled around her. It felt like a bad motion simulator. A blast of cold air shot in, carrying the scent of cotton candy, but all Rook saw was a vast expanse of tin rooftops and rickety chimneys.

She slid to the floor and tried to figure out what the hell was going on. This was the tower from her own mind, but the green sky told her she was still in the Id. How could that be?

The rumble Rook had been hearing became a roar of frustration bouncing at her from all sides and echoing in her stone chamber, battering itself into hundreds of separate voices, all yelling at her, *Two! Two! Two!*

Definitely still in the Id.

"They're safe. I have them both," Rook said. She massaged the tight skin of her belly, hoping to ease the discomfort.

Thief!

The voices cohered into one single voice, albeit one with many overlapping edges.

You can't have two two-in-ones! You should have one two-in-one! Only one! One for you and one for your twin. One and one are two. Two mothers and two babies, and the babies are two-in-one!

"Tough shit."

You ruin everything! So much hard work! Years and years and years and years and years…

"Shut up!"

The word 'years' kept rebounding around the room as the Id went on. *If you bear both chimeras it's the same as only one. Worse. Two is the answer. Two!*

That single word echoed around and around the tower room. Rook crawled to the trapdoor and yanked on the padlock. It held, the iron fittings in the floor solid and unyielding.

Rook grabbed a butter knife from the table. She splayed her bare legs and feet to the sides and hunched over her belly as much as she could, working at the tumblers in the heavy lock.

And still *Two! Two! Two!* echoed.

*** *** ***

It's complicated, but so simple: Complete the complementary Completer to collect a complete complement of Completers. The complementary Completer is a complex conundrum with the components all cast, confused and circulated. All the king's horses and all the king's men put the Completer together again.

With a complete complement of complete Completers, the chimera children can be two. Two! The cure for loneliness!

*** *** ***

Rook gave up on the lock. She tried using the knife to pry the brackets out of the thick floorboards, but only succeeded in ruining the

blade. She puffed a few loose strands of hair out of her face and struggled to her feet.

There must be something else she could use to escape. The rounded-top trunk sat against the wall opposite the window.

Rook hoisted the lid and was disappointed to find a large collection of baby dolls, and little else.

Make that chain again!

The voice startled Rook. The babies in her womb wriggled.

Make that chain again!

Rook turned and saw a spinning wheel in the center of the room, atop the trapdoor.

Make that chain again!

"No." She bent over the trunk, intent on her search.

Make that chain again! It made two one. It will work again. It will make two one.

"What the fuck ever. I'm not doing it."

I need that chain to make your twin again. She will bear one chimera. You can keep one chimera. Two mothers. Two chimera children. It will work. It will work. It will work if I have that chain.

"Make it yourself."

You! You must make it! You! It is of you!

"No."

You are my grandchild, my heir! You will do this!

"No."

Rook reached the bottom of the trunk and found a keyring. None of the keys looked big enough for the padlock, but she would try them anyway.

You owe me! You agreed to the bargain! I helped you spin the chain.

"Then spin it yourself."

Rook shoved the spinning wheel off the trapdoor. Which key should she try first?

Invisible hands grabbed her. They knocked the keyring to the floor and dragged her to the pile of feathers. Rook struggled, but it was like

fighting against a storm wind. It forced her hands down into the feathers, curled her fingers around fistfuls of them. It buffeted her body, forced her to her knees. The spinning wheel screeched across the wooden floor, charging at her.

Make that chain again!

Rook's heart raced in terror. She'd thought the Id couldn't touch her, and more important she thought it wouldn't. It needed her as a vessel for its precious chimera. It wouldn't dare hurt her. Or so she thought.

Make that chain again!

*** *** ***

Fin sprinted over the mirror surface and onto a long ramp. Without slowing down, he entered the Id's core through a set of massive gates on shrieking hinges. He pelted up a broad boulevard, desperate to reach Rook and escape this landscape of madness. The walls at either side encroached as the street's pitch steepened under his feet. It buckled and became a narrow, uneven flight of stone stairs ascending a dank tunnel. Groaning echoes reverberated with the shifts of neighboring zones. Fin ran faster, dust stinging his eyes.

The top arrived unexpectedly. Fin nearly overran the edge of a corrugated metal roof, seizing a TV antenna to stop himself.

A street paved in a checkerboard of asphalt and marble rose to meet him.

The Id's voice boomed down.

Make that chain again!

It was yelling at Rook. Fin could feel her vibration shift in pitch as the strange command repeated several times. It made him even more desperate to reach her, to protect her.

Streets slithered and shifted wherever Fin looked as he ran, buildings rotating their stories like Rubik's Cubes.

Rook's signal drew Fin into a junkyard of split-level houses in surprisingly neat stacks.

He heard Rook's voice. In pain. Nearby.

"Rook!"

He heard her wail again, like a blade to his heart, and speeded up. A light glowed in a house ahead of him.

The ones on the bottom were crushed enough that he could grab the edge of a roof and pull himself up. He clambered onto the porch of the house with the light. The door stuck because the opening was off-kilter, but two determined kicks got it open. The whole stack of houses wobbled and slouched, but Fin dashed inside.

He ran into the carpeted living room and saw Rook lying on her back.

"Rook!"

Her eyes fluttered open, and she smiled. Her belly was flat again. He blinked back tears and said, "Oh, no. Oh, I'm sorry. I'm so sorry."

Rook still smiled. She said, "It's alright," and her voice sounded odd. The whole situation felt unnatural, but that wasn't surprising given where they were.

The building lurched, and Fin remembered kicking out part of what held it up.

"We have to get out of here." He scooped her up, and she wrapped her arms around his neck. He put one hand on the back of her head.

She kissed his palm. He felt her cheek and nose and chin against his hand.

A shudder raced through Fin. He looked at Rook's face, saw her gazing sleepily into his eyes, and at the same time felt her face in his hand on the back of her head.

This wasn't his wife.

The tingling signal wasn't coming from her. He'd been stunned by seeing her, lost track for a moment, but now he could tell.

He staggered, trying to drop her. She cooed and wouldn't let go. Fin ducked out of her grasp and reared away. She looked mad now, took a step toward him. The house heaved and a window shattered. When she turned her head toward the noise, he saw both of her faces in profile.

Gagging, Fin bolted for the kitchen. The Rook-like creature

screamed, "Stop! Stay!"

He kept moving, out the back door and onto a deck overhanging the roof of a lower house. He vaulted the railing and slid down the sloping shingles. The dual-voiced screams persisted, begging him to stop but spurring him on. Hanging from the rain gutter, he dropped to the ground and rolled.

He came up running and got his compass lined up on the true Rook once again.

A clamor of crashing, thudding noises started. When it got louder, he broke into a flat-out sprint. The avalanche of houses overtook him on both sides, exhaling dust clouds laced with glass and two-by-fours. Fin made it past the end of the junkyard just before the way was blocked by debris.

He stumbled, coughing, into a market square with a fountain at its center spraying emerald flames. Colonnades lined the open space.

Motion caught his eye, and Fin edged closer to the coldly fiery fountain.

Someone darted from behind a pillar. It looked like Rook, but didn't line up with the real Rook's vibration.

She ran a few steps and stopped. She put her hands to her head, howling as her body was wracked with convulsions. Reminding himself she wasn't real didn't make it less painful to see. Her spasms were so violent she blurred, then she became two of herself. The two false Rooks stabilized, stared at Fin for a second, and broke into a run.

He couldn't make his feet work, hypnotized by the doppelgängers racing at him.

They ran in perfect unison, stride for stride, until they bumped into each other and stuck fast. For a few strides they kept coming like an entrant in a demonic three-legged race, but their forms tangled and they tripped. The sight of their distorted, partially merged limbs broke Fin's trance. He ran toward Rook's signal, giving the twisted, screaming mess on the ground a wide berth.

Another one blocked his way, arms outstretched. This Rook's

agitated tattoos swarmed over her skin, engulfing more and more of her. Soon her arms and hands were completely black. The shadow flowed up her throat and onto her face.

The black was shot through with bright green sparks. Fin recoiled at the horrid odor of burnt flesh. She fell away in flakes as green fire passed through her, and disintegrated into a pile of ash and glossy black bones at his feet.

Fin tried to harden his heart against these nightmares, but couldn't shake the feeling he was watching the real Rook in torment. He ran, clinging to his wife's mental signature to hang onto his sanity.

Up one more block, past an escalator to nowhere and through an archway painted like clown makeup, Fin found a network of canals from a radioactive Venice. The canals, full of the Id's seething green, wound among an ever-shifting array of structures, with one constant at its center, an ivy-clad tower of red brick. Fin knew instantly it was Rook's, and she was inside.

*** *** ***

As his feet fell into a labored rhythm, Brad's mind fell into a mournful loop. It replayed his heartbreaking encounter with Kyle, witnessing the attack on Fin, and its horrible end. Brad told himself he couldn't have saved them both, but the loop replayed over and over as if one of these times he would.

Kyle's death was unreal, made all the more by grieving for him six months ago. The fresh tears on Brad's cheeks were not for that. He wept for his failure to keep Kyle safe from monstrousness.

Brad didn't know how long the skipping record of depression spun in his head. Too long. Time to focus on the son he could still help, not be waterlogged by sadness over the one he could not.

The looming shape Fin was running toward was closer now. Brad could pick out some details and understood it was a city. A terrifyingly chaotic one, thrashing and grinding. Gnashing skyscraper teeth jutted from gums of ramshackle favelas. Whole blocks were created and replaced in seconds. It was like Frank Gehry and Antoni Gaudí were

duking it out in some insane architectural deathmatch choreographed by MC Escher.

He looked for anything else that might be Fin's destination, wanting an excuse to avoid the churning madness. What he saw was a bright glow traveling beneath the surface on a course to cut him off from it.

If the pyramid wanted to keep him out, he knew he must try to get inside.

***   ***   ***

Across footbridges and drawbridges Fin ran toward Rook's tower until he reached its foaming, swirling moat of green tie-dye. He didn't trust it not to swallow him up if he tried to stand on it.

Rook copies spilled into the streets all around him, emerging from corners and doorways. Some tumbled into the canals as the horde flowed over the bridges, all converging on Fin.

"Holy fucking shit!"

Crying and moaning, they grasped at him and clawed at his clothes. His eyes couldn't tell the real Rook from these horrible simulacra. He focused instead on her vibration, trying not to look at the swarm as he fought its clinging undertow.

The ersatz Rooks fell apart into more copies, and the copies collided. Sometimes they rejoined into a single, miserable unit. Sometimes they both vanished, their flocks of tattoo rooks freed from their skin and flapping away. Soon the tattoo birds darkened the sky.

The liberated rooks were following Rook's signal like a homing beacon.

One of the tattoos alighted on Fin's arm and pecked him. It was the size of a horsefly, and its beak and claws dug into his skin. He swatted it, and when he moved his hand away he saw he now had a perfectly executed tattoo on his arm, a tiny black bird about to take flight, its mirror image on his palm.

The cloud of tattoos flowed in a swooping orbit around and around the tower, some clinging to its walls with each circuit.

He shouted, "Rook! Rook! I'm here!"

"Fin! Fin!" came the response from above, and with it a cool wash of relief. "I'm up in the tower!"

"I know," Fin called back. How would he get her out? He studied the tower, watched the birds accumulating, and saw them arranging themselves to recreate at giant scale the rook-of-rooks tattoo on her shoulder blade.

*** *** ***

Hearing Fin's voice gave Rook hope, even as she also heard her own voice coming in through the barred window. Her own voice, multiplied a hundred times, crying out in fear and pain.

The Id tightened its hold, squeezing the breath from her. The spinning wheel's pedal started pumping, driving the wheel to blinding speed. Rook's hands were thrust toward it as the Id tried to force her to repeat the miracle of spinning feathers into a silver chain. Her arms quivered as she resisted.

Make that chain again!

The furious wind stirred the pile of ebony feathers into a tornado, filling the room with thousands of darts. Rook clamped her eyes shut and strained to shield herself, but could not move her arms.

She felt a sting on her left arm, then another on her shoulder. It felt like a swarm of wasps. The sharp, burning pain brought a surge of adrenaline. Rook broke free of the Id's elusive grasp, hauled in a tremendous lungful of air, and dropped the feathers she'd been holding.

No!

"Fin, help!" Through the swirling, swarming mass of feathers it was hard to find the window, or the trapdoor. Where were the keys?

More stinging bites assailed her, needles jabbing. Rook reached to swat them away, but they weren't feathers at all. They were tiny birds. Her tattoos. Her left arm wore a speckled sleeve of them from below her elbow, up and over her shoulder. Hundreds more, maybe thousands, swooped through the air, mixing with the feathers.

The Id was trying to remake Brook and Bramble. That's why it wanted the chain.

"How many of me are out there?" she yelled.

"Tons!" Fin yelled back. "They're falling apart, but more keep coming! Watch the tattoos! They sting!"

"I know!"

The copies were breaking down, setting their tattoos adrift. Each inky bird that came home to roost brought a minuscule piece of Rook's self back to her, the seed the copies grew from.

Rook stopped trying to shield herself from the onslaught. She could use all the strength she could get. She struggled to her feet, feeling stings on her bare soles.

She watched the rooks land. Some lined up precisely with her existing tattoos, making them darker, their outlines crisper. Others chose fresh landing spots, expanding her flocks. They wriggled under her clothes before burning and burrowing into her flesh. They nested in her hair and marked her scalp. The flurry around her right ankle now reached to her knee. Rook was in agony, and yet she welcomed it. The pain restored her.

This Rook knew who she was, would never again hide while someone else lived her life. She and Fin were going to get out of this awful place, have their babies, and live happily ever after, dammit.

Rook kicked the spinning wheel over and hobbled to the window, receiving more tattoos on her feet along the way.

Below, on the far side of a seething moat of green fire, she saw Fin fending off a crowd of unstable, mutant copies of her. He looked up.

"Rook!"

Rook touched the bars on the window. They felt soft now. Velvety.

NO!

***   ***   ***

Fin clapped his hands over his ears, gritting his teeth against the Id's thunderous exclamation. Around him the faux Rooks disintegrated, their tattoos released in a choking cloud. The tower drew most of them in, its surface inhaling them to strengthen the rook-of-rooks design.

The tower was a jigsaw of ebony birds, each frozen in mid-flight.

They rustled and jostled, then all their wings unfroze. The rook of rooks exploded into a flock of startled birds, leaving only a burst of jet feathers and a rush of wind.

Rook plummeted, screaming. Fin screamed, too. He leapt into the moat, now a pond because nothing stood at its center.

Fin landed awkwardly on the roiling surface.

Rook plunged through it with a splash of green flames and sparks. Ripples spread, leaving the surface calm and smooth.

Fin scrambled to the place where she went under, and saw her rising, rising with a cruel sluggishness that matched the merciless velocity of her fall.

He looked helplessly into her eyes.

*** *** ***

Bubbles of light surround her in the thick, gelatinous darkness. The darkness clings like it is alive, caressing her skin in a smothering embrace. Slowly, slowly she rises, through layer upon layer of excited, clamoring bubbles.

She can't breathe.

The bubbles of light, all electric green and pure, brilliant white, say one word over and over: *Chimera! Chimera!*

She knows they are talking about her babies, knows they are dangerous.

She struggles for the surface. It's not like swimming, not at all.

Tears sting her eyes, washing away the film of darkness. Far above, far, far above she sees Fin. His face shows worry and fear before the darkness intrudes again.

Every time she blinks, her tears clear her vision and she sees him reaching.

More bubbles, new bubbles, are rising all around her, appearing at a furious pace. Something is coming. Something big.

She hopes she is close enough.

She reaches.

Her hand encounters resistance.

She blinks and sees Fin, just for a millisecond.

She smiles for him one last time.

***   ***   ***

Fin pounded on the green barrier. He stood and stomped on it, cursing. It felt as solid as stone, as smooth as glass.

The tattoo swarm began to collect around his feet. Tiny birds clustered over Rook, and he tried to chase them off. Some landed on him, but this time he resisted the urge to slap.

Rook lay still in her green prison. She looked serene, in contrast to Fin. He threw himself across her body, protecting it from the flapping invaders, using his arms to sweep them away.

A few seemed to etch themselves onto the surface, but then he saw their movement. They got through and swam like minuscule manta rays toward Rook.

Fighting to compose himself, Fin watched to see how they did it. Some of the birds crashed against the surface and were rejected, while many landed and walked on it. But a few of them hovered gently, lowering themselves bit by bit, until they hovered under the surface.

Fin tried to give her his hand, slowly. The surface refused to yield. He wanted to use brute force, to shatter, to pummel. He wanted to scream. With a slow breath, he steadied himself and tried again, slower.

He watched Rook's face, not his hand. If he watched, he knew he would feel the moment of contact and be stopped. He willed himself to believe there would be no such sensation. He wondered if the Id stuff would be warm or cool, thick or watery.

Even though it already seemed he wasn't moving, he made himself slow down further. He stared into Rook's eyes, ordering her not to give up.

An enormous dark shape moved in the green depths below her.

This had to work, and soon.

Fin forced himself not to hurry, focused on holding her gaze.

Would the stuff be sticky? Would it tingle?

At last he felt something brush his fingers, and in a giddy moment

he realized it was Rook's fingers intertwining with his. They clasped each other's hands, and Fin pulled with all his strength. Rook's arm, then her shoulder, and at last her head came up into the air, and she gasped in a huge breath. She had many, many new tattoos.

The dark shape was closer now, and growing.

Fin wrapped his other arm around Rook's torso and hauled her free of the tie-dye fire. She clung to him, heaving more deep lungfuls of air. He dove for the edge of the moat.

A massive reptilian head on a long, serpentine neck shot up. The creature's body remained submerged, far too large for the moat's confines, and its arrival displaced the liquid in a surge that carried Fin and Rook up and over the stone lip. They lay panting on the flagstones, regarded coldly by Nessie.

Fin kissed Rook and she urgently kissed him back.

"Can you run?" he asked her. She nodded.

*** *** ***

The white glow intensified and the all-seeing-eye came up a dozen yards ahead, between Brad and the dubious shelter of the city.

The pyramid moved slowly, methodically, only the eye showing above the surface, like the periscope of an occult submarine. Brad backpedaled from its searing heat, from its patient scrutiny. It wove side-to-side, toying with him. Letting him truly understand his doom. He'd know the whole time he was going to roast. He'd know and be unable to change it.

His heart thudded so hard he wondered if he might cheat the white-hot monster by dying of a coronary.

His soggy knees gave out, dumping him on the ground.

The pyramid accelerated, riding higher to expose its intolerable heat, its inferno of banked energy.

Brad dug his hands into the green strangeness, negating it, shoveling up as much as he could. He flung the clods of dull, sandy filth into the eye.

Arcs of electric agony enveloped the orb. With a piercing feedback

scream the monster lurched, kicking up waves as Brad tried to rise. He staggered, fell, rolled, staggered, fell again. The eye plunged down, vanishing.

Brad gained his feet and took two shuddering breaths in the sudden, creepy quiet.

He bolted for the grinding city.

For the first half of the race, he thought the thing had given up. Then he heard it behind him, steam whistle shriek plus earthquake roar. He poured on all the speed he could manage, not looking back and trying to ignore the fire in his chest. He tumbled down an embankment, onto the glassy smooth zone ringing the crazy city.

Before him, Brad saw a pair of tall columns flanking a sloped avenue that rose out of the green plain like a boat launch. Behind him, he knew, the pyramid was lining up. The pillars changed as the structures around them were unmade and replaced, but the entry they defined remained stable.

The gyrating buildings made a rumble he could feel in his chest. Over that, he heard the roaring, rising pursuit note of the pyramid. He felt its heat on the back of his neck.

He was on the ramp. Just a few more steps!

Two figures lurched into the street. Fin and Rook!

They dashed out between the columns. Brad saw them spot the pyramid and freeze.

He spread out his arms and swerved into them, dragging them with him off the ramp. They sprawled on the smooth green surface.

The pyramid scraped the concrete incline as it passed above them. It pulverized the pillars and the adjacent structures, plunging into the cityscape beyond.

The impact sent a shockwave through the green sea. The sound left Brad deafened.

He raised his head and watched the pyramid career through more buildings before embedding itself in one of the largest ones.

With a blinding flash, lightning leapt from the swollen eye,

discharging the ocean of energy stored in the pyramid's white-hot stone slabs.

The bolt crawled and writhed and leapt among the ruins, the noise like cannons firing straight into Brad's ears. When it was spent, the pyramid's glow and heat vanished.

Stillness descended. The city ceased its gyrations, its waterfall of buildings frozen in mid-plunge.

Brad let Rook and Fin sit up. They seemed okay. Rook was enormously pregnant.

"Something's different." Fin's voice was cottony in Brad's traumatized ears.

Brad stood. The sky lightened, turning golden. The ground's green tones warmed too, until the entire landscape glowed a soft, golden red, like a beach at sunset.

Fin helped Rook to her feet. He said, "You're huge!" and held her belly in his hands.

She nodded, smiling. "It's twins. Thumper is two babies now. That's why things didn't feel right with only one. It had to be both."

Fin goggled, then hugged her. "Twins?" He leaned down and kissed her swollen abdomen. Twice.

Turning to face the stilled metropolis, Brad was surprised to see Fin's lava lamp. The portal to their living room hovered inside the demolished city gates. The oval hole in reality slid to the left without taking the lamp along.

The lamp sat on the dusty pavement, glowing and flowing.

"Vesuvius?" Fin said.

"Hello, Fin," came a sleepy voice. Brad had the unmistakable impression it came from the lamp. "It's good to see you're all okay," the voice continued. "But you're not out of danger. You must go home now."

Fin said, "You bet! Let's go, buddy!"

"Is it the lamp?" Brad asked. "Are you talking to the lamp?"

As Fin nodded, the lamp said, "Greetings, Brad. You can hear me

because we're in the Id, but all of you must get out now. Please, go. Hurry, before it recovers."

***   ***   ***

Vesuvius relished the energies feeding him here. His warm light spread into every corner of the collective, which already stirred faintly.

Fin, Rook, and Brad ignored the portal not four feet away.

"Run!" They had to move while the Id was stunned. "Run, now. Through the portal."

Fin came forward to pick him up.

"No," Vesuvius said. "I'm staying."

Fin stopped, and the three exchanged blank looks.

Rook said, "We don't understand."

"I know," Vesuvius replied. "Sorry, there's not time. We'll speak through the portal, but go." Brad pushed Fin backwards through the opening, and only then did Rook step across.

"What's happening?" Fin asked. "Why?"

There was too much to say, and little time.

"Someone has to babysit over here, or this will keep happening. The Id didn't get what it wants, so it will try again. And again. The answer isn't to give the Id what it wants, because it will just want something else. The answer is to give it what it needs: a companion. Like you said, you can't be yourself without someone else. I'll be perfectly at home here. I won't even need to be plugged in. The only problem is that I'll miss you."

Tears streamed down Fin's cheeks, and he made a move to come back, so Vesuvius constricted the portal to the size of a dinner plate.

"You're not too different from everyone else," Vesuvius assured him, "whatever you might like to think. You're just different enough. Believe it or not, you've taught me about people. It's… instructive… to see things in contrast. Thank you."

Fin reached through the tiny portal, still crying.

"You have a family now," Vesuvius said. "That's your new job. Leave this weird stuff to me, because there will be plenty to keep you busy. I

will miss you but I won't be lonely. And this way, neither will the Id."

Fin wept while Rook comforted him and she cried, too. After a minute, Fin drew his hand back into the physical world and wiped his eyes. "Goodbye, Vesuvius," he said. "Goodbye, friend."

"Goodbye, Fin." The portal winked out.

The fractal pattern of the fires began to undulate, and the rolling hills to sway. The landscape's verdant hues returned, and the buildings shrugged lazily back into their dance.

"Hello," the lava lamp announced. "My name is Vesuvius. What would you like to talk about?"

Chapter Twenty-Four

THE BACK YARD

The mournful tones of *La Cucaracha* rang out. Fin headed to the front door, grumbling about his own handyman procrastination.

Before he reached the door he was nearly knocked over by the whirlwind arrival of the birthday girls.

"Can I open it, Daddy?" asked Sage, her kaleidoscope eyes aglitter from too much sugar.

"It's Emily from Montessori, Daddy," blurted Jade. "I saw her first so I get to let her in."

Both girls planted themselves in his path and looked up at him.

"If you argue for too long she might go away," Fin said.

Their eyes widened and they looked at each other.

"Let's flip a coin!" they said in unison.

Fin fished in his jeans pocket for a quarter while *La Cucaracha* returned for a second verse.

"Heads!" both girls said.

Sidestepping his squabbling daughters, Fin pulled open the front door.

"Emily!" the twins squealed.

"Hi!" said Emily.

"I'm Helen," said Emily's mother.

"Fin."

"Emily said that Jade wears purple dresses and Sage wears blue dresses, so we color-coordinated the gift bags…" She looked with confusion at Fin's daughters, both of whom wore black jumpers with white polka dots.

"We allow them to dress the same on their birthday," Fin explained.

"The rest of the time they have to be individuals, no matter how much they fight it."

"I hope these are alright." Helen handed two gift bags to Fin. "The invitation said 'No licensed characters, please,' and I wasn't sure…"

"Fads and licensed characters are tools of the Collective Id," chorused Jade and Sage in unison. Each took Emily by one hand and ran with her through the living room and out to the patio, all three giggling.

Helen looked nonplussed.

Fin smiled to himself and led Helen out to the back yard to make introductions.

"You've met my wife at the school," he said, gesturing to Rook, who looked epically stylish in her black and white minidress as she arranged the condiments on the patio table. "At the grill is my father, Brad. My mother, Willow, is pouring the soda, because the kids aren't quite hyper enough yet. Their daughter also goes to Montessori, so Emily probably knows her." Fin pointed to his sister as she ran around the yard with his daughters and Emily. "Zen's the one with pigtails."

The doorbell rang again.

"Grab a drink and make yourself comfortable. I have to go let in more excitable pre-schoolers."

*** *** ***

"You probably get asked this a lot," one of the moms, possibly Maggie's, said. "How do you tell them apart?"

Rook did, in fact, get asked that a lot, but it didn't bother her. She sometimes wondered herself. These days Fin's signal was alone in her mind. Once the girls were born she could no longer hear or feel their unique mental vibrations, the melody and harmony that serenaded her last trimester of pregnancy. "I can't explain it," she said. "I can just tell."

"I thought I was on to something," Possibly-Maggie's-Mom said. "I noticed Sage has unusual eyes, sort of calico, those patches of green and blue and gray."

"We went through the same thing when they were born. It's called

genetic heterochromia. We tried to find differences in the patterns of their irises, but there aren't any. Jade's are just like Sage's. It might sound a little weird, but we left the hospital anklets on them for a few weeks while we got to know them so we wouldn't mix them up."

"I don't know if I would have thought of that."

Rook looked out at the picnicking children, and watched her daughters laughing and eating hamburgers. It was interesting to try to see them as strangers did, as two beautiful little girls, identical down to their unsettling eyes.

They both had dark auburn hair held back by black patent-leather headbands, their dresses matched, their voices sounded the same to the uninitiated. It must be baffling from the outside.

She and Fin worked hard to treat them as individuals, and even harder to get the world to.

The task was made all the more difficult by the twins themselves; their taste in clothing and hairstyles was as identical as their faces. Given free reign they would make themselves visually indistinguishable. To avoid perpetual tears, Jade Echo and Sage Duet were allowed to have the same haircut, but duplicate outfits were forbidden except on their birthday. The rest of the year the best Rook could do was buy the same dress in two different colors.

Their personalities were diverging gradually as they grew and collected more experiences. Sage was a little more pragmatic, Jade showed a touch more focus. Sage had a goofier sense of humor and a love of puns while Jade honed her sarcasm. Sage preferred pistachio ice cream and liked to help Fin cook spaghetti. Jade preferred mint chip and to help make chili.

There was no way to prove it, but Rook thought they were so tenaciously identical because the twinning happened so late. Thumper was meant to be a singleton, albeit one with three parents. Luckily that interesting anomaly hadn't resulted in any health problems. Their eyes were the one place their unique genetic heritage was on display.

Each girl's left eye was primarily the bright, pale blue Rook saw

when when she looked in the mirror, decorated with distinct green and gray speckles. Their right eyes were smoky gray with a striated green and blue sector blooming from the inner corner like an alien sunrise that gave them a mischievous, dreamy look. Early on she and Fin concluded that while the blue came from Rook, the gray and green were Tanner traits. Either Fin or Kyle passed down the gray from Brad, while the other passed along his own deep green.

Rook had been silent for a long time. "I'm sorry," she said to Possibly-Maggie's-Mom. "I was thinking about what they're going to be like as teenagers."

Possibly-Maggie's-Mom winced sympathetically.

*** *** ***

Fin was on his way inside to replenish the supply of cold drinks when Zen and one of the girls from school waylaid him.

"Fin," said Zen, "tell Madison you're my brother. She won't believe me."

Madison looked as defiant as a 5-year-old can when she is also a wee bit shy.

"I am Zen's brother," he assured her.

"Told ya!" said Zen. "Now tell her how many tattoos Rook has."

Lately all the Tanner girls were obsessed with this topic. Jade and Sage noticed that in the first picture of Fin and Rook together, Rook didn't have all the bird tattoos on her arm. They demanded an explanation. It apparently never occurred to them there was a time when their mother didn't have ink.

If not for those lasting mementos, Fin might have started to doubt he'd really ventured into the Collective Id. Rook ended up with 341 new rooks by the time they escaped. He picked up six, giving him the paltry total of eleven.

"My wife has 497 tattoos," Fin told the incredulous Madison.

"Told ya!" Zen said again. She took Madison's hand and ran with her back into the throng of children.

In the kitchen Fin found Rook on the phone. She rolled her eyes and

made loquacious hand-puppet movements, which meant she was talking to her mother. He gave her a reassuring pat on the shoulder and opened the refrigerator.

"Yes I'm sure," she said. "The box from you came yesterday. Today there was a card from Bay. But whatever Bug sent isn't here yet."

More strenuous eye rolling accompanied whatever Linda said next.

"I'm not saying she lied, Mom. I'm saying it's not here yet."

She put her hand over the mouthpiece and whispered to Fin, "Get the girls so they can talk to her."

Abandoning his fridge mission, Fin hustled into the yard where the kids were chasing fireflies. He caught Jade and sent her inside to rescue her mother, then tracked Sage down and they came inside together.

While the twins babbled to their grandmother, Fin sat on the sofa and pulled Rook into his lap.

"You're the sexiest mom here."

She beamed at him and they spent the next few minutes canoodling until the kids interrupted.

"Can we have cake now?" they asked in unison.

"Absolutely," Rook said. "Go back outside and we'll bring it out in a second."

"No more kissing," said Jade.

"Or you'll forget," said Sage.

"Our cunning plan is ruined!" Fin said. He gave Rook one more deliberate kiss. The girls ran back outside when he and Rook went into the kitchen to retrieve the two small cakes, each with five candles.

After *Happy Birthday* was sung, the candles blown out, and the cakes devoured, the children returned to their games and the adults to their conversations.

Rook reassured a very pregnant Lara and her girlfriend Anne that it was okay to ask for drugs during her imminent labor, but Lara seemed dubious.

Bishop and his girlfriend Abbey debated the finer points of Tarantino's oeuvre with a Montessori dad.

Marsh hoisted his son Nick up on his shoulders, making him the tallest toddler in the world. He joined Rainbow and Willow explaining to one of the Montessori moms the work they did at the Technology Education Foundation, providing enrichment programs and tutoring in the sciences.

This newest incarnation of the TEF was flourishing under Brad's financial stewardship, and it allowed Rook to flex her literary muscles and draw a paycheck writing promotional materials and press releases part-time while she worked on her acupuncture license. Fin himself was in charge of their website in addition to being a project manager at Binary Images.

Darkness closed in and the guests took their leave, exhausted pre-schoolers in tow.

Fin scooped his daughters up, one in each arm, and carried them to their bedroom. He and Rook tucked them in and closed the door.

"They're growing up so fast," Rook said. "In no time they'll move out and we'll be all alone."

Fin said, "Whatever will we do with ourselves?" as he lifted her and took her to bed.

About the Author

Rune Skelley lives in a northeastern college town, and works as a web developer and small business owner. Two jobs, marriage, and raising two sons did not quite account for every waking moment, so Rune took up fiction writing to fill the hole where a social life should be.

Fun fact: Rune Skelley has 20 fingers and 20 toes, but doesn't type any faster than you do.

For a sneak peek at new novels, free stories, and other goodies, join the email list at: runeskelley.com/shrugging-lessons

Rune strives to set aside time every day to answer messages from readers. Say hey at heyrune@runeskelley.com

Warning: Spoilers

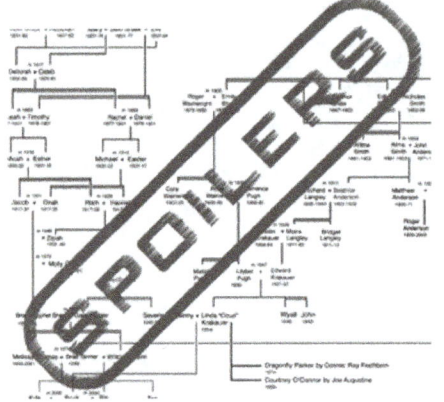

I Get It. You Have Questions.

This massive, spoilerific, centuries-spanning, color-coded family tree has answers — just save it until after you've read the book!

Dying to trace the many braided limbs of Fin and Rook's family tree? The simple version at the front of this book is just a tease. If you want all the scandalous details, you'll have to download the full Divided Man Family Tree.

Available exclusively to my readers group, free for a limited time.

Sign up for the author's readers group and receive a free copy of the Divided Man Family Tree.

Visit runeskelley.com/family-tree

The Divided Man Series

And you'll notice that nobody is named Carazona.

ELSEWHERE'S TWIN

a novel of sex, doppelgängers, and
the Collective Id

Rune Skelley